LOOK WOT I DUN

DON POWELL

My Life In

SLADE

LOOK WOT I DUN
DON
POWELL
My Life In
SLADE

LISE LYNG FALKENBURG
+ DON POWELL

OMNIBUS PRESS
London / New York / Paris / Sydney / Copenhagen / Berlin / Madrid / Tokyo

Exclusive Distributors
Music Sales Limited,
14/15 Berners Street,
London, W1T 3LJ.

Music Sales Corporation
180 Madison Avenue, 24th Floor,
New York,
NY 10016,
USA.

Macmillan Distribution Services
56 Parkwest Drive
Derrimut, Vic 3030,
Australia.

Every effort has been made to trace the copyright holders of the photographs in this book but one or two were unreachable. We would be grateful if the photographers concerned would contact us.

Typeset by Phoenix Photosetting, Chatham, Kent
Printed in the EU

A catalogue record for this book is available from the British Library.

Visit Omnibus Press on the web at www.omnibuspress.com

Contents

Foreword By Don Powell

Getting older, most people can look back and think about the different episodes, different people and different circumstances that have shaped their lives in so many ways. I have now reached the age of 65 and I have lived a very unusual life. Much of my life I don't remember, though. I know that's quite normal when you get older – to forget, that is – but in my case it has nothing to do with age. To remember things has been a problem for me since I was 26 years old.

I suppose to most people, writing the foreword to a book that is meant to document your own life doesn't seem a problem and should be an easy thing to do. But in my situation, believe me: nothing could be further from the truth.

My life has truly been an adventure in so many ways and I have been so very lucky, but it has not been an easy life and not as glamorous as many people would think. Born in 1946, right after the war, into a working-class family from the Black Country. Falling in love with music in the fifties. Working hard to follow the dream of making a living playing drums during the sixties. Reaching fame with Slade in the seventies, and living the rock'n'roll life since then. It has been a fantastic but also scary roller-coaster ride, which most people only get to dream of.

There has been a lot of sex, a lot of drink, a little bit of drugs and a whole lotta rock'n'roll, but… also a lot of loneliness. My life hasn't always been easy for me, or for my family and closest friends down the years.

In 1973, at the height of my career, I was lucky to survive a horrendous car accident. Since then, I've had to cope with amnesia and all the challenges, frustrations and insecurities it brought along with it. I had to develop certain 'survival skills' such as hiding behind a mask, pretending nothing was wrong.

Over the years, people have told me I should write a book about my life since I had to keep diaries in order to remember anything. So, after years of thinking about having my biography written (and with the encouragement and support from my wife, Hanne), my dear friend Lise was my first and only choice to put pen to paper, and when I approached her, she was up for it straight away.

Then for some reason I became very sceptical. Not with Lise, though, far from it, as I have the utmost respect for her – also, we have a very strong friendship, which I value extremely highly. No, I was sceptical about myself, thinking, what have I got to say that really hasn't already been documented? But then again, thinking about it some more…

During the heyday of Slade, I very rarely did interviews and if I did, it was always about the band's activities. So to talk about myself was a bit of a challenge and really not as easy as you might think. But having my life documented in a book would be interesting for *me* and enable me to remember many forgotten things from all the different and sometimes strange paths I have taken. It would also force me to jerk my memory and in many ways let *me* and also my family get a better (or worse) picture of what has shaped me to be the person that I am today, and to understand why I am what I am.

A big help has been keeping my diaries from all those years back (well, most of them) since my car accident in 1973. My diaries were my lifeline and what I wrote in them was exactly how I felt or what had happened to me on that specific day. Handing them over to Lise was a very easy and comfortable thing to do. I thought, well, the project has to be with 'warts and all' so to speak, although I was aware that many of the notes in my diaries were not to be published as *everything* was documented there, otherwise I could be in big trouble by hurting and losing many friends. *My aim was only to dish the dirt on myself!* Hanne and myself read the diaries together and, would you believe, it was the first time I have read them since they were written. As far as I remember (pardon the pun!), Lise is the only other person to have read all of them. And I thank you, Lise, from the bottom of my heart, for all your incredibly hard work and patience throughout.

Because of my amnesia, reading Lise's book has sometimes been like reading about a complete stranger (does that seem weird?), but believe me, having the memory problem is 'in itself' a very strange animal to deal with and I think, for anyone who's never had that experience, it's going to be very hard to understand.

I just hope you'll enjoy reading this as much as I did!

I would like to thank all my dear friends who have contributed to piecing my life together. Also I want to give my wonderful family, Hanne, Anne Kirstine, Emilie, Andreas and Rocky a big kiss… for finally giving me peace in my life. "You have made my life complete, and I love you so!" as Elvis sang in 'Love Me Tender'.

Don Powell, October 2011

1

The Boy From Bilston

Earls Court, London, July 1, 1973. The concert hall is full to the brim with 18,000 youngsters dressed in tartan, top hats and silver, screaming their lungs out in anticipation of seeing Slade, the most popular band of the moment. The Wolverhampton-based rock band have gone from rags to riches within three years and the concert at Earls Court will cement their popularity.

As the four band members take the stage, Don Powell feels the rush of adrenaline. The tall, well-built drummer with the long, dark hair is known as the powerhouse of the band, hitting the drums so hard that sticks break between his fingers. It is difficult to believe that he is the quiet one of the bunch. Don smiles in disbelief at the eager crowd and mounts his drum stool.

Ten days later Don wakes up, shivering with cold, not realising that he is lying on a bed of ice. Tubes and pipes are sticking out of him and he doesn't know why. He feels a panic rising. He has no idea of where he is or how he got there, his memory is blank.

Later, when the tubes have been removed, Don gets to look in a bathroom mirror. He still doesn't know what has happened and is wholly unprepared for what he sees. His face is bruised beyond recognition, teeth are missing and his body is covered with deep cuts. His hair is gone. He

1

has a huge crack across the top of his head and his skull is held together with metal clamps. The shock of seeing the distorted face blows him across the floor and into the back wall.

Almost 40 years later, Don Powell still suffers from amnesia, but nowadays he knows what happened back in 1973. He knows that, three days after the Earls Court concert, he was in a horrendous car crash, a crash that cost the life of his girlfriend and left doctors with little hope that he would survive. He still doesn't remember the crash as such, but his permanent loss of smell and taste as well as his amnesia are daily reminders of that fateful night.

When talking to Don it is difficult to believe that he still suffers from the effects of the crash so many years ago. His disabilities don't show and he comes across as an attentive man, unusually kind and considerate, with a sharp sense of humour. He is very down-to-earth, and had it not been for his full head of unruly hair, nothing would indicate that this mild-mannered man is one of rock's great drummers. He is just an ordinary guy with an extraordinary job in what happens to be one of the most famous bands of its era. There are no airs and graces and no bitterness surrounding the limitations that his handicaps have caused. On the contrary.

"I've been so lucky," he says, displaying the gratitude that colours his outlook on life. "I have the best job ever, travel the world, doing something that I love and getting paid for it. I've been so lucky, *so* lucky, and I always appreciate it."

★　★　★

Donald George Powell was born on September 10, 1946, in Bilston, Staffordshire in central England, the second of five children of steelworker Walter Powell and his wife, Dora. The couple already had a daughter, Carol, born in 1940, and a year after Don's birth came a second son, Derek. A younger sister, Christine, died in infancy before the last of the Powell children, Marilyn, saw the light of day in 1953.

Walter Powell was a strict father but also a bit of a ladies' man, with a beautiful tenor voice. During the Second World War he served as a Desert

Rat in North Africa, but on his return suffered from malaria and declined the medals to which he was entitled because he hated every minute of his military service. Even in the forces, Walter's unusual voice had been noticed and there were suggestions that, with training, he could become a professional singer, but money was scarce and it never amounted to anything. Instead, he worked hard in a foundry all his life in order to provide for his family and give them what he had never had himself. Henceforth, his singing was saved for parties and sing-songs in pubs.

His wife, Dora, was quiet but possessed a sharp sense of humour that showed itself in brilliant one-liners. She loved her children, but had her quirks. For one thing, she didn't want to have her boys' hair cut. Both Don and Derek had beautiful hair and she was afraid their curls would disappear if she took them to the barber. She used to dress the boys alike, to the extent that she got them mixed up and called them both Dorek. She'd put them in the pram together and wherever she wheeled them around, people would stop and say, "What a beautiful pair of little twin girls." Eventually, Walter demanded his sons be freed of their long, curly hair.

Walter won that one, but generally Dora knew what she wanted and how to get it. At the time of Don's birth, the family lived with their gran, Dora's mother, in Chapel Street, Bilston, but Dora wanted a home of her own. The problem was that Gran had too much space for Dora and her family to be offered a council estate home, so Dora solved the problem by moving her family into a small one-up one-down in Temple Street. After 18 months in the tiny quarters the family got their desired house. The move is one of Don's earliest memories.

"What I remember more than anything was the day we went to see the house in Green Park Drive for the first time," he says. "It must have been in the early fifties because Marilyn was born in that house. After the Second World War there was a baby boom in England, so the council built big housing estates and we got a house in Bilston. Although our house was built, the whole estate was not finished. None of the landscaping had been done, like the turf and the greens, just mud everywhere. My mum and dad took us there and dad carried me. There wasn't even a bus route, so we had to walk all the way, but I could see mum and dad's excitement and I always remember that picture of dad carrying me."

3

Coming from the tiny Temple Street residence, the house in Green Park Drive was a vast improvement. The family was very happy there, although the country had been marked by the war.

"The Midlands had been very heavily bombed," Don notes. "Not so much Bilston, but in general all of the Black Country had been affected because of the coal mines, iron foundries and steel mills that had given name to the area. The same goes for the rest of the Midlands, where Birmingham and especially Coventry were completely flattened. I think it was rebuilt pretty quickly, but other effects of the war lingered. I remember Mum had ration books for food and coal and had to use stamps to buy certain goods. It must have been quite difficult for families back then. You got a certain amount of stamps each week depending on how big the family was. The bigger the family, the more ration stamps."

The Powell family boasted six members after Marilyn's birth and with four children, each child had its own part to play. Marilyn was the baby of the family. "Because of Christine's death, Mum was very close to Marilyn," Don says, "but I guess we all spoiled her."

His sister Carol agrees. "I used to dress Marilyn and feed her and take her for walks in the pram. When people saw me with her in the pram they would look at me in a certain way. I was a very young teenage girl, and I could see what they were thinking. 'She's not mine!' I used to say."

Being the oldest girl of the family, Carol became the baby-minder. "I was a surrogate mum," she admits. "I was taking the boys with me everywhere. I didn't have to do housework or cooking or anything, but I had to take care of the kids. So I brought the boys along wherever I went, to the park, for walks, to the pictures, everywhere. I didn't mind, though."

Meeting Carol and seeing the love she has for her family, you don't doubt her.

Of the boys, Don was the better behaved, an intelligent, independent boy who knew how to carry himself and be a proper eldest son.

"Don was the only one in the family with a brain," Carol admits. "He was a very clever boy. He loved puzzles and stamps and he was the quiet one of the two boys."

"I *was* a quiet child," Don seconds. "Almost too quiet, maybe, whereas Derek was loud."

"You'd have thought that of the two of them Derek would have been the one to go on stage," Carol agrees.

"Although only one year separated us, Derek and I were very different," Don explains. "We didn't even attend the same junior school. I was four and a half years old when I went to the local school, Villiers Road Primary School, which was about five kilometres away."

"When Don started school, he didn't want Mum to pick him up," Carol recalls. "He used to say, 'I'm not a little boy any more,' but Mum didn't like the idea of him going on his own. One time she went to get him and she couldn't find him because he'd gone another way than the one he was supposed to. After that, Mum didn't go any more."

"The year after, a new school had been built and Derek went there," Don continues. "In this way we never mixed as brothers. Derek had his friends, I had mine, and we went in different directions."

"The thing was that Don and Derek didn't want to play with each other unless there was no one else to play with," says Carol, "and then they fought all over the house, especially when our dad was not there. Dad worked shifts, so I used to be the one to be sent in to stop the fights. Then the boys would call me Bossy Boots. Their fights were horrible. I remember that Don's nose used to bleed easily in those days and Derek knew that if he could get Don's nose to bleed, he'd have won the fight. It was madness."

Even though the brothers fought all the time, they weren't quite able to avoid each other, as Don explains: "The house in Green Park Drive was a big house for the time. It had two rooms downstairs, a kitchen, an outside toilet and a toilet and bath inside, and then three bedrooms upstairs. Marilyn slept with Mum and Dad to begin with, then she moved in with Carol who had her own bedroom, and Derek and I shared the last one. The two of us fought every night when we had to go to bed; whenever we heard Dad on the stairs, however, we pretended to be asleep. But he knew! Today Derek and I are a lot closer than we were back then."

5

"It was a madhouse," says Carol. "But at least Derek always fought Don's battles. Don was never aggressive. In a row he'd walk away from the situation, whereas Derek would get stuck in."

Despite the fights with Derek and a father who, according to Carol, was too strict towards the boys, family bonds were tight in the Powell household.

"I come from a very loving family," says Don. "Dad worked in a foundry in Moxley. He took the bus to get there in the mornings and he worked there all his life until he retired. Mum worked as well, at Woden Transformers making electric components. We were just an ordinary working-class family, where both parents had to work, but Mum and Dad were fantastic. They always made sure that we went on holiday every year. They would save up all year so we could go to the south coast of England, always the last week of July and the first week of August. We stayed at bed and breakfast places, all of us in one room. That was how it was back then, but those holidays were wonderful. I've always appreciated that they insisted on taking us each year."

Carol also remembers those holidays fondly. One especially comes to mind, the one when she and Gerald, her husband to be, had started courting. "Gerald went with us that summer. We stayed in a summerhouse by the sea, but of course in those days Gerald wasn't allowed to sleep there too, so he and Don had a house for themselves. They spent the days with us, but in the evenings they had to go back to their own place."

"When we got back to our place, I went to the toilet and Don went into the bedroom," Gerald recalls. "After a while he came out and said, 'There's something wrong. There's a pair of ladies' panties on the bed.' And we looked at them and realised that we'd gone into the wrong house. We sneaked out very quickly without anybody noticing, but afterwards we couldn't stop laughing."

The annual holidays were only one of many traditions in the Powell family. Another was breakfast in bed on Sunday mornings.

"Sunday mornings, either Carol or I would do the tea and toast," Don says, "and then we would all sit in Mum and Dad's bed and have breakfast. Marilyn would sit in between Mum and Dad and then Carol, Derek and I would sit in the bottom end. That was wonderful. And we would talk about what we would do. Sunday afternoons in those days we went to the local common, Penn Common actually. There was a café there and people went to the common to play football or have picnics and just spend the afternoons. There were lots of families at the common on Sundays and we always had a good time."

Out of Don's childhood memories, the fondest ones revolve around Christmas. How else could it be? "Christmas mornings were the best, of course," Don admits. "Derek and I always tried to stay awake as long as we could on Christmas Eve to get a glimpse of Father Christmas. And whenever we heard a noise, we thought it was him and his sleigh. But we could never stay awake and when we woke up the next morning, all the presents were already there."

"The boys would stay up for as long as possible," Carol confirms, "but when they'd finally fallen asleep, I'd put the presents at the end of their beds for them to have in the morning. Often they woke up in the middle of the night and then they would open the presents, as they couldn't wait for it to be Christmas morning."

During Christmas Day, the home was filled with people cooking, singing and having a good time, much like in the lyrics to 'Merry Xmas Everybody', Slade's 1973 Christmas hit that still haunts not only Britain, but all of Europe during the festive season. Christmas will forever be connected with Don and his band because of that song, but Don doesn't mind, as he is fond of both the song and the season.

Don and Carol have disparate memories of the family's leanings towards music. All Don can remember is hearing the music of Rodgers and Hammerstein around the house while Carol recalls the arrival of rock'n'roll. "Sunday morning was the house cleaning day," says Don. "We all helped out except for my dad, who went to the pub. I used to do the hoovering, but of course my mother and sister did the bulk of it. That was when the records went on the record player. It was always the albums from *Oklahoma!*, *Seven Brides For Seven Brothers* and *South Pacific*, and as a child I never heard any other kinds of music."

Carol doesn't quite agree: "It was in the fifties, you must remember. So we used to listen a lot to Elvis. We loved Elvis! And Dad did his singing, so there was plenty of music around. Besides, Don was always drumming. Already as a boy he was always going bang-bang-bang on something. At the breakfast table he would sit tapping and banging on everything. It drove us crazy! I don't know where it came from; he was just at it constantly."

"That's right," says Don. "At the table I used the knife and fork to bang on everything and Dad would say, 'Be quiet!' and then he'd clip me."

Don's love for drums was soon to become more tangible as he joined the Scouts. Carol explains: "He was in the Cubs first, when he was seven, and then the Scouts, and he loved it. He went on jamborees and he got all his merit patches and everything. He was indeed very clever. And then he started playing drums."

"That was when I was 11 or 12," Don recalls, "but in those days in the Scouts I was with, you had to play bugle first, and I couldn't do that. I would just stand at the back puffing my cheeks, pretending to play. They found me out and said, 'OK, you can play the drums.' That was how it started. I was taught the rudiments, like the different rolls, and I didn't find it difficult. It came quite naturally to me. If there was something that I didn't know, I used to ask the older Scouts and luckily they were very nice and showed me what to do. I learnt a lot from them and it was like a revelation when I learnt to do certain rolls. It was a fantastic feeling.

"With the Scouts we had the Sunday morning parades around my hometown. Then my parents used to come to watch and they were always waving to me. Oh dear! I was trying to keep a straight face, as it was always *so* embarrassing!"

At the age of 11 Don entered the Etheridge Secondary Modern School, a secondary school for boys. He was a good student who did well, especially in English, history and athletics, but his academic achievements were overshadowed by his friendship with Graham 'Swinn' Swinnerton, who became a lifelong comrade and eventually Slade's tour manager.

"We were both shy and the pair of us hooked up and gave one another confidence," Swinn explains. "A friendship developed and it's still there today."

"We became really close friends," says Don. "At first we were pretty well behaved, but after a couple of years we became more or less the rogues of the school. We used to sit in the back and mind our own business."

Exactly how Don went from quiet boy to rogue is a matter he has difficulty explaining. Maybe it had to do with his wicked sense of humour, inherited from his mother. Or maybe it stemmed from his inborn restlessness.

"Don is restless by nature," says Carol. "Even as a boy he always had to do something new. He always had to go out. He had a paper route for a couple of years and then he did his training. Every day he went out. He was into athletics and whenever he did anything, it was 100 per cent. He used to go out every morning in his shorts to train, even when the weather was freezing."

"I left the Scouts when I was about 14 and then I got interested in athletics," Don explains. "I used to do long-distance running for Bilston and it was so strange, because girls didn't exist in my life back then. I trained seven days a week. Sunday morning in the stadium working out, Monday in the gym, doing rope training, Tuesdays and Thursdays in the stadium, Wednesdays and Fridays in the gym. I was just getting ready throughout the week for the event on Saturday. I always ran on Saturdays and then, on Sunday, it started all over. Girls were the furthest thing from my mind back then; I just wanted to run at the Olympics. That was the whole purpose of my life in those days."

Knowing Don's track record when it comes to women, it is indeed strange that girls were not on his mind back then, but in the long run Don wasn't able to close his eyes to the fairer sex.

"When I was about 15, Swinn and I started to go to the youth club together in Moxley where Swinn lived," Don recalls. "That was where I had my first kiss."

"The youth club was all that there was in those days," Swinn adds. "They did a lot of things with the kids, but the trouble was that they were always connected with the church."

For the two friends who were taught religion at school by a registered Communist, who used to campaign at every election, this connection was not ideal. "It was the Bourne Methodist Youth Club and to be a member you had to go to church on Sundays," Don sighs. "It was some sort of bribery, but we went anyway, in order to be members. In the club we used to listen to records and play table tennis; actually, I was the youth club's table tennis champion. They used to have dances there as well and the last dance was always a slow one, with a kiss in the end. One time, this girl came up to me for the last dance. Her name was Irene and I sometimes used to walk her home from the club. As it was the last dance, I had to kiss her, but I didn't know that you were supposed to have your eyes closed and somebody actually shouted, 'Close your eyes!' It was hilarious."

Although Don was later known as a ladies' man, he didn't start dating until he was 17. Instead, he went into another kind of contact sport. "At the age of 15 I got interested in boxing," Don explains. "I joined the boxing team at a youth club sponsored by the local police force, but when I started out, I boxed left-handed, as I'm ambidextrous. I write with my right hand, but I throw with my left and I kick with my left foot as well. I'm backwards with my knife and fork, I wear my wristwatch on my right wrist and I play snooker both ways. When I started off boxing left-handed, my trainer made me turn round to get the fight at a balance when you go against another boxer. I didn't find it particularly difficult to use the right, but it was the first time I really thought about being ambidextrous.

"I hadn't told anybody except Swinn that I boxed. Towards the end of the term at school we had gym all morning and our gym teacher, Mr. Hawkins, said, 'We'll get the ring out and do a bit of boxing today. OK, the first ones up are Powell and Swinnerton. In the ring!' Swinn objected and said, 'But he *does* boxing! He boxes for Bilston!' Mr. Hawkins asked, 'Is that right?' 'No,' I said, and Mr. Hawkins went, 'That's it! Get in that ring!' And I smashed Swinn all around. I think he got in one good punch and that was purely by accident! But I must admit that my boxing career was pretty short lived."

"Dad wouldn't let him," says Carol. "Don had inflammation of the mastoid and is quite deaf in one ear. Dad was afraid that it would get worse."

"My mum took me to the doctor's and I was advised to stop boxing because there was a risk that I would get permanent damage," says Don.

"I was so disappointed, so gutted, because my trainer wanted me to carry on as he saw the potential in me."

But Don had already found other things to hit than a punching bag. The love of drums was still there, so Don longed to replace the old knife and fork with proper drumsticks. He didn't have any though, so he decided to make them himself, out of a Christmas tree. "I didn't know about different types of wood back then," he says, "or where to buy wood at all, so I used the stem of a Christmas tree. I carved it and, although it must have been very crude, I made the sticks with tips and everything. I even varnished them. I was so proud and I spent such a long time on making them. But the first time I used them, they broke. I was *so* disappointed!"

During their last year of school Don and Swinn were made house captains, Don for the house of Wedgwood, Swinn for the house of Vincent.

"I thought, 'What? Us? Prefects?'" says Don. "We didn't understand why they wanted us to monitor the other kids, because we were rogues. We would do anything to get away from the books for a while. Once we even went on a commando course. The rest of the boys at school thought we were mad. But it was great. We had a week's training in the outskirts of Wolverhampton and then we went to the mountains for three days."

"The commando course was actually called an adventure course," says Swinn, "but I don't remember that much about it any more. Only that we had to get up at six o'clock because we realised that we had to have our shower first in the morning when the water was still warm."

"We were probably 30 boys from different schools," adds Don. "We didn't take the training that serious though, we were always joking and laughing, but we were taught how to pitch a tent on a slope and we did a lot of climbing and tunnelling and things like that. We were to use Primus stoves heated by methylated spirits and we were being taught how to use them in the hall of the camp. The teachers then put the lights off and said, 'This is how it will be in the mountains.' And all you could see was silhouettes of people running around with their hands on fire because they had spilled the fuel.

"After the training, they dumped us in the Welsh mountains, not that far from Wolverhampton, but we were in the back of the van so we didn't see where we were going. They gave us the maps and compasses and said, 'See you in two and a half days…*maybe.*'

"Swinn and I went together and we had our tent and cooking things. On the first night we were pitching the tent on a slope, but Swinn had forgotten to put the pegs in around the bottom and I rolled out in my sleeping bag during the night. The ropes of the tent stopped me and I remember waking up under a beautiful clear black sky full of stars, thinking that I was dead. I was absolutely certain that I was dead and in heaven. It took me a while to realise that I was alive and outside."

Both Don and Swinn survived and made it back in time. Swinn still hangs on to his adventure course certificate, which shows that the course took place from October 23 to November 1, 1961.

Don finished senior school when he was 16 and, for the last day of school, he and his fellow rogue prepared one final prank.

"At school we had a piano in the hall where we used to sing the hymns," Don recalls. "The night before the last day of school, Swinn and I shoved newspapers down the piano so the keys couldn't hit the notes. On the last day of school the prefects were on a stand above everyone else and Swinn and I just held our heads down, because we couldn't stop laughing when the music teacher tried to play the piano. Finally, the piano was being wheeled out and a new one was wheeled in.

"Afterwards, we said our goodbyes to the teachers. When we reached our music teacher, Mr. Price, we said, 'We have a confession to make,' and he pointed at us, 'It was *you*, wasn't it! I *knew* it was you two!'

"Then we spoke to our headmaster and asked, 'How come we got made prefects?' and he said, 'We basically get the biggest rogues and make them prefects. Whenever something happens they know what is going on, and as they get power-mad, they turn people in.' So we realised that we were nothing special, we were just the biggest rogues in school given a bit of power."

"We were the crooks, so we became prefects," adds Swinn. "That was how the system worked."

From Etheridge Secondary Modern School, Don went to Wednesbury Technical College to study metallurgy. "That came from my father," he says. "He was on the factory floor in the steel works and he said, 'That's what you should do, become a metallurgist. It's a good job, really interesting,' so I consented. But my college career didn't last long. The thing was that Swinn and I went to different colleges. He was doing the GCEs, the General Certificate for Education, that is. He went to a college in Bilston and I went to one in Wednesbury, so we didn't really see each other. We went for probably six months and one day we happened to bump into each other and we never went to college again, ever.

"We would go through the motions, though. I would leave my house in the morning and he would leave his and we would meet in a coffee bar, spend a few hours there until 11 o'clock and then go to Swinn's place. Swinn only had his mother and she used to leave the house at 11 to go to work. She worked at a school doing the school lunches and when she had left, we went to Swinn's house and stayed there for the rest of the day, until I was due to be home from college.

"Because we had dropped out of school, I used to get up early on Monday mornings to get the post before my parents got it so they wouldn't see the letters from college saying, 'Why isn't your son at school?' I didn't tell my father about the letters until many years later and he said, 'Do you think that I didn't know?' How stupid of me to think that I could keep that from my parents!"

Don's neglect of his education turned out to mean nothing. Already, even before he admitted his absence from college to his father, something had happened that would change his life forever.

"I was playing table tennis in the youth club one time when these two guys came in," Don recalls. "It was Johnny Howells and Mick Marson. They were a bit older than me, but I knew them from the Etheridge Secondary Modern School. Johnny was a singer and he played guitar and Mick was a guitarist as well. They'd heard that I played drums and wanted to get into a band, so they came down just to introduce themselves and ask me if I would like to play drums with them. I said that I would love to, although I didn't know what that involved. I didn't even have any drums of my own and in fact I had no idea of what I was getting myself into. All that I knew was that I wanted to play the drums."

2

Becoming A Vendor

By the age of 16 it was clear that, although Don was a bright boy, he wasn't going on to a college education. He may have thought 'he wanted to become a drummer' instead, but Johnny Howells, who nowadays prefers to be called John rather than Johnny, recalls it differently. "At first Don didn't want to join the band, but eventually we did get him cornered and got him interested."

Mick Marson confirms that. "It took a bit of persuading, but we persuaded him. We wanted a new drummer because at that time we had another one and he was getting on a bit. I remember his name was Kenny Ashbury. He was much older than we were so we wanted a younger one, and we got in contact with Don through Dennis Horton."

"I knew Dennis Horton from the youth club," Don says. "He had a group where he played guitar and the introduction to Mick and Johnny came through him. I don't really recall being reluctant when they approached me, but they probably had to persuade me because I was afraid of my parents, thinking about what they'd say if I told them I wanted to be a drummer. And maybe I was unsure. Would it be the right thing to take that step when I was supposed to do college?"

In the end Don joined the band, which was called The Vendors, because the first thing John and Mick had learnt to play was Moisés

Simons' 'The Peanut Vendor'. At first Don played on telephone directories as he didn't have any drums, but eventually he borrowed a kit from a school friend, Dave Bowdley. "He had an Olympic drum kit," Don recalls. "He lived on the same estate as my parents and we'd been in junior school together. I went to ask him one day if I could borrow his drums and he said, 'Yeah, just take them. I'm not using them.' I used those drums for about 18 months, because he never asked for them back."

Being ambidextrous didn't show when Don played the drums. Although he kicks and throws with his left leg and hand, he can't play left-handed. "It is a bit strange," he admits, "but I play the orthodox way and I use my right foot as well for the bass drum."

Although at first not much happened to The Vendors career-wise, John Howells partly ascribes their later success to their origins. "It was probably a good thing that we knew each other from the Etheridge Secondary Modern School," he says, "because that school produced quite a few bands. There was another band from there that was quite famous; they were a couple of years older than us. Eventually they played the Royal Albert Hall. They started out as Danny Cannon & The Ramrods and then went on to be Herbie's People. It was a popular school when it came to forming bands."

"To begin with we never played anywhere; we just rehearsed at Johnny's house," Don recalls, still referring to Howells as Johnny. "Johnny's father had a small bed and breakfast place. There used to be an old repertory theatre nearby and the actors would stay there. We were rehearsing in the front room. It wasn't that big, but the toilet joined the main lounge. So we put the drums in the toilet and then Mick would be off in the corner somewhere and Johnny would be off in the other corner, so we used to shout to each other what we were gonna play."

"Everything was music back then," says Howells. "Perhaps we were interested in music because of the theatre people staying in my dad's boarding house, but I don't really think so because what they did was fifties music hall and we were into early rock."

"Mick and Johnny introduced me to that kind of music," recalls Don. "The only music I knew was what I had heard in the youth club, which were the records of the time, like Billy Fury and Joe Brown. But Johnny and Mick being a few years older were into the early rock stars like Gene Vincent, Eddie Cochran and Buddy Holly, so that was what we played.

"Eventually we started playing at weddings, youth-club dances and the occasional sort of small pub. We didn't get paid. It was just a hobby to us. But then came an offer from a local cinema. Saturday mornings was the kids' programme and they used to have either a singer or a duo play on the stage before they started the cartoons and all the films for the young kids. They asked us to play one Saturday morning. I remember when we met Johnny that day he'd seen the people at the cinema, and they said they were gonna pay us. I said, '*Pay* us? We get *paid* for doing this?' 'Oh, yeah, we're getting £5.' It was amazing! The cinema was only just around the corner, so we could carry our equipment from Johnny's house. We got paid the £5 and I think we had £1 each. Because we rehearsed at Johnny's house, we used the extra £2 to pay Johnny's father for the teas and the milk and sugar and the biscuits."

"When we did start to get bookings we used to take Don's borrowed set of drums with us on the bus," John Howells recalls. "The first time we got a decent payment for a gig must have been at the Prince's End working men's club in 1962. We got £18 between us and that was good. At least I paid my dad for what equipment he had assigned for me. That must have been like three weeks' wages."

Originally the band consisted of Don, John and Mick only, but after a while there was a coming and going of musicians. At one point Dennis Horton played guitar with The Vendors, while Johnny Shane joined the band from March to April and again from September to December 1963. His real name was actually John Howell, but he called himself Shane and had been the singer of his own group, Johnny Shane & The Cadillacs. With The Vendors he became the lead guitarist, as John Howells was the singer. On bass they had Walter Diffy, better known as Bill.

"I introduced Bill to the band," says Swinn. "At that time I worked at Woden Transformers where Don's mum worked. Don's brother,

Derek, used to work next to me for a while and Bill Diffy was also there, so that was how I knew him."

"We became a five-piece band and we were very lucky to get the support of our parents," says John Howells. "Our parents didn't know what was in store for us, but the music was what we wanted. It was a challenge that we had to meet. Between us we had parents that could understand that. One of the obstacles was that we were only teenagers, supposed to be back home with the last bus at 11 o'clock, but when we were out playing, we just couldn't make it. I remember the first time when we tried and were late. When I got back my dad asked, 'Where have you been?' and he wanted to stop me from playing any more. When I'd gone to bed, he came in and said, 'I didn't really mean that.' And from there on it took off. He could have stopped it so easily, but I think he could see that we wanted this. Our parents were willing to nurture our dream and they were very proud, obviously. They could see that life could be better for us."

Don's parents were also OK with their eldest son's decision to become a musician, as Carol recalls. "We were all thrilled. That was something he wanted, so we all supported that and I think it was a great thing of especially my dad to do. Don didn't have his drums at home, anyway, so we never heard anything of the racket. He never practised at home. But it was a bit ironic. Don was the only one in the family with a brain, he was the only one of us to go to college, and then he used it on this! On drumming!"

Mick Marson wasn't that lucky. "When we started playing, my mum threw me out. We'd done a gig and came back to Bilston in the morning. I saw my mum and she threw me out. I followed her around town, but she wouldn't talk to me. She disowned me, so I went to live with John for quite a while until she forgave me."

The Vendors were influenced by some of the local groups, notably The Redcaps, who were regarded as the best of the beat groups in the area. They originated from Walsall, but were regulars at Birmingham beat venues. To match up with them and other local groups, Don wondered if he needed proper drum lessons.

"I went to this teacher in Wolverhampton," Don recalls. "I don't remember his name any more, but I was 17 at the time and he tried to teach me the proper way of holding sticks and things like that, but I already knew what he was trying to teach me. So I only went to try to learn how to read drum music, but then I thought, 'What do I need that for? I don't need drum music,' so I only went a couple of times. I wasn't being advanced in any way so I didn't really bother."

The Vendors did all right anyway, and one of the places they were very popular was at the St. Giles Youth Club in Willenhall. "We used to play at their youth-club dances on Thursday nights," Don remembers. "It was so nice there. John Squire was the youth-club leader and we became members. A couple of times a year John had a big dance, as it was in those days at the local dance hall, and there we would always support whoever was playing at the time. That was when they were having the big groups of the time like The Hollies."

The Vendors entered and won a rock'n'roll contest organised by the St. Giles Youth Club. First prize was a gig as support to The Hollies at Willenhall Baths in November 1963.

"We learnt something off The Hollies," Don laughs. "We learnt to wear make-up! We saw The Hollies wearing that on stage, so we had a go of it as well.

"The Hollies had recorded the George Harrison song 'If I Needed Someone', and I was so naive that I said to Graham Nash, 'You only recorded that because you knew you'd get a hit.' If I'd done that today I would have got a punch in the face! But Nash only said, 'We recorded it because it is such a great song,' and it is. But in those days The Beatles were so successful that if you recorded one of their songs, you were guaranteed a hit and I thought that had been their motive. That night we were paid £4 and The Hollies got £75. That's quite a difference!"

Although the pay was not the best, The Vendors enjoyed being able to play with some of the big names of the time. "We were playing with all the Liverpool bands like The Fourmost and The Merseybeats," Don recalls. "It was a great time for us, because where else could we play with these bands? We never got to play with The Beatles though, but I think I saw The Beatles once! There was a TV programme filmed in Aston on Sundays called *Thank Your Lucky Stars* for broadcast the following Saturday. I was by the bus stop going down to Swinn's house, and a big car drove by and I thought it was The Beatles inside, obviously going to *Thank Your Lucky Stars*. I felt really excited about seeing them.

"When The Beatles were cracking it, we sometimes played in Liverpool, just working men's clubs and things like that. It was only one and a half hours away by driving, but we would go there already after lunchtime, hoping to see The Beatles. And whoever we bumped into we would ask, 'Do you know The Beatles?' It was mad!

"We never played with The Rolling Stones, either. They played at the same baths, but I never went to see them. I remember walking by the Willenhall Baths to get the bus home, and there were queues there going around the block by 5.30 p.m. to see the Stones that night. I don't remember why I didn't go see them. Maybe it was too expensive. I was very envious when I was walking by all those kids!"

But even without supporting The Beatles and the Stones, The Vendors were doing very well and came up with fancy stage names for each other. "Johnny Howells was Johnny Travelle, Mick was Snowy Vance and I was Sticks Powell," Don remembers. The Vendors performed regularly and before they knew it, they had an agent called Chalkie White.

"We were playing at a working men's club when this guy came up to us," Don explains. "He said, 'I can get you work.' That was Chalkie White. I don't think Johnny's father liked him, but he did get us a lot of work."

"We used to call him Mr. Ten Per Cent," Mick Marson adds, as that was the fee that White demanded for his services.

In December 1963, Johnny Shane left The Vendors for good and the band needed a new guitarist. Chalkie White called one David John Hill, who'd played in the school band The Young Ones and, after that, a pub band led by drummer Mac Wooley.

"We first met Dave at Johnny's father's house," Don recalls, "and Dave had his girlfriend, Pat, with him as well as his father. At that point Mick and Johnny only played three-string chords, but Dave played the full barre chord like Chuck Berry and I had never seen that before. We had the audition in the front room at Johnny's father's and we asked Dave to play. He played the full barre chord and said, 'Aren't you gonna play with me?' He didn't know that he was more advanced than we were! At that particular time we were only playing other people's songs, the pop tunes of the time, really. When Dave joined us we started to play a few Chuck Berry songs. He knew that kind of thing. That was his style."

"First time I met Don was at Johnny Howells' house in Bilston," says Dave. "I was being taken across to Johnny Howells' house to the audition as they were looking for a guitarist. I was introduced to them and Johnny and Mick were the first ones to approach me. They were doing all the talking; they seemed very friendly while Don sat there at the back of the room and didn't say anything. He seemed very quiet and possibly shy."

"I said to Dave the other day, 'I probably know you better than my own brother,' but back then when we first met, it took weeks before we spoke to each other for the first time," Don laughs. "It was crazy. We were in the same band, but we didn't speak! Back then Dave was very clean-cut and quiet, nothing of the flamboyance of later years. He had a job as an office boy at Tarmac and he thought I was just a pale-faced, spotty kid who never said a word to anybody, so he didn't bother to talk to me either."

"Later, of course, when we starting playing together and I got to know him better, I realised how funny and witty he was," Dave admits. "He looked good too, with his dark, combed-back hairstyle. I didn't give it a great deal of thought at the time, but as soon as we played together I realised how good he was. The main thing about Don is that he has always had an original style, a solid drummer with great timekeeping and also very energetic. His drumming played a very important part in our music."

Having placed Dave with The Vendors, Chalkie White had more or less outlived his role and Maurice Jones became their new manager. "We knew Maurice Jones as he managed a band from Wednesfield called The Sonnets," says Don. "We had played a couple of the same youth clubs on the same nights as them and Maurice Jones started getting us work. Soon after he began booking for the Astra Agency, which Stan Fielding and Len Rowe ran in Wolverhampton, so we went with him to Astra.

"At the Astra Agency in Wolverhampton, all the bands used to get there Friday morning for their money. It was always like that. We would play a pub, but the pub would send the money to the agency, so the bands would have to go to the agency every Friday morning to get the money. If it was *there,* you know! And then we used to pay Maurice Jones £5 a week of our money as a back-hander to help us get more work."

Through Astra, The Vendors were introduced to Ma Regan's circuit. Ma Regan also managed many local groups and had four ballrooms in Birmingham: The Brum Kavern, The Plaza at Old Hill, The Plaza at Handsworth and The Ritz at King's Heath. "She used to put six bands on a night and then they were taking turns at the different places, so six bands were going around to all four ballrooms," says Don. "She paid peanuts, but it was a good circuit with lots of exposure."

"We went to audition for her and sat waiting our turn while The Redcaps were on," says Mick Marson. "We listened, then looked at each other and thought, 'No!' No way could we have followed that group! So we went to the manager and said, 'We have to leave.' 'Why?' 'We ain't good enough.' So off we went to learn new stuff!"

"I think it was good that we recognised this," John Howells says, "but we were angry with ourselves. We played all those fifties numbers and the other bands were playing quite different things, like Beatles songs. We realised that this was the thing to head for, with sort of a commercial feel to it."

"But we could never really play Beatles songs," Don admits, "because we didn't have the voices to do the high falsetto or the harmonies. And then we started playing blues anyway, because the bluesy sound suited Johnny's voice."

"We looked into the bands that had a market and lifted a bit from them," John Howells says, "and when we saw The Yardbirds we thought, 'Ah, that's nice, that could be us.' The Yardbirds were a good band and we liked the way they projected themselves, so we tried to lean a little bit towards that. And consequently when we went along that road we were booked as support act of some of the big names such as Georgie Fame, Alexis Corner, Zoot Money, Spencer Davis, that type of band, like blues with a commercial touch."

The new style went down well with the audience, so although still only teenagers The Vendors were pretty popular. And as they got more bookings, a driver was needed.

"Johnny Shane's father sometimes used to drive us to gigs," Don explains, "but after Johnny had left, we had a guy called Mark driving us in his van. Mark used to work at Tarmac where Johnny and Dave worked and he lived in the same estate as my parents. He used to charge us £2 a night and when we played weddings and pubs he always brought his wife so they could have free drinks. They could drink all night and eat as well, free of charge. Furthermore, Swinn came along to help us with our equipment. He wasn't exactly a roadie, but he helped us out. Back then people only had one roadie anyway, and the bands carried the equipment themselves."

"Once we were playing a wedding and afterwards we left in the van," Mick Marson recalls. "Swinn was in the back of the van and suddenly he said, 'Anybody want a piece of cake?' He'd nicked the wedding cake!"

"We lived off that wedding cake for a week!" Swinn laughs. "Another time I stole all the cutlery and put it in the case with the leads and the cables. When I came down walking across the hall, the case fell open and all the knives and forks fell out. That was embarrassing!"

"We did a lot of crazy things back then," Mick Marson admits. "A couple of years later we were to play at a hotel, but they didn't have a dressing room there so we were asked to change in one of the hotel rooms. But what we did was that instead of changing, we all went to bed."

"We climbed into bed, all of us together," Don seconds, "just to see what it was like. We weren't used to hotel rooms; we hadn't even seen an en suite bathroom before! So we were all lying in this bed with the covers to our noses, thinking this is the life, and in walked Steve Brett

& The Mavericks! That was one of the first times I actually met Noddy Holder."

"The Mavericks were to play the same hotel and change in the same room," says Mick Marson, "but they didn't know what to think of it, with us lying in the bed!"

Despite the tomfoolery, Astra believed in The Vendors and wanted to expose them further. It was suggested that they do an EP for promotion purposes, so off they went to make a private demo tape at the Domino Studio in Albrighton. The demo was then pressed up by the studio as acetate EPs.

"We bought some time at the studios," says John Howells. "I think the agency suggested that we did an EP with four tracks. It was 'Peace Pipe', 'Twilight Time', the Buddy Holly song 'Take Your Time' and 'Don't Leave Me Now', which Dave and I had penned. It was never distributed or promoted, but it was the only one we got. Today I have the only copy left. The tracks can be found on the CD *The Genesis Of Slade*, but I didn't really make any money off it. If I wanted to have done that, I'd have released it in 1973!"

"I also have a copy," adds Mick Marson, "but it is broken!"

Another move to expose the band was to get them an audition for a TV programme called *For Teenagers Only*.

"We went to the audition at the ATV studio in Birmingham," John Howells says, "but when we got there, there was no bass player. The time was moving on, so we made a call to where Bill Diffy worked and he came on the phone. He was still at work. 'What are you doing there?' we asked and he said, 'I can't come. My foreman won't let me go.' 'You didn't call in sick like the rest of us?' No, he had turned up for work. So he cost us a TV appearance. Things were never right between us after that. Bill had to make his choice if he wanted an ordinary life or be on the road with us. That was his choice and soon we were looking for a new bass player."

"Bill was much older than us," Don explains. "He didn't think that the group was making any money. He was going to get married so he wanted to settle down and he decided to leave the band."

Luckily, Maurice Jones knew of a bass player who was available following the dissolution of another of the bands that he managed. "His name was Dave Jones, but we used to call him Cass," says Don. "Cass was short for Casanova, because he was a good-looking guy who appealed to the girls, but he was never that fond of the name. Often he then went by the name 'Big Dave', as opposed to Dave Hill who was 'Little Dave'. Dave actually liked the name 'Little Dave' back then. He thought it was cute!"

"Cass got the job right away," adds John Howells, "because he was good. He was probably the best bass player of the time. From then on the band was Dave, Don, myself, Mick and Cass."

When Cass joined he didn't particularly like R&B music, but after a while he changed his mind as they had plenty of gigs and a good following. It was clear that something bigger was in store for The Vendors.

3

'N Between Times

Since Don had dropped out of college he hadn't done anything but play, but in 1964, when he was about to turn 18, he had to find a job.

"I looked through the jobs advertised in the newspaper and I saw one that said junior metallurgist wanted in a foundry in Willenhall," he recalls. "It was at the BICC, British Insulated Callender's Cables, where junction boxes for telephone cables were made. 'That's a good job for you,' my dad said, so I just applied for the job on what I had learnt in college. I didn't have the qualifications, but luckily the main boss there, his name was Don as well, liked me. I came for an interview and he gave me the job. I didn't say anything about me playing in a band and my hair was pretty long for the time, so I combed it back so it didn't look that bad.

"I worked for about a year at BICC's laboratory testing metals and it was a nice job and nice people. Both Don and his assistant Ivor were nice guys to work for, although we worked in different departments. After a few months I got to talk to Don during a tea break and he said, 'You never told me that you played in a band.' I was stunned. 'How did you know?' 'You played the local dance hall last night and some of the guys from the department were there.' And I thought, oh God! But I said to Don that I thought it might hinder my chances of getting the job and that was why I had never mentioned it. He then went, 'No, no, no!' and he was really interested in the band. When we had to travel away to places like one hour away from Wolverhampton, he let me finish early. He said, 'As long as you get your work done, it is OK.' So I got in early in the morning or weekends if we weren't playing to catch up with my work."

As soon as he started earning money, Don bought his first set of drums. It was a standard Premier kit, but he couldn't purchase it without his father's blessing, "I had to pay for them in instalments and in order to do that in those days you had to have the parents sign the hire purchase papers. That was what I was dreading, but Dad signed them, no problem."

Towards the end of 1964 it was felt that a new name was needed for the band, as The Vendors sounded a bit dated. "It happened at a gig in Walsall," John Howells explains. "As The Vendors we came across as a nicey-nicey band, but we had developed our own different styles and the hair was getting a bit longer, so we weren't completely nice any more. We played in a club and Spencer Davis was there, talking to Maurice Jones. He said we ought to change the name, but the question was, to what? We sometimes worked under different names such as Johnny Travelle & The Travellers, but that was always mispronounced as Johnny Travel, so that name didn't fit either. But then Maurice Jones said that we were sort of in between styles, so what we did was drop the 'i'. And that's how we became The 'N Betweens and we all found that it sounded good."

In the spring of 1965, The 'N Betweens started bonding with a young secretary, Carole Williams, who worked at Astra. "My cousin Vicky and I used to go to all the local dances and Vick knew the sons of Stan Fielding, one of the owners of Astra Agency," explains Carole. "I had just turned 18 and we were chatting to Stan at one of the venues. He asked me if I wanted to change my job and would I like to go and work for him? This sounded much more interesting than working for Goodyear, the tyre company, so I left there and went to Astra. At that time they were based in the basement of an old house, which had been converted into offices. The land is part of the Ring Road now and it was just down the road from the Molineux football ground.

"I started work there on a Monday in this virtually underground office, which had a window facing down the back garden. Friday was payday for the bands and on the first Friday in my new job, two guys came walking down the garden. One was small with long brown hair; the other one was much taller with black hair. I remember they came into the office and the little one was obviously the more outgoing of the pair. He was full of questions. Who are you? Where do you live? Do you go and see local bands, etc., while the taller guy, who had these incredible eyes, was very quiet and just stood there chewing. The talker introduced himself as 'Little Dave' and told me they were in The 'N Betweens and the other guy was the drummer, Don."

"I'd started chewing gum by then," Don comments. "When I was playing on stage I got a dry throat and I couldn't stop to take a drink. I had chewing gum one night and it kept my mouth moist and I thought this actually works! So I continued with that and later I got quite famous for it."

"Dave asked if I had seen the band," Carole Williams continues, "and I said yes, they were very good. Then he said, 'Next time you come to see us, let us know you are there.' And they went off to get their wages. After that the Friday meetings were regular and soon both Vick and I were part of the gang that surrounded the band."

The 'N Betweens' 'gang' had by now turned into a decent following, which the band members themselves ascribe to their being a bit different from other groups. "All bands of that time, like the very popular Montanas, were cover bands, but they concentrated on the Top 10," John Howells says. "Probably the first tribute band was The Californians, although they didn't realise it. They did all Beach Boys material. As for us, we also looked at the American market, but not the Top 10. We went to Birmingham to a place called The Diskery, where they got all the imports, and we bought some and learnt them. So although we were covering other bands, too, not many people had heard of them. We were probably the first to do songs by, for instance, Sonny & Cher."

"The one lasting memory is when they did 'I Got You Babe'," says Carole Williams. "Mick Marson and Johnny Howells as Sonny & Cher!

I can't be sure any more, it was a long time ago, but I think it was Mick who dressed as a woman."

A tender vision, to be sure! Actually The 'N Betweens were regarded not as the local Sonny & Cher, but as the local Rolling Stones, because their taste in music didn't match the normal beat group repertoire. Soon they had their own fan club, run by Carole Williams. "I was asked by their manager, Maurice Jones, if I would run the fan club," she explains. "It was only a small fan club, but I sent out monthly newsletters and gig guides so that the members could plan their nights out."

The 'N Betweens went back to audition for the Ma Regan circuit and she liked this new, improved band. "Ma Regan was quite powerful," Don says "and she offered us a residency in King's Heath every Thursday night. It was fantastic as they got prestigious gigs there. We also played The Plaza in Old Hill now and again, as Mondays were blues nights. The Plaza had a revolving stage, which was a revolution at that time. But it was very useful, because at the Plaza they sometimes had up to 10 bands a night and with a revolving stage one band could set up while another one was playing."

"After gigs the band used to stay with us," says Don's sister Carol. "Then Don would go upstairs and bring blankets and whatever and mum would make them tea. They all liked mum."

"Dora was a bit of a character," Mick Marson admits. "Both of Don's parents were, actually."

"They were lovely people," adds John Howells. "Salt of the earth."

"My memories of Don's family were that they were always cracking jokes," says Dave. "Don's mum had a deadpan humour; she would say something funny, but keep a straight face. His dad was a bit the same. This is where Don gets his wit. That's how Don is, says a one-liner and it's absolutely hilarious. When I went round his house there was always toast and tea on the go, and there would be Don's dad, standing in vest and braces and he would ask, 'Dave, do you want some toast?' 'Yes, Mr. Powell,' I would always reply. But the thing about the toast was it was cut thick, the size of doorstops! So that's how it was."

"Everybody was sleeping in Mum and Dad's front room after gigs," Don recalls. "Mum always used to get mad at me because I let the other guys sleep in the armchairs and settees and then I would go to bed. She went, 'How can you leave them downstairs? You could at least have offered somebody else your bed!'"

The 'N Betweens played on a regular basis at many venues in the area. They were the most popular group to play at The Woolpack in Wolverhampton, mostly on Tuesday and Friday nights. "The Woolpack was like a restaurant and part of the old Wolverhampton market," Don recalls. "The windows went all across the wall and the stage backed the windows out into the market. It was the only place where we had to do two-and-a-half hour sets. It was a tiny place and it got incredibly hot in there."

The Ship and Rainbow on Dudley Road in Wolverhampton was another haunt where The 'N Betweens made their mark. It had an upstairs ballroom called The Dudley Suite, where the bands played. "To get there we had to use the fire escape," says Don. "I never understood why we couldn't use the stairs that were in the foyer of the pub below. Maybe they wouldn't let us carry our equipment through the pub. But it was dangerous using the fire escape. Especially when it was raining."

The Ship and Rainbow offered entertainment five nights a week, with Sundays being R&B nights promoted by Astra in the early days. Bluesy groups were very successful there. The 'N Betweens used to alternate with local band The Soul Seekers on Sunday nights and supported artists like Manfred Mann, Spencer Davis and Alexis Korner.

"He was a lovely man, Alexis Korner," Don says. "A wonderful man. And we were in awe of these people. But I remember once he said to me, 'What am I doing here? I usually don't do things like this. I could have been at home writing letters.' I just couldn't believe it. He was so popular and then he would rather stay at home!"

What Don remembers most, however, is a show The 'N Betweens played at the Civic Hall in Wolverhampton, again promoted by Astra. "The Civic Hall was one of the most significant dance venues in Wolverhampton, with room for around 1,000 people," Don explains. "Playing there was a big deal, although the acoustics were horrible. We were on the same bill as Georgie Fame, Zoot Money, Alexis Korner and The Soul Seekers from Wolverhampton, and we got autographs from all the big names. It was such a great night."

As they became more successful, so the number of gigs increased and eventually the five 'N Betweens lads realised that they couldn't keep up the pace. "When we started out, I'd gone to work less than 12 months in an engineering shop at Tarmac," John Howells recalls. "We couldn't keep it up, working during daytime *and* playing at nights. We didn't get home until very late and the next morning Mick would come to my house, because we went to work together. We didn't work in the same place, as he was a butcher, but it was on the same route. We were still in a daze from the night before and then we said, 'See you tonight at five o'clock.' Eventually we had to stop working. Something had to go."

"Dave had turned professional in 1964, way before the rest of us," Don says, "but in late 1965 we realised that we had to become professionals as well. Ivor was my immediate boss at BICC and when I left, I asked him if he was interested in working for us, but he found it too risky. Later BICC closed, so he probably regretted his decision."

Now that The 'N Betweens had turned professional, Maurice Jones felt that changes were needed. For one, he wanted the boys to be better groomed. On their first day as fully professional musicians Maurice Jones told them to get perms at Joanna's, a ladies' hairdresser in Bilston.

"The hairdresser was opposite John's," Mick Marson says. "It is still there, by the way, not the same people, but the store."

"We were a bit reluctant at first," Don remembers. "Especially Dave and Johnny, I think. Cass and I went first and had our hair washed and set. The three others were afraid of being caught at a ladies' hairdresser, but eventually Maurice Jones talked them into it. I think some of them felt that the new hairdos looked like Beatles wigs!"

The next thing Astra did was to organise an audition at the Marquee Club in London, a prestigious venue where German club managers came to listen to the bands. "There was an opening for British bands in Germany because of The Beatles," Mick Marson recalls, "but Germany was way behind England musically, and R&B had no real place there. The top band in Germany back then was called The Lords. They were terrible. 'Baby Baby, Balla Balla': that was what their hit song was called and those were the only words in it!"

"It was just crazy," adds John Howells. "At the audition we only did one song, I think it was a Chuck Berry song that was popular in Germany, and we got the job on that. But we were really excited about going to Germany, as it was the first time out of England for any of us. We left by the end of October 1965 and stayed for a month."

"We went over with the ferry to Ostend," Don recalls. "On the ferry we accidentally bumped into Noddy Holder and his group, Steve Brett & The Mavericks. They were on the ferry going to Frankfurt. Noddy's real name was actually Neville, but nobody called him that, except for his mum who used to call him Nev."

Neville John Holder had been with the band The Rockin' Phantoms, who changed their name to The Memphis Cut-Outs in May 1964. "They were playing the same pubs and clubs that we were," Don recalls, "and in late 1964 they started backing a cabaret singer, Steve Brett, calling themselves The Mavericks, the name of his former band."

"I think Noddy was thinking of leaving," says John Howells. "The Memphis Cut-Outs were a band like us who went into cabaret. They were offered a lifeline in the shape of backing Steve Brett as his new Mavericks, but as it was all cabaret we thought they'd sold their souls. That was probably why Noddy wanted to get out."

In Dortmund The 'N Betweens were booked at the Habenera club for a month playing six hours a night, seven nights a week for £14 a week each. "They had two clubs; one in Dortmund and one in a small town called Witten, a few kilometres away," Don recalls. "Another English band called Four Steps Beyond was playing there and the deal was that we were to play Dortmund for two weeks while they were playing Witten and then we swapped over. The club in Witten was a bit more posh and they didn't like us, but in Dortmund they didn't like Four Steps Beyond either, so we swapped back. This way we only played one or two nights in Witten and the rest of the time in Dortmund.

"Four Steps Beyond were good. They used to do Hollies-type stuff, and we stayed together with them in this farmhouse in the middle of nowhere. It was awful. In the room where we slept there was one double bed and three small single camp beds. Johnny and Mick had the double bed and Cass, Dave and myself had the single ones. Across the hallway, Four Steps Beyond stayed in a room similar to ours. There was no heating or hot water and I don't think I had a shower for a month. We had to boil the water, so we only boiled enough to have a shave."

"It was *freezing* in that farmhouse," John Howells recalls. "When we first arrived I went into the bathroom and the pipes were made with cardboard inserts and I thought, 'This is ridiculous!' We went back to the club and we said, 'If there are no improvements, we go back to England.' So they put a stove in the bedroom, like a wood burner. That was the improvement! But I guess in those days that would have been common."

"All we got to eat was chicken and chips for nearly a month," Don continues. "We bought that from a caravan near the station. 'Hänschen und Pommes Frites', it was called. That was the only German I knew! One day a week we used to treat ourselves to a meal at a restaurant in a department store, otherwise it was only chicken and chips every day. But there was a big army base in Dortmund and the soldiers came into the club at night. They used to buy us drinks and look after us a bit. They took us to the base one day and brought us to the mess and we had roast beef and everything. That was fantastic."

"There were many Brits in the club and the Americans were coming in every night as well," says John Howells. "If you knew the songs that they wanted, they'd bring you a tray of drinks, so we had drinks all the time. It was long hours though, and the other bands had told us that if we needed a break we just had to say, 'Eine kleine Pause.' That's a saying that I still remember in German. Working long hours every day was exhausting, but we never went to drugs to keep up with it. We were never offered anything anyway! That was a good thing. In the late sixties, early seventies it would probably have been different, but back then the only thing we had was Dexedrine to keep us awake. Compared with today we were probably a sad band!"

Mick Marson celebrated his 21st birthday over there. "That was a manic night, that was," he recalls. "It was only us and the guys from

Four Steps Beyond celebrating at the farmhouse, but the next morning the chandelier was full of beer. There was beer everywhere. I think it was the drummer of the other band who'd done it. The next morning I found him in the wardrobe. I'll never forget that birthday, it was totally insane."

The 'N Betweens returned to England at the end of November and went straight to the Pye studios in London. "Before we left for Germany, we had gone to London to do some tracks for Barclay Records," Don says. "It was Bobby Graham who spotted us. He used to be the drummer with Joe Brown & The Bruvvers, but he left the band to go into record production and he was a talent scout for Barclay Records, their French label. He was doing auditions at Le Metro Club in Birmingham and lots of bands went. He liked us so we went down to Pye studios in London."

The 'N Betweens recorded the four tracks 'Can Your Monkey Do The Dog?', 'Respectable', 'I Wish You Would' and 'Ooh Poo Pah Doo', but they were never released. After returning from Germany the band went back to record another four tracks. "Bobby Graham was a session drummer as well," Don remembers. "He had done some of the early P.J. Proby things and big records of the time. He said, 'I have a session guitarist friend who has started to write songs, so I've asked him to come along and bring some.' And that was Jimmy Page. He had short hair and came there with his guitar and his little amp and he played this song called 'Little Nightingale'. That one we recorded along with 'Feel So Fine', 'Take A Heart' and 'You Don't Believe Me'. When we had recorded all four tracks, we never heard any more of it. But later we found out that an EP had been released in France only, with us on the one side and a band called The Hills on the other side. They had passed the audition like us as well and Barclay Records had decided to put both bands on the same EP."

With local fame, a good following, their own fan club and an EP out in France, things looked pretty good for The 'N Betweens, but Don and Dave were not content. They wanted more than just to play the blues. Around this time, Cass Jones left the band. "The month in Germany had taken its toll," Don admits. "Those particular bookings would either make or break a band and basically we started to fall apart after that. Cass had met a girl called Jenny. Her grandfather was the greengrocer at the estate where my parents lived, so my parents knew him, and that was how we met Jenny. Her family actually ran a string of greengrocery shops all over Wolverhampton, so Cass could see that was where he was gonna go.

"As for Dave and myself, we were getting a bit disillusioned. We were sick and tired of always playing blues. We wanted to take the music somewhere else and we had already talked about splitting up the band. I remember that Johnny had learnt a whole album by Muddy Waters or somebody like that and I said, 'If you're gonna play that, I'm leaving!' Johnny was into the blues and that was what he wanted, to go further with that, but I hated the blues situation. I could just sit back doing nothing. It was the same drum thing for every song. With Cass gone, Dave and I decided that if we were to form a new band, the time was right."

4

The Magic Line-Up

By the end of 1965, Don found himself in a tricky spot. Being in a locally successful band but wanting to change both the music and the line-up that had made its success was not an easy manoeuvre. The next few months were filled with secrecy and double-dealings and eventually it would cause some hurt feelings.

"It was all a bit underhanded," Don admits, "because Dave and myself wanted a four-piece band like The Beatles. It looked great on stage. I remember at one point we talked about getting Robert Plant as our singer. Looking back it was a bit strange, because we had already worked with Jimmy Page when we recorded for Barclay Records, so we kind of had a connection to half of what was to become Led Zeppelin. But we thought, if we got Robert Plant we also had to get another guitarist and we didn't want that. We wanted the four-piece band.

"At that point Robert Plant was in a band called Listen and later in Band Of Joy. Noddy's old band had been playing with Robert Plant and when Nod was not working, he used to roadie for them in his dad's window-cleaning van, as his dad was a window cleaner.

"Noddy wasn't a lead singer back then, he was a guitarist, and as Dave and I also had the idea of forming a band with two lead guitarists, like

The Allman Brothers, I said to Dave, 'Do you remember that guy, you know, Noddy Holder? I wonder what he's doing now?'

"Noddy was a great frontman. He was even then. Steve Brett was the main singer of their band, but Nod used to sing maybe one or two songs before the start of their show to warm up things. He didn't have that loud a voice back then. It came later, but he had impressed me because he reminded me of John Lennon in the way he talked and the way he sang. Before he joined The Mavericks, I'd also seen him with The Rockin' Phantoms at St. Giles' and I had already noticed him then. The Rockin' Phantoms were very good, especially Nod, but I remember Johnny, Mick and me being a bit jealous, as they were stealing some of our glory. When I suggested Nod to Dave, he thought it was a joke though, because Noddy was now in this cabaret act."

The pieces fell into place when Don and Dave bumped into Noddy in Wolverhampton and went for a coffee at Beattie's Coffee Bar. Here they learnt that Noddy had left Steve Brett & The Mavericks, so they promptly offered him a job with Don and Dave's new band. Noddy thought over the job offer, then accepted it.

There was also a vacancy for a bass player to replace the departing Cass Jones. Maurice Jones placed an advert in the local newspaper, the *Express & Star*, and many prospective bassists turned up to audition. "When Dave 'Cass' Jones said he was leaving, I helped arrange the auditions for his replacement," Carole Williams remembers, "and I think almost every bass player in the area wanted to try out! The auditions were held in The Blue Flame, a club run by Astra, and this school kid turned up. He was wearing a long scarf and looked really young. But the guys were in no doubt he was *the* one. Enter Jimmy Lea."

James Whild Lea was a musically gifted child who had played the violin since the age of nine and been the youngest member of the Staffordshire Youth Orchestra for a number of years. He liked rock as well as classical music and at the age of 14 became the bass player of a school band called Nick & The Axemen. "The first time I met Don was at The 'N Betweens' audition for a bass player," Jim recalls. "I was extremely nervous while I was playing, but when Dave broke a string we paused for a few minutes. Don called me over and cracked a couple of jokes, which immediately put me at ease."

"Typically wry, Don enquired of Jim if he played anything else other than bass, keyboard and violin," adds Keith Altham, then a rock journalist with *New Musical Express*. "'I used to play the cello a bit,' said an unsuspecting Jim. 'What went wrong?' asked Don. 'Did the spike keep getting stuck in your neck?' Don's infamous dry wit broke the ice and Jim joined the group as a result."

"We didn't know Jim before the audition at The Blue Flame club," Don says. "He showed up with his bass in a polythene bag and we picked him because he was a great bass player. He could play *so* fast, and the rest of the guys at the audition were crap. Some of these people, how could they think that they could play? Jim struck me straight away as being the one for the job, but Astra didn't really want him. He was just a school kid and they probably found him too young to fit in with the image of The 'N Betweens. But we didn't want him in The 'N Betweens, we wanted him in a new band with Noddy as the frontman, although Jim didn't know that. He thought he was to join the original band.

"When we came over to Jim's house in Codsall to ask him to join, we told him that the idea was to get members for a four-piece band. Jim was very disillusioned about that, because he used to be a big fan of the old band. He really liked Johnny Howells and the blues and, just like Dave, he thought that Nod was a joke. But he accepted and we went for a tryout with the new line-up straight away."

The first rehearsal with the new four-piece band took place at the Three Men In A Boat, a pub near Noddy's home on the Beechdale Estate in Walsall. "It was done in secret," Don says, "as Johnny and Mick didn't know. Dave and myself got our equipment together in the van. Dave was the only driver at that time, so he used to drive. We picked Jim up and went down for Noddy and then on to Three Men In A Boat, where we'd played a lot of times with The 'N Betweens. We knew the guy who ran the pub and he said we could rehearse there that afternoon. So we had a secret rehearsal just to see if it would work.

"For the first song we had to think of something that Nod's band played and that our band played and this way the first song we ever played together was 'Mr. Pitiful' by Otis Redding. And it worked! Straight away it worked! We were all like young kids, laughing and giggling because it was working. Then we just leapt into other things, like soul and some Tamla Motown, and that worked as well. It was fantastic."

As fantastic as it may have seemed to find the right guys for the new band, there was still some dirty work to be done. "Both Dave and I felt that Mick had more or less lost interest," Don recalls. "That didn't fit well with me and Dave, who wanted to branch out, so we had to tell him that we wanted to replace him with Noddy."

In the end, they approached John Howells and asked him for a meeting. Howells wanted to bring Mick Marson, but was told no. Don and Dave then made it clear that they wanted Nod to be in the band. "That confused me," John admits. "Did they really want a fourth guitarist? But no, they wanted Mick out. Furthermore, they wanted to take the music in a different direction." He went away to think.

"I think they approached it the wrong way," John Howells states. "They could have said, 'Mick, you need to do this or that,' or, 'We want to take the music there.' They could have talked about the problems. It was a bit awkward that they wanted to let Mick go, because we had quite a following. I could have turned around and said, 'I'm sorry, Mick, but you are going and I am staying,' but I had this loyalty and I couldn't do it. And I couldn't figure out what kind of music they wanted, either, as they didn't really say so."

"I think Johnny was very, very disillusioned," Don adds. "He may have thought that we wanted to carry on with him as a frontman, but that was never the idea. We just wanted to be a four-piece band consisting of Dave, Nod, Jim and myself."

"When Don and Dave kicked me out of the band, I was a little upset at the time," Mick Marson admits. "John and Don and I had been so close, so it was a little underhanded. But that's water under the bridge. Don is still a mate."

When Jim joined The 'N Betweens, he played a few shows with Mick before he was replaced by Noddy. The shows had a difficult atmosphere about them. Mick Marson and John Howells were on the point of leaving and the fans were discontented. So were the soon-to-be ex-members and their families.

"Pam, Mick's girlfriend of the time who later became his wife, poured a pint of beer in Dave's suitcase," Don recalls. "He had all his stage clothes in there. We used to wear matching suits and Cuban-heeled boots and Dave's things were ruined. I think it was the last day that Mick played with us, because I remember him getting pissed."

"There was a bit of conflict when Nod joined the band," agrees Carole Williams. "That was the end for John and Mick. I remember being quite upset and angry at the changes, but it soon became obvious that something magic had happened. The music changed, the band went from strength to strength and was certainly the most popular local band at the time... although there are other groups who like to think they were!"

The new line-up was indeed eventually going to perform miracles, but it took another six months before they could become the four-piece band of their dreams. "We already had some bookings at the time," Don recalls, "and our agent said, 'Well, you can only do these bookings with Johnny Howells. They like him as a singer, so you can't let him go quite yet.' Because of that, Nod joined the band as a guitarist only, but he used to sing a few songs with us before Johnny went on."

The first gig without Mick Marson was on March 19 1966, at Walsall Town Hall. Contrary to common belief, the gig did not take place on April 1, because the venue was closed due to local elections, with all dances being cancelled. In any case The 'N Betweens played The Majestic in Newcastle on that particular April Fool's Day. The band even played a few other gigs before April 1 and the myth about Slade being founded on April Fool's Day didn't surface until 10 years later, apparently as a promotional gimmick.

All spring The 'N Betweens performed with John Howells as their singer, until finally in June something happened. "In those days in England in the holiday resorts, we used to play a ballroom or a club every night for a week, and we were to play at the 400 Ballroom in Torquay," Don says.

"It was an annual engagement arranged by Astra. We had done that for two seasons already, and now came the third season.

"We stayed in a tiny caravan because it was cheap for the week. It used to cost £15 for the whole week, which was perfect, even though the caravan was situated in Paignton. One night Johnny didn't want to play. He asked us if we could do it on our own because he had met this girl and he wanted to take her out that night on a date. And of course we said, 'Yeah, we'll try it.'

"That was the first time that we could play together, just the four of us. And it went *fantastic*! We were in such high spirits. As we drove back to the caravan we thought that we'd better be careful when we got back with Johnny. He was not going to be very happy because of our high spirits. It got even worse when we got to the caravan, because the girl he was seeing that night didn't turn up, so he'd spent the night in the caravan on his own. It was a total contrast to us, who were all jubilant because the gig went so good."

"In the end it worked out," John Howells says. "The split with The 'N Betweens didn't further our relationship at the time, but no matter what has been said in the past, I'm going to stick up for the band. Nod and Jim are great guys obviously, but we never bonded that much. And with Dave, there might have been a bit of a battle between us at that particular time when we split, as it wasn't done well, but it is water under the bridge. When I left The 'N Betweens it was in my interest, musically. I joined The Blues Ensemble, as I wanted to get on with blues. I wanted to sing with a full blues orchestra with horns and everything, and I could do that with the new band. It couldn't be different. It was fate."

With Howells gone, Don found himself in the four-piece band that he and Dave had wanted, but a new line-up playing a different kind of music also meant a lot of work. "We rehearsed just like *crazy* for months and months," Don recalls. "We started learning a lot of Tamla Motown stuff and arranging them just for us."

"Don was always extremely friendly and willing to help out in any way he could," Jim recalls. "I used to work out the musical arrangements for the band and while Nod and Dave were learning their guitar parts, Don would make buckets of tea for us. He pretty well always knew what to do on the drums, but should I have any fancy ideas, he was always very quick on the uptake. If not, he would graft until he had nailed it."

"In the rhythm section, Jim and I worked everything out together and we played *so* close together," Don recalls. "We got that from The Hollies, because I'd noticed how drummer Bobby Elliott and bass player Eric Haydock played close together and I thought it was incredible. It was so tight and that was exactly what Jim and myself did when we formed. Furthermore, although Noddy was the lead singer, Dave and Jim sang as well, and Nod and Dave played lead guitar together, like twin lead guitars. Jim also played his bass like a guitar, the three of them playing with different harmonies. It was quite revolutionary for its time, so we figured we just had to have a few weeks to work this out on our own.

"Then, through Astra, this offer came up for us to go to Germany. That would be great; then we could get our act together, so to speak. So we got booked to do a month at the Star Palast in Kiel. The manager there, I'll always remember his name, he was a guy named Manfred Woitalla. He was a real *gangster*! In those days we got £17 a week each and accommodation. We were playing a ballroom, which was a big old cinema that had been converted. The old cinemas in those days had the big stairways round the side going up to the balcony, and our accommodation was the landing. We had four camp beds on the stairway landing and we had to get cleaned up in the club's toilets.

"Manfred Woitalla *hated* us. 'What are you doing?' he said. 'You're playing too loud!' He didn't like the material we were playing either. Because in those days if you did that kind of booking you had to play the Top 20 material, but we weren't playing that. We were playing old Tamla Motown stuff and certain soul hits of the time. He *hated* us. He used to stand down the front, shouting at us and throwing his keys on the floor, yelling, 'Too much treble, too much treble!'

"Usually, when you did those kinds of bookings, you'd get a bit of money within the first few days, but Woitalla didn't give us any. We didn't have any money at the time and nowhere to crash, as we had to wait for the club to close to get into those camp beds. And every night

Woitalla made us finish after the first 45 minutes because he didn't like us.

"The top of the bill at that particular club was a group called Paul Raven & The Boston Showband. Now Paul Raven is better known as Gary Glitter. He and his band had proper living quarters and he used to take us out for a coffee and cake, because we had no money. Manfred Woitalla wasn't gonna pay us; we *knew* he wouldn't give us any money, so after a week we decided to leave and come home.

"During the day, Woitalla's kids used to play cowboys and Indians in the club with toy bows and arrows, and Noddy got an arrow off one of them. The equipment we used on stage wasn't ours, it was supplied by the club, and as Nod is a person who won't let anything go, he pushed the arrow through the speaker cabinets of all the speakers before we left.

"We got in our van and hightailed it from Kiel to the ferry in Ostend. We were really worried in case Woitalla would send someone after us. We had it all timed just right to get to the ferry, but when we got there, the ferry was just leaving. And we were going, 'No, no, no!' But then they brought the ferry back! It was only a few metres out and they brought it back. And we all went, 'Thank *God!*' We were really terrified in case anybody came after us."

The 'N Betweens survived without any reprisals from Woitalla, but soon after they bumped into another striking individual whose personality was quite different from that of the hated German club owner. It all started when the Astra Agency got The 'N Betweens a shot at playing the Tiles club in London.

"When they got their first London gig, at Tiles, I arranged a small coach to take a crowd of us to see them," Carole Williams recalls. "It was a really big night for the band, and we wanted to share it with them. That was the night Kim Fowley saw them."

"It was in late August 1966," Don explains, "and we didn't know there was this guy in the audience called Kim Fowley. He had produced The Hollywood Argyles and he *was* Napoleon XIV. 'They're Coming To Take Me Away Ha-Haaa' – that was him. Kim was much taller than me and *so* skinny, and he came up to us and said, 'You guys are gonna be famous,' and we went, 'Who's this freak?' He introduced himself as Kim Fowley and said, 'Stick with me. You're gonna be stars.' 'OK, Kim.' 'I'll make a record with you. It could be a massive record.' 'OK, Kim.' We'd heard all this before. 'OK, Kim.' And then we went back to Wolverhampton.

"Back in Wolverhampton, we found out that the agency that Kim Fowley was with had actually contacted Astra. So we went back to London and into Regent Sound in Denmark Street to make a record. It was a tiny studio, a real dump, but The Rolling Stones had recorded there.

"We didn't really write our own things then and Kim Fowley said, 'Well, what are some of your favourite things that you play on stage?' We really liked a song called 'You Better Run' by The Young Rascals, so we recorded that with him. He was *mad* because he said, 'We'll do it as a fade-out. So when you finish the song, just keep on playing and then you'll give me time to pull it back.' But he never did. If you listen to the record, it just falls apart in the end. You never thought that was the ending.

"Then Kim said, 'Now we'll write a B-side together.' We'd never written before, but he took another song that we liked playing on stage, 'I Take What I Want' by The Artwoods. Kim said, 'OK then, we'll just put new lyrics to it,' and we did that. We called it 'Evil Witchman', but we all went, 'Can we call it that?' Kim assured us, 'Yes, as long as it is the B-side it is normal.'"

The band did three more recordings, 'Hold Tight', 'Ugly Girl' and 'Need', with Fowley on additional vocals on the latter two, but those tracks weren't released and wouldn't see the day of light until the 1996 CD *Genesis Of Slade*. A recording of Otis Redding's 'Security', which the band also made with Fowley, was issued in America as a promotion-only single with 'Evil Witchman' as the B-side.

'You Better Run' was eventually released on December 2, 1966. Says Don: "Even though the single got plenty of airplay, it didn't sell well. As luck would have it, the song was also released by Robert Plant's group Listen at the same time and, although their version didn't sell either, their production was more professional than ours. So that was the end of us working with Kim Fowley."

5

Bonding

The meagre sales figures for 'You Better Run' probably had something to do with the new line-up. It was still only six months since John Howells had left the group and many of the old fans were still not happy with the new arrangement.

"It didn't go down with the fans very well that we had changed," Don recalls. "It was a bit unnerving, because we'd had quite a good following with the old band. At the time we didn't think it would be a problem until it came about and then people said that they would never come and see us again. We basically had to win a lot of people over. It was not just a new line-up but also a different style of music, but we'd kept the name, because if we had a new name we would have had to start all over. It wasn't easy for the Astra Agency either, when it had to book us, because we were quite a different band from what people expected."

A few loyal fans stuck with the new 'N Betweens though, among them Carole Williams and her cousin Vicky Pearson. "I got involved in all this through Carole," says Vicky. "There were so many small clubs where we could go and see bands back then and The 'N Betweens were our favourites. We soon bonded and the bond exists to this day. We followed them all over, just because of the friendship."

"We were really close," says Carole Williams. "Back then, Don appeared to be very shy and thoughtful, but he had a wicked sense of humour, which only a few of us lucky insiders ever really saw. He drank lemonade by the pint and made a fortune in profits for Wrigley's! In the early years he was the quiet one, always happy to be in the background, although not so quiet when the background was on stage. He must have been the loudest drummer in the West Midlands!"

"In the sixties everybody got bigger and bigger equipment, and it was the days before monitors so I had to play loud," Don explains. "I thought that was the way to do it. I had to keep up with the rest of the band and it just carried on. I've always played like that basically, there's no formula, no hidden thing. It's just the way I play."

"His drumming became louder over the years," Jim adds, "and I am sure at one point he became the loudest drummer in the world – I pitied his broken drums!"

"Don was only the second quietest in the band," Vicky Pearson states. "Jim was obviously quieter. Nod and Dave were always the ones that you looked at – Noddy obviously because he was the frontman – but Dave also had his own persona."

"We were all really good mates," says Carole Williams. "Jim brought his girlfriend, Louise, along, Dave had his girlfriend, and we were really like one big family. If there was a gig within 20 miles of home we were all normally there. After local gigs, it was quite common for us to have a lift home in the van, and we would stop at my house for hot drinks and toast. If my stepfather was working a night shift, we ate in the house. If he was home, the food and drinks were consumed in the van so that we didn't wake him, as he had to be up early. My mum always knew when the boys had been back. Then she had to go to the shop over the road for bread for breakfast!"

"Back then there weren't any phones at private homes," says Vicky, "so when the chaps played down south, Carole and I could tell our mums individually that we were at each other's house. Then we would actually get the train to London, go watch them and we couldn't come back in the van, as there was no room, so we'd take what we called the milk train back in the morning."

The girls did indeed get close to the band; Vicky even helped shape their personal appearances. "I used to cut the chaps' hair, as I'm a hair-dresser," she says. "I had to do it after hours, because obviously I couldn't do it when the boss was there. The boss used to go home every day at three o'clock and we had a secret place where the chaps would stand and if the boss was still there, they would wait; if not, they would go in.

"They'd have a shampoo and, although it was before women's hairdressers were doing men's hair, it coincided with when men found their feminine side. I could suggest new hairstyles to them, 'Can I do this?' 'Oh, yeah, go on.' It was all very good fun. But they were so young. Jimmy looked like a 12 year old and Don used to have dreadful acne, so he always wanted me to buy him spot cream. He wanted the women's spot cream for his skin, so we used to go shopping together. I was getting him in touch with his feminine side!"

"In his youth Don had bad acne," Don's sister Carol confirms. "It was really unfair. He was very clean, but he always came out in spots, whereas Derek's skin was flawless although he never wanted to bathe. We had to hold Derek to sponge him down! Don tried everything on his skin, but nothing worked. It was so unfair."

"It started with the usual teenage pimples on the forehead," Don says, "and then it spread to all over my face and my back. The others used to joke that they could read Braille off my back! And when I had to shave, it was really difficult, because those things were all over. I saw so many specialists and doctors and they gave me cream and different things, but it was always the same. They all said that it was basically my age, that it was teenage pimples. But this was slightly more. It was really big boils! And when they burst, I got blood and pus all over my T-shirts, but when I finally stopped with all the different treatments and cream, it cleared up. I still have marks all over my back though, from where they burst. They're like craters and the guys used to joke and call my back the Dark Side of the Moon!"

According to Carole Williams, Don's acne didn't seem to affect his chances with the ladies. "He was very dark and handsome," she says, "and I am sure he had no idea of just how gorgeous he really was!"

★ ★ ★

The band didn't just bond with fans; they bonded with each other as well. That involved quite a lot of teasing. "It was Noddy who started calling Dave 'H'," Don recalls, "H being short for Hill. Dave hated it. And I used to call Jim 'Little Plum'. There was this cartoon character of a Red Indian who had a very red nose and he was called 'Little Plum'. When Jim joined us at the age of 16, he used to always have a red nose. Jim was three years younger than the rest of us and we always made fun of him. He was very unworldly back then.

"Nod and I were friends and he used to go with me to Swinn's house on Sunday afternoons, and then we'd sit there and listen to the records of comedians like Tony Hancock and Bob Newhart. It was like a ritual."

"We were into comedy, I really don't know why, but we loved Tony Hancock," says Swinn. "My mum had quite a big collection of LPs that we used to listen to. We also used to play chess a lot in those days as well. We became chess fanatics. And then of course Mondays we would go to the Queens Ballroom together."

"Monday nights, if there was no gig, they would take themselves off to the ballroom to see whichever act was performing there," says Carole Williams. "Vicky and I would be there as well, dancing away. We would then see them on the balcony and spend the rest of the evening watching the band with them."

"One night, Pat was there with her friends," says Don. "Pat used to be Dave's girlfriend, she was the one whom Dave had brought along for the audition for The Vendors, when he first joined the band. Noddy had his dad's window-cleaning van, so we took Pat home in that. She lived in Penn, like Dave. That night she asked us in for a cup of coffee at her mum and dad's place, and that was when we started seeing each other. She became my steady girlfriend and we used to go out a lot with Jim and his girlfriend, Louise. Dave was the only one whom I didn't associate with outside the band. He never went out."

While Don had won Pat's heart, the band now started to win back the hearts of many of their old fans, as well as gaining some new ones. They did a string of memorable gigs, one of them in October 1966 where they supported Cream at the Willenhall Baths, along with Robert Plant's Listen.

"In those days, all bands were sharing the same dressing room," Don says. "It wasn't really a dressing room, but a store room basically. When playing with Cream, Ginger Baker had this big double Ludwig kit in the room, so we could hardly move. And he was dancing all over his drums and jumping around and kicking them, and I thought, 'God, he must be rich!' But no, he was stoned out of his brain. And Eric Clapton used to stand there like a zombie, all glassy eyed, and I couldn't get it together at all. I was trying to hold a conversation with him, but he totally ignored me. He was obviously stoned as well, but in those days I didn't get it.

"Cream were amazing, because the stage at the Willenhall Baths was a sloping one. They had a drum riser, so the drums could be flat, as the drummers needed that, but not Ginger Baker! He had the drum riser taken away so he was on the sloping stage as well. I had never seen anything like that then."

Another gig that Don remembers fondly was at the Queen Mary's Ballroom, although that particular booking is not remembered because of the bands playing, but because of someone in the audience. "The Queen Mary's Ballroom in the zoo in Dudley was like a restaurant during the day, but they turned it into a ballroom at night," Don recalls, "and we used to play there Sunday nights. We had to drive through the zoo and we could hear the animals roar at us as we passed them. The audience had to walk through the zoo as well to get there. Robert Plant came that night, and we hadn't seen him for a while. We got to talk and he said, 'Jimmy Page has asked me to join this band. Jimmy Page of The Yardbirds. I don't really like The Yardbirds, but they are going to America, so I'm gonna take the job just to go there.' And the rest is history. Led Zeppelin was born."

The band also witnessed another major group in the making, Deep Purple. "That came because of Kim Fowley," Don recalls. "He was connected to Derek Block and Drew Harvey and they got us a few gigs down south together with the band Roundabout, who later became Deep Purple. I remember watching Ian Paice on the drums from the side of the stage. He looked like a little kid, but he was really good."

★   ★   ★

Although the single 'You Better Run' hadn't done very well, Block and Harvey hadn't quite given up on The 'N Betweens. In the spring of 1967, they were given a new chance to record.

"Drew Harvey said, 'I got your new record,'" Don remembers, "and it was 'Delighted To See You'. It was all pop and we didn't really like it, but we recorded it anyway. In the end nothing came of it."

The recording was made on April 20 1967, at London's Abbey Road studios where The Beatles were working on *Sgt. Pepper's Lonely Hearts Club Band*. "When we arrived at the studio we could see the white Roller, the Bentley, the Aston Martin and Mini Cooper or whatever it was," Don says, "and we went, 'Oh God, The Beatles are in!' We walked in and saw a couple of guys on a settee in the hallway sleeping. They were The Beatles' chauffeurs.

"The Beatles were in studio two and we were in studio three and we used to sneak up to their control-room door having a listen, and we couldn't make head or tail of what was going on, with backwards tapes and all the things like that. And every time we heard any movement, we used to run away like little kids.

"One thing I remember – and I wish I had a photograph of it – was George Martin walking out of the studio. He went, 'Aarghh!', burying his face in his hands and crouching down, obviously frustrated at what was going on inside. In those days it was still only four-track studios, so they were bouncing down and overdubbing. It must have been a complete mind game for him. I actually do believe that George Martin was an integrated part of the band. With him and two brilliant songwriters like Lennon and McCartney, there was no way they could fail."

The track The Beatles were actually recording was George Harrison's 'Only A Northern Song', which ended up on the 1969 album *Yellow Submarine* instead of *Sgt. Pepper*. As for The 'N Betweens, they hoped that The Beatles' magic would rub off on them a bit. "The guy who produced our song, 'Delighted To See You'," was Norman Smith," Don explains. "He used to work as an engineer at some of the early Beatles recordings and we asked him about what things they did in the studio. A few years later he himself had a hit record called 'Don't Let

It Die', but at that time he called himself Hurricane Smith. I remember seeing him on *Top Of The Pops* and I thought, Hurricane Smith? His name is Norman!"

The 'N Betweens worked steadily throughout 1967 with a series of gigs in England and Wales. "In the early days we could only afford to stay in guest houses," Don recalls. "Once we were playing a club in Whitehaven, a fishing port in the north of England, and we had found a guesthouse where the owner had told us, 'You'll have to share a room.' We were used to doing that among ourselves, so we climbed the stairs and walked into the room, only to be greeted by about 30 beds, four free ones for us! We had back-combed hair at that time and were wearing tight jeans and women's boots. All the other beds had dockworkers and miners sitting on them, cleaning their hob-nail boots! We left and slept in the van that night!"

While on the road, Don got to know guitarist Andy Scott, who was to become part of rival band The Sweet. "Don and I definitely crossed paths in Wolverhampton when he was in The Vendors," remembers Scott, "but my first real recollection was when he was with The 'N Betweens. I was in a band called The Silver Stones and we used to say 'hi' or meet on a motorway somewhere. I'm from North Wales, which is not far from Birmingham, so we often went there. It was a good scene at that time and I remember when playing in Birmingham someone said, 'You should have played with Don's band instead.' In any case, we were doing so much work. What happened in a month would probably take a year now!"

One week in every four, The 'N Betweens visited Scotland, sometimes staying on the Isle of Arran on the west coast. "We used to play three small village halls there," Don says. "One was in Lamlash, then there was one in Brodick and the last one was in Whiting Bay. They were basically within walking distance of each other. We used to play there during weekends and all the kids would go over on the ferries to the island to get drunk and see the shows in these three towns. We used to go over on the boat with everyone else and stay at a guest house for three nights. It was just a drunken weekend. I remember one time there was a dredger that would go down the coast, cleaning the coastlines, and its crew were in a pub that we used to go into in Whiting Bay. The pub was about to close, so they said, 'Let's get some beers and go down to the boat and have a party.'

"We went with them with a few other people from the pub in an old rowboat and we had to climb up a rope ladder to the dredger. When one person had climbed up, he had to hold the ladder for the next. Dave climbed the first, but he didn't know that he had to hold the ladder and the next one was a crew member, a really tall bloke who had his best suit on. Dave just walked off and this tall bloke went SPLASH! into the water. He was swearing, but we were just killing ourselves laughing! We got drunk on that boat, but it was really filthy. When we got back to England, after a few days we all started scratching, and we'd got rashes everywhere, so we had to go to the doctor. It turned out we'd all caught scabies! We caught scabies on that boat and it was so contagious that we couldn't go anywhere. We couldn't see our girlfriends and all the bed linen had to be washed every day. It was just dreadful!

"But in general, we always had a great time in Scotland. The guest house where we stayed was run by a retired army officer, on the main street in Glasgow. We were all in one room and we paid like £1 each for the bed and breakfast, so this retired army officer always used to get us up for breakfast every morning, even if we got in late, like three or four in the morning! We didn't have a key to the room so he just slammed the door open. We said, 'Can't we just stay in bed? Just keep the money!' But he said, 'No,' and made us get up and eat and then we could go back to bed afterwards!

"In Scotland we got paid in cash, so we could pay our instalments on our equipment and it worked perfectly. Some of the money we got in Scottish pound notes and some banks in England would only give you 98p to the pound, although they should give you the full amount. When we split the money between us, we then used to give Dave the Scottish pound notes and he never noticed!"

The long distances that the band now covered meant that they had to have their own transportation, instead of relying on hired vans and drivers. "Before that, Dave's father sometimes used to drive us in a big old Daimler," Don recalls. "We could take the back seat out and put all the equipment in there and we could all get in as well. The Daimler had indicators that came out on the side when we went left and right and whenever we got out of the car, we would break them off, because they would stick. So we always had to pay money for the repair of the indicators. Sometimes Dave drove the Daimler, but because it was such a big car he couldn't see over the steering wheel. He had to sit on a cushion. The first time I saw it, I thought, is it my eyes, or has he become taller? But in the end we bought our first van for £90. It was an old J2 van and only Nod and Swinn could pack it. Everything had to be packed with millimetre precision to fit in between the two wheel arches in the back."

"I remember the amplifiers were all worn away by the wheel arches," says Swinn. "I used to call the van Betsy. I don't know why. I'd say, 'I'm gonna take old Betsy out.' All our vans were called Betsy, but this particular one was always breaking down. One time we were on the motorway coming from Torquay and the fuel filter blocked up, so whenever we went uphill it would stop. We had to drive in reverse up the hills."

"Dave's father was a fully qualified motor engineer and he kept the van going for us," says Don. "The handbrake was a piece of string tied around where the connection was and we pulled the string to brake. The petrol tank had a hole in it so we could only get around four gallons in it. We had to stop at almost every petrol station and we knew exactly how far we could go. The engine was between the driver's seat and the passenger seat in the front and, as the heater didn't work, the engine got hot. It was a race to get in the front so we could have a warm. We used to swap round when it was freezing.

"To begin with, only Dave and Nod drove, while Jim and I made ourselves comfortable in the back. We didn't have driver's licences then. I got mine during 1967 and then I purchased a blue Mini and Jim got his licence a week after mine. But Jim didn't drive anyway; he always went to sleep. He had his sleeping bag with him and, after a gig, he curled up in the back and that was the last we saw of him."

★ ★ ★

It was during this period that Swinn and Noddy came up with a pioneering idea to develop the sound of the band. "Back then we had the classic AC 30 box amplifiers and two 12″ speakers in each cabinet and they were placed on either side of the drum kit," says Don. "PAs weren't a featured thing back then, so you couldn't get a balance. That had to be done from the stage. To get a more even sound, Swinn and Nod split the speakers so Nod and Dave had one speaker each in both cabinets; this way two guitars were coming out of each cabinet and that was quite revolutionary."

"I remember we did a show in Walsall Town Hall with The Fortunes," Swinn adds. "Their equipment hadn't turned up so they borrowed The 'N Betweens' equipment and they couldn't figure out what was happening. They were totally bewildered by it. The agency then started advertising 'the stereo sound' of The 'N Betweens."

The first steps towards the band's massive wall of sound had been taken. It was a sound that was to be developed further in the years to come.

6

The Grand Bahama Island
Stories Carry On

In September 1967, after a year of going steady, Don and Pat decided to get engaged. "That was on my 21st birthday," Don recalls. "In those days, we used to get the whole family together for birthdays and go to the pub for a meal, so all my family was there and Pat's as well, and that was when I gave her the ring. She accepted and it was all set. We were engaged to be married." With the prospect of a wedding, the last thing that Don needed was to be separated from his lovely fiancée, but that was exactly what happened. In the first half of 1968, the Astra Agency came up with a deal the band couldn't refuse.

"On Fridays we used to go down to the Astra Agency to get our money," Don explains, "and one time they called us to the office and said they'd had this letter with an offer for us to go to the Bahamas. It was from a guy called Ken Mallin, who used to be a member of the St. Giles Youth Club. He'd watched us there, but now he was living in the Bahamas and he wanted us to go and play there. The Bahamas might have been the moon as far as we were concerned. The Bahamas? It was something you saw in a film in those days.

"The agency then said, 'He's got contacts there and you can play in a club for eight weeks. They will fly you out there' – we sat with open mouths – 'and they'll pay you $100 a week each and it is with board and food.'

"*What?* This was like… this is it! We've struck it, we've made it! None of us had ever been on a plane before, nothing like that, and we flew out on a Sunday. I remember it was May 19 because my sister Marilyn's birthday is May 23, so I was a bit disappointed, as I would miss her birthday."

The 'N Betweens played the Connaught Hotel the night before their flight and directly after that they went home to say their goodbyes. "I said goodbye to Pat and then Swinn picked us up and we drove all night to Heathrow airport," Don recalls. "Our equipment went as excess baggage, paid for by the businessman in the Bahamas who was going to finance us.

"It was an eight or nine-hour flight to the Bahamas, stopping off in Bermuda. We were all neatly dressed in shirts, ties, jackets and trousers and we were all very excited. Wow, Bermuda! I remember getting off the plane there and jumping straight back in again. I thought the jet engines were still on, with the heat. But they weren't. I just didn't realise it would be so hot outside. So we got rid of all the jackets and ties and we thought, 'We haven't even got there yet, and even Bermuda airport is like paradise!'"

From Bermuda, The 'N Betweens flew to Nassau, where Ken Mallin awaited them. He took them to Grand Bahama Island on one of the tiny inter-island planes that flew regularly like airborne bus routes. On landing in Freeport, Don and his bandmates were amazed. "We drove to the hotel and on the way we couldn't believe what we were seeing," Don recalls. "We had never seen anything like it – palm trees, blue skies with no clouds, beautiful buildings. We were just totally in awe, with our mouths open.

"We went to the hotel, and we had never been in a place like that before. It was amazingly luxurious and we had adjoining twin rooms. Jim and I shared one and Nod and Dave shared the other. We always shared rooms that way, I don't know why. It was like an unwritten law, but this time at least we got a bed each. We never had that before.

The rooms had big French double doors looking out over a big lagoon. It was amazing. We were just these four blokes, these scumbags from Wolverhampton, and here we were sitting in the Bahamas! On this luxurious island in a hotel!"

Their amazement was far from over. Coming from working-class families in the Black Country, this new and improved world demanded quite a bit of adjustment. "Ken took us out that night," says Don, "and as we left the hotel there was an electrical storm going on. I couldn't understand it. There was all the lightning, but where was the thunder? I kept on waiting for the thunder, because in England when you have lightning, you have thunder. And I said, 'How come there is no thunder?' Ken said, 'These are just electrical storms.' I'd never heard about that before. Then he took us for drinks and dinner and we had different cocktails. We didn't know what that was either. I got one called Yellow Bird; I'd never tasted or seen anything like it, with the straws and everything.

"That night, when we got back to the hotel, we couldn't sleep because of the time change and the excitement of being there. And it was so hot at night; I couldn't believe it. In England it was always cold at night, but here it was the same heat at night as during the day.

"The next morning Ken came to the hotel and said, 'What would you like for breakfast? I'll just call room service.' Room service? We never knew what room service was. Ken said, 'Just pick up the phone and tell them what you want and they'll bring it to you.' 'You don't have to go and fetch it?' 'No, no, they'll bring it to you.' We didn't really get it. The waiters then came with their big trolley and Ken signed the bill for the breakfast. I said, 'Aren't you gonna *pay* for it?' 'I already have.' But I hadn't seen him give the waiters any money, so I didn't understand."

It was when Ken Mallin drove The 'N Betweens to The Tropicana Club, where they were to play, that it began to dawn on them that not everything in the Bahamas was as luxurious as they first thought. "As we went along, all the luxury hotels vanished behind us," Don recalls. "We went into the jungle and got to the club and there were cockroaches all over the walls; it looked really run-down. The club manager was a black guy named Duke and there were a few Bahamians in there, all stoned.

We set our gear up and checked everything, then we changed and the dressing room was behind a curtain at the side of the stage. We had bought new stage clothes for this trip and I remember that mine was a red frilly shirt and red pants. We were unsure how we would go down, as this was not our usual audience. After all, we had been booked to play there for eight weeks, so we wanted to do well.

"As it turned out, there were some American kids dancing and the Bahamians were all sitting in the back. The American kids aged 18 and under had to leave the club at 10 o'clock because of a curfew, so for our second set only the black Bahamians were left. We were a little worried, but they actually liked us. We were playing soul music and they had never heard white kids play that before. They could make fun of us, but it was their kind of music, as James Brown was God over there.

"We played for the first week and then Ken said, 'Well, not so many people are going to the club, so we can't give you $100 a week each, but we can give you some.' We didn't care. We really didn't need to buy anything, anyway, as we'd got the hotel and we could eat there. Furthermore, we had come to know everybody at the club and the American kids wanted to know us as well, because we were from England. They used to pick us up at the hotel and take us out to their houses to meet their mums and dads and have coffee. So we didn't need that much money in our pockets. None of us even smoked then, and we still hadn't found out that we ought to tip people. In England tips weren't given, so it was only after a couple of weeks we started to realise that something was wrong. We needed a taxi once and, when we reached our destination, we gave the driver the exact amount of money. He waited for a tip, but we started to walk away so he asked for one. We said, 'But you've been paid!' He threw our money back at us and just screamed off!

"We had the same problem at the hotel. When we ordered something we signed for it and the waiters were then hovering over us, waiting for a tip. We'd say, 'That's it then,' and they would walk out very annoyed. As the weeks went by every time we ordered room service it took longer for them to come and it was a new waiter every time. Then it started to hit us that we probably had to tip these guys. We gave them a few cents and that didn't go down too well either."

The 'N Betweens were not the only English band in the Bahamas in those days, as Andy Scott recalls. "We had split The Silver Stones and turned ourselves from a seven-piece soul band into The Elastic Band, a four-piece progressive rock band, which was what other bands would do at that time, and somebody suggested that we do a residency in the Bahamas. I had just turned 18, so I thought, 'Well, *yes!*' Most people were only there for a month, but we were there for three months. All of a sudden you realised you'd got lucky. We came together, the two bands, on the same island, the same very small piece of land, yet one was playing in what was predominantly, should we say, a rather run–down, native kind of area, and the other played the slightly better areas – to people who had escaped the draft in America or moved down to avoid tax. So we had these two bands from England in the same place and we used to meet up on the beach, where we got up to quite a few things."

"We had a fantastic time," Don expands, "by the swimming pool, on the beach every day, hanging out."

"Don, of all of them, was the one I got on with the best," continues Andy Scott. "Of course, Noddy and I got on really well too, but Dave and Jimmy were difficult. Jimmy is a thinker and Dave is, well, Dave, so obviously Noddy and, especially, Don are the most approachable. We never saw Dave Hill very much. He must have gone home white, as he was never with the others on the beach for the day. Our drummer, Shaun, was like that as well. He used to keep out of the sun.

"One day, we took a lilo and the six of us were hanging off it. My brother Mike, the singer Ted Deaton, Noddy, Don, Jim and I grabbed the lilo and we started floating in the lagoon. You could see the sand and the rocks and the fish below you. It wasn't deep. We were chatting away and then someone mentioned that the beach looked rather further away than it should. We looked down below us and it was dark. We had gone beyond the edge of the reef. We thought we'd better get back and we started to feel the sea moving us a bit, because the further out you get, you go where the sea wants to take you and not where you wanna go. The six of us were paddling in the right direction and somebody mentioned the kind of fish that were down there, barracudas and stuff like that, and we got a bit more frenetic. Obviously we got back to the beach, otherwise I wouldn't be here to tell the story."

Water didn't seem the kindest element to Don though, and especially not its inhabitants.

"One of the kids had a party once because the parents were away," he recalls. "There was a pool in the garden and we all got in to play ball, but it got a bit crowded, so we decided to go down to the channel to swim there. The rich people on the Bahamas usually had the canals down the garden where their boats were. We all dived in and played there for hours, but one by one everybody got tired and I was left there in the water holding the ball. I thought, I might as well get out now, and I climbed up the ladder and stood there looking at the water and then this enormous, three-metre long mantaray appeared. It turned out that when the tide came in, everything came up with it, but nobody had told me. I never went to the water again.

"You really had to be careful with the ocean. Another time, we met this Portuguese guy called Veno. He was stoned out of his brain permanently, was always in swimming shorts and was covered from head to toe in scars. While you were talking to him, you couldn't help looking at them. In the end, I had to ask: 'Veno, what happened? Did you get caught in a boat propeller or what?' It turned out that when American tourists visited the Islands in their boats, they used to hire Veno to go out on the ocean and find a shark, minding its own business. Veno would jump in and fight the shark so the tourists could film him with their cine cameras, hence his scars. We all went back to his hut once and it was like a scene from *Jaws*, with jawbones adorning his walls. I wonder if he's still alive…"

Playing the club in the evenings was equally eventful, as Don explains. "The MC there was a black guy called Eric Roker who was a drunk, gay junkie and he was *so* funny. He was a great piano player as well, and he used to jam with us. He was also the one to introduce us to marijuana. We were all a little apprehensive in the beginning, but anyway, we decided to try it and we all thought it was *fabulous,* except we weren't the type of band that could go on stage and play when we'd had a smoke. Our set was too energetic. But I remember having the munchies so bad, walking up and down the hotel corridors, going through the remnants of food left on the room-service trays outside doors to be collected, taking cold French fries and hard bread, anything that was edible!

"In the club, I was almost married off at one point. There was this guy there who imported cigars from Cuba and apparently his daughter fancied me. He called me over to his table one night and said, 'I'll set you up in a house, you can have a car and everything that you want, but if you cross her, you're dead.' It was a bit ridiculous, as I never had a relationship with his daughter. Nothing ever happened between us."

Dave also got in a clinch with a lady, but in quite a different way. "A lot of guys in the Bahamas wore kaftans," Don explains, "but we didn't really have the money to buy any. We met a girl who wore a dress that looked like a kaftan and Dave got her to go to the bathroom to take it off, so he could try it. He wore it the same night on stage at the club and then a girl came in with the same dress on! She came to the front of the stage and said, 'I don't believe you! You're wearing the same dress as me!'"

After six weeks in paradise, Don and his bandmates woke up to face reality. It really did start with a wake-up call. "The phone rang early in the morning," Don says. "We were still in bed and from the other room Nod shouted, 'Pick that bloody phone up!' and I did. It was the hotel manager's assistant. The manager's name was Dan Darrow and the assistant said, 'Mr Darrow wants to see you in his office in half an hour. Be there.' Nod shouted, 'Who was that?' 'The manager's office. They want to see us in half an hour.' 'Oh, fuck off, we're still in bed.'

"Half an hour later, the phone rang again, '*Mr Darrow needs to see you straight away!*' Well, we'd better go and see what he wants, we thought. So we just put our swimming shorts on and T-shirts and got down there and sat in his office. He was very smart, with a suit and everything, and we said, 'What's wrong?' I'll always remember Dan Darrow's words. He said, 'You've been here for six weeks now, living like *kings*. When am I going to get some money?' We looked back at him and said, 'What do you mean? Ken Mallin said that it's all been paid for.' He listened to that and made a phone call. His assistant came in with all his paperwork and, looking through it, he said, 'That wasn't the deal.

You came here on a charter flight, which included accommodation for two weeks. After that you had to pay for it yourself.' I went, '*What?* Explain that again!' He did and then we told him about the situation. That we were going to get $100 a week each and they would pay for the hotel and food. 'I'm sorry,' Dan Darrow said, 'That's not what I've got written down here. You've been here for six weeks now, and everything has been signed to the rooms – room service and things like that – and you have to pay.'

"Well, we got a bit worried, because we had nothing. All we had were the return tickets back home, so we said, 'What's the bill, then?' And he checked it and it was $35,000! This was 1968! We just went into hysterics. We couldn't stop laughing. It was just totally unbelievable. Dan Darrow said, 'This is not funny! You can't stay here any more either.' We got rather timid then. 'What's... what's happening with us? Where are we gonna go?' 'I'll tell you now,' Dan Darrow said, 'I've been over at the club. It has just been bought by two American guys from Miami.' 'Yeah? We didn't know about that.' He continued, 'They are willing to pay you $100 a week between you, of which I will take $75 to help pay this bill off. You'll have $25. I'm moving you out of the hotel and into one of our staff apartments and you'll stay there until this bill has been paid off.' 'But we only have two weeks left here!' we objected, but Darrow said, 'I'm sorry. You're staying.' I thought we were never going to get home."

The 'N Betweens moved into an apartment complex that didn't even come close to the standard they had become used to at the hotel. "We had a small one-room apartment with a kitchenette in the corner and four camp beds and a separate toilet and bathroom," Don recalls. "That was it. That was a big difference from the luxury hotel. But luckily we had made a lot of friends among the American kids, so we explained to them what had happened and they said not to worry. They'd help us out with food and pay for things and drive us everywhere.

"We then realised that we hadn't seen Ken Mallin for quite a while, but we hadn't really taken any notice. Now it turned out that he was gone and that nobody knew where he was. He'd just left us on our own and we thought, *bastard!*

"We then went down to the club to meet the new owners. They'd kept the manager and the bar staff and we told them what had happened. We only had two weeks left, but the owners let us continue playing at the club, so we could work off the debts. They didn't particularly like us though, and thought we were playing too loud, but they paid us our $100 a week and every Friday night they'd come from the hotel and get $75."

When the eight weeks for which The 'N Betweens had originally been booked were coming to an end, the band started wondering what to do. "Our plane tickets were only valid for three months, so we had to get home at the end of August," Don explains, "but we had no money to pay for having our equipment sent back and we weren't going to leave it, as we didn't have anything else. We were still paying for it in instalments actually. We wrote to the Astra Agency to send us some money and help us out, but they blanked us. They gave us no help whatsoever, so we just played on at the club to save money.

"I wrote Pat as well. I used to write her because at that time we didn't have any telephones at home, so I couldn't call her. I told her about our situation and how we tried to save up money to get our equipment back and she wrote back, 'Sure.' It was the absolute truth that we were stuck, but back home people thought that we were living the good life in the Bahamas."

"The 'N Betweens would come wandering down the beach and sit with us," Andy Scott recalls. "We'd have an Esky of cokes and soft drinks and I think it was Jimmy who said, 'You wouldn't think how we look forward to coming down to sit with you on the beach at lunchtime because you have that Esky of cokes.' I didn't realise until later when they told me that they had to carry on playing in order to get home. We had our airline tickets and that was almost like having a million pounds in the bank, because we could get home, but they couldn't."

Stuck in this situation, The 'N Betweens could do nothing but work, playing at the club eight hours a night, seven nights a week. "Every weekend the owner would bring American acts over from Miami," Don recalls. "Fire dancers, female impersonators, soul singers and things like that. So we had to rehearse with them and play with them Friday, Saturday and Sunday. The acts did their shows, we backed them and we played our own things in between.

"The first act to come over was William Bell, who'd had a hit record with Judy Clay called 'Private Number'. He had this fantastic guitarist, Harold Beane, who sounded like Jimi Hendrix. It was probably the best weekend we did at the club. Then there were three girl singers called The Twans, who did a Surpremes routine, and a lot of other soul acts. But whoever came over from Miami never had a drummer, did they? So I was engaged with them. I used to go down every Friday afternoon to rehearse with them. I never got any money for it, apart from the deal. I used to be on stage from eight o'clock in the evening until four o'clock in the morning, without a break. Sometimes I'd fall asleep on my drums. Just collapse over them and sleep. Then someone would come out and say, 'Wake up, that's it now!' 'Well, OK.'

"Most of them played standard soul things and everybody had a hit record called 'Hitch It To The Horse'. The first time somebody asked me, 'Do you know my hit record?' I answered no. Then I was told, 'Of course you do! It's called "Hitch It To The Horse".' It was just a 12-bar thing, and after that I played with a lot of singers who had the same hit. When they asked me if I knew of their hit I'd always say, 'Don't tell me – "Hitch It To The Horse".' And they all went, 'Ah, you *do* know it!'"

During weekends the club operated as a cabaret. That was what the new owners aimed for, and the crowds were bigger as a result. "A lot of more grown-up people came to see the fire-eaters, limbo dancers, transvestites and whatever," says Don. "The problem was that the acts were never there when they were supposed to get on stage. They were in the bar drinking. So while we were playing, Nod used to go and get them: 'Come on you lot. Get on that fucking stage! You're on now!' It's incredible when you think of it.

"There was also a fire dancer there called Prince Badu, but his real name was Sidney. He was always at the club anyway. He didn't have to travel in. I used to play tom-toms for him while he was dancing. He had this big pole of fire and it was only a tiny stage. He used to dance around sort of limbo dancing with this thing and I learnt to duck while playing, to avoid the fire.

"Prince Badu was to come on stage with his fire act one night and the MC, Eric, wanted to play drums. I said, 'Fine,' and he was just playing around on the drums. Then he said to Jim, 'Do you know some Latin American?' 'Yes,' and then he went into that. But Prince Badu sometimes painted himself all silver, leaving only a small part so his body could breathe. Then he called himself Silver Man. He was waiting to go on stage all painted as Silver Man, but Eric didn't care, he was stoned, and continued on the drums until Prince Badu passed out. He almost suffocated because his body couldn't breathe.

"When finally he came on stage that night he brought a tin tray that he used for the equipment for his fire show. He threw it on the floor and stormed off. Eric just got off the drums and came up to the mike and said, 'Prince Badu will not appear on this stage again tonight because he is a baby.' Things like that were going on all the time. It was crazy."

When The 'N Betweens had saved enough money to get their equipment back, their plane tickets were close to expiring and they decided to go home. "There was no way we could pay all the money to the hotel, anyway," Don says, "but the problem was how to get the equipment out of the club to get it back to England. If the people at the hotel found out that we were going to leave, they'd kill us. They'd murder us. They'd shoot us. What were we to do?

"Somebody must have been watching over us because it was just a pure stroke of luck that the new owners of the club told us, 'This weekend after you have finished playing on Sunday we want all your equipment out of the club. We are closing for a week, as we are going to redecorate.'

"We couldn't believe it! We got our equipment out and we took it straight down to the airport, paid on the plane back to England. The equipment went home a week before we did and then we just partied for a week in the apartment, getting drunk and having a great time. The apartment got completely trashed.

"The night before we left, we said to the American kids, 'Now listen, we've got to skip the island tomorrow.' We were going on the 4.45 flight from Nassau back to England, so we had to take the inter-island plane from Freeport to Nassau at three o'clock. We had it all timed and we told the kids that because of the money that we owed they couldn't tell anybody that we were leaving. 'So don't see us off at the airport, otherwise it'll attract attention,' we said to them.

"The next day, we went to the airport and all the kids were there to see us off, and we went, 'No! No! Go away! Go away!' but in the end we got on the plane from Freeport to Nassau.

"When we reached the airport, the plane for England was delayed for four or five hours. We were sure that the hotel people were going to get us. We were really scared. So what we did was that for all that time, we went to four different parts of the airport and hid, even lying down so no one could see us. And those were the *longest* hours I have ever spent!

"I remember looking out and seeing our plane coming in from England and we *ran*! We all checked in and got on that plane. And that was it. We got off the island. But it was strange flying over it, a bit sad. We had been there for three months and then looking down and thinking, God, we'll never see this place again. This place is like paradise… and we will never see it again.

"It had been the most amazing experience that four kids had ever had and it had made us *so* tight as people, because we only had each other. We were very different personalities and we had to be together 24 hours a day for months. We went through a lot, us against the rest of the world, and we came out of it still together. That made us as a band. On the plane back we were all very positive and we thought, well, this is it now. We've had our hardship. We're gonna try to make it now. We're gonna work our *damnedest* to make it. We'd been through all that shit together, so we're gonna go for it now."

After The 'N Betweens returned to England, letters arrived from the hotel in the Bahamas demanding the money they owed. "When we had first checked into the hotel we put our actual addresses in the registration," says Don. "We didn't think at all! We still had $23,000 that we owed them, but they never got their money. After a couple of months, the letters stopped. Then we went to see the agency and they had the nerve to ask us for their commission from the months in the Bahamas. We said, 'You fucking what? You left us there, you never even offered to help!', but they didn't believe us. They thought we had tried to pull a fast one. That was when we decided to leave Astra."

7

Ambush Shake

The Bahamas ordeal strengthened the relationship between the four members of The 'N Betweens to the extent that Don still tends to say "we" when he speaks of his years with Dave, Nod and Jim.

On their return, they found themselves in a changed situation, feeling betrayed by Astra but with new, strong bonds within the band. At the same time, their music had taken a new turn.

"I think because we had to live together, sharing that small apartment in the Bahamas, it had made us bond much better," says Dave. "We got to know each other, obviously, and as we'd worked regularly it also tightened us musically as a group."

"We kept playing everywhere," says Don. "Astra still got us bookings, but our music had changed. We did all the soul things we'd learnt in the Bahamas and we did 'Born To Be Wild', which was a big hit for Steppenwolf, and a song called 'Journey To The Centre Of The Mind' by The Amboy Dukes, which featured Ted Nugent. Back in England people didn't really know of those songs, as they hadn't been released yet, but they went down well. I guess you could say we went through a hippie phase after the Bahamas, but it was really short. We dressed up in flower-power gear and Pat and her sister, who was a dressmaker, made my stage clothes, and Louise made some of Jim's clothes as well, as she was a window-dresser.

"We had psychedelic stage lights with variable colours on a circular Perspex filter and we used to burn incense as well. I remember once we played in The Woolpack in Wolverhampton. We'd put the incense in ashtrays on top of the cabinets and, because of the smell, everybody thought it was drugs. The staff then came with long sticks, trying to knock the ashtrays off the cabinets. But we never did do drugs when playing. I remember one occasion when we were playing at a club somewhere. There was no-one in and the manager said that it wasn't worth us playing, but that he would still pay us our £15. Anyway, we had some hash and we decided to have a smoke, so there we all were sitting in the dressing room, *zonked*, when the manager burst in and said that a big crowd had just walked in from the closing pubs, so we could now go on stage and play. We all screamed to ourselves, 'WHAT?' I couldn't even tie my own shoelaces! I still remember Jim and myself walking around outside the club taking deep breaths, trying to straighten up – but to no avail.

"We eventually went on stage playing everything so slow and laid-back. My drumsticks felt and looked about two metres long! At one point, Nod was trying to tune his guitar. I can still picture the string he was trying to tune suddenly hanging loosely between his legs, close to his knees. He then turned to me saying, 'I'm out of my fuckin' brains.' We carried on, all finishing the songs at different times to each other. We never, ever did it again before going on stage! I seem to remember the club manager saying it was the best gig ever at his club!"

"They were progressive times and I remember one show in Wolverhampton where I spent hours putting balloons on the stage and flowers," Swinn says. "The music of The 'N Betweens became more progressive as well. They went through a period where they did the Who thing of smashing instruments, except they never smashed any guitars. Instead, Jim used to do a number with a violin on stage, so we bought cheap violins and when the time came to smash it, he would change the good one to a cheap one.

"Something *had* happened though, during their stay in the Bahamas. Upon their return they were very different people. In some ways it had always been strange that the four of them were together in a band, as they had very different personalities, but I think they were all insecure. That was why they worked as a unit. They gave one another security. Now they came back from the Bahamas, all changed and highly professional, and I couldn't really relate to them myself. Because of that, I sort of lost contact for a while."

"Astra couldn't relate to us any more either," Don says. "They didn't care for us much and we didn't care for them, so we wanted to switch agencies."

There was a new agency in Wolverhampton at the time – the Nita Anderson agency – and The 'N Betweens decided to try their luck there. "The agency was run by Andy and Nita Anderson," says Don, "but because Andy was a policeman, he couldn't be seen to have a business, so the agency was in his wife's name. They ran it from their house in Sedgely and, as Andy and Nita also ran a few pubs in Wolverhampton, we knew them and were quite friendly with them. We asked if we could come over to them and they asked whether we had a contract with Astra, but we didn't. They never even signed us. It was a pure mistake on their part, but we never said anything. We wanted to keep that up our sleeve, because you never know what will happen.

"We then approached Astra and said, 'We're not staying with you any more, we're leaving,' and they said, 'You can't. You're under contract.' 'So will you find it?' They said, 'No, we can't just find it like that,' so we went, 'We'll come back next week.' We came back and they didn't have the contract, so we walked away. It worked perfectly."

"Astra actually tried to sell the band," says Carole Williams. "I was really upset by this, as I always had the feeling something big was around the corner. To make matters worse, I was given the letter to type, making the offer! I really made my opinion known, and not long after I was asked to leave, as my 'interests' were no longer loyal to the company. The boys asked me to keep running the fan club and said nothing had changed, so I carried on."

"At Nita Anderson's, Roger Allen became our new manager," says Don. "He was an influential promoter who managed quite a few of the really good pop bands around the area at the time, like The

Montanas and Finders Keepers. He used to run some of the big hotels in Wolverhampton as well – the Park Hall Hotel, the Connaught Hotel and a few others – and he would get all the bands from Astra to play there. He joined forces with Astra to form the Astra-Allen Agency for a short while, but he had left in 1967 to work with Nita Anderson instead.

"Roger Allen managed to arrange a recording deal with Fontana for us. He talked Jack Baverstock, head of A&R for Philips Records and its subsidiary labels, into looking at us and we went to London for a studio audition. We just did what we had learnt: 'Born To Be Wild', 'Journey To The Centre Of The Mind', 'Nights In White Satin', things like that. Jack Baverstock really liked us, so he said, 'I want you to make an album.' We went, '*What?*', but he meant it. 'You've got a week.' We just couldn't believe it."

Although Baverstock liked The 'N Betweens, he didn't care much for their name. He felt that it implied an element of homosexuality, so that had to be changed. The group came up with the name Knicky Knacky Noo. "That phrase came from Graham Bond," says Don. "We'd done one of the shows at the Wolverhampton Civic with the Graham Bond Organisation, a soul show with Georgie Fame and other acts. They were staying at a guesthouse for the night and Graham Bond went, 'It's the best thing since the Knicky Knacky Noo.' We'd never heard that before, we couldn't stop laughing and we've used the phrase ever since."

Baverstock couldn't see the fun in that, so he came up with his own name for the band. Unfortunately, that name was just as crazy as the one the band suggested. "He had this secretary who used to name all of her things, like her pens and shoes and handbags," Don explains. "They all got names. One of her things was called Ambrose and another Slade. Jack Baverstock put the names together and said, 'You're gonna be called Ambrose Slade.'"

The band changed their name officially on December 12, 1968. "It took a long time to get used to it," says Don. "There were a few obstacles that we had to get over and it took quite a while. Dave and I had tried that once before when we went from The Vendors to The

'N Betweens. In those days it was almost a kiss of death if you changed your name. We were known as The 'N Betweens and that was how we got the work, so Nita Anderson's agency had to put it out that we were now Ambrose Slade.

"We didn't particularly like the name, anyway. The 'N Betweens was bad enough, but Ambrose Slade? It was always misspelled, as people couldn't figure it out. We were billed as Ambush Shake, Arnold Shed, Amboy Spade – it was horrible.

"We did do some good gigs though, and people liked seeing us because of our choice of songs. They didn't know what to expect. One of my particular favourites was 'Goin' Back' by Dusty Springfield, which was really nice. We also did Neil Diamond's 'Cherry Cherry' with Jim on lead vocal, and that was a good stage song. We'd heard The Move do it at the Marquee Club in London and it worked so well that we did it, too. Another one was Harry Nilsson's 'Cuddly Toy', with Dave on lead vocal. It was a hit for The Monkees and Dave wanted to sing that, but it was only a simple little pop song, so we didn't do that for long.

"Then we did the theme from *Skippy The Bush Kangaroo*. When we played the clubs and pubs in Wolverhampton, this guy Melvyn used to come and see us. He used to stand in front of the stage with a glass of beer, always spilling it all over, and Nod would use Melvyn when he talked to the audience, saying, 'Have you got a girlfriend yet?' or whatever. One day Nod asked, 'Would you like to come up and sing, Melvyn?' And Melvyn's eyes lit up, so he came on stage and we asked him what he wanted to sing? 'Skippy The Bush Kangaroo'. Oh, my God! But he sang and we played, and as this was repeated whenever Melvyn was in the audience, we actually learnt how to play that song. Just for Melvyn's sake. He was so serious when he sang that tune. It wasn't a joke to him, but while he was singing we used to hop around behind him like kangaroos without him knowing. I mean this was Slade, hopping around like kangaroos! People just couldn't pigeonhole us."

In February 1969, the band now known as Ambrose Slade spent a week in the Philips studio at Stanhope Place near Marble Arch, recording their first album. "There was only us in the studio, with an engineer

70

called Roger Wake," Don recalls. "What we did was more or less our stage show of the time. 'Born To Be Wild', 'Journey To The Centre Of The Mind', 'Ain't Got No Heart' by Frank Zappa, 'Martha My Dear' by The Beatles, Jeff Lynne's 'Knocking Nails Into My House' and things like that. We had blocks of wood in the studio to make Lynne's song, knocking them together to make the sound of a hammer knocking nails.

"Jack Baverstock really believed in us and it gave us so much confidence. He wanted us to write our own songs as well, and we came up with one called 'The Knicky Knacky Noo', of course. Baverstock came and listened and he said, 'Are you taking the piss out of me?' But we were actually quite serious. We then wrote an instrumental called 'Genesis' and another one called 'Mad Dog Cole', which was a nickname for Roger Allen. Jim and Nod wrote 'Pity The Mother', with Jim on the violin. Those were our first attempts to write; with all the rest of the songs, we just used to mess around in the studio.

"Around that time, Jim was teaching me to play guitar. I bought an acoustic guitar off Nod for £40. That was typical Nod. I think I was paying what he paid! Jim taught me to play a few chords and a 12-bar, but I didn't have the patience. I wish I had kept at it.

"Although I can't sing or play any other instrument but drums, I *can* tell if something is out of tune. One time in the studio, probably a few years later, we listened to a playback and I heard something and said: 'Is something out of tune?' Jim sat by me and we played it and then I couldn't hear it. Then we took some things out and there it was. Jim said, 'None of us heard it!' With things like that I have a certain ear. Like harmonies. I used to sit at the front when the others were singing harmonies and I would say, 'This needs to be done' or 'That needs to be done'. I don't know the terms musically, but I have a certain ear, I suppose."

Recording an album was a major event for Ambrose Slade, but things would soon become even more exciting, as Don explains. "During the time that we recorded, Jack Baverstock said, 'You need London management,' but we didn't know any. He said, 'Oh, I'll put the feelers out, I'll see if I can find out who's around.'

"One day in the studio, while we were recording, I looked up from the drums and through the window into the control room I could see

Chas Chandler. I was like mouthing to the others, '*Chas Chandler!*' That was the guy who *found* Jimi Hendrix, and he'd played bass with The Animals and everything. He was like a real hero of ours, and I actually got goose bumps from seeing him right there in the control room. Chas was impressed with us and wanted to see us perform live, so it was arranged for us to perform in Rasputin's Club."

The live performance went well and Chandler liked the way Ambrose Slade carried themselves on stage. To him they were "a breath of fresh eayer", as he used to express it in his thick Newcastle Geordie accent.

"He said that we should come and see him in his office and he gave us his address," Don recalls. "We just couldn't believe it. *Chas Chandler liked us!* Many years later, he revealed to us that the main reason why he liked the band back then had been Nod's singing."

Ambrose Slade went back to Wolverhampton after they finished recording the album, but were soon back in London to meet with Chandler. "We got to his office address, which was on 67 Brook Street in London," Don says. "We drove up in our old van and it was the Robert Stigwood Agency. They handled bands like The Bee Gees and Cream and we were just in awe. We went in – they had this amazing reception area – and we said, 'We've come to see Mr. Chas Chandler.' The girl in the reception replied, 'Have a seat, he'll be with you in a minute. Do you want some coffee?' Oh! We'd never been to a place like that before!

"Then Chas came downstairs to meet us and we went up to his big office with him and there was John Gunnell, another big name. He and his brother Rik used to run all the prestigious clubs in London in the sixties like Rasputin's, The Bag O'Nails and The Speakeasy, and they looked after Georgie Fame, Alexis Corner, Zoot Money and other big acts.

"Chas introduced us to him and, again, we were in awe. Then Chas said that he would take us over and manage us. He and John Gunnell had just set up a management company as part of the Robert Stigwood Organisation, and Gunnell was to become our agent, with Chas as our manager. Chas then told us that what Jack Baverstock had done was unheard of – to put an unknown band in a studio and let them record whatever they wanted. He'd never heard of that before and I think that impressed him.

"But Chas didn't like the idea that we were on Fontana, as he felt it was a dwindling company. He told us that Fontana would probably put the album out and there was nothing he could do about that, but he'd try to get us away to a bigger company. We couldn't believe it. It seemed totally unreal.

"Then he asked if we had a telephone number, but no, none of us had a private telephone, so he said, 'I'll tell you what we'll do, we'll put a telephone in one of your houses, pay for it and pay the bill.' It was unbelievable! We decided that Jim was going to have the telephone and I remember John Gunnell saying, 'Have they got telephones in Wolverhampton at all?' We were all laughing, but at the same time it hurt a bit. Still, we were amazed at what was happening. Within a year we'd been to the Bahamas, we'd been through all that shit together and decided that now we wanted to make it, and the next thing we knew we were recording an album and Chas Chandler wanted to manage us. It was *unreal*."

8

A Breath Of Fresh Eayer

With Chas Chandler managing them, Ambrose Slade had to switch agencies again. Nita and Andy Anderson went to London; on their return, Andy Anderson met with the band.

"When Nita and Andy came back from seeing Chas and John Gunnell, a deal had been made," Don recalls. "Andy said to us, 'We've done what we could for you and I think you should go with a bigger agency. They've got more to offer.' We found it very thoughtful of Andy and Nita until much later, when Chas and John asked, 'Did you ever get a share of that money we paid?' 'What money?' '£400.' It turned out that Chas and John had paid for our contract, without Andy and Nita ever telling us!"

Roger Forrester at the Stigwood office now handled their bookings and their first gig was a big show at Newcastle City Hall supporting Amen Corner and Dave Dee, Dozy, Beaky, Mick & Tich among others. "There were two shows that night and each band used to play 20 minutes," Don says. "We were hired to warm up, with two or three songs, and we thought that was amazing. So we all got in the van to drive up to Newcastle, but on the way the van broke down. We found a pay phone and called Chas and he said, 'You've *got* to get there.' Somehow we got the van repaired and we got there, although we missed the first show. We were just in awe of all the equipment that was on stage. We played our couple of songs and there was no response really, as it was a teenybopper audience and we were hippie underground, but it was good exposure for us. Chas also rang a few people from the press and we were all on our best behaviour, as we had not met any of them before."

Chas Chandler was set on getting his new protégés noticed, so he commissioned photographer Gered Mankowitz to take a series of shots, and appointed a press agent, Keith Altham, who used to write for *NME* and now ran a PR company with pop journalist Chris Williams.

"My first glimpse of Don in action came when their manager Chas Chandler, with whom I had a long friendship, first convinced me as a press agent to come and see Ambrose Slade rehearse across the road from my office in London. It was at a dive that had once been Ken Colyer's Jazz Club," Keith Altham recalls. "Louis Armstrong and Kid Ory still stared down from one peeling wall in an old black and white photograph, and their trad-jazz counterparts like Terry Lightfoot, Acker Bilk and Chris Barber stared back from the other.

"My first impression of Ambrose Slade was that they were a motley crew, with a singer with bugger lugs grown down to his chin, a flash guitarist with teeth like a beaver and a shy, but highly accomplished bass and fiddle player with a dodgy eye. The only possible pin-up (I had served my apprenticeship on teenage mags and *NME*, and knew looks were not everything but they helped), with his deep-set eyes, dark, shoulder-length hair and high cheekbones, was the drummer. He counted the band in and then practically flattened me against the rear wall by sheer volume, with one wallop of the bone-juddering bass drum, and then thundered around his kit and led the band into their set. My ears were still ringing a day later, as Chas led me from the dungeon-like rehearsal room, intoning in his usual understated Geordie style, 'Yoos have just heard the new Beatles.'"

In early May 1969, the single 'Genesis'/'Roach Daddy' was released on Fontana. A week later, the album *Beginnings* followed. The record featured a very young band who hadn't found their own particular style and, although the mix of cover songs and self-penned tracks showed promise, it wasn't the world's most astonishing debut album. The cover, showing four bare-chested youngsters reaching out to the camera, didn't say much about them either.

"I remember doing that cover photo," Don says. "They had sent up a photographer from London to do it and we were in awe. Gosh, we'd hit the big time! The photographer came to Wolverhampton from London by train, so we met him at the station and took him in the van. We had all bought real trendy gear to wear for the photograph session.

"The photographer wanted to find a quarry and do the shots there. There was one near where Noddy lived with his mum and dad in Walsall. It was called Pouk Hill. When we got there, the photographer said, 'Now, take your tops off.' We had to do it, and it was freezing. There was actually snow on the ground. It was the first time we met a real photographer and they take forever. They take so many shots, like 100 rolls of film, and they only use one of them. We were so cold and so disappointed, because we had dressed up special. And in the end you could hardly see that we had our tops off anyway. But at least the album was the first one made by any Wolverhampton group. It was incredible. We thought that albums were only for big bands."

Beginnings was released in the USA later that year with a different cover, re-titled *Ballzy*, but neither the album nor single charted, so Ambrose Slade concentrated on playing live, particularly in London. They did a wide range of prestigious London venues, not only smaller ones like Tiles and the Ram Jam Club, but also all Gunnell's clubs as well as the Redcar Jazz Club, The Temple and The Marquee, where they went on as support for Yes, who had a residency there.

"Mick Tucker and I saw them play for real during that period," Andy Scott says. "I'd moved from The Elastic Band to having a couple of other bands and I started to look at ads in the paper. The Sweet advert was in *Melody Maker* one week and the next week I was a member of the band. I had only just joined The Sweet and we'd heard about this band coming through, so Mick and I made a journey to the old Kew Boat House in London. It was a big boathouse that held about 1,000 people and they were playing there. The last band that we had seen playing there was The Who. When we went in the place, the atmosphere was electric and they had a fantastic sound. They had this big PA, and ours was rubbish. The energy was fantastic, with Jimmy running all over the place and Noddy at the microphone singing. Coming away from that gig, I said to Mick, 'We need to re-think some things.' That was a defining moment. I never really saw them play live again."

Another acknowledgement came when Ambrose Slade played one of Gunnell's clubs.

"We used to do the Zappa song 'Ain't Got No Heart'," Don remembers, "and one night at The Speakeasy, Frank Zappa was in the audience. He liked the band, especially Jim's bass playing. He said to Jim, 'That was great bass playing, man,' which was a great compliment."

During this period, Ambrose Slade were booked to play at Eastnor Castle in Herefordshire. "It was at a wrap party of a film called *One More Time* with Sammy Davis, Jr. and Peter Lawford," Don recalls. "Jerry Lewis directed it. We got there and played in the main hall and everybody wanted Sammy Davis, Jr. to sing. So he agreed and said he just wanted the drummer and bass player to accompany him. I don't remember what he sung now, but it was one of his standard songs and he said to Jim and me, 'Just do the rhythm.' But both Jim and myself really knew the song. We came to a part where on the original the band stops, and me and Jim did that. Sammy turned around and said, 'How did *you* know?' That was quite something!

"But a week later, we were all sent for by the local Special Branch police. When we got there, it turned out that a lot of the silverware and different artefacts and antiques from the castle were gone. They had been taken and, obviously, the band gets the blame! They interviewed us individually, like you see it in films, with light shining in our faces. We were all in one room and got called in individually; when we were finished, we were sent into another room, so we couldn't talk about what was asked. When I had been interrogated, I went into this other room and, waiting, I could hear Nod through the door: *'I ain't took your bloody silver!'* I always remember that!

"We were totally innocent this time. We could honestly say that. But still they grilled us individually. That was the last we heard of it until 1974, when we met some of the film crew doing the film *Flame*. They said, 'We remember you. You played that party with Sammy Davis, Jr. at Eastnor Castle.' And we said, 'God, yes! We got accused of stealing the silver from that castle!' The film crew just laughed and said, 'It was us!'"

Ambrose Slade might have been on a tight budget, but they didn't go around nicking silverware. Despite bookings and records, nothing happened in the way of getting closer to fame and fortune. Like so many others, they were into the progressive look and failed to stand out from the crowd. That was soon to change. In the autumn of 1969, press agent Keith Altham came up with what Chas Chandler thought was a brilliant idea.

"Chas and John Gunnell sent for us and we drove down in our van to the office in Brook Street," recalls Don. "We knew something was wrong, because Chas got a bottle of whisky out and offered us a drink. He never did that. He poured us a drink and said that with what was happening in the country with skinheads, he thought we should cut our hair off. He said we had no identity basically, and we needed something to set us apart from other bands. We would get that by becoming skinheads. We were all horrified. It took me *so* long to grow my hair – no way was I going to have it cut! And we were dressed all trendy; we didn't want to replace that with the boots and braces of the skinheads. But Chas said, 'Well, why don't you go and have a cup of coffee and a think about it, because I believe that is what you need.'

"So, we went to have a think and we were a bit scared, because we thought that if we said no, Chas probably wouldn't want to manage us any more. Now we had finally found someone who was a proper manager, and were we to lose him because of a haircut? So we agreed to do it.

"When we came back to the office, it turned out that Chas already had the hairdresser booked. It was a guy named Harry, who'd actually done Hendrix's hair. We then had all our hair shaved off. Oh God! From hair down to the waist one day to, like, nothing the next. And we had to wear all those horrible things, Dr. Martens boots, braces, collarless shirts, etc.

"We still lived with our parents back then and when I had left my mum and dad's house in the morning, I had hair down past my shoulders. Now I went back, totally bald. It was late when I got back, so Mum and Dad were already in bed and I went straight to bed myself. My mum always used to bring me a cup of tea in the morning and when she came up with it the next morning, she went, 'Here's your cup of tea. *OOHH!*' and she poured the tea all over me. She thought I was a stranger. When she realised it was me, she was so upset: 'Your lovely curls!' It didn't go down well with Pat, either, and in fact everybody around Wolverhampton couldn't believe what we had done."

"I struggled to keep them in the pages of the music press," admits Keith Altham. "Right from those early days, I knew Ambrose Slade had a 'sound' and they were tight. What they did not have as yet were songs of their own, which was essential, and I was driven to the lengths of suggesting they become skinheads to get attention. It worked but, as Don understatedly said at the time, 'Dave is not happy with his short back and sides, and the BBC are scared to death of us and won't book us because they think we are going to incite a riot.' Don, like the others, saw the publicity value, but was uncomfortable with the yob-like comparisons and more violent aspects of the skinhead cult. However, as a publicity gimmick, it worked after a weird fashion, because it got them media attention."

The first new publicity photos appeared in *NME*. By then, Chas had abbreviated the band's name to Slade and, according to Don, that was much more popular than the old Ambrose Slade. "I remember we played somewhere and the black bouncer said, 'I like the name Slade. It sounds like *spade.*' I couldn't stop laughing.

"Chas would do anything to get us noticed, and he and John Gunnell came up with the idea of booking us into one of the big, posh hotels in London with a view to us getting kicked out. Then we would get press. We were booked into just one room and when we walked in at the hotel, we got looks from everybody there. When we reached the room we were supposed to cause a commotion, but could we? We tried everything. Turning the TV up loud, shouting, slamming doors, banging on the walls and sending furniture down the lift to the reception area, but nothing happened. They knew what we were up to at the hotel, as it was so obvious. After an hour, we called Chas to say that it was a waste of time, but he said that we had to get kicked out as the press was alerted. So we tried, but we weren't good at that kind of thing. It didn't come natural, as it wasn't in our hearts. We were too nice. We could just as well have said, '*Would you throw us out of the hotel, please?*' In the end they came to throw us out, but then they took us through the kitchen and out of the back door, so nobody noticed. It totally backfired.

"Our first gig as skinheads was in The Melody Room in Norwich. We had played there many times before we had our hair cut, but now we dreaded going there. When we turned up there were hundreds and hundreds of skinheads outside and we went, 'Oh, shit!' And we weren't playing their music, either. Skinheads usually listened to ska and blue beat, and we did our usual stuff. As far as the skinheads could see, it was a bit of a con, which in a way it was. We were crapping ourselves because of the audience. It was really frightening.

"There was a big mirror in the back of the room, so we could see ourselves on stage and, although we didn't feel like it, we looked really hard. Especially me. Whenever we played anywhere they used to send me in for the money, because I looked so hard that the club owners wouldn't dare turn me down. It was always, 'Send the quiet one in for the money, he'll frighten them!'"

Having changed the band's name and image, Chandler next demanded that Slade write their own material. The band had never really done that before – except for the few stumbling attempts on *Beginnings* – but as Chandler kept telling them to do it, they agreed. They paired off in writing teams the same way they used to share rooms – Don and Jim in one team, Nod and Dave in another.

"Don's songwriting is very good, especially the early ones, like 'Dapple Rose', 'Know Who You Are' and 'Look Wot You Dun'," says Dave. "He is really good with lyrics and has very interesting ideas in that respect."

"Jim usually wrote the melodies, but I did come up with some of them as well," Don points out. "It was not just the lyrics. There was a melody there, or the basic idea for it anyway, and then Jim used to take it from there. But it was a long process, in a way. Because I don't play any instruments except the drums and I can't sing, if I had any ideas for a melody I'd try to sing it to Jim and have him sing it back to me. It took a lot of time!"

"Don was very keen on the songwriting side," Jim recalls. "He would come over to my house with lyrics and a tune of sorts. Unfortunately, he always came across as completely tone deaf and, although he tried very hard, he did have difficulty with mumbling the intended tune. It was during this time with Don that I learnt to write melody on the spot, and I would always rewrite whatever his hazy tune may have been. He never seemed to complain, so it must have seemed OK."

Slade's next single, 'Wild Winds Are Blowing', was released on Fontana in October 1969 with the B-side, 'One Way Hotel', penned by Don and Jim, with the help of Noddy. Chandler got them on TV – *Scene At Six,* the six o'clock news programme for London only and *Monster Music Mash* on BBC1, hosted by Alan Price. They promoted the single and also played 'Martha My Dear', with Jim on violin.

"There's some old footage around from that time," Don says, "and when I see it now, I can't believe it. Seeing the four of us playing on a TV show without any hair and Jim on violin, it seems so abstract!"

The second single didn't chart either, but Chandler stuck to his skinhead idea and, although reluctant, the Slade members understood. "In a way it was the right thing to do to turn us into skinheads," Don ponders. "I always remember a gig where we were booked at a college of art. When they had the end-of-term balls, they had like 10 bands booked, and it was the student union that handled it. All the bands turned up and the people from the union tried to find out who they were and which room they were going to go to. Then we walked in and they went, 'Slade! You go in there!' So it worked, we had an identity.

"We got a lot of publicity and that was what Chas wanted, but in those days skinheads were associated with violence and a lot of places wouldn't let us play. They were afraid they were going to have the places smashed up. So here we were, all dressed in jeans and boots and everyone was scared to book us. We got no work whatsoever, and some of our bookings even got cancelled."

"I met Don around that time," guitarist and manager Len Tuckey remembers, "and he and the rest of the band were so different from their image. I was with a band called The Nashville Teens and we played at a college or university in Wales somewhere. Slade were on the bill and we shared a dressing room with them. They were all nice to talk to, especially Don, and we liked them very much. Don seemed a little shy, but they were all really nice guys. I think they would have been in a bit of trouble with the real bovver boys!"

Slade appeared on TV again when their third single was released by Fontana in March 1970. The A-side was Mann and Weil's 'Shape Of Things To Come', with Noddy's 'C'mon C'mon' on the B-side. Chas Chandler pushed for them to appear on *Top Of The Pops*, but again they ran into trouble, as *Top Of The Pops* was reluctant to allow skinheads on the show.

"The producer's son had been beaten up by skinheads," Don explains, "so they didn't really want us there, but eventually we got on to promote 'Shape Of Things To Come'. By then I had a standard Ludwig kit, and in those days on *Top Of The Pops* you could take your own equipment, so I brought my drums. On this particular kit I had the drum skin painted. Jim was into art and he had a friend who went to art college, so he painted *Tondal's Vision* by Hieronymus Bosch on the skin. I thought that would look great and I paid him £6 to paint it for me."

Following the release of 'Shape Of Things To Come', Chandler arranged for Slade to be moved from Fontana to Polydor, another label within the same corporate structure. *Beginnings* was therefore the only Slade album released on Fontana.

Despite problems getting gigs and an album and three singles that had bombed, Slade were oddly enough chosen to represent England in a European radio show that was broadcast from the German island Heligoland on August 15, 1970. "All the European countries got together to do this pop show on Heligoland," Don says. "Apparently, they had to broadcast the show from there as it was the only place from where every country could receive the radio signal. We went from England, Golden Earring went from Holland and there were a lot of other bands as well.

"Polydor flew us to Hamburg, then we got the boat out to Heligoland as it was too small an island to land a plane there. It was a duty-free island and we could buy a bottle of whisky for 50p. Oh my God! I bought a bottle and I was just slugging it back. We all were, but I was probably the worst for wear.

"We did three songs: 'Shape Of Things To Come', Alvin Lee's 'Hear Me Calling' and 'Know Who You Are', which we wrote ourselves. We also did a live radio interview, which was broadcast all over Europe. We had all this crap because we were skinheads and when it came up in the interview I said, 'What the fuck is wrong with skinheads?' And that was broadcast all over Europe! I got kicked out of the studio. Still, it was a good experience appearing on the show and we were all very impressed with Golden Earring. What a fantastic band.

"I still don't know why we came to represent England though. We were not an obvious choice because of our skinhead image and we hadn't even had a hit. Maybe it was because we used to do a lot of Radio One live sessions. Back then, the radio stations used to play a lot of live music as well as records; they played maybe one song a day and, as they owned those tapes, they could repeat it whenever they wanted. We used to record in BBC's Paris Studio in Regent Street and we did that really quickly. We used to have three hours to record five songs, and there never was any trouble with us. Maybe that was the reason why they chose us to go to Heligoland."

After the release of 'Shape Of Things To Come', Slade began work on a new album in Olympic Studios in Barnes, West London. Chas Chandler wanted them to write at least half of the songs for the album and it took them three weeks to record it. "It was great being at a big label like Polydor," Don says, "and it was the first time that Chas took us to the big Olympic studio, which was just about to open. That was a fantastic experience. They had a normal eight-track Studio One, and Studio Two, where we recorded, was the new 16-track studio. The new baby, so to speak.

"We basically christened that studio, as we were the first ones in there to do an album. And, of course, as we had 16 tracks, we were going mad, weren't we? We did everything, cowbells and door slamming and things like that — anything just to use up the tracks. There was a little village hall or church hall where we always used to rehearse back in Wolverhampton. Sometimes we would have an afternoon there, just to go over things or get the basic idea, and then leave it to work in the studio and get more ideas there. We used to go out to Chas' house near Gatwick Airport, so he knew our ideas as well.

"Sometimes we rehearsed there too, but basically we rehearsed in the studio when we had the songs written, not realising how much studio time we were wasting. We could have done four albums! Normally, what would happen would be Dave, Jim and myself on the instruments and Nod would always sing on the basic track. He would wear his guitar to get the feeling that we were on stage, but he never really had it plugged in. Then he would overdub his guitar later.

"Nod sang live as a guide vocal, to get a nice live feel. More often than not we actually kept that vocal. He maybe did another couple of takes afterwards, just him doing vocals, but then Chas said, 'Forget it! We've already got the vocals.' It happened so many times that the guide track was the finished one. So we recorded *all* together. We all got together in the studio and just did it. And it was *mayhem* in the control room, trying to control things, but that's what it was.

"That particular album was done pretty quickly, because we were still finding our way in the studio. We didn't really understand studio techniques then. We would just go in and do it with all four of us playing at the same time. And then the overdubs, piano or whatever it was, were done afterwards."

While Slade were working on the album, Jimi Hendrix approached Chas Chandler to resume managing him. "We were doing a radio session in London, when Chas asked us to come and see him," Don recalls. "He said, 'I'm managing you now and that is not going to change, but Jimi has asked me to manage and produce him again. What do you think?' And we thought it was fantastic, having the same management as Jimi Hendrix. That would be so good for us.

"Chas then went to visit his parents in Newcastle for the weekend and he said he would sort things out with Jimi when he came back. We went to the BBC to do a radio session and during one song the BBC producer said on the intercom, 'Have you heard the news? Jimi Hendrix is dead.' It was such a shock. Chas was on the train to Newcastle and didn't know about it. It was terrible. We didn't see Chas for weeks after that. He and Jimi had been like brothers. They had this respect and love for each other, and Jimi had lived with Chas and his wife when he first came to England. It hit Chas pretty bad."

Soon other great rock stars were to follow Jimi Hendrix. Both Janis Joplin and Jim Morrison died within a year, with all three of them aged 27. It didn't scare off Don and Slade though. Their first release through Polydor Records emerged in September 1970, a single with two tracks from the album sessions: 'Know Who You Are' and 'Dapple Rose', both written by Don and Jim.

"Actually, the A-side, 'Know Who You Are', is the same as our old instrumental 'Genesis', so Nod and Dave are credited for that one as well as

Jim and myself," Don explains. "I wrote the lyrics for it and some of them are about Dave. I don't know how it came about, but the first line that I came up with was 'H, old babe, sing a song to make out that your playing is easy.' Another line goes: 'Tired of your socks, trying your father's on.' That came from an actual experience, as I used to nick my father's socks. If I had holes in mine, I used to take my dad's. Dad would then shout, 'Don! Where's my bloody socks?' He knew where they had gone!"

Although both songs were of a higher standard than any of their other self-penned releases, the single didn't chart and neither did the new album, *Play It Loud*, when it was released in November 1970. Chas Chandler had produced it and he acquired the publishing rights, too. "In the beginning Chas wanted the publishing," Don remembers. "He was signed to the label and we were signed to him. We wanted our own publishing company, but we agreed that Chas got it, as we didn't want to lose him. Not to put Chas down, but we were in the palm of his hand. We didn't want to upset him."

Apart from a few cover songs, Jim and Don wrote the entire album with the occasional help of Noddy. "Nod finished a lot of the songs for us, lyrics-wise," Don admits. "I can write lyrics but, back then, Jim and myself sometimes couldn't finish the songs, so we'd take them to Nod to have him help out. But basically it was Jim and me who wrote the album. We wrote nine of the album's 12 tracks. We were still living at our parents', so I'd go to Jim's parents' house, or he'd come to my parents' house."

"Don's parents were pure salt of the earth and always extended a genuine warm welcome whenever I went to his house," Jim recalls. "There were always buckets of tea. During the Don/Jim and Nod/Dave writing era, Don and I were far more prolific, providing most of the songwriting imput."

"One of them was 'Pouk Hill', where I wrote the lyrics about the very freezing experience we had had when we shot the cover photo for the *Beginnings* album," Don says, "but the strangest track, looking back, was probably 'I Remember'. In hindsight, it is spooky that I would write a song about a man who loses his memory, three years prior to the accident where I got amnesia. I didn't even realise until a couple of years ago. I'd never thought of it before, and I don't even remember what the inspiration was at the time when I wrote the lyrics to that one. It is indeed very weird!"

Play It Loud was not a typical Slade album as it had a melancholy, nihilistic feel to it. In Don's opinion, they tried to be too clever when they wrote it. When 1970 came to an end, Slade realised all too well that although they had been managed by Chas Chandler for two years and had a live following and lots of press, they still hadn't had a hit.

"Again, it was us against the world," Don says, "but this time at least we had Chas. When we first started with him, I remember he said to us how close we were as a band and as people. He said, 'Even I can't get into your little circle.' We couldn't really think what he meant, but he continued, 'You four are so close because of the experiences you've been through,' and he said he had never seen that in a band before, except maybe The Beatles. He said, 'You'll make it as a band, because the tightness of the four of you is unique.' Chas always had so much faith in us, although a lot of people were saying that we would never make it."

The camaraderie within the band was largely responsible for Swinn having been left behind in 1968, but he was not forgotten and was now hired as their first full-time roadie, leaving Woden Transformers to do so. "I remember going to see him to ask him if he wanted to be our roadie," Don recalls. "I honestly thought he would say no, as he had a steady income, but he said yes. He wanted to be paid the same as at Woden, which was £28 a week. We usually paid £4, but we all agreed."

Swinn's services were sorely needed, as Slade worked 11 months a year. No matter how hard they tried, however, a breakthrough still lingered somewhere off in the distance. In the end, Keith Altham resigned as their publicist.

"Keith Altham did actually say to Chas, 'They are never going to become successful,'" Don recalls. "He said, 'I don't believe in it. I feel I'm taking your money off you. Forget the publicity. It's not working. I think you should take the account somewhere else.' He left, but later regretted it. He actually said that it was the biggest mistake of his life."

John Halsall, who ran the photo agency Popwire, was hired to replace Altham. Halsall got Slade favourable press reviews from the writers that he invited to see them live, but it was still without the boys denting the charts. But, as always, the darkest hour is before the dawn.

Don lays it down; recording at Command Studios, London, 1971. MICHAEL PUTLAND/GETTY IMAGES

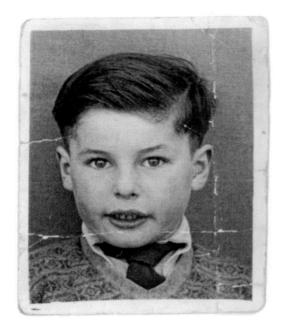

Don's first school photo, at Villiers Primary, aged five. DON POWELL

On the playing field in Bilston: "It looks like I'm wearing a pair of Dave Hill's trousers!" says Don. DEREK POWELL

Outside Don's house on Stowlawn Housing Estate, Bilston, in the 1950s: Don's sister Carol and baby sister Marilyn, cousin Dave with brother Derek and Don himself (on the left), and an unidentified little girl. DEREK POWELL

Don aged 15, on holiday at Brean Sands: "My 'Fonz' period!"
DON POWELL

Don and his dad during their drinking days. DON POWELL

Dora and Walter Powell in 1973. DON POWELL

The original 'N Betweens trying their best to look "hip" at St Giles Youth Club in the early 1960s. DON POWELL

A dressing-room shot from the early days. Don: "I can't work out what Nod's doing. Has he just had a curry?" CAROLE WILLIAMS

One of the first publicity shots after Slade reluctantly became skinheads. Don: "Don't our expressions tell you how we felt?" GERED MANKOWITZ

A dressing room in 1973, with Dave and Jim in the mirror. GERED MANKOWITZ

Slade manager Chas Chandler: one of Don's favourite photos of the man who took Slade under his wing. ANDREW BIRKIN

"Unusual for me to be not doing anything!" says Don. "Nod must be talking to the audience or taking the piss out of Dave."
ANDREW BIRKIN

"Backstage... my zip is stuck!" GERED MANKOWITZ

In concert somewhere in the US in 1974. "When we didn't know where we were," says Don, "we used to say TOWN HALL whichever country we were in." ANDREW BIRKIN

Jim, Dave, Noddy and Don during the heyday of Slade. REDFERNS

9

It's Alive!

What makes a band rise to fame is always a mix of different elements. For Slade, who had years of experience, a good live following, a record deal with a major label and one of the most expert managers in the business, it should have been a piece of cake. But they still needed that extra *something*, that one song that would make them break through. It came to them by accident.

"We used to play the Connaught Hotel and the Park Hall Hotel," says Don, "and our former fan club secretary, Carole Williams, had a boyfriend who was a disc jockey there. He always finished his show with Bobby Marchan's 'Get Down And Get With It', which had been a Little Richard hit. The crowd used to go mad when they heard it, so we wanted that for stage."

"I recall Jimmy coming to my house one day to ask if I could get them a tape of a record they had heard my boyfriend playing," says Carole Williams. "I got the song taped for them and the rest is history."

"'Get Down And Get With It' became part of our stage show," Don expands. "We used to finish our shows with it and then Chas said, 'It goes down so well on stage that it's gonna be your next single.' That was a *great* idea! We never even thought of that."

The song was recorded in Olympic Studios and released in May 1971, with 'Do You Want Me'/'Gospel According To Rasputin', both penned by Noddy and Dave, on the B-side.

"In those days you only got on *Top Of The Pops* if your record was in the Top 30," Don remembers. "They used to have a new-release spot, but it was always the established artists of the time, like Tom Jones, who got that. 'Get Down And Get With It' went to the charts in the 40s, I think, and crept up to 32. We thought, *next* week! We're gonna get it on *Top Of The Pops* next week. Next week it was 32 again and I thought, no, it is never gonna do it now. But Chas said, 'Well, you'll get in the Top 30 next week.' The following week it was 29 and we were on *Top Of The Pops*. Eventually 'Get Down' went up to number 16 and that was the start."

This time *Top Of The Pops* didn't mind letting Slade perform. They had started to grow their hair by then and brighter clothes had replaced the skinhead uniforms. Or, as Keith Altham puts it, "They took the skinhead trousers, adapted the skins' girlfriends' hairstyle and somehow concocted a happy-go-lucky, futuristic *Clockwork Orange* persona."

"At TV shows like *Top Of The Pops* we had to re-record the songs," Don recalls. "I think it was the Musicians' Union that started that. As I understand it, if a record had brass features or something, they had to use the *Top Of The Pops* orchestra for that, to give them work. And it was also to prove that it was the artist on the record. So even if it was just the band, like Slade, who played, we still had to re-record the song, otherwise the union put the boot in. We used to go into the studio two days before and re-record the song, which was a joke really. They sent a representative down to watch that we really re-recorded it, but half the time he'd say, 'I'll just go for a drink; you'll have recorded it when I get back,' meaning you're just gonna give me the tape of the record. I remember one time we had this really strict union man and he wanted to watch us recording it, but then the engineer just put on the master tape of the record and we were miming to it, and he didn't even notice! I actually dropped a stick and bent down to pick it up while the music was still playing, but he didn't notice! It was a total waste of both studio time and costs. It was absolutely dreadful."

★　★　★

'Get Down And Get With It' was a hit in Holland before it was in the UK' so, at the beginning of July 1971, Slade went there for a few days to do a TV show. "What I remember most of that trip was the last night, which we spent in a haunted house," Don says. "It was a guest house and we didn't get there until midnight. The guy who ran it waited up for us and he let us in while wearing his dressing gown. We told him that we had to leave early in the morning to get the ferry back to England. We paid him straight away and, as we wouldn't be there for breakfast, he'd put some sandwiches and orange juice for us to take with us when we left.

"We then had two rooms with an adjoining door between them. Jim and I shared one room, Nod and Dave the other as usual. We went to bed straight away, to get as much sleep as we could, as we were to leave at five or six the next morning. It was so hot in the rooms that I couldn't sleep. I could hear somebody walk down the corridor, like footsteps up and down all night. And then I could hear Nod and Dave talking in the next room and see the light underneath the adjoining door. They went on and on and I thought, 'Stop, stop, stop,' because we had to get up early. I was about to throw a pillow at the adjoining door, when suddenly the talking stopped. And then the light was not switched off, but dimmed down. I thought, 'Great,' and went to sleep.

"The next morning we got up, got the sandwiches and went off. There was quiet in the van, nobody spoke to each other, so to break the ice, I turned to Nod and Dave, who were sitting in the back, and I said, 'You two! You knew we had to get up early in the morning, why did you keep talking all night?' They were quite surprised. 'We weren't talking.' 'But I could hear you!' But no, they'd done the same thing as us, gone to bed straight away. Then I said, 'But I could see the light through the adjoining door!' And then they looked at each other and said, 'What door?' There'd been no adjoining door between our rooms!

"It then turned out that we had all heard the pacing footsteps in the corridor and we all went, 'Oh God!' Furthermore, Jim had actually thought he saw a man standing at the end of the bed with a big axe during the night. We just took the sandwiches and threw them out of the car window and got the heck out of there!"

The scary experience didn't keep Slade from going back to Holland. Later in the same month, they returned to do two live appearances in Amsterdam, one in the Paradiso Club and one in Vondelpark. "They had a bandstand on an island in the middle of a lake," Don remembers. "Well, it was more of a pond actually. When we got on, the kids went crazy and tried to cross the pond to get to us. That was a great gig. But there were some trees there that blocked the view and Chas wanted them cut down. He had quite an argument with the promoters. It was a typical manager thing, wanting the group to be seen."

"I mainly remember that gig because the police pulled a gun on me," Swinn adds. "They said we had played over time. The police officer actually brought out his gun and said, 'You will stop the band!' 'OK!'"

By now Swinn had become Slade's tour manager, while the rest of the crew consisted of sound engineer Charlie Newnham and Johnny 'JJ' Jones. Soon after, the Scot Robbie Wilson came on board.

The rest of the summer was spent touring Scotland and England and setting up a new fan club. The Slade Fan Club was run out of Chas Chandler's South Molton Street office by John Bright, who wrote the newsletters under the pseudonym Diana. The first newsletter covered July/August 1971 and was a mix of concert date information, competitions, news updates and written contributions by the individual band members. Or at least that was what the fans were led to believe.

"We actually didn't write those ourselves," Don reveals. "John Bright did that. We never had anything to do with the fan club whatsoever."

The fans didn't know and they flocked to the South Molton Street office to get a glimpse of the band and the mysterious Diana, who was always out to lunch when fans came calling. Over the years, the club became a huge success and, at its peak, had 30,000 members. The collated fan-club letters were released as the book *The Slade Papers* by Barn Publishing in 1976.

With 'Get Down And Get With It', Slade had their first whiff of fame, but with a cover song. Chas Chandler wanted their next single to be their own, and this time, Noddy and Jim teamed up with stunning results. "Nod and Jim came up with 'Coz I Luv You'," says Don. "I think it only took them a few minutes to write it. Both of them were always big fans of Django Reinhardt and Stéphane Grappelli and they used to play around in the dressing room, because of Jim playing the violin as well."

The dressing-room shuffle, which was used to tune up Jim's violin, was added to a chord progression influenced by the legendary Hot Club de France. Slade went in the studio to record the song and, when stomping and hand clapping were added, hey presto! It came alive. "As for the drum sound of the record, it came from one time when we were rehearsing," Don says. "It was such a tiny room, so I just went on the snare drum. Jim said, 'Remember that,' because he'd got an ear for that type of thing, and I used that particular style on all of our early records, only snare drum and bass drum and occasionally a cymbal crash. That's where 'Coz I Luv You' came from. Not until later did I realise that Ringo Starr used the same thing on 'Get Back'!"

The single was recorded at Olympic Studios, but Slade were not quite satisfied. For one thing, they found the title too 'wimpy'. "Back then, the title was spelled 'Because I Love You' and it looked so wet," Don recalls. "In order to heavy it up, we decided to spell the title in Black Country dialect and it came out as 'Coz I Luv You'. But we did get in trouble with the educational authorities because of that. We were accused of misleading the kids and teaching them a wrong way of spelling. The funny thing was a few years later they actually started teaching phonetic spelling at school, so in the end, who was misleading the kids?"

Nevertheless, the controversy with the schoolteachers was good press for Slade and the Black Country misspelling became a trademark of the band. But even with the new spelling, they were still not satisfied with the recording. "We didn't want the song out," Don says. "When we recorded it, we weren't sure. I remember Chas said, 'You've got your first number one,' but we couldn't see it, because it wasn't what we used to play. We actually never played it on stage. But Chas said, 'I don't care what you think. It's coming out!' He then took the master to Polydor and they freaked."

'Coz I Luv You' was released in October 1971, with Noddy's 'My Life Is Natural' on the B-side, and it got plenty of radio play before the release date. "And that was it," Don states. "Then the roads were closed for going back. It was just incredible."

The music, the spelling, everything worked in Slade's favour, making them a band that rose above others. This was, of course, noticed by their fellow musicians. "Slade were slightly after us with 'Coz I Luv You'," says Andy Scott. "We were just a year ahead of them, with a completely different kind of music. At that time, The Sweet were a sickly sweet pop band, even though with the musicianship and the capability of the band, we could do more than what appeared on the record. But Slade came in at exactly the right time, with that slightly stomping, harder kind of music. I remember The Sweet thinking, 'That's what *we* should be doing!' And then the next year the glam-rock thing started to break and, of course, The Sweet were very keen on putting the eye make-up on!"

Slade's own fashion statement came with 'Coz I Luv You' in the shape of platform boots, which they first wore on *Top Of The Pops* while performing the hit. They became synonymous with the band, since few others were wearing them at that time. "It was Dave who started with the platform shoes," Don recalls. "We used to get them at Kensington Market. There were two guys there who did all our clothes for us, especially a guy named Julian. In years to come, the platform shoes got higher and higher and more outrageous, but at the time of 'Coz I Luv You', it was a first."

So was their single. "When it came out it went to number 26 and next week it was number eight," says Don. "We just couldn't believe it. The week after it was number one and it stayed there for four weeks. All in all, it was on the Top 20 for 10 weeks."

The next move came a couple of weeks after the single release, when Slade were booked to record a live album. "Live albums didn't mean that much in England at the time," Don recalls. "The Who did *Live At Leeds*, which was quite a successful album, but in general, live albums weren't that big a thing. It was Chas' idea, anyway. He said, 'You're a great live band, so you have to record a live album.' Then he booked the Command Studios in Piccadilly.

"Command was a theatre studio where the BBC used to record radio plays and things like that with a live audience, so the studio was wired up for live recordings. We recorded three nights with an invited audience, basically from the fan club. I think there were 300 per night, and all the material that went on the album was recorded on the second night. We had come directly from *Top Of The Pops*, where we had pre-recorded 'Coz I Luv You' for broadcast the following evening, and every track on the album was from that night. We were just on a roll."

After recording the live album, Slade went to Europe. Because of the initial success all over England, they had a week booked on European territory doing TV shows, but on the ferry to Holland they hit a hurricane.

"Instead of being on the boat overnight, we spent three and a half days," Don laughs. "The national press in England wrote, 'Slade lost at sea!' I think one of the quotes was, 'Good!'

"The force of the weather made it impossible for the boat to turn, so it kept on going north. We nearly ended up at the North Pole! Then it turned back.

"Three and a half days was a long time on that boat, but it was all free – food, drinks and whatever. We didn't have to pay anything, but of course nobody wanted to eat, as everybody was seasick. It was terrible. You couldn't go outside, the weather was too bad, and you couldn't really sleep either. I remember I tried to sleep, but I couldn't stay in bed. I kept being thrown out of the bunk.

"Jim and I went to the bar and there was this old sailor. We kept being thrown around, but this old guy was just standing there. He didn't move an inch. He said, 'Put a towel on the bar, wet the towel and the glasses will stay on the towel.' He was just standing there, drinking.

"We were all seasick, but it was particularly bad for Dave. I remember one time we were all in the bar, drinking. We were talking and I said, 'Where's H? I haven't seen him all day?' Then Swinn got up and fetched a glass of water and put a stomach powder in it. He walked to a settee, which stood in the room with its back to us, and we saw Dave's hand come up, take the glass and then it went back down. He'd been there all the time. He was *so* ill."

"He was actually green in the face," quips Swinn.

"When finally we reached the Continent we did a TV show in all of the different countries," Don continues. "Holland, Belgium, Germany and so on, and that TV tour was our first taste of the big time. Living out of suitcases and travelling around, just us and our equipment. Being picked up by cars and taken to the next place. I enjoyed it."

Slade didn't rest on their laurels. In January 1972 their next single was released. Don and Jim had written 'Look Wot You Dun' with the help of Noddy, and the single charted at number four.

"I wrote the lyrics to that one," Don recalls, "but I couldn't really finish it, so Nod came up with the chorus, 'Hey hey, hey, look what you're doing to me' and so on. The song is recognisable because of the heavy breathing in the chorus and I think that was Chas' idea. Don't ask me why! It just came. It's actually me doing the heavy breathing, and I also used a matchbox, making the sound on the sulphur of the box. The B-side of that particular single was 'Candidate', which Jim and I had written as well.

"I always remember when we first started working with Chas, because in those days the B-sides were considered throwaway songs. Like a song you would never use on an album. But Chas said, 'No! It's gotta be just as strong, it's gonna stand up in its own right.' He actually took that from The Beatles. On Beatles records, all the B-sides were almost as good as the A-sides, so when kids bought a single they obviously did it because of the A-side, but they'd get just as good a product on the B-side.

"It was the right thing to do. When I would buy records and the B-side was great as well, that was like a bonus. I got two great songs for the price of one. You got value for money, basically. I think it is a good policy to have, instead of what they call album fillers. I hate that expression! Album fillers? You're supposed to be making a product – every song is going to stand up on its own and not be throwaway. Otherwise, it's just a con. When I buy albums, I like to get something out of each track, not put the album on and go, 'Oh, that's just a filler.' It's a horrible description. The same thing goes for B-sides. Oh, it's just a B-side. We always tried to make our B-sides as good as the A-sides."

In March 1972, the live record that became Slade's most successful album was released. *Slade Alive!* peaked at number two and stayed in the charts for 18 months. The seven songs on the album were from Slade's live set and included Alvin Lee's 'Hear Me Calling' as well as John Sebastian's 'Darling Be Home Soon', which Noddy made notorious because he happened to do a massive burp in the middle of the song.

Two new self-penned songs found their way to the album, one of them a medley of upbeat 12-bars called 'Keep On Rockin'', a phrase that became a mantra and greeting among Slade fans. All four band members were involved in the writing of that, whereas Don and Jim wrote the other original track, 'In Like A Shot From My Gun', with the aid of Noddy.

Praise for the album did not just come from the fans. The album sleeve boasted a series of adulatory quotes from the press and from fellow musicians, including Paul McCartney and Richie Blackmore. Slade themselves took their success in their usual down-to-earth way. They continued gigging at clubs, universities and pubs all over England during the first months of 1972. "We honoured everything that was already in the book," Don explains. "A lot of people wouldn't do that when first they got success, but we honoured everything that had already been paid for, although it was chaos. If we were playing a 500-capacity club, there would be the same again outside, waiting to get in. It was a great feeling though."

"We were all thrilled to bits when they finally made it," Don's sister Carol remembers. "It was so exciting. We used to go and see them, all of us getting backstage."

"Don's sisters had the shyness of youth, they were always friendly and perfectly polite," Jim adds. "His brother, Derek, was really good-looking, which belied the fact that he could and did swing the odd punch or two. Once again though, always gushingly friendly."

"Derek only attended a few times," says Don, "but when we played the small clubs and pubs, Dave's younger sister Carol came to see us quite often, with her girlfriends. Nod was an only child, but Jim had three brothers, an older brother named Raymond and two younger ones, Frank and John. Raymond came to see us a couple of times but Frank and John were too young then. When Frank got older he used to come quite often, and eventually he got my Ludwig kit.

95

"The thing was that I wanted bigger drums, but I couldn't afford a big Ludwig kit. They were out of my price range, so I went to Hayman. They were good drums as well and I could afford them. They had a big bass drum and tom-toms and I used them from early 1972.

"My sticks I got from William Shaw. They were based in the north of England, near Bradford, and they said they could make sticks in any design, any weight, any size that I wanted. I was using Premier sticks at the time and I said, 'If you can copy these, that would be perfect,' and they did."

Slade ventured out of England again in April 1972 to tour mainland Europe. Mostly they did TV shows and a few one-off concerts in Scandinavia and Belgium. They also did promo videos to send to Australia and other territories to which they couldn't go. Finally, they went on their first real concert tour playing all major cities in Britain, with Status Quo as the opening act.

"Mel Bush promoted that tour." Don recalls. "He approached Chas and said he wanted to promote Slade's first tour and make it a good package. Status Quo had had success before with the 1968 song 'Pictures Of Matchstick Men', but they'd gone down and were trying to build their name up again, playing universities and things like that. Mel Bush said it would be a great package with Slade and Quo, and the ticket prices were quite low. It was like 50p. Status Quo had been a *Top Of The Pops* band and they were hellbent on getting rid of that image. Once we played with them at a university. They turned up in a limousine dressed quite straight, and then they changed into all the ripped jeans and old T-shirts. They wore the scruffiest things I had ever seen, in order not to look like a *Top Of The Pops* band any more."

"Mel Bush was a really important person in the early progress of both Slade and Quo," recalls Bob Young, who became Status Quo's tour manager/harmonica player and songwriter in 1968. "Three years later, after hundreds of gigs in clubs, bars and universities in the UK and Germany, we were still struggling. Then we met Slade for the first time on January 7, 1971, at The Flamingo Club in Hereford. That night, we all partied hard back at the hotel and it was the start of a friendship and mutual respect that continues to this day."

"They were the first band that we called our friends," Status Quo guitarist Francis Rossi agrees. "The first time I ever saw Slade was when they released 'Get Down And Get With It'. They were the first English band that I saw that had this high energy. There weren't that many bands that were into high energy and that intensity. I really did like Slade a lot and we did a lot of things with them. Most of it was day-to-day stuff, but we were having fun. We were touring and we enjoyed the travelling. I just remember good times with Slade, as they were the one band that we had... kinship with. I don't know why, but we were really, really comfortable with them. I particularly liked Don. I got on extremely well with him, although we didn't have sex or anything together. I could tell if it had happened, it would have been quite a good story to tell," Rossi laughs, and continues with a grin. "We may have had sex together, but none of us remember!"

"That's so typical Fran!" Don chuckles.

"In any case, Don is a very loud drummer," adds Rossi. "I'm not gonna say that he's the best drummer in the world, but he is perfect for Slade. It's a synergy. That's what seems to happen with those kinds of bands, bands like us. It's not necessarily that any individual is particularly good, or particularly brilliant, but something works. There's a chemistry, so when they got together, something happened."

During the tour, Slade's next number one single, 'Take Me Bak 'Ome', was released. The single came out during May with 'Wonderin' Y' on the B-side. "Jim and I had written the B-side, but the A-side was by Nod and Jim," Don says. "It was much better when they started writing, because it just happened so quickly. It was like the perfect formula and that format was kept, signed and sealed, so the idea of Jim and me writing sort of dropped out basically. A lot of the songs that I had written with Jim still surfaced as B-sides, though."

"Slade's *Clockwork Orange* persona that took off with "'Coz I Luv You' found its feet when Don combined with Jim Lea to write the lyrics for 'Look What You Dun'," says Keith Altham. "Don contributed a few more Slade songs, like 'Wonderin' Y' and 'Know Who You Are' (the first example of sock and roll), but once Slade were on a run of hits with Holder/Lea compositions, Don was characteristically content to take a back seat and concentrate on playing his indispensable anchor role."

"There was a big difference between what Jim and I wrote and what Nod and Jim wrote," Don ponders. "I think Nod was more down to earth. He wrote about what the guy next door did, what the kids could shout on the streets, and not so much the contemplative things that I used to write. And that was great for the band actually. It worked fantastic.

"Some of the things that Noddy wrote made me laugh. Even Chas used to laugh so much over the things he was writing. And sometimes when it got a bit too close to the mark, Chas said, 'No, no, no, you can't say that! Forget it! It'll get banned! You won't get radio play, so you have to rewrite it.' That was quite funny sometimes, because Nod was always trying to be so adamant. He wanted to keep the naughty things in."

As part of the UK tour, Slade and Status Quo were invited to play at the Great Western Festival at Bardney near Lincoln in May 1972, before an audience of 50,000 fans who were unlikely to be devotees of *Top Of The Pops*. Also on the bill were Joe Cocker, The Beach Boys, Rod Stewart & The Faces, Roxy Music, Lindisfarne and the *Monty Python's Flying Circus* team.

"Chas said that one of the big festivals was going to crack us as a top group," says Don, "and I think he had to pull some strings to get us on the Great Western Festival at Lincoln. It was a three-day event and there were a lot of big names on. We really weren't sure how we would be received, because we didn't play the same music as the rest of the bands. We were more *Top Of The Pops* music, like Status Quo had been, but Chas wanted to get us that credible name."

It was a bit ironic that, only three years earlier, the underground Ambrose Slade had tried to break though with a teenybopper audience, warming up for Amen Corner, and now the successful pop band Slade had to prove their worth in front of an underground crowd. As expected, they were booed when they went on stage, but within minutes they'd turned the audience around.

"Chas did it right," Don says. "He got us on when the sun was going down and we were the first band to use the lights that day. And it just worked miracles for us. The *coup de grâce* was when Nod introduced the festival's backer, Stanley Baker. He was standing at the side of the stage and Nod said, 'This is the guy who made this festival,' and the crowd just went mad. It was a great thing that Nod did, and he got the crowd to do the war chant from Baker's best-known film, *Zulu*. It just went ballistic after that."

"The Lincoln festival was amazing," Swinn agrees. "It gave them credibility. Up until then they had been a pop band. They weren't regarded as a serious band, a musician's band, but a fun band, probably because their music was always upbeat; it was always a good time. At Lincoln, that was the first time they were taken seriously by the business and given due credit for the band that they were."

"We totally took the festival and we were on the front pages of all the music papers the next week," says Don. "It was really an important breakthrough for us."

10

Riding High

The Lincoln Festival proved what Slade's followers had always known. They were an incredible live band. Their records may have placed them among the pop bands, but their live performances meant they were taken seriously and ranked among the top musicians. As if to prove the point, they went to the Granada Studios in Manchester in 1972 to film the TV show *Set Of Six*. The 25-minute studio performance, including the four cover songs from the *Slade Alive!* album as well as their self-penned hits 'Coz I Luv You' and 'Look Wot You Dun', showed how the many years of playing pubs and clubs had paid off. The sheer energy of the band, as well as the banter from the stage, made even the perplexed young studio audience get out of their seats. No wonder Slade would go down in history as one of the best live bands ever.

"The reason that all started was that some of the bands we used to see were heads-down and never communicating with the audience," Don says. "We decided we were never gonna be like that. Nod was a great frontman obviously, with the command of his voice. I have never seen anyone to better Noddy, but we all gave what we had in us. Also, with our talk on stage, how we used to make fun of each other, we always had that thing with each other and if people could see that we were having a good time on stage, then it reflected on them. That policy we always stuck to."

Slade toured Europe from Finland in the north to Spain in the south during the summer months of 1972. Being on tour meant drinking, smoking and indulging in the pleasures of the road to be found at red-light districts in cities such as Hamburg and Amsterdam. The rock'n'roll lifestyle crept up on the band, which Swinn still vividly remembers. "We did a club in Benidorm in Spain for a week and they put us up in a little fishing village called Calpe just a few miles away. Don, Nod and I shared lodgings and we used to sit in the window overlooking the harbour with the fishing boats. We would smoke dope and sing 'When You Wish Upon A Star', all high."

"I always thought somebody must have spiked our drinks!" Don admits. "Dave and Jim shared an apartment, because they didn't want to go out, but Swinn, Nod and myself had been out drinking and, when we came back, we couldn't even walk. We tried to get up the stairs to our apartment, but we could only get that far up, then one of us would roll back again. It happened in what seemed like hours. In the end, we were laughing so much that we couldn't move at all."

"In the lodgings there was a full-length window going all the way from the floor to the ceiling," Swinn continues, "and that night I got out of bed, naked and stoned out of my mind. I was going to the toilet, but I walked out of the window instead. It was about three or four metres down. I was passed out outside, still on my hands and knees where I had landed."

"I remember being woken up by a thumping on the door by the groundsman," Don says. "He was shouting, 'Your amigo! Your amigo!' I got up, wrapped a towel around me and went out. There was Swinn, lying stark naked in the courtyard, hands and knees bleeding and this big window was open. I couldn't stop laughing. Being a true friend, I ran in and got a camera and took a photograph of him."

"I could have killed myself," Swinn reflects. "If I had been sober and straight, I probably would have been dead. That was life on the road back then. Oh, happy days!"

Although Slade enjoyed their massive success and everything that went with it, it didn't alter their everyday way of life. They drove an old Vauxhall Velox to gigs and lived at home with their parents in

Wolverhampton. When possible, they preferred to go for a beer at their local pub, the Trumpet, in Bilston, rather than hang out in fancy clubs in London. They did have to spend more time in London though, but then they stayed in The Grantley Hotel in Shepherd's Bush.

"It was not a nice place," Don recalls. "It was like £1 a night with breakfast and we shared a room… the four of us. The bathroom and toilets were down the hallway. We stayed there when we did *Top Of The Pops*. Then Chas would take us out to Tramp, *the* exclusive place in London. All the tables there were in long rows, so everybody was sitting together, basically. One night I looked down at the bottom of the table and Keith Moon was there with Marianne Faithfull. I looked at him and he looked back at me the same way. We were sort of acknowledging each other and that kept going for hours. I looked at him and he looked back, nodding. Then he got up to leave with his party. He came over to say hello and shake hands and he took out a bundle of £20 notes and called the waiter over. He threw the money on the table and said, 'Buy them all a drink. They will soon own the place.' Then he walked out.

"Keith Moon was a funny fellow. I remember once in Tramp, he and Dave were sitting talking all night and The Who's Pete Townshend said to me that he had never seen Keith talk to anybody for so long before. Usually he wouldn't bother to concentrate on long conversations, but then I realised that the reason was probably that he and Dave were just the same. They were both sitting there talking about themselves all night without listening to each other!"

By around mid-1972, the band members were finally starting to make serious money from Slade, not that it affected their lives that much. A few new cars were bought and Jim married his long-time girlfriend, Louise, and bought a house in Wolverhampton, much to the dismay of Chas Chandler. "He always wanted us to settle in London," Don explains. "He never understood why we preferred to stay in Wolverhampton. But our friends and families lived there and we could keep out of the public eye a bit."

By then, Slade had achieved the status of key ambassadors of the glam-rock movement, which they had helped start. Glam or glitter rock, as it was sometimes called, stemmed from younger fans becoming bored to death by prog-rockers' 20-minute epic songs. It dominated rock during the period 1971-1974 and was characterised by a hard-rock, raunchy, high-energy sound. Lyrically, it centred on standard rock themes. In Slade's case, the main issues were drinking, pulling girls and having a good time, with only occasional hints at the darker side of life.

Visually, glam rock combined science fiction, nostalgia, camp, theatre and transvestism. Defined by both music and fashion, glam included British names like T. Rex, David Bowie, Roxy Music, Gary Glitter and the Chinn & Chapman-produced The Sweet, Mud and Detroit-born Suzi Quatro, as well as American acts like Lou Reed, Alice Cooper and The New York Dolls.

Don, Jim and especially Dave wore glittery clothes on stage, whereas Noddy stuck to tartan trousers and a top hat with mirrors glued on. He made it himself, inspired by a dress he had seen Scottish singer Lulu wear on TV. On stage, Nod's top hat had the same effect as a disco mirror ball, throwing light in all directions. No matter how colourful the clothes or high heeled the platform shoes, the four ugly buggers from the Black Country never looked feminine like The Sweet or Marc Bolan.

"It showed itself in the fans we got," Don laughs. "We never used to get the beautiful women. We got the people from the bar in *Star Wars!*"

Slade's main rivals in the UK singles chart were Marc Bolan's T.Rex, and eventually their record labels decided to co-ordinate the release dates of their singles so they wouldn't compete for the number one spot. "Marc Bolan was great," Don recalls. "When we had all our big hits I remember him saying, 'It's all over to you lot now.' He realised the success that we were having and how difficult it was to match."

The rivalry between the glam bands only included record sales, as there never was any competition on a personal level. "It's funny, because people always think we didn't like each other, but in the bands it was never anything like that," Don says.

"When we saw each other at *Top Of The Pops*, we used to spend more time in Slade's dressing room than in ours," Andy Scott agrees. "I used to go in the dressing room and when Dave wasn't there, Noddy would go, 'Now this is a good band, isn't it?' and then I'd go, 'Yeah, between the four of us. Sleet or Swayed.' I do like Dave a lot though!"

"We only ever saw the other bands when we did *Top Of The Pops*, anyway," Don goes on, "so when people were saying, 'Oh God, the competition between you!', they only talked about our state on TV shows. The competition was more between the fans. In those days you were only a fan of one band, T. Rex, Slade, The Sweet or someone like that; you couldn't have more than one favourite band. It was like that in the rest of Europe as well, but not with the bands being aware. Still, it kept the records rolling."

Slade had quite a different sound from the British 'Chinn & Chapman' stable of glam bands anyway, because they wrote their songs themselves, but they were perceived to be the same by the press. Slade felt the comparison and, to cater to the young glam audience, who were reading about their idols in teenage magazines such as *Melanie*, *Jackie* and *19*, a few years were shaved off their ages. Henceforth the birth dates of Don and Noddy would alter to between 1949 and 1950, whereas Jim and Dave were reportedly born in either 1951 or 1952.

One of Chas Chandler's strategies for keeping his boys in people's minds was to have a new single ready as soon as one dropped out of the charts. Slade's next was 'Mama Weer All Crazee Now', with 'Man Who Speaks Evil' on the B-side. The latter was written by Don and Jim, whereas the A-side was by Jim and Noddy. Noddy came up with the lyrics after seeing how fans had wrecked Wembley Arena at a Slade concert. Originally the song had been named 'My My Weer All Crazee Now', but Chas Chandler misheard the title and thought it was called 'Mama'. That mistake was kept.

"I think it was Jim who said, that 'My My' didn't ring true," says Don. "It didn't match the other titles that we had. 'Mama' sounded a lot better."

The single was released in August 1972 and became Slade's third number one. "Then I insisted on a pay rise," Swinn recalls, "and I went up to £30. I was travelling first class around the world and I didn't have a clue as to what I was doing!"

At that point Swinn was with Slade in America, where Chas Chandler had found them representation. "Chas had an American partner named Peter Kauff," Don explains. "Chas had met him in his Animals and Hendrix days and they were really good friends. Peter Kauff used to be a booker at the Premier Talent Agency, the biggest agency around, and Chas used Peter to get us in there. It was headed by legendary booker Frank Barsalona, who was huge in that business.

"We were not very worldly at that time though, so when we first went over to Los Angeles, we made a bit of a blunder. We had the crew with us and when we landed in L.A. a guy from Polydor met us. We went to the cars, but back then we didn't know of band limousines, because we had never experienced anything like that. There was a small minibus there for the crew, but we were used to driving in vehicles like that so we climbed into the minibus. Then the road crew had to get into the limousines! The guy from Polydor was scratching his head, 'I don't believe these guys! These guys are ultra-cool! They let the roadies go in the limousines!' But it was purely a mistake on our behalf!"

The first concert was in San Diego, where Slade opened for Humble Pie, but after that first gig Slade had to fly straight back to London, to the Sundown Theatre in Mile End Road. "That was an old booking that we had to keep," says Don. "Within 24 hours we flew to London with all the equipment, opened the Sundown, then flew back to Los Angeles with the equipment to continue the US tour. It was crazy. I didn't even alter my watch back to English time. It wasn't until three days after we got back to America that everybody collapsed because of the time change.

"On the tour, we were booked to support Humble Pie and sometimes we were billed third, with The J. Geils Band as second. Other times we were billed second, with Peter Frampton as third. And then we did some small headline shows on our own.

"When we were in Chicago, Jerry Shirley, the drummer of Humble Pie, was going to Ludwig to pick up some things as he was an endorsee. And I said, 'Can I come with you?' He took me with him and introduced me to Kay Holsten, who was Bill Ludwig I's secretary. Kay asked if I would like to see the factory and I said that I would love to. I was like a kid at Christmas.

"Ludwig was one of the very few family businesses still remaining in America. There was Bill Ludwig I and Bill Ludwig II. Bill Ludwig III was only a small child then. It wasn't that big a factory in Chicago, but I almost freaked out because Bill Ludwig I was checking snare drums himself. I couldn't believe that the man himself was there in the factory checking to see if the drums were OK. It was amazing.

"Then they made me this deal. I could buy my equipment from them for 40 percent off the factory price, which was like *nothing*. I told them what I would like, like the big drums I had imagined in my head, and they made them and shipped them to England for me. So I became an endorsee then, although it was not a full endorsement. But I got my big chrome kit.

"Unfortunately, the tour didn't go well. Humble Pie's audience was very different from the type of audience we were used to. We tried to take the English thing over to America and do what we did in England, and that didn't work at all. There were a few good nights around Chicago and other Midwest areas, but the West Coast was a total failure for us."

Slade went back to England for their second UK tour in late 1972, and in November released their next single, 'Gudbuy T'Jane', written by Noddy and Jim, with the B-side 'I Won't Let It 'Appen Agen'. It reached number two in the charts.

"'Gudbuy T'Jane' refers to an actual girl," says Don. "On our American tour we'd done a chat show in San Francisco and the host of the show was a really old hippie from the sixties. He had this little dolly bird sitting by his side and that was Jane. She had shoes that she used to call her '40s trip boots' as they looked like they were from the bouncing forties. That was where the lyrics came from.

"Jim wrote most of the song on the plane back to England from America and he nicked the drum intro for it from the signature tune of the German music show *Musikladen*. Jim wrote 'I Won't Let It 'Appen Agen' completely on his own, lyrics included. If you listen to the start of that, you can hear somebody shout, 'Yeah!' That's me shouting, because it felt so good when we started that I just couldn't help it. And it was kept. That's the kind of thing that I like. The human thing, if you like."

The second UK tour took off in November, with Thin Lizzy and Suzi Quatro as support. Suzi was very new to the business. "Before I had any recording success myself, I was added to the bill as a favour to Mickie Most by Slade's manager, Chas Chandler," she says. "I had 15 minutes at the beginning of the show, followed by Thin Lizzy and then Slade. What a learning curve!"

"I was with the Suzi Quatro band when she toured with Slade," says Quatro's guitarist, Len Tuckey. "We got to know the band better then, as well as the guys from Thin Lizzy. We did about six songs, opening for Slade, and it was a very good tour. All the bands were very friendly."

Things got more than friendly between Len and Suzi, as Don explains. "On that tour Suzi Quatro met her husband to be. She had a hired backing band where Len Tuckey played guitar and they married a couple of years later."

"By then our concerts had evolved into big parties," Don continues. "They involved loads of audience participation, bog-roll throwing, people invading the stage and the football anthem 'You'll Never Walk Alone' as a compulsive singalong at all our concerts. For some odd reason we had this football following, which was strange because none of us were into football. I remember once I was invited to a match and I sat there reading a drum magazine among all the football fans. Then I realised I'd better put the magazine down before they got angry with me.

"It was a great tour, but Dave broke his ankle at Liverpool Stadium. It was a boxing stadium and it was actually built as a ring. It was mayhem at the concert, because of the success we had in England. Dave just tripped, went over and broke his ankle. He had the cast covered in silver foil to match with his stage clothes. He was on walking sticks and he looked like an old pirate, so I wanted to buy him a parrot for his shoulder. I couldn't get a parrot, though, so I bought a seagull. When I bought it, people would say, 'What do you want that for?' It was difficult to explain!"

December saw the release of what would become Slade's first number one album, again recorded at Olympic Studios: *Slayed?*

"On the *Slayed?* album, 'How D'You Ride' was a big contender to be a single at one time," Don recalls. "Chas really loved that song; he wanted it to be a single, but it never was. Both 'Mama Weer All Crazee Now' and 'Gudbuy T'Jane' were on that album as well. 'Gudbuy T'Jane' was recorded in half an hour. We had a little time left in the studio and Chas said, 'Do you have anything else?' You know, just to use up the studio time. And Jim had this tune, it wasn't even really finished, and we got it together and recorded it. Jim had come up with the title 'Gudbuy T'Jane', but Nod wanted to change it to 'Hello T'Jane'. He was outvoted."

The album also featured what many think to be Slade's best cover version, Janis Joplin's 'Move Over'. Noddy's voice was every bit as strong and strange as Joplin's, like a male counterpart to hers, and Don and Jim were an extraordinarily efficient rhythm section.

"It was a great stage song," Don recalls. "It always went down extremely well. Nod did a great job on that – also on the quiet bit, when he used to ad-lib some things. As for Jim and myself, we used to work very hard on getting our parts together. It was a good song and it was an obvious choice to record that."

Slayed? was the first album not to feature any songs by Don, but he didn't mind. "The thing was that our last studio album, *Play It Loud*, didn't do anything. In a way, it wasn't particularly *us*. The right thing for us, the right formula, was Nod and Jim's songwriting. At that point, we had started doing overdubs. We did just bass and drums, some vocal or piano, and overdubbed the guitars afterwards. A lot of the time the drums would be put on again, depending on what kind of sound we wanted. If we couldn't really get it in the studio, we put the drums in the toilet to get the big echo sound. It was purely by accident. At the Olympic Studios, I went to the toilet one day and there was this echo. It was like the tiles all the way around made a live sound and I said, 'Oh, let's try the drums in the toilet.' So we did that, just like in the old days when I used to rehearse with Johnny and Mick in The Vendors. We put microphones down and that's how it all started with the massive sound of the drums.

"The first time I tried it, I was halfway through a take and then the toilets flushed! I thought, 'Oh, no!' and we had to turn all the toilets off.

But that was also when it started to take a lot longer to make albums, sometimes too long. Some things we could have done in probably one third of the time. It was the time of learning, of experimenting really. But we were the kind of band where it was much better when the four of us just went in and played. Playing like we were playing on stage really, because we weren't very good at being clever. We were never good at being clever! But I enjoyed working for Chas. It was so nice. He had us in the studio every day from 12 to six. After six o'clock he'd say, 'Go home. Go to the cinema, relax, get the studio out of your mind and get in the next day with new energy.' And it made sense. I liked his discipline.

"Chas was in the studio, basically, for discipline, and he really proved to be right. We once did some recordings throughout the night. We got back the next day to listen to them and we said, 'Oh, it's a pile of shit!' We had been half asleep and had let things go. There was no discipline there. So Chas proved himself wise on that. It was so true – only work from 12 to six."

The formula seemed to work. At least Slade won the Band Of The Year category in *Disc* magazine's 1972 readers' poll.

11

Glam Kings

In early January 1973, Slade played the London Palladium as part of the celebration of Britain's entry into the Common Market.

"In the sixties, there was a big TV show in England called *Sunday Night At The London Palladium*," Don recalls. "It was top of the bill, all the fancy names. It was *the* biggest variety show in England. The whole country was glued to it. It was always the same format: a comedian, a singer, the top of the bill, which in those days would be Frank Sinatra, or someone like that. When The Beatles were on, it was just a total revelation that a band was actually playing at the London Palladium.

"When we played there in 1973, I think we were the first rock band that ever did a regular concert there. But never again. They never had a rock concert there before, so they didn't know what to expect."

"They did two shows in the London Palladium, but they almost took the band off stage, because of the balcony bouncing," Swinn seconds. "We were all on stage watching the balcony bouncing from the stomping of feet."

"It was quite frightening, seeing how the balcony swayed," Don adds, "and all the seats downstairs were wrecked. We got totally banned from there after that."

During January, the band went on a two-week package tour of Australia, headlining over Status Quo, Lindisfarne and Caravan. "We were informed that we'd be making our first trip to Australia and New Zealand," says Bob Young of Status Quo. "We would be supporting Slade and I remember the excitement we all felt at the prospect of travelling to the other side of the world for the first time. So January 1973 came and all four bands, their managers and crews met at Heathrow Airport with great anticipation and excitement. We didn't care that we were flying for 36 hours in the uncomfortable economy seats at the back of the plane. The pleasures of first-class, five-star travel were still a couple of years away for all of us. Anyway, we could smoke and drink our way to New Zealand and enjoy several hangovers together on the flight."

"When the plane landed in Sydney, we saw all these TV cameras and we thought, 'Who's on the plane?'" Don laughs. "Who are they waiting for? And obviously they were waiting for us, because at that time *Slade Alive!* was triple gold in Australia. It was number one and had been so for a while, and *Slayed?* was number two. We had singles in the top three places on the Australian charts as well, but nobody had told us. Everybody knew our songs, and every second song on the radio was one of ours. Lindisfarne would say, 'Oh, shit, not you lot again!' We got played all the time."

"The Australians regarded them as the new Beatles," Swinn adds. "*Slade Alive!* was the first album to outsell *Sgt. Pepper* in Australia, and they played very big outdoor venues with loads and loads of kids in the audience."

"The huge audience was treated to some seriously good music," Bob Young states. "Also, back at the hotel later, the local girls were treated to some good old British rock'n'roll. The rest of the tour continued in much the same way of travel, gigs and parties. It's amazing just how much trouble you can get into in a short space of time, when you're in a band on tour… Aaah, such sweet memories."

"I remember lots of good times in Australia," Francis Rossi adds. "We went on a bus and we used to have this song, 'Hi-ho, hi-ho, we are the Status Quo, we're number one, we'll have some fun, hi-ho, hi-ho.' Then we went, 'Slade! Wonderful Slade!' Just to pass the time. We had so much good fun. It was always fabulous."

"I remember Alan Lancaster always going, 'Gudbuy T'Don' or 'Gudbuy T'Nod' to the tune of 'Gudbuy T'Jane' whenever they had to go somewhere," Don grins. "It was such a great tour. We played open-air sports stadiums with 30 to 40,000 at each show. Everything was so vast. I remember playing arenas in the middle of nowhere. There was nothing around for hundreds of miles and then, out there, there would be an arena. People travelled from all over the place to get there and see us; there was just nothing around, no towns or anything. It was incredible.

"When we were doing an open-air show in Adelaide, something unforeseen happened. It hadn't rained there for more than 30 years, I think, but what happened the day we played? The heavens opened! It wasn't just rain, it was torrential rain. We had to stop the show and move the equipment back, because the stage wasn't equipped for rain, but it didn't matter to the audience. Most of the people there had never seen rain before. We might as well not have been on stage. Everybody was just dancing around in the rain and jumping in the mud. We had to take big mats of straw and throw them out to the crowd because the ground became so soft. It was like a big party, so we were just background music to the rain dance they were doing. We always said that we caused it. Slade brought the rain to Australia. It was fantastic."

After the Australian tour, Slade released the first of their singles that went straight into the chart at number one in the UK. 'Cum On Feel The Noize' was a song about how Nod had literally felt the noise of the audience pounding in his chest at a gig on the tour.

"The single was released in February 1973," says Don. "Chas, his management assistant Johnny Steel and Polydor boss John Fruin came up with a plan together, to get the single straight to number one. Singles were released on a Friday. Chas would get *Top Of The Pops* for us on the Thursday, the day before the new release, so they had Friday, Saturday and Monday's sales, then the charts would come out on Tuesdays. Chas saw to it that we had the record played on the radio at least a week before release and, because of our success at the time, people would pre-order it. The shops would stack the records a week before, so they would be there on release day. It was a marketing scheme that actually worked.

"Usually, when a record was released on a Friday, it wouldn't be in the shops until a week later, but this way it was there the day of release. The kids could buy it from Friday and, because of that and the pre-orders, we could enter the charts at number one. That hadn't been done since The Beatles.

"By then it was a standing joke that we were the house band of *Top Of The Pops* because we had singles out every few months. At *Top Of The Pops* they used to call us the resident band. We were on first-name terms with all the crew and had a laugh with them. We had a good relationship with them, the producers and everybody else as well. We always made sure that we were there on time. We were never late or anything. I hate bad timekeeping anyway.

"Dave always changed in the toilet," continues Don. "He knew what would happen: we would ridicule him. He had all these costumes gone mad. One we called 'Foghorn Leghorn' because he looked like that cartoon character, like a big chicken, and there was the 'Metal Nun' and a lot more. Jim *hated* that. When he complained about Dave's costumes, which he found ridiculous, Dave used to say, 'You write 'em, I sell 'em.' Jim wrote almost all of our music, but Dave and his costumes made us stand apart visually from other bands."

Dave's fashion sense really made him the face of Slade. Nod was the lungs, Jim the brains, Don the backbone, or at least that was how the fans saw them. Dave's mad costumes had become a trademark of the band, making them easily recognisable. In a way, he echoed the lyrics of the B-side of 'Cum On Feel The Noize', 'I'm Mee, I'm Now And That's Orl'. Both sides were penned by the efficient Holder/Lea-team.

In the spring of 1973, Slade toured Europe, visiting Scandinavia, Holland, Belgium and Yugoslavia. They didn't earn much, as the fans used to trash the venues and the band had to cover the damages. Another episode that didn't go as planned that spring was Don's engagement.

"Pat and I split up in 1973," Don says. "I've always wanted a small farm to live on and Pat and I found one, just off the motorway, north of Wolverhampton. It was perfect. I remember we went to look at it, but then came this guy in his sheepskin jacket and we thought, 'Uh-oh.'

We could see from the looks of the old couple who lived there that he had offered them more money. There was quite a bit of land with the farm and the rich guy wanted to buy it and build a bigger house. Now there is a beautiful, massive mansion there. We were so disappointed, as we were all set to buy it.

"After that, we decided to buy a flat in Wolverhampton. I remember that once, after we had rehearsed, I dropped Jim home in the van and on the way to his house I saw these flats for sale, so I bought one. But after the fiasco of buying the farm, Pat and I had started to drift apart. In the end, we decided to finish. When I split with Pat, I gave her the blue Mini."

"I was working in a butcher's shop on Oxford Street at the time," Mick Marson recalls. "Don's mum used to come and buy meat off me. And one day, Don pulled up in his blue Mini. All around were all the kids. You could hear them. And then he just came into the shop. I think it was hilarious. Nobody expected to see Don Powell in a butcher's shop on Oxford Street here in Bilston. The next time I saw him, he was driving a Bentley. He had obviously split with Pat."

"It was a shame when Don and Pat split up," Don's sister Carol adds, "but Don said that they'd waited too long to get married. They'd become like brother and sister. Pat was such a nice person. She fitted right into the family and we still see her. But it wouldn't have worked in the long run. All Pat wanted was to settle down with a husband and children. She couldn't have had that life with Don's job and she's married to somebody else now.

"After Pat, Don dated a lot of women. Each year for Christmas he brought a new one along. But there was no harm in it. He was single, he could do as he pleased, but it was a bit difficult each year to have a new girl there. Don is quite a ladies' man. He takes after Dad. He was good looking, he could charm the women."

The first girl Don dated after Pat was a 20-year-old secretary named Angela Morris. "Angela was a friend of Dave's sister," Don recalls, "and Dave dated Angela for a short while. It was a joke within the band that I would get his cast-offs."

In April 1973, Slade were about to embark on their second US tour. By then, Chas Chandler had dispensed with the services of John Halsall

114

as the group's publicist and hired the most respected rock PR agent in London, Les Perrin, who represented three ex-Beatles and The Rolling Stones. He came up with the idea of Slade going to America as headliners.

"This time we were on our own basically," says Don. "We did the headlining and, at most of the places, there weren't that many people. In hindsight, it was the wrong thing to do. Chas said, 'You headline, then you can take all your own equipment, your own PA, the amplifiers and things like that.' But it was the wrong thing. It was too early. Chas had been warned about it, but I could understand his motives. He said, 'If you could be seen under the right circumstances with your own equipment, you'll come across,' but it was too early to top the bill."

"It was nonsense," Swinn agrees. "It cost a lot of money to take our own equipment and it didn't amount to anything. The crew was Charlie, J.J., Robbie and myself, only the four of us. I still hadn't got used to how things were in America. Once, I sent the crew to the right town but unfortunately the town was in the wrong state! I hadn't quite grasped the idea that so many towns were called the same. I never told the band!"

To be fair, Slade always did well on the East Coast and in the Midwest, but on the West Coast only San Francisco was worth the trip. "It had to do with the way that the concerts had been booked," Don explains. "Frank Barsalona from the Premier Talent Agency was so powerful in the States. He had everyone on his books. Bob Meyrowitz, who, along with Peter Kauff, was our representative in the US, later told me about the stand-up rows they used to have with Chas about the way he wanted us promoted in the States. He wanted us topping the bill straight away, whereas they wanted us for the first few tours to go in through the back door, supporting big names and making a name for ourselves that way. But no – Chas, with his powerful demeanour, insisted we topped the bill more or less straight away. So when our tour was booked, it was like, 'You can have The Eagles if you have Slade,' or, 'If you want Peter Frampton, you have to book Slade.' If the promoters wanted a particular act, they were forced to take us as well. It was kind of a blackmail thing, a totally wrong thing to do, but we didn't find out until later that some of the promoters didn't want us. I think it left a lot of bad taste with the promoters for us.

"Because of Chas insisting that we top the bill, a lot of big names came to support us on that tour. Iggy Pop was one of them. Frankly, I never understood about the relationship between David Bowie and him, as Iggy Pop had no aesthetics at all. He was always drugged out of his mind, but the same thing could be said about Lou Reed in those days. He also supported us on that tour and he was very off the wall.

"My favourite moment of the tour was at the Philadelphia Spectrum. It held 20,000 people and we headlined over The Eagles, Lou Reed, Stevie Wonder and Steely Dan. The Eagles were second and we were top of the bill. I had never heard of The Eagles then and I watched from the side of the stage. Who are these guys? They're fantastic! They've been my favourite band since then. But imagine *The Eagles* supporting Slade!"

On Slade's first American tours they had been signed to Polydor, but now Chas Chandler shopped around for another label in the US. "Chas wasn't happy with Polydor, so we signed with Warner Brothers," says Don. "We went to San Francisco to play Winterland, and afterwards we attended a party held by a guy whom Chas knew from his Animals days. This guy was still an old hippie. He lived in San Francisco in a small chapel, which had a pulpit and all. We stayed there for the weekend and he had a party one night in this chapel.

"I went to have a look around and there was this rope fixed to the roof that came to the balcony. I had a girl with me and I said, 'Are you up for a laugh? Get on my shoulders!' We could look down at the party – there were a few hundred people there and we would just swing down between them. But what Chas told me later was that because we had just signed to Warner Brothers, there were two or three of their executives there. They were talking to Chas and they were asking him what we were like in the band. When it came to me he said, 'Don never really says anything, he's pretty quiet,' just as I was swinging by like Tarzan with this girl on my shoulders! And the executives said, 'Who's that?' 'That's Don.' '*He's the quiet one?*'"

Nobody knows what Chas Chandler told the executives about the rest of the band, but Slade's road crew had started calling Jim "Midlands

Misery", because he always seemed to be miserable. A shy person, with a fragile disposition, he hated the attention that came with the fame.

"Actually, both Jim and Dave were always miserable," Swinn recalls. "They never really enjoyed themselves on the road. It was a duty to them, something they had to do. I think they disliked not being in control of things when we were touring. That made them insecure."

Insecure or not, Jim didn't doubt his abilities as a musician and songwriter for one minute, and he shared that self-confidence with Noddy. He, too, knew of his own worth as a singer and songwriter, although his character was different – cheeky and outgoing. Add flashy madman Dave, who based his self-esteem on his skills as a guitarist, into the mix and this sometimes led to a battle of egos, but then Don would step in as a mediator. "I used to go in light-heartedly," Don says, "make jokes and things like that to ease up the tension."

In this way, Don became the glue that held the band together, the true backbone of Slade. He, for one, had learnt the lesson that Chas Chandler taught the band when success beckoned. "It is almost impossible to make new friends when you've become a household name, because you never know if they are genuine or not," says Don. "Chas said that as well, 'The only friends you have got are the band.' And it is true. Everybody else always wants something from you. You walk into a place and people act like they have known you all your life, but you've never met them before. They just want to be your best mate, because of the success. They just want to make money out of you. Frightening, but true."

Don didn't mind being famous, though. He enjoyed the success. "All those years we'd wanted to become a success, and then ultimately having it was amazing," he states. "As Chas once said, 'When you get your first number one, you want another one and another one and another one. You won't settle for anything but number ones.' With 'Coz I Luv You' we were just happy to get a hit, but he was right. When you get a taste of success, you want to keep on riding it. You know at some point it is going to stop, but when it is there, you live it all. You enjoy every minute of it, but it comes with a price.

"Success will take away your independence. You can't just go out to a café or visit your family or anything. I remember once, I was visiting my sister Carol, and I had parked outside her house. That was a bad mistake. The kids were coming out of school and they were totally blocking the street. I was completely surrounded, and had to fight my way to the car. It's things like that. You do lose the normal things. If you want to go to a pub or go see a band, that is taken away from you. It really is. You are no longer a normal person. The person you might want to be is taken away from you.

"I remember a time when I was sitting in a pub with a drink and this guy came up to me and said, 'What are you doing here?' 'I'm having a drink.' 'Well, this place isn't good enough for you, is it?' They expect to see you at the Hilton or something like that. All the normal things are taken away from you.

"Instead of a normal life, you are presented with another kind of world, with hangers–on, tough businessmen and a lot of drinking and drugs, although we were never particularly a drug band. Personally, it frightened me. I always thought it was the unknown. So although we had smokes and things like that, we were more a drinking band, because with drinking, at least you know what happens. You wake up in the morning and have a bad headache, but at least you know why."

On their return from the second American visit, Slade embarked on another UK tour. By then they had added a new member to the road crew, Midlands-based Haden Donovan. "My brother David knew Don before I did," Donovan remembers. "He's a musician, so he knew all the people in the Wolverhampton bands. It was through him I met Don and I saw him a few times while working as a roadie for my brother's band."

"I met Don in 1965 or 1966," says Dave Donovan. "I didn't know him at all, but he played with The 'N Betweens and we were supporting them. I was with a band then called Samantha's Moods and we played at Willenhall School, which was close to where Don lived, but I didn't bump into him again until later. I used to go and watch Slade in the early days, before they were famous, in local halls like the George Hotel in Walsall. I suppose you could say we were on nodding terms. I got to know him very well around 1970, just as they were breaking. I used to see him occasionally and we would go out for a drink in Wolverhampton."

"When Slade needed somebody in 1973, they got me and Robbie Wilson," Haden says. "Slade's crew was incredibly loyal. It was the best time of my life and if we could do it again tomorrow, I would."

"When Haden used to drive us, he talked," Don recalls. "He got this drone in his voice. It's almost like a monotone; he just talks and talks non-stop. Your eyes glaze over and you go somewhere else. The car we had at the time was a Rolls-Royce limousine with a glass partition between the passengers and the driver. When Haden started talking, we would press the button and the window would go up, so we couldn't hear him. We'd let him talk for a few minutes, then the window would go up. We always used to do that!"

"On the tour, they came home to Wolverhampton to do a few gigs," Vicky Pearson recalls, "and they were just gods. I think it was lovely that they returned, now that we had seen them conquer the world."

"But my mum didn't understand the success situation," adds Don. "To her, I was still a little boy. She came to the concert at the Civic Hall and she was waving to me on stage, just like she used to do when I did the morning parades with the Scouts. She was not very happy with me, because I didn't wave back, but I couldn't see her! I also remember that, in the Civic Hall, all the kids were trying to get on stage and Haden Donovan was down the front, trying to get them off. Haden was actually a schoolteacher, and there were quite a lot of his pupils there. Gradually they realised who he was. 'Oh, hello sir! What are you doing here?' It was hilarious!"

During the tour, Slade's next number one was released. 'Skweeze Me Pleeze Me' made Slade the first act to go straight to number one with successive releases. Jim got the idea for the song at The Trumpet in Bilston while listening to Reg Keirle playing the piano and the crowd joining in on the chorus. "Sunday lunchtime at The Trumpet, the audience was men only," Don explains. "Reg Keirle used to play piano and sing really rude songs."

The B-side of the single was the Hot Club de France-inspired 'Kill 'Em At The Hot Club Tonite', with Jim mirroring Stéphane Grappelli's violin. Both songs were penned by Holder/Lea.

This particular UK tour was Slade's biggest to date, and playing Earls Court on the final night, July 1, was to crown their achievement. Slade were the very first rock act to book show dates at Earls Court, although David Bowie managed to play there a month before them. Bowie's concert hadn't been a success, but Slade's was. Eighteen thousand turned up to see them and DJ Emperor Rosko introduced the band.

"I remember driving up to Earls Court in the black Rolls-Royce limo," Don says. "There were all the kids going to the concert, with top hats with mirrors on. It was an amazing sight. Someone told me that they were even wearing glittery costumes on the Tube.

"At Earls Court we had a special stage made. When David Bowie had played there, one of the criticisms of his show was that the stage was too small for the size of the arena, so Chas had this big stage constructed. We came through a door at the top of the back and the audience was below us.

"The Sensational Alex Harvey Band had been our support throughout that tour, and every night Alex Harvey had been booed off. Even in Glasgow, his hometown. At Earls Court, I was standing with him at the side of the stage before he went on and he turned to me and said, 'You know, Don, if we get booed tonight, it'll be the loudest boo you have ever heard.' And sure enough, they got booed, but they always stood their ground.

"Playing Earls Court was the highlight of our career really, but I remember not being that happy with it, because it was a *big* concert. I always think that with big concerts, there isn't any real communication with the audience. That's why I don't really like it. It is so hard to get good communication, although Noddy was a master at that.

"But, of course, the concert was an incredible adrenaline kick, especially when we were waiting behind the door to go on stage and we could hear the crowd going mad. It was difficult to take it seriously. It was like it wasn't us. It was totally unreal."

The concert could have been Don's last. Three days later, he was fighting for his life in hospital.

12

Crash

In the early hours of July 4, 1973, Don picked up his girlfriend, Angela, from the Dix nightclub in Wolverhampton, where she worked. The two of them drove off in Don's white Bentley. A few minutes later the car left Compton Road, flew through a hedge and smashed up against a tree and a brick wall adjoining a local school. Both Don and Angela were thrown out of the car in a way that made it impossible to tell who had been driving. Angela was killed on the spot.

By chance, two nurses passed the accident scene minutes after the crash and helped to save Don's life. They called the hospital and requested an ambulance.

"There was an ambulance nearby, dealing with a pregnancy," says Don, "and that's why, when the nurses called the hospital, they knew the ambulance was in the vicinity. In the ambulance, they dropped the baby and came for me. If it hadn't been for that, I would have been dead. The nurses were holding my head together, as it was split open. It was a miracle that I survived.

"I don't remember the crash, but I get flashbacks of being wheeled into hospital on an upright stretcher. My head fell to one side and I didn't feel like I was lying down, so it must have been an upright stretcher. But after that, I don't remember anything."

Don was brought to the Wolverhampton Royal Hospital, where surgeons worked on him for hours. They had to drill into his skull to ease the internal pressure, and many broken bones and deep cuts had to be attended to as well. Afterwards, Don was put on a bed of ice to keep his soaring temperature down. He was more or less in a coma for five days. When he did wake up, he still wasn't quite conscious at first.

"One time, I panicked," Don recalls. "I vaguely remember it. I woke up shivering, not realising that I was on a bed of ice. There were tubes everywhere and I just panicked. I didn't know where I was, or why I was there. I pulled out the tubes and got out of bed, and that was when the nurses came rushing in. They put me back to bed and I asked, 'What am I doing here?' and they said I had been in an accident. But it didn't sink in. It didn't mean anything to me. I kept drifting in and out of consciousness.

"At one point, a doctor came when I was in bed and he also said, 'You've been in a car accident.' And it was strange, because I must have still been aware of certain things. I *did* remember that I was in a band, and my recollection was that we had been coming back from a gig and I thought the rest of the guys were in the same position as me, somewhere in the hospital. I thought we'd all been in a crash, so the rest of the guys must be there somewhere. The next thing when I came round again, they were all sitting at the bottom of the bed in hospital gowns and that freaked me."

"Don's accident was horrible," says his sister Carol. "Just horrible. Mum broke down completely. It was so strange. I'd dreamt about it the night before. I'd dreamt of Don, a very unpleasant dream, and in the dream I kept reassuring Don that it would be all right. It would be OK. And then I woke up to learn that Don had had his accident.

"And that poor girl died. We didn't know her, as she and Don had just started dating, but it was awful. My dad went to the hospital and they asked him if Don did drugs. There was nothing of that sort back then, but they had to ask, as they were afraid that he was dying. It was awful. Dad cried.

"News got out very fast. Everybody in the street was talking about it and the fans were literally invading our home. They were all over. I'd married Gerald by then, but they even invaded our house. They were crawling the drains and they ruined my garden. But they sent Don so many nice get-well cards. He had hundreds and hundreds of them."

"The support from the fans was incredible," Don agrees, "and the support from the rest of the guys as well, Nod, Jim and Dave."

After a while, Don didn't need the tubes and pipes any more, but still, the details of the accident were kept from him.

"I was there for quite a while before anyone told me what had happened," Don recalls. "When I didn't have the tubes any more, I got to the toilet. Afterwards, I washed my hands and came to look in the mirror. I had no hair, my face was all smashed, with black eyes and teeth missing and that big crack in the head, held together by clamps. I was so shocked that I fell into the back wall. It was terrible. I thought, somebody has got to tell me what's going on. I kept asking, 'Please, tell me what has happened!'

"Dad told me about the accident. Then he said, 'Your girlfriend has died.' He didn't say Angela, so I thought it was Pat, because I didn't remember Angela, as I'd lost my short-term memory. I only remembered Pat."

"When Don had his accident, Pat was away," adds Carol. "She didn't learn about it until she landed at the airport. It was on all the front pages; she saw it at the airport and broke down completely. She would have wanted to be there for Don."

"Pat actually came to see me in hospital," Don explains, "but she was told, 'You can't see him yet, because he thinks it is you who has died.' The press wrote that my fiancée was dead, but I had never been engaged to Angela, as I had only known her for a few months. Pat was the one I had been engaged to, and only gradually did I understand that it was Angela who had died. That freaked me, because I didn't remember her. It got out in the press and, of course, her parents saw it and that was not very good. When I got out of hospital, I went to see them obviously and explained about my amnesia, that it was the reason why I didn't remember their daughter."

Don's friends and colleagues were all shocked by the accident and the death of his girlfriend. "The phone rang in the early hours of the morning," Jim recalls, "and I was mortified by the dreadful news for days, until I saw him in the flesh, just to make sure he was still there. A lifelong tragedy for Don, but a mortal tragedy for his lovely girlfriend, Angela."

"I knew Don's fiancée, Pat," Carole Williams says, "but I was not aware that they had split, so the morning I heard about the accident, I really thought it was Pat in the car with him. I had been friends with her younger sister; I used to take her to football matches and had got to know the family. It was only when I rang them that I knew Don was with someone new. I really followed the news to see how he was, as it did not seem right to intrude when we had not seen each other for a while."

"It was horrible when Don had his accident," says Vicky Pearson. "It was weird, because the chaps had become so big, and you do lose touch. They were on a different planet, but you know when you have a friend and Don was my friend. The grief was enormous. I used to work with Angela, and to learn that she had died was appalling."

"The first time I heard about the accident, I was at my parents' house," Dave says. "The call came early in the morning. My sister Carol answered the phone. It was a neighbour who said Don had been in an accident, but we didn't know till later that it was serious. Angela had been killed and Don was in hospital in a serious condition and was not expected to survive. Well, I was in shock, and so was Carol, as Angela was her best friend. It's hard to explain how I felt. All I can say is it was a dreadful time. Things had been going so well, we were number one in the charts, we had just done a big show at Earls Court in London, and then suddenly this happens! I was absolutely gutted. All my thoughts went to Don, just hoping he would pull through."

"Don's accident was frightening," echoes Swinn. "The first time I saw him in hospital he was unconscious, tubes everywhere. His head had been shaved. And for a week we didn't know if it was touch and go."

"When I learnt about Don's accident, I was in tears at the thought that he was not going to survive," Andy Scott admits. "The car was wrecked and he was in hospital. I think it was a huge shock, which obviously nobody would have wanted or wished."

"I remember when Don had his accident, we heard about it through the musical grapevine," Len Tuckey adds, "and, of course, everyone was devastated. We thought it was all over for him. We really did think that this was the end. We were all very shook up that Don was so badly injured."

"I learnt about it in a very strange way," says Haden Donovan. "I was back working with my brother's band, because there was a gap between Slade gigs. We were playing a week in a club in Somerset and, when we got to the gig one night, we were told, 'People have tried to get in touch with you lot all day. Can you phone this number immediately?' That was how we found out, because we hadn't seen the newspapers and we hadn't heard the news on the radio."

"One of my very good friends was J.J., John Jones. He possibly called me," Dave Donovan expounds. "When Don had his accident, I was in Weston-Super-Mare doing a week with Screaming Lord Sutch and they called me to come up and have a rehearsal with them because they had two Isle of Wight shows. The first time we met after the accident, Don looked quite poorly. It was desperate times. Don did die a couple of times, didn't he?"

"We went to see him in hospital and that was frightening," Haden Donovan recalls. "He didn't remember the girl who was in the car. Instead he kept saying, 'They didn't tell me about Pat. How is Pat?'"

"I went to Don's mum and dad's," John Howells remembers. "Nod came that day to say hello and we talked. You put things aside in the past when a thing like that happens. We just wanted to get Don back and fit again. In the early years, Don never even smoked or anything; all he did was drink coke and had his Wrigley's Spearmint gum. He was a fit lad, a county runner. But he'd had some success, he got a bit of money in his pocket and he had acquired a taste for the good life, and that's what happened to him. Normally he would never have bought a car like that. He would probably have got a Mini or something, but when you get a bit of money you get a bit brash, like Dave, a bit of an extrovert, show what you got. If Don had never bought that car, the accident may have never happened, but who knows. It is fate, ain't it?"

Don's accident affected many people, making them realise how quickly everything could come to an end. That thought made Dave marry his girlfriend, Janice, while Don was in hospital. They were wed in Mexico in July 1973.

"The four of us, Dave and Jan and Angela and myself, had planned to go to Los Angeles for a holiday after the English tour," Don explains. "Dave called my father after the accident and asked if it was all right that he and Jan still went. My dad said, 'Of course it is. Don wouldn't want you not to go because he is in hospital. You go.' And that was when they got married in Mexico."

"Everybody was so considerate," Don's sister Carol states. "They were great with us at the time of the accident. We only had one bad experience. When Don was still at hospital, somebody called us and said she was a nurse. She said we should hurry to hospital because Don was dying. And we got all hysterical. There were only us women in the house, Mum and me and my sister, Marilyn, and when we got to the hospital, we found out that it was just a very nasty prank. That was really unpleasant, somebody doing that."

"I remember another unpleasant incident," says Don, "although that came out of thoughtlessness rather than ill will. I got a lot of mail from fans and friends and I read that in bed in hospital. Then came a letter from Chicago, from Ludwig drums. I was really ill, almost lying on my deathbed, and they had sent me the details of a funeral service! It turned out that Bill Ludwig I had died and it was so typically American that they sent out the whole funeral service, with the prayers and the hymns and everything. Only in America! And I thought, *What the fuck*! I'm on my deathbed and they send me a funeral service!"

Six weeks after the crash, Don was released from hospital. He went with Jim and his wife, Louise, to Bournemouth for a week, staying at the home of their tour promoter, Mel Bush, before going home, where his family took care of him.

"The first long time was awful," Carol says. "Don's memory was all gone, he couldn't remember a thing and kept repeating everything. He could tell you the same thing 12 times over, without knowing that he had just told it. It was frustrating. But Don then gave the whole family a trip to Malta, and it was the first time I had travelled outside England. It was so generous of him. He said it was his way of thanking us for taking care of him."

"I felt so inadequate," Don admits. "I didn't know what else to do. Before, I used to have such an impeccable memory, but now! It was horrible. At least I found out that I used to fancy one of the nurses at hospital. I didn't remember anything about it, but apparently when she came over to tuck me in, I used to grab her and hold her by the bed. So when I went to visit the staff at the intensive care, after I had been released, she just looked at me with squinting eyes and said, 'You! What are you doing here? Get out!'

"Still, it was awful, as my memory was really, really bad. I didn't remember a thing about the accident but, as the specialist said to me, 'What do you want to remember that for? You'll never remember it. Don't even try. The brain switches off just before an accident and it switches on again after.' And he was right. The accident happened near where I used to live, in Wolverhampton, and when I got out of hospital, I had to drive past the wall and the school every day, but it didn't mean anything to me."

The question of who had been driving Don's Bentley on that fateful night remained.

"When Don finally came out of hospital, he remembered nothing," Andy Scott says. "He didn't even know who was driving, for all the speculation in the world."

"Perhaps one of the most spiteful early rumours about Don in Fleet Street concerned his revelation on leaving hospital that he had lost his memory following the horrendous car crash," Keith Altham adds. "'Very convenient,' one jaundiced Fleet Street scribe described his condition to me. 'You just don't know how severe his injuries were,' I told him. 'He nearly died and you do not know the man,' I added angrily. 'He could not be more genuine.'"

"It said in the media that it must have been Don driving that night, because Angela never drove the car," Haden Donovan says. "That was a lie. When Don was in America the first time with Slade, I had to take my brother David in my uncle's car to Don's parents to pick up the Bentley and drive it over to Angela's house. She used to drive it to work. Also, there was talk about a person who saw the car go past on the night of the accident, and he said it was a pretty young girl driving.

I think the autopsy said that she had bad bruises from the steering wheel as well."

Don attended the coroner's court, although he was not called to give evidence as he couldn't remember the accident anyway. Dix's owner, Richard Brownson, said that he had taken the car keys from Angela and given them to Don before the couple left the club. On the other hand, a witness had seen Angela climb into the driver's seat outside Dix but could not swear who was at the wheel when the car drove off. Coroner Walter Forsyth said there was doubtful evidence as to who drove the car and the jury brought in an open verdict.

The nurses who had helped Don at the accident scene hadn't been called to give evidence, as no one knew who they were, but eventually Don was to find out. "Many years later, I got in touch with one of the nurses who had helped save me," he says. "There was this guy who was doing an article about the crash and he asked, 'Would you let me try to find out who the nurses were?' He then got the number of one of them, gave it to me and said, 'She would love to hear from you,' and I really wanted to say thanks to her.

"She explained that it was she and her best friend of the time who had saved me. She said, 'When we found you, you were very poorly and the reason that you are very lucky is that, not only did we happen to go by, but the ambulance was just around the corner'.

"I spoke to her about the article and the photographs, but she said that she didn't really want to do it. And I was glad, actually, because I didn't want to either. If Angela's parents were to see it, they'd have to relive it again, so I'm glad it didn't happen."

The day after Don's accident, Chas Chandler had come up from London to meet with the band. "Chas came to stay with me in Wolverhampton for a few days," says Swinn. "He was shocked by the news, but he also saw the promotion advantages in it. Everything was a story to him. And then, of course, he was concerned with the gigs that had already been booked."

"He met with the rest of the band at Jim's house," Don says. "Jim's younger brother Frank was there, fixing some plumbing, and when

Chas said they might have to cancel some gigs on the Isle of Man, Frank said that he could play. I'd given Frank my first Ludwig kit to develop his drumming."

"I'd come up from the Screaming Lord Sutch tour to rehearse with the band for the two Isle of Wight shows, but by the time I got up to the Midlands, Jimmy Lea had got his brother to do it," Dave Donovan says. His brother Haden expands: "David didn't mind, but it was a bit ironic, as my brother was a much better drummer! David would have loved to do it though, because it was for Don. For his mate."

"The shows were in late July and I got a kick in the backside from that," Don recalls. "I thought, 'What is going on here? Somebody else is playing!' And in a way it helped, because people didn't realise that I'd got so insecure. I felt I was letting everyone down. I felt absolutely useless. If I had been in a normal profession, it wouldn't have been so bad, but doing what I was doing, I felt absolutely worthless."

"It was awful," Mick Marson agrees. "The band had Jim's brother on the drums for a while and Don came to see me. He said, 'I think they want me out of the band. They have Frank on the drums now.' I said, 'The best thing you can do is go talk to them.' It must have worked out all right, because I didn't see him again until 1991!"

A couple of months after the accident, Don was back with Slade. His speedy recovery surprised everybody and only his fit condition made it possible. Many years of athletics, boxing and the exertion of being a drummer helped him recover physically, but mentally it was not that easy. "Don got back to working rather quickly," his sister Carol comments, "but only because the rest of the band helped him. He couldn't remember a thing."

"After the accident, we as a band and a close-knit unit rallied round him to help," Dave seconds. "It must have been difficult for Don, not being able to remember the day before, but we supported him as a group, helping him to remember things. But Don had such a good sense of humour, which seemed to override a lot of things. I think the camaraderie, as we called it in the band, and Don's sense of humour helped."

"I dealt with it by making fun of myself," Don agrees, "and very quickly, I got back in the studio. I remember that Chas would cue me through the control-room window, because I couldn't remember the simplest things. I was doing the beats and he was counting and then, sometimes, I'd drum something else that I knew. It was about being reminded of things. Just cue me in."

Slade were recording their next single, 'My Friend Stan', with 'My Town' as the B-side. By then, all songs were penned by Nod and Jim, and the single was released in September 1973, reaching number two in the charts. "When we first went back in the recording studio to do 'My Friend Stan', our engineer, Alan O'Duffy, understood my problem," Don recalls. "He was so nice. He had worked with us on most of the early hits. It was him who suggested I keep diaries. He said, 'You write down what you have done and what you have to do. That will help exercise your brain.' I always used to have a soft spot for Alan because of that."

"I then started buying him a diary each year," says Carol, "a big book where he could write down everything."

After Don's discharge from hospital, he went to the Brands Hatch motor-racing circuit in Kent. "There were a lot of people there, like Cozy Powell and Keith Emerson, and they took part in a charity race," Len Tuckey explains. "Don was there and, although he wasn't fully recovered, he was smiling and everything, so he seemed to be OK, which was a relief for everybody. We knew he was going to be fine. He just had to heal, basically. Everyone was very, very happy with that."

"In reality, I felt like shit," Don reveals. "I wasn't prepared, neither physically nor mentally. I was on walking sticks, I had no hair, my skull was held together with clamps and I really didn't want to be there. A lot of bands attended that gathering and I remember just sitting down in a corner. Everybody was drinking and partying and I felt terrible. Then Olivia Newton-John came over and sat with me and she was fantastic. She was holding my hand and talking to me. I'll always remember that, because she was great."

With Don back on the drums, Slade undertook a postponed US tour in September 1973. Don was still walking with the aid of sticks and he had to be lifted onto his drum kit. His short-term memory was blank. "I remember this quote in a newspaper where a reporter said, 'Why is Don Powell back on the drums so early? You'd have thought that he would have been resting in the Caribbean Islands somewhere,'" Don says. "The reporter wrote, 'What is the normally faultless Chas Chandler doing, making Don Powell go on stage?' But it was good for me. It was the best thing I did. It was the specialist who said it: 'Get him back to work as soon as possible – otherwise he never will.'

"And it was so true. It *was* the best thing and I would say that to anyone under the same circumstances. No matter how inadequate you feel, do it. And I *did* feel inadequate. Things were never the same after the accident. My spontaneity disappeared for many years, as did my confidence. I felt it especially when we were touring and I woke up in different hotel rooms. I'd wake up in the morning and didn't know where I was. So I always had to have adjoining rooms with Swinn or somebody, so they could come in and tell me where I was and what I was doing. The only thing I remembered was who I was and that I played drums. But the everyday things were gone. If I had an appointment somewhere, I had to leave half an hour early in case I forgot on the way where I was going. Then I would get lost. This earned me the nickname Mr. Memory Man."

"Don's amnesia was very frustrating for all of us," Swinn agrees. "It was driving me crazy. He would call me 10 times a day with the same question. I was going out of my mind."

"I was repeating myself all the time and when I realised, I started to withdraw into myself," Don recalls. "If I had anything to say, I thought, 'I've probably already said that, so I'm not gonna say it again.' It was, indeed, very frustrating. 'Why can't I remember this and why can't I remember that?' I knew I played drums, but it was actually remembering songs that I couldn't manage."

"On his return to the stage, Noddy and the boys had to coax him through the set on stage," says Keith Altham, "as the anxious enquiry of 'How does it go?' would be perplexedly asked of them, as they introduced another hit he had played only a few months before."

"Imagine what it is like to go on stage and we were going to do, say 'Cum On Feel The Noize', and I went, 'How does that go?'" Don sighs.

"People don't realise the extremity of what was happening. I couldn't remember anything and, to me, it seemed even worse, because I used to have this impeccable memory. I used to remember just everything. Now I felt useless and I said, 'I'm a total waste of time for you.' I was letting everyone down with my amnesia, forgetting everything, songs, etc, taking a long time in getting everything to sink in, so I decided to leave the band. I got our road crew to bring all my drums to where I lived in Wolverhampton, so I could store them. I then told the crew what I was going to do and J.J., one of our roadies, started to cry. I then called Nod, H and Jim in turn to say the same. H said he would probably do the same then, Nod couldn't believe it, but Jim wasn't too bothered. To prove it, Frank Lea came to my flat shortly after to say, 'Looks like I've got the job then?' I tried to get hold of Chas Chandler at home to tell him, but I couldn't get through for some reason. Then I went and got thoroughly pissed. I'm not sure how long it was before Chas got the train to Wolverhampton for a meeting at Jim's house with us all. I knew how much I was letting them down *and* I did give them the chance to get someone else, but after the meeting I was persuaded to stay in the band. A part of me still wonders what I'd be doing now if I'd left in 1973. I don't think people realised how difficult it was."

"I remember one time when they had just finished a show and were coming back for the encore," says Swinn. "It was their new single, but on the way back to the stage to do the encore, Don said, 'I can't remember it.' And they had to run through the number before they went back on stage."

"When we were on stage, Noddy would be announcing the next song or just talking and Jim would come up to me and say this and this comes next and you have to do so and so," Don says. "It was a big help. We could do that, because we knew each other so well. That was essential, that the band were there and they knew. I don't know how I would have dealt with it if they hadn't been there. I hate to think what that would have been like. When I met people, they always said that they had no idea I had amnesia, because it was covered up very well."

"It is significant that had Don not recovered sufficiently from his horrendous car crash in the seventies, singer Noddy Holder was on record as saying that Slade could have not carried on without him," Keith Altham adds. "'I always swore that if Don had not made it through his terrible injuries, I would break up the band,' said Noddy, some years later. 'He was our anchor.' A testimony to just how important Don was to the band's overall sound. By virtue of the fact that most drummers sit at the back on stage, there is a likelihood of being overlooked, but a drummer can make or break a band. Just ask Jagger and Richards about the importance of Charlie Watts sometime, or Roger Daltrey if he believes The Who were ever the same band after Keith Moon's demise, or Paul McCartney if The Beatles would have secured their recording contract without the expertise of Ringo. Don Powell was the indispensable engine room for Slade and one of the essential ingredients of their success. You only have to listen to a Slade hit single to realise that Don is an integral part of that 'stomping' sound, which became the signature for Slade's musical identity. He has a unique style, which is the secret for success with all great drummers."

"But after the accident, Don changed," Haden Donovan ponders. "There was no doubt about it."

"Every time I've seen Don subsequently, he is not quite the same as he was before the accident," Francis Rossi adds. "There's a certain vacancy. You realise that there is not always a link to him in conversations, because of the accident. Suddenly he's not there, *whoopsadaisy*, and then he is all right again. That feels awkward, and I could never be with Don as I was before the accident, because he isn't like he was before and that's a bit of a fuck. He's not the same any more, but you couldn't say it to him. That's quite frightening."

"I think it's psychosomatic," Dave Donovan says. "Don's long-term memory has always been fabulous, but he had his problems with his short-term memory. I think he blocks things out."

Although frustrated by his amnesia, both Don and Slade learnt to live with it and even to see the funny side of it. "After the accident, Don was eating a lot of food and putting a little weight on," Dave recalls.

"When we were touring I'd go for breakfast, but because of the amnesia, I'd go back and have another breakfast!" Don explains. "It is funny thinking about it, although it wasn't at the time. Did I have breakfast? I don't remember. I'd better go and eat. I was quite popular at restaurants!"

"That was definitely where the weight gain was coming from!" Dave sniggers.

"There were often some moments of light humour during his early amnesiac condition," Keith Altham agrees. "I can recall one occasion during a tour of the UK when he awoke from a deep sleep and found himself he knew not where and ran, panic stricken, into the hotel corridor. The night porter was startled out of his wits a few minutes later, when a naked man arrived at his reception desk, wearing only a card over his private parts, bearing the inscription 'Do not disturb', to be asked more worryingly if he knew who he was and what he was doing there."

To Don, the physical hardships that followed his accident were easier to live with than the amnesia, although they caused trouble as well. "When I first went on stage, my ribcage was really hurting whenever I stretched, because I broke five ribs in the accident. I thought there was still something wrong with the bones, so I went to the hospital and they did X-rays and they said, 'There's nothing wrong with the bones, it's just the tissue in between that is still stretching. There's nothing to worry about.' Later it stopped and that was about it, really.

"I also used to have headaches a lot, but that was because of the fractured skull and I guess that's a normal thing. That was just for a few months after the accident, then they disappeared. But I still find it hard to brush my hair – I have to be careful because of the scar on my head – but I seldom brush my hair anyway!

"Finally, there was the matter of some of my senses being gone. I talked to our manager Peter Kauff in New York, and told him that I had lost my sense of smell and taste. It was a real major thing and he arranged for me to see his neurologist friend, Dr. Goodgold, and he paid for it. The neurologist talked to me and – only in America – he said, 'I know how it's like when you've lost the sense of smell and taste and you want to taste a good teat,' and I thought, *what?* That was the last thing on my mind!

"He then wanted to do a test on me with a light bulb and he said, 'Open your mouth and I'll put the light bulb in.' I thought he was crazy, but he switched the light bulb on and it lit all of my head up. He could then see the nerves in the nose and he explained that it couldn't be fixed. The nerves that come down from the brain and into the bridge of the nose were severed, because I had smashed my nose. The doctors could have saved it, had it been done straight away, but the way I was smashed up, the doctors wouldn't even think about it. They had so much else to do on me that was vital, so they left it and the nerves withered. They were just thinking of keeping me alive.

"I'd had an operation in London, as a doctor had said that he could fix it. I'd gone to his surgery and he charged me £200. He did the operation and he said that if it was going to work, it would be OK in a couple of days. But nothing happened. When I told Dr. Goodgold, he said, 'That was a total con. There's no way you can fix it. Don't even think about it.' And when he said that, it was great. Then I accepted it.

"Before, I had put so much weight on. I was trying anything and everything, just to get a reaction. I couldn't understand why I could taste sugar and salt and things like that, but not everything. Dr. Goodgold said, 'Sugar, salt, sweet and sour they are from the receptors of the tongue, that's why you can taste them.' At least I know that now. But I don't take sugar and I don't take salt, so I'm not in a very good position. I always put a lot of pepper on my food and I remember saying, 'I hope there's nothing wrong with fucking pepper!' But in a way, it's amazing how lucky I was. I could have lost my eyesight, my sense of balance, the ability to tell the difference between hot and cold, a lot of things that I didn't know about. In that way, I truly consider myself lucky."

Don's way of being able to see the positive side of even the most horrendous events is one that never ceases to amaze. "The overriding fact about whatever difficulties Don experienced, post-accident, was that he never lost his warm personality, or his extremely wry, dry, quick-witted sense of humour," Jim comments.

That exposed Don as a true fighter and survivor and, although the door was closed on his hopes of regaining the ability to smell and taste, another door was opened in New York. It was a door that equalled immortality in the rock chronicles.

13

Back On Track

While in New York that summer, Slade recorded their third single that would go straight to number one: 'Merry Xmas Everybody', which became their greatest hit ever. Jim had always wanted to write something like 'Happy Birthday', a tune that never dies, and when his mother-in-law asked why he didn't write a tune like 'White Christmas', the idea of a Christmas tune came to him in the shower. He used the chorus from an old song written by Noddy in 1967, a psychedelic-tinged tune called 'Buy Me A Rocking Chair', and then wrote music for the verses, after which Noddy added new lyrics. The song was recorded at the Record Plant studio, while John Lennon was recording *Mind Games*.

"It was very hot when we recorded 'Merry Xmas Everybody'," Don recalls. "There was a heat wave; it was over a hundred degrees outside and we sat there, recording a Christmas tune. And the engineers went, 'Very strange!'

"Again, Chas was cueing me through the control room window. The drum pattern that I had put on before wasn't working that well, so I put the drums on top of the track again. If you listen to the record, there is just one drumbeat where I forgot to stop.

"We weren't sure about the record at the time. We didn't think it would work, as the whole record was a total overdub, so we didn't want it out. I think only Nod's voice was an original. We recorded the drums again, the guitars, everything. But Chas went, 'I don't care what you say. This record is coming out.' And the rest is history."

In the end, 'Merry Xmas Everybody' got a silver disc before it was even released, because of advance orders of 500,000 copies. More than 30 years later, it still enters the charts every Christmas.

While in the States, the single 'My Friend Stan' was released along with *Sladest*, a compilation that went to number one in the album charts. In the autumn of 1973, Slade went on a European tour that took them to Belgium, Switzerland, France, Norway, Sweden, Denmark, Germany and Austria.

While they were playing the National Forest in Brussels, on October 25, the Royal Observatory of Belgium detected a small but not insignificant earthquake in Brussels. This earthquake was immediately announced on radio and TV, with scientists assuming it might be the first sign of an even bigger quake. The epicentre was located and, when a scientific team was sent out to investigate, they discovered there hadn't been an earthquake at all. What had been measured was simply Slade playing much louder at the National Forest than any other band before, along with 7,000 fans at the sold-out venue clapping their hands and stomping their feet.

While in Europe, the band went on all the major music programmes, including the German *Beat Club*, *Musikladen* and *Disco* as well as *Top Pop* in Holland. "We were on those shows all the time," Don says. "We used to leave from Birmingham in the morning and fly to Amsterdam and drive to Hilversum, which was not that far away, to do *Top Pop*, their equivalent to *Top Of The Pops*. We always did two takes, so we always brought two sets of clothing. One take was just normal, but the second was in front of a blue screen, so you couldn't wear anything blue or you'd disappear into the background. Then they could project different things to the blue screen. We did that for every release that we had and then we went back again the same day."

By Christmas, 'Merry Xmas Everybody' had sold more than a million copies and, on American national news, the single was proclaimed as the only good thing to come out of England during this period. Optimism sneaked into Don's life again, as Slade were on top of the world with a bestselling single, constant TV shows and earth-shattering tours. They were more than ready for their next album, *Old New Borrowed And Blue*.

'Merry Xmas Everybody' had featured 'Don't Blame Me' as a B-side and that track, along with 'My Friend Stan' and its B-side, 'My Town', were re-used on the new album. "That album was quite different from what we had done before," says Don. "The glam era was coming to an end and we wanted to change. It was the one of our albums that I enjoyed doing the most, because it felt like a live thing when we did it. I especially remember the track 'Just A Little Bit'. If you listen to that, just around the quiet bit, Nod does a little giggle. Because I pulled a face at him! We could all see each other, we always liked the closeness when we recorded, and Nod tried to be so cool that I just pulled a face at him. Then he did that little giggle and it was kept.

"Tommy Burton plays piano on 'Find Yourself A Rainbow'. In the sixties in Wolverhampton, Tommy Burton & His Combo were a big band and they did a lot of gigs. They attempted to capture the original rock'n'roll sounds of Bill Haley and others, before Tommy turned to his first love, jazz, in 1965. He was a big name. He used to play with Reg Keirle as well.

"When we were doing the album, we were just jamming in the studio, me, Jim and Tommy, to put the track down, Tommy on piano, Jim on bass and me on drums. While the sound engineer was getting the sound together, we were just playing around, and Tommy was an amazing pianist. I think Jim still has a copy of it actually. It was *so* good!"

Old New Borrowed And Blue was released in February 1974 and went to number one in the album chart. By then Don had bought a new car, a silver Jaguar, and had started drinking.

"Don lost his senses of smell and taste when he had his accident; food-wise, it takes it all away," Len Tuckey says. "That was probably why he started getting into the drink, because he could actually *feel* something."

"But after the accident, Don's tolerance for alcohol disappeared," Haden Donovan reveals. "He only needed one drink, then he was on the way. He was quite drunk. Don would go to the clubs in

Wolverhampton and people would go, 'Come on then, Don. Your round,' and Don would pay and forget it afterwards. People caught onto that and had Don buying drinks all night, because he couldn't remember. Don has always been so keen to please people, to be Mr. Nice Guy, so he would do it. My brother David used to be very, very angry about it; the more drunk Don got, the angrier David would get. When Don used to come and fetch him to go out, what David used to do was say, 'Come on, Don, you sit there and I'll go to the bar for you,' and that way it stopped. Don used to drink gin and tonic, but David would just give him tonic and Don wouldn't know."

"Dave didn't drink and he hated me drinking," Don agrees. "He didn't like me drinking at all."

"I was really naughty with Don," Dave Donovan says. "I always made sure he had a drink, but he couldn't taste it, so…"

"One or two people really had a go at David in the clubs over it," Haden Donovan explains, "because if Don wasn't drunk, he wasn't gonna be a fool."

His brother adds, "Don used to say to me, 'You know, it's great coming out with you, Dave, because when I go out with anyone else I'm absolutely pissed brainless, but with you I'm quite sensible.'"

"I think I started drinking out of insecurity," Don admits. "I felt so inadequate that I started drinking after the crash. A lot, I mean. Before that it had never been anything silly or out of hand. It *was* now. Most people think that I had started drinking earlier, because I always had a huge whisky bottle with me on stage, but the thing is that it wasn't whisky in it. It was just coloured water. Even in my drinking days, that was one drink I could not drink. It was always the whisky that went last, if there was a minibar in my hotel room. I never really liked it."

In January 1974, Slade went on a four-week tour of America, followed by their second trip to Australia and a short tour of Japan. "I think it was on that tour that some of our gigs were cancelled because of snow," says Don. "It was probably in the Midwest, because they used to have bad winters there. I had a room on the ground floor and Swinn gave me a call in the morning to tell me that tonight's show was off. I was still in bed and I asked him why. 'Have a look out of the window,' he answered and I got out of bed and opened the curtains. The snow went past the windows! So we were stuck there."

Brownsville Station supported Slade on the American part of the tour. At that point their hit 'Smokin' In The Boys Room' was at number one in the US charts. "They were supporting *us*," Don recalls. "We did quite a lot of shows with them in America and we had a good relationship with them. They were nice guys, very funny, especially their singer, Cub Koda. He was excellent as a frontman. He is gone now, but I still keep in touch with their drummer, Henry 'H-Bomb' Weck."

"Slade liked to add an "e" to Henry, and call me 'Enery or Henery," Henry Weck recalls. "They were so much like Brownsville Station, as we both had incredibly talented frontmen, and all wore rather over-the-top stage clothes. Each band worked the crowds into a frenzy, so Slade were one of the few bands we socialised with on the road. Slade weren't afraid to let us go on stage before them, because they knew it would make them work even harder to win over the crowd."

"On that trip, Robbie Wilson, Slade's Scottish roadie, got in trouble," Don says. "Actually, he was a great roadie. He took care of everything. He could sort things out. We used to have a truck in which a couple of the roadies went and then a small minibus for the rest of the crew. They were late one morning and Robbie was driving, and three squad cars couldn't catch him. That was how fast he was going. They had to put a roadblock up for him, as it was the only way they could stop him. He was dragged out of the car like in a typical American film and he was thrown in jail. In California in those days, you were automatically thrown in jail for five days for speeding. Peter Kauff then got him out on bail.

"At that time we only had a week or two left of the tour before we went to Australia, and we had the last five days off in Los Angeles. The sheriff then said that when we'd finished touring in America, Robbie had to go back to jail. And sure enough, as soon as our last show ended, there were two sheriffs waiting for him and they took him straight off. So while we were lying in the sun in Los Angeles, he was in jail. He was a different man when he came out. It was only a petty offence, but he was thrown in a cell with five or six others, all real criminals.

"After that, we went to Australia and that was quite a contrast. I particularly remember one day when I came back from the beach and I called my parents. There was a recession in England at the time. It was really horrible. There was a fuel shortage and you were only allowed to heat one room of your house. It was almost like World War III. Because of the time difference, when I called my parents it was five o'clock in the morning in England. I talked to Dad and in England there was snow on the ground. Dad said he had to leave early for work, because he couldn't put fuel in his car as he had already used his quota. He had to walk to work and that was about seven miles. Then he said, 'What are you doing, son?' I said, 'I've just come back from the beach and my sunburn is killing me!' I won't repeat what he said to me!

"This second time in Australia, we did many indoor venues. It wasn't as chaotic as it had been on the first tour and we only did four or five concerts."

"Still, the band were huge in Australia," Haden Donovan recalls. "When we came in, the day before the band, we were in a car from the airport as the record company sent a car to pick us up and take us to the hotel. A DJ came on the radio at 9.30 in the morning and said, 'I'd just like to say hi to the Slade road crew. They're probably on their way to their hotel now.' It was amazing. I mean, who'd want to know that? We went to the airport the next day when the band came in, but we couldn't get anywhere near the airport. It was huge. Like The Beatles."

After the Australian gigs, Slade flew to Japan to play four concerts: two in Tokyo, one in Osaka and one in Kyoto.

"It was great that I was with Ludwig by then," says Don, "because no matter where I was in the world, I could just call Chicago and talk to the secretary, Kay, and explain what I needed. So when in Tokyo, she'd just look up in her directory and tell me which shops distributed Ludwig in Japan. Then she would send them a fax straight away and I could go and pick up the stuff that I needed. It was a fantastic situation.

"I enjoyed the trip, but Australia and Japan were totally opposite countries. Australia basically has got no history as such, whereas Japan was steeped in history and culture."

"When in Australia, you felt on the edge of the earth," Swinn ponders. "You were very conscious of how far away you were from home. You also felt that in Japan, but in a different way. In Japan you never get behind the veneer. You never get close to anyone as they don't open up."

"Japan was crazy," Don states. "At the first concert I went down to sort my drums out before the others got there. Between the stage and the floor where the kids would be, there were three big Japanese guys holding a piece of rope between them. I said, 'What's with that rope?' and they said, 'You'll see tonight.' What happened was that the kids went crazy in the audience and when they stood up and started to move forward these three guys would pull them back to their seats with this rope.

"There was a Beatles copy band playing at one of the concerts. They were called The Bad Boys and singing 'She Roves You'. Obviously they didn't look like The Beatles, but they had their suits and their hairstyles and the band members were called John, Paul, George and Lingo. I cracked up!

"Another incident that I recall was when I was having a cup of tea in the hotel lobby in Tokyo. There was a big TV screen in the lobby surrounded by Japanese, and they were all curled up laughing. I went over and on the TV screen was this elderly man in a tatty ripped uniform, standing to attention. I asked the promoter what this was all about and he said, 'They've just found this soldier on an island and he thinks the war is still on.' Apparently, he wouldn't believe that the war had ended, so they had to get his commanding officer of the time and fly him to this island to dismiss him and tell him that he could go home.

"He had this big ticker-tape parade. This poor guy was looking around and he didn't understand a thing. Thirty years he had been on that island, and he was totally confused. I remember saying to the promoter, 'I wonder if he is going to get his back pay!' But I understood that he was taken back to the island, because he couldn't cope with modern civilisation."

Slade were in Japan less than a week, but Don managed to meet a model at the reception after one of the concerts in Tokyo. "Her name was Mari and her father was German, whereas her mother was Japanese," he recalls. "When I went back to England after the tour, we used to write to each other and spoke a bit on the phone. I actually stopped drinking when I met her, and soon after I moved to London. Mari couldn't settle in Wolverhampton, but she had been to London a few times, so that was why I moved there. I was the first member of the band to actually leave Wolverhampton, although both Jim and Nod had bought houses in London as well. They didn't really live there, but I did, in my flat in 37 Platts Lane in Hampstead. I lived in London for almost 20 years and I never thought I would move away from there."

Fittingly, Slade's next single was a ballad. It was a waltz, more or less written by Jim's wife, Louise, fine-tuned by Jim, with lyrics added by Nod. Titled 'Everyday', it was released in March 1974 and was the first Slade single to have been taken from an album that had already been released. Up until then, Slade singles had often been included on later albums, but not the other way around.

"It was Chas' idea that our singles weren't appearing on albums first," Don says. "He took that from The Beatles. He said, 'They have never ever had a single on any of their albums except for their soundtracks.' And it is true, because it takes away sales. If people buy the album, why buy the single? When we released 'Everyday' it didn't do so well, because it was on *Old New Borrowed And Blue*. In America, you have to have a single off the album, as it is a totally different market, but in England it was like the kiss of death if you did that. I don't know why Chas suddenly wanted 'Everyday' out as a single – maybe to cater for the American market – but I do remember Jim being very much against it."

Dave was too, but he had his own reasons. He thought that anything with a piano on it was doomed to fail. Tell that to Elton John!

'Everyday' reached number three in the charts. Its B-side, 'Good Time Gals', was another track from *Old New Borrowed And Blue*. Slade toured the UK in April and the next single, 'Banging Man', was released in June. It charted at number three as well, although it had no piano on it. "The B-side for that one was 'She Did It To Me'," Don recalls. "I really like that. It's such a nice song. I think it is one of the best that Nod and Jim ever wrote."

Shortly after, Slade expanded their line of work beyond records and tours, as they went into the making of their first and only feature film.

14

Slade In Flame

Don is a natural storyteller, and a natural-born actor as well. When talking about his life, he jumps out of his seat to act out the different events, playing the parts of all the characters, changing his voice into theirs. His gestures and facial expressions are so vivid that you can almost see the events taking place before your eyes. This acting skill was captured in 1974 in *Flame*, a film whose plot centred on the rise and fall of a sixties rock'n'roll band, its principal focus being the darker side of the music industry.

"Chas suggested that we do a film," Don says, "and it was great. Another string to the bow, so to speak. Chas used to model our career after The Beatles, so the next step would be a film. I remember him saying it was so easy doing *A Hard Day's Night*. That was no problem, but it would have sunk as soon as it had been released, so we didn't want to do that kind of thing.

"Then Chas' assistant and friend John Steel came up with the idea of us doing a spoof of the old BBC sci-fi serial *The Quatermass Experiment*, with Noddy as Professor Quite-A-Mess, but Dave wouldn't have it. According to the script, he was to be eaten by a triffid within the first 15 minutes! So very early on, we decided to do a realistic portrait of the music business, instead of a slapstick comedy. When we decided to do that sort of plot, I thought, 'Great.' I really wanted a gritty film."

144

The first order of business was to record a soundtrack album at Olympic Studios in Barnes. "When we did the *Slade In Flame* album, we wanted to have brass on it," Don says. "The storyline of the film was set in the sixties, so we wanted a slightly different sound from ours. Chas obviously knew a lot of people, so the brass section was from the sixties, Georgie Fame and Zoot Money bands. At that point they were in a band called Gonzalez.

"Chas contacted them and the main guy in the band, Mick Eve, came to the studio to listen to the tracks that we were going to have brass on. He played sax and keyboards and was musical arranger as well. He wrote down the notes that he wanted and then the band came and did all the brass in one session. It was incredible; they did ad-lib as well. In the track 'How Does It Feel?' there's a high contra-melody, and that was Mick Eve's idea. He just did that in the studio. It was quite amazing.

"The album was mixed in the Record Plant in New York, the same recording studio that John Lennon used. When Chas was mixing the track 'Standing On The Corner', Lennon walked in and he said, 'I like that singer. He sounds like me.' That was like the greatest compliment he could give Noddy."

Slade In Flame is widely regarded as Slade's most coherent album and remains a favourite among fans.

It was while Slade were recording the album that Mari came to England to live with Don. The relationship was very intense; a true emotional roller-coaster ride, from which Don got a short break when he had to leave to tour America. "When we went on that particular tour, screenwriter Andrew Birkin and director Richard Loncraine went with us," says Don. "It was Richard's first film and Andrew… I liked him, but he was a weird fellow. He used to write in churchyards. On gravestones. He was always into the supernatural. He was a type who never pushed himself though. He was always in the background. I remember Andrew and Richard falling out one time, because Andrew is the brother of Jane Birkin, who did 'Je T'Aime' with Serge Gainsbourg in 1969. Richard was sort of asking him questions like, 'Was that really happening in the studio?' and Andrew didn't particularly like that. He was probably fed up, because all people did was talk about that record.

145

"Andrew and Richard didn't last long on the tour. Only two weeks, I think. They were different men when they went back, totally wrecked. I don't think people realise how heavy the schedule is when you are touring, especially in America. But it was good that they went."

"Although all four members of Slade made our trip an amazing experience, it is Don who I remember best," Andrew Birkin recalls. "He had a slightly other-worldly quality, as though sleepwalking through this temporal experience. One time in Los Angeles, he and I went exploring in the old Cahuenga Pass near the Hollywood Freeway, and suddenly found ourselves inside the Hollywood Bowl. I'd seen The Beatles there back in 1964 – free of charge, of course, having clambered over someone's garden wall – but now it was deserted and all ours. Don wandered about the stage in a sort of daze, wondering if he'd ever get to play here. I didn't feel he was particularly lusting after the spotlight, more a vague curiosity as to what the future held. He'd survived the auto accident a year earlier, and perhaps this detachment was a consequence of that, but to me it seemed inextricably entangled with his own very idiosyncratic personality: warm, funny, kind, infinitely touching and totally lacking in ego."

"Andrew and Richard went with us everywhere to get the stories for *Flame*," says Don, "and while on tour we headlined over 10cc, Aerosmith and The New York Dolls. The New York Dolls were crazy. They had 'dead' baby dolls strapped to their backs. When we headlined over Aerosmith at the NY Felt Forum, Gene Simmons, Dee Snider and Joey Ramone came for the show. Later, they all admitted to having been influenced by us. It was a 6,000-capacity venue and it was totally sold out."

On their return, Slade started shooting the film. Filming was completed within six weeks at the Pinewood Studios, with additional scenes on location in Shepperton, Sheffield, Brighton, Tenterden in Kent and the Rainbow Theatre in London.

"None of us took it *that* serious," Don recalls. "It was just a bit of fun for us. But of course, it was a different routine to work like that. After a couple of weeks, you get into the flow of things. Up at five, get ready and be on set around seven-ish to work. Then eventually, Andrew or

Richard would say, 'Break for lunch.' Break for lunch? I thought it was the end of the day! We did around six hours, that was a full day for us, or it would have been in the studio, and then you had all afternoon to go! Plus most of the time we spent hanging around, while they set lights, set the cameras, just for two seconds on the screen basically."

Acting came naturally to Don, mainly because *Flame* is a fanciful version of Slade's own story – at least with respect to their early days – as Andrew Birkin puts it. "I was the drummer, Charlie," Don says, "and in the film, I work in a steel factory and pay instalments on my drums, like I used to do in real life. Jim was the bass player, Paul, who is married and he carries his bass in a polythene bag. Noddy played the singer, Stoker, and Dave was Barry, a foppish guitarist who gets all the girls, although he is in a steady relationship with a girl named Angie."

Although Don's character was named Charlie, like Charlie Watts, and Jim's Paul, like Paul McCartney, Birkin recalls that the naming of the characters had nothing to do with the music scene. "Noddy was called Stoker because he reminded me of boiler-room stokers on board the Titanic. Barry sounded a bit slicker and fitted Dave's character, Paul seemed gentler and more introverted, and Charlie just felt right for Don."

"It fitted my character so well," Don laughs. "He is a right Charlie, a bit of a fool, always dropping things and getting into trouble."

"If The Beatles were John, George, Paul and 'Bongo', Don was Slade's Bongo!" Jim states. "His performance in the film looked completely natural because it was just pure Don – just like 'Bongo'."

"Don's acting in *Flame* is really good," Dave adds. "It is fantastic, really, because it wasn't long after his accident. I don't know how difficult it was to learn the lines. I know it is difficult for anyone to learn lines, but in the end product, what Don did to the film was really good."

"Because there were stops all the time, the making of *Flame* wasn't that difficult with my amnesia," Don explains. "I'd do one line and then stop. Even in my long scene, where I talk to my boss under the bridge by the river, I just did a few lines, then they stopped to change the camera angles and then I'd do a few lines more. Furthermore, Patrick Connor, who played my boss, was very patient. If I forgot something,

147

he just said, 'Don't worry. We'll just go back and do it again.' He was very nice and helpful. A real gentleman."

"Years after we made *Flame*, I watched the film on DVD with my sons," Andrew Birkin recalls, "and all of us thought the scene with Don under the bridge was not necessarily the best, but by far the most memorable. Like Don himself."

To Andrew Birkin's way of thinking, lines shouldn't be learnt anyway as the idea of the scene is what matters. One advantage of having Don and his fellow Slade members play themselves was that they didn't really need to have any acting talent, just the ability to be as natural as possible in front of the camera.

"We didn't have to act that much," Don agrees. "At least Jim and I played more or less ourselves. We did have to learn how to project to the camera though, and it sometimes seemed to be over the top, but it worked and Andrew even let us alter little bits now and again. I could say, 'I don't think Charlie would do that,' or 'I don't think Charlie would say this,' if it was a bit intellectual, and then we also added some of the local slang.

"In any case, with the many similarities to our lives, it didn't feel much like acting because we had been through it for real. For instance, Nod takes over Dave's girlfriend, Angie, in *Flame* like I did with both Pat and Angela in real life, and in one particular scene Dave celebrates his 21st birthday. In reality, we were all made younger to cater to the teenage girls, especially Dave. But I remember that one of the criticisms of the time was that Dave was the only one not to have a background in the film. I was seen living with my parents, Jim had his wife and Nod was living with his grandmother, but Dave? He just sort of fell from the moon! You never hear anything about his background. I guess they couldn't use his real situation in the film, as his marriage to Jan was still kept away from the fans. All in all we played ourselves, except for Nod. His character didn't have very much to do with him. In the film he is doing boot sales, he's living with his grandmother and he has a shed in the garden with pigeons. That's a bit of a northern thing and it had nothing to do with Nod in real life. But Noddy was really great in that film, it was a true vehicle for his acting skills."

As for their fellow actors, Don is full of praise. Some of the colleagues in *Flame* were rather new to the business, while others repeated roles that they had already done before. "The casting director was fantastic really," Don says. "All the actors were perfect. Tom Conti, who played Flame's manager, Mr Seymour, was the '*ac-tor*' of the bunch and he carried himself like that. A bit highbrow, but very nice. I always thought that *Flame* was his first film, but later he told me that he had done one before, but as he said, it was not worth mentioning. I think it was *The Killer Bees* or something like that! He always seemed to forget his lines on set and that's why he did all the long pauses in the film.

"Kenneth Colley, as his assistant Tony Devlin, really fitted the part. He was in a few episodes of *Star Wars* after that. Johnny Shannon, as the mean two–bit agent Harding, that was pretty much the same part he played in *Performance* with Mick Jagger. That's the part that he always played! He did a lot of sitcoms in England and it was always the same kind of character. He looks the part and he carries it really well.

"But Alan Lake, as the singer Jack Daniels, more or less played himself. He was dressed in the same way in real life as in the film. And we thought, '*God!* He can't be serious!' When our original singer, Johnny Howells, saw the film, he was not happy. He said, 'That's supposed to be me, isn't it?' because in the sixties he looked a bit like Alan Lake.

"In real life, Alan Lake was married to Diana Dors and he had a drinking problem. On our very first day of shooting, he started a fight with the owner of the club where we did the first scene. He was fired on the spot, but Diana came to his rescue and promised that from then on, Alan would behave himself, which he did. Ten years later he shot himself, because Diana had died of cancer.

"Then there was Anthony Allen as Russell, the roadie. We never got to know him though, as he was a bit of a loner."

"Russell in the film was kind of like my counterpart," says Swinn, "but there was nothing in his character that was like me really. I remember I had to teach him how to roll joints! All the actors who were seen smoking, I had to teach them how to roll joints."

"As for the girls, Nina Thomas played Jim's wife, Julie, and Sara Clee played Dave's girlfriend, Angie," Don continues. "Sara Clee had been in *That'll Be The Day,* where she'd played more or less the same part as in *Flame*. I don't know what happened to her, or most of the actors later on. We had that joke that whoever worked on *Flame* never got any work afterwards. One shot himself and the rest didn't work! But… at least Tom Conti came out well."

Andrew Birkin went on to enjoy a successful career after *Flame,* writing screenplays for *The Name Of The Rose, Joan Of Arc, The Fifth Element, The Lost Boys* and *Finding Neverland*. He has been Oscar-nominated and won a Silver Berlin Bear but, in 1974, *Flame* was only his second screenplay.

"I liked it, because everything that happened in that film was based on real life," Don says. "Every scene is true to life, either it happened to us or to other bands. The coffin scene with Noddy, that did actually happen, but not to us. That was Screaming Lord Sutch. He once got stuck in his coffin. The shooting at the radio station had happened too, and that came from Chas. He'd tried something similar in his days with The Animals, as there were illegal radio stations back then. It was so exciting: pirate radio! People used to pay money to have their records played and the pirate radio stations used to fight each other. During the shooting in the film, you hear Kenneth Colley say, 'Mention the bloody group!' and that was also taken from Chas. It was supposed to mirror that concert in Holland back in 1972, where Chas wanted some trees cut down because they blocked the view. It was a typical managing thing; get the group noticed at any cost.

"The guy who plays the DJ in that shooting scene is Tommy Vance. He came from pirate radio in real life. So did Emperor Rosko, who MC-ed our Earls Court concert; in *Flame*, he's also the MC of Flame's big concert.

"In that concert scene, there's a girl who throws herself at me on stage. In real life, she proposed to me in a letter! She was one of them girls who used to hang around no matter where we went and they were always friendly. I don't know how it happened, but she got my phone number when first I moved to London. When she phoned me the first time, I was surprised how she got my number, but I said to her, 'I'll tell you what. You keep it to yourself and then you can call when you want.' She said OK and immediately after that I contacted the telephone company and changed the number to a new one, ex-directory again. Then this girl called again and said, 'Why have you changed your number?' That freaked me out. I said, 'How did you get my number? It's ex-directory.' But she just laughed and put the phone down. I never heard from her again, except she sent me another letter saying, 'You've had your chance. Now I'm marrying someone else.' That was wonderful! It was so funny. *You've had your chance!*

"But some fans are scary, because they imagine things and they live in a fantasy world. There was one female fan and I think I had spent a night with her, but afterwards she was telling her friends that we were living together. She went to the extent of buying clothes that matched mine and leaving them all over her home. When her friends came for a visit, she used them as proof of me living there. If they started asking questions, she told them that I had just gone out, or that I was on tour or something. She even took the step of telling people that she was expecting my baby and had photos made with a pillow under her dress, so she looked pregnant. It's so frightening, It's a mystery to me how fans become that obsessed."

The fans' obsession was evident during a tour of Europe that autumn, where Slade visited France, Germany, Iceland and Denmark. At the K.B. Hallen venue in Copenhagen, Denmark, so many chairs were smashed by eager fans that Slade were never invited back and gigs in other parts of Scandinavia were cancelled. It was getting close to madness.

Madness also seemed to prevail on set and, as in all films, scenes had to be re-shot for *Flame* when things didn't go as expected. "I remember, in the film, when we are racing from Nod's band," says Don. "That was shot at a proper club and there was this house right next door. When we were fleeing, this guy popped out and yelled, 'WILL YOU FUCKING SHUT UP! I'm trying to get my kids to sleep!' He didn't know what was going on.

"I remember another scene at the start of the film, with me in the factory, when I walk out of the driveway because I'm leaving work. All the workers were proper workers from the factory and they kept looking at the camera. And Richard said, 'Don't! Don't!' And what he did was, he stood on a wall on the opposite side and he started singing something stupid at the top of his voice, so that all the workers looked at him to see what that was. He was fantastic!

"I'd love to see those out-takes, but I don't know where they are, if they are still there. At least back then, if you had done a take or two, they just wiped them because of the cost of tapes. Minor mishaps were kept in the film though. In the coffin scene, Nod gets locked in the coffin with a glass of beer, but where does that go? In the next scene it isn't there, instead he has three hands! I don't know where that came from, but suddenly there's a hand waving behind his head within the coffin. Things like that are great!

"Then we had to overdub in the studio, if there was background noise or if the diction didn't come off right in the film. That was strange. You have the screen in front of you and you stand with some headsets, and when it is your turn to say something the line goes across. When it comes to the end, you say it and then it fits in sync with the lips. The voice of Noddy's grandmother was a complete overdub. You never see her in the film, except for her eyes, and it was actually one of the technical crew who played that part."

In October 1974, while the film was in post-production, the first single from the soundtrack album was released. 'Far Far Away' was an instant classic, reaching number two in the charts. Noddy wrote the lyrics on a trip to America, with Jim contributing lyrics for the chorus as well as the music. "That song is actually my favourite Slade song," says Don, "mainly because of Nod's lyrics. When it came out, we *had* been touring the world non-stop and the lyrics were a reminder of where we had been."

The B-side was another track from the *Slade In Flame* album, 'O.K. Yesterday Was Yesterday'. A month later, *Slade In Flame* was released and it reached number six on the album chart.

In January 1975, a month prior to the film's release, John Pidgeon's book, *Slade In Flame*, was published. In many ways it was a typical book of a film, an easy read with scant attention paid to literary merit, with both the narrative and the characters quite different from the film. "In the film, Dave and myself were in charge of the comic relief, doing slapstick sort of things," Don says," whereas Nod and Jim did the heavy stuff. But in the book, Jim and myself are the main characters."

Actually, most events in the book are seen through the eyes of Jack Daniels and Don's character, Charlie Spencer. Gradually, Charlie's point of view diminishes, to be replaced by the thoughts and feelings of Jim's character, Paul Harris, who turns out to be the hero of the book. The storyline emphasises the professionalism and friendship of Charlie and Paul and leaves it to Nod and Dave's characters, Laurence Stoker and Barry Jenkins, to bicker about girls and egos. Barry and Stoker thus come across a lot less sympathetically in the book than in the film.

"I think the book is really good," Don comments. "The storyline is better and there is more depth to the characters. It was closer to us as we had been in the early years. I don't know how he did it, John Pidgeon, but it is as if he knew us really well when he wrote that book. Had the book been made prior to the film, I think we should have filmed that instead of the screenplay. It would have been so much better."

A week before the premiere of *Flame*, a second single taken from the soundtrack album was released: 'How Does It Feel?' coupled with 'So Far So Good'. Jim allegedly wrote 'How Does It Feel?' in 1969 on an old, out-of-tune piano with half the keys missing. The single only reached number 15 in the UK charts, thus underlining Dave's argument that anything with a piano was doomed to failure as a single. In the years since, however, it has consistently been rated the best Slade song ever in fan polls. Many musicians, including Noel Gallagher from Oasis, agree on that.

Flame premiered in London on February 13 1975, at the Metropole Rialto in Coventry Street, but before that it was shown at a cinema in Sheffield. "I don't know why Sheffield was chosen," Don admits, "but it probably had something to do with the fact that many of the scenes, such as the one with the factory and the one with me living with my parents, were shot there. For the first night, Dave and I had arranged with the owner of the cinema that we could sneak in and sit on the last row after the lights went down, in order to see the reaction of the audience. We were with a whole bunch that went – me and Mari, Dave and Jan, some of the road crew and some friends as well. When we got to the cinema, Dave put on a false beard in order not to be recognised, but it wasn't even the same colour as his hair! It just looked so phony. And, of course, when we went into the place, the first thing that happened was this guy coming up to him, saying, 'Hi, Dave!' To make things worse, when Dave got the false beard off he had a rash all over his face from it.

"Things weren't that much better at the premiere in London. We arrived on a fire engine, because Chas wanted to do the big Hollywood arrival. I always remember going there on that fire engine, because The Sweet passed us in a limousine going to the cinema and they rolled the windows down and went, 'I bet you lot are cold!' And we *were*! It was freezing!"

Andy Scott remembers the episode with a grin, but says, "I thought *Flame* was fantastic, but Mick Tucker, my dear, departed drummer, made a *faux pas* after seeing the film. Chas said, 'Well, guys, what did you think?' I said, 'Great film. Fantastic,' but Mick went, 'Yeah, it was all right.' 'All right?' Chas seethed. 'What fucking films have *you* done?' And Mick said, 'All I meant to say was that it was great.' I really liked the film. I think some thought had gone into it and Don was brilliant."

Flame went on general release three days after the London premiere and Don's parents saw it in Wolverhampton. "As they were coming out of the cinema there were some kids in front of them, and obviously they didn't know that Mum and Dad were my parents," says Don. "Then one of the kids said, 'That drummer is an idiot!' and Mum hit him with her handbag! That poor kid, he didn't have a clue what was happening."

While Dora was defending her son's honour, Slade had their own troubles promoting the film. "We went to different towns in a big, black Rolls-Royce and we were driving up to Manchester to promote *Flame*," Swinn recalls. "We were stuck in traffic and as we were running really late, I decided to go across the island, but of course the car got caught in the mud. The first thing I did was to get the Rolls-Royce washed before we got to the cinema, but Chas went crazy. He'd been on to the newspapers and there were all these cameramen, waiting to take photographs of the Rolls-Royce covered in mud. Everything was a story to Chas."

Don is still very fond of the film. "I'm glad we did it. At that time, it was possibly the first film to show the underside of the industry. David Essex had done some films like that, but they were a bit more glossy, I think. Because he was that kind of character. With *Flame*, it has kind of set a standard. Just think about *The Commitments*. It's sort of a parallel to *Flame*, isn't it? But when *Flame* was first released, it probably wasn't the right thing to do, because at the time it wasn't what Slade were. I remember we talked to Robin Nash, who produced *Top Of The Pops*. He said, 'I really admire what you have done. You've done the right thing, but do you really think that the kids want to see that? That side of the business?' I know what he meant, because when it was released it got very mixed reviews from the general public. We weren't really down, we were more contemplating, have we done the right thing? We were proud of the finished product, but was that the right direction? People hadn't expected that kind of film from us."

The problem was that those who hadn't read the book didn't expect the bleak streak that runs through the film, and those who had read the book were disappointed that the inside stories featured in the book weren't in the film. All of the sex and much of the violence was left out, and so was an explanation of the internal relationships between the four group members, as well as a timeline that was easy to grasp. The book made it clear that the career of the band spanned several years, whereas in the film it all seems to happen within a few months.

"In the film you can only tell that years are passing because the hairstyles and clothes are changing," Don states. "Especially Sara Clee's Angie; she represents the passing of time with her different hairdos, headbands and everything. I guess it is difficult to create that illusion of time in a film, but it is so important to do that. And *Flame* didn't.

"Another criticism of the film was that it only runs for 86 minutes. We had to cut something, and we couldn't have anything distasteful in it because that would restrict the age group. We wanted a PG rating, so our younger fans would be able to see it, and I remember there were so many things that had to be cut out for that reason. Like in the party scene at the hotel, where Nod's drunk and Sara Clee picks him up. There was something more there that was cut. There were quite a few things where we were told, 'You can't do that,' because with the censorship we had to be so careful. For instance, the scene where Alan Lake gets his toes demolished. That could not be shown because of the censorship, but it would have been totally different if things like that had been kept."

Probably the biggest obstacle was that in the film Stoker and Paul fall out and, eventually, the band splits up. "The thing was that people couldn't separate Slade from *Flame*," Don sighs. "They didn't understand that we played characters. So every time we did TV interviews or whatever we had to say, 'We're not Slade in the film! We really like each other and we're not about to split up!' I guess the whole storyline confused the fans. People in the music business liked it,though, because they knew what it was all about. They knew what we were trying to get across, but not the fans. Because of that, the film wasn't around for very long and the actual general release wasn't everywhere, like you'd see with a major film that gets a nationwide distribution. But that didn't happen with *Flame*. Only certain towns would show it.

"In the late seventies it was shown again in a few special cinemas, like a tiny cinema in Wardour Street in London. When it came out in America it didn't do that well either. We were actually quite big in the Midwestern states, concert-wise, but with *Flame* they couldn't understand what we were saying, because of our Black Country dialect. They talked about subtitling it! I still think the film is good though. Because of the story, I think it still stands up."

Slade never made another film. All the band members had proved themselves capable actors, but with the criticism of the film as well as the band not making any profit from *Flame*, further plans of filming were discarded.

"We never got any money from it," Don reveals. "Chas had told us that, once the original investment for the film had been covered, we would get a cut of the profits because of us contributing stories to the manuscript, but of course we never saw that money. Chas' company financed it and I think it was half a million pounds. It's difficult to see where the money went, but of course it's a matter of the crew, the equipment and expenses like that. It probably was a pretty low budget. At least it got shown on British television a couple of times and it has also been released on DVD."

For the re-release of the DVD in connection with Slade's 40th anniversary, in 2006, Don, Dave and Jim all went to London and, along with Tom Conti and Richard Loncraine, filmed comments on *Flame*. Noddy had already contributed his commentary interview to the film in 2003.

"That's the first I've heard of Richard since we did *Flame*," Don says. "Apparently he lives in Hollywood now and has done the film *Firewall* with Harrison Ford. I saw the interview with Richard and he didn't look any different. Tom Conti hadn't changed much either. He's such a nice man. It was great doing those comments and having the film re-released. There would have been no way that it would have been released again, if we had done a thing like *A Hard Day's Night*. I am indeed very proud of what we did."

15

An American Sojourn

With a feature film out and a solid following throughout Europe, it was a thorn in Slade's side that they still hadn't conquered America. British bands often had a hard time over there, but many had succeeded in a big way.

"Both Led Zeppelin and Queen had done it, so why not us?" Don asks. "Obviously, we were friends with the guys from Led Zeppelin, and Brian May from Queen was one of my friends, too. We had met during a TV show in Germany and we started going out together, Mari and myself with Brian and his wife, Chrissy. I remember I once called Brian to ask if he and Chrissy would fancy going to a concert with us. He said it sounded really nice, but I didn't tell him who we were going to see. I picked him up, and he had his white suit on and looked really smart. We went to Earls Court and I always remember his face when he saw who got on stage: Jimmy Osmond! I had taken them to see The Osmonds, and there was this look of horror on Brian's face. It was priceless."

Queen's album, *Sheer Heart Attack*, had gone gold in America in 1974, and Led Zeppelin were now rated as the biggest band in the world, so Slade spent two years trying to win over the vast country as well. "We moved to America to crack the market," Don says. "It was stated in the press that we moved because of taxes, but that was not the ultimate reason. We did pay a lot of taxes in England, so it did help, but it was not the real reason. Reggae and disco had become 'in' in England anyway, so we found that it was the right time for us to make the move."

In early 1975, Slade started touring in America, often headlining big arenas in front of audiences that didn't always appreciate what they heard. At the Memorial Auditorium in Dallas, Texas, in March, it got a bit out of hand.

"We were doing a really good gig in Dallas, except all kinds of fruit like oranges, apples and bananas was being thrown on stage," Don remembers. "We thought, what's the matter? Where does this come from? After the show, we walked off stage and as soon as we walked to the dressing room, John Bonham and Robert Plant walked behind us. And we went, '*You!* You fucking bastards!' They had bought fruit especially to throw at us. We didn't know Led Zeppelin were in the audience. We'd heard that they'd been there a few days before, but we didn't know they were staying over.

"There was a big hotel in town and the guys from Led Zeppelin all got suites there. John Bonham then said, 'Let's go to my suite and have a party.' So we went there and they had a lot of booze and stuff, and that was when Bonham tried to kill Jim.

"Led Zeppelin were so huge in America, and Bonham was saying, 'You lot are mad topping the bill of these arenas. You should do what we did on our first tour: just go second or third on the bill and really show yourself against the other bands.' Jim was never that good at explaining things, so what he said was, 'It's OK for you lot.' What he really meant was that Led Zeppelin already had the crowd with them, even before they go on stage, but Bonham took it all wrong. He was already out of his skull on whisky and cocaine anyway, and he said to Jim, 'Do you mean to say that I don't try when I go on stage?' Bonham took his walking stick with this big silver tip and took a swing at Jim. He was not playing around. He was serious. But because he was so out of it, he fell on the floor and missed him. Otherwise, he would have killed him."

"Jim could be obnoxious without realising it; a very insensitive person," Swinn adds, "and Bonham attacked him with a cane. I just threw myself at him. I wasn't being brave; I just did it automatically. So

I was on the floor with Bonham and everybody just stood staring and I said, 'Jim! We're out of here!'"

"Actually, Swinn calmed Bonham down," Don continues. "Led Zeppelin's tour manager said they'd never seen anyone calm Bonham down like Swinn did. Normally, he would have wrecked the room to get at Jim."

"I got thanked by Chas a few days later and was told what a great job I did," says Swinn. "I didn't get a raise though, or a 'thank you' out of Jim. I always said to Chas that I should have let Bonham have that go at him. He might have learnt something."

Despite the violent incident in Texas, John Bonham remains Don's all-time favourite drummer. "I knew him from back in the sixties, when he played in a cabaret band. That is hard to imagine! And I couldn't believe it; he didn't need microphones, he was *so* loud. But, basically, he was a natural drummer. He had no tuition, he didn't go for lessons; it just came from his heart. Amazing.

"One time when we did an American tour, we went to Tower Records in Los Angeles, this enormous warehouse full of records, and we were told, 'Help yourself.' It was pre-CD days, so it was like a big factory full of records. I think I probably got 75 or 100 albums; it felt a bit strange, just to take them. But apparently, when Led Zeppelin got the same offer, they took a big lorry down there and took *every* record – hundreds of thousands of albums. After that, Tower Records stopped offering free albums to bands."

Slade were back in England in April for their next UK tour. This time, they were followed by a radio crew from BBC1 and the result was the revealing radio show *Six Days On The Road*, which was transmitted as two one-hour programmes in August 1975 as part of the *Insight* series. By then, Wrigley had noticed Don's huge consumption of gum.

"Wrigley had these adverts on TV with a guy walking with this big gum packet," Don recalls, "and Wrigley actually sent me one. It was a blow-up one, and I brought it with me on stage. That was a laugh."

The single 'Thanks For The Memory (Wham Bam Thank You M'am)' was released that May. It went to number seven in the charts, but Slade got into trouble with the censors because the song contained what was thought to be obscene language. "Nod had to change some of the words," says Don. "I think it was the line; 'Have a love smell on your sheet.' What he came up with to replace it ['Have some honey with your meat'] was almost as bad, but nobody seemed to notice."

'Raining In My Champagne' was the B-side of the single. Straight after the UK tour, Slade went back to America to tour with Black Sabbath.

"We knew them from the pubs and clubs back home, before they became Black Sabbath," says Don, "and their singer, Ozzy Osbourne, was quite a character. He would go on stage in his white satin trousers and, more often than not, they would burst open in the front and he would walk off again to change. When you see him on television nowadays, that is how he is. There's no acting or anything. But he's the nicest bloke and he's a gentleman as well. In the company of ladies or children, he'll behave himself.

"I remember a classic Ozzy comment when we toured with them. We were sitting in a hotel somewhere having a drink and Ozzy said, 'Is it right, Don, that you can't smell or taste?' and I said, 'Yes, that's right.' Ozzy then said, 'I'd throw myself off a fucking cliff if that was me!'

"I think it was on that tour that I started wearing gloves when playing the drums. Before that, the sweat always made the sticks fly out of my hands; I started putting sticky tape and plasters on my fingers too. I bought some while we were over there, but I was allergic to the adhesive. All my fingers went sort of poisonous. Then I went to a doctor and he said, 'Why don't you try wearing gloves?' And I said, 'I need very tight gloves so I can actually feel the sticks.' 'Simple,' said the doctor. 'Use ladies' gloves.' So now I go to ladies' shops to buy gloves, as they have to be very tight. I get some strange looks! I say, 'It's OK. It's for my wife. We're the same size!' I also go to charity shops to find them. Sometimes I have to take the lining out of the inside to get them even tighter. At one point I tried to use golfing gloves, but they only make one! So I had to find a left-handed and right-handed golf pair. It's much easier with ladies' gloves and I find them much better than sticky tape. Especially with the sweat. When you're soaked, you always seem to lose a stick at the most important point, or you're breaking a stick and you go, 'Oh no!' as you don't have the time to change it.'"

Slade spent most of 1975 touring the US and Canada with acts like Aerosmith, ZZ Top, Kiss and Ten Years After. Slade had known Ten Years After since their 'N Between days in the sixties, playing the Mansfield Palais with them. Ric Lee, the drummer from Ten Years After, remembers that, when touring with Slade, he didn't see much of Don. "I used to hang out with Noddy and Jim. Don was still not awfully well memory-wise. I remember asking the guys, 'How is Don?' They said that he was OK, but still recovering. He was playing great though!"

What Ric doesn't remember is Slade covering 'Hear Me Calling'. "I forgot they covered that," he admits. Slade had heard and fallen in love with the song in the Marquee Club in London in the late sixties.

"The DJ played it," Don recalls, "and we just looked at each other and said, 'That would be great for us for stage,' and since then it was always our opener, but not on that tour."

"Because we were there," Ric catches on.

"Yes," Don laughs. "We couldn't go on before you and do it, but Alvin Lee was on about it quite a lot. He said that he had made quite a bit of money off our version of 'Hear Me Calling', because *Slade Alive!* was such a big album. He said that he'd probably made more money off our version than on his own. 'Hear Me Calling' did a lot of good for Slade and Ten Years After were the first band we bonded with in the sixties."

If Slade were buddies with the British bands Black Sabbath and Ten Years After, they were role models for the American group Kiss. "One thing I always say about Kiss is that they actually admitted that they had been influenced by Slade," Don says. "Gene Simmons told me that when he came to see us at the Felt Forum in 1974, he and Kiss would get our show and take it further. He actually admits it."

"We were always big fans of Slade," Gene agrees. "They were a band that went the distance and the extra mile. You've gotta tip your hat to a band like them, who made the money you spent on a ticket worth it. To this day, when I talk about Slade I can't stop talking about Noddy

Holder's incredible voice, his mirrored top hat, Dave Hill's Superyob guitar or their platform boots. They wrote simple but extremely effective meat and potatoes rock'n'roll songs, and that's very hard to do. And they wrote a lot of good songs."

As for the other bands on the road, Don says, "ZZ Top were a fantastic band to tour with. We used to open for them. We were told before the tour started that they were the most difficult band to work with – we wouldn't get anything, no soundchecks, nothing. But we got anything we wanted. When we toured with them, they didn't look like they do now; they were clean-shaven. They were great guys, but people don't realise how big a name they were. They were the biggest band in the Southern states, but anywhere else they didn't mean anything. When we toured with them on the West Coast, the Midwest and the North East, they were doing so much promotion to get their name known, almost like a new band. It took them a long time to really break America."

"When we toured with ZZ Top, they put Slade on the bill to help ZZ Top draw on the East Coast," says Swinn. "They couldn't draw the North East. They were great live, ZZ Top, in those days. On the centre stage they had a map of Texas, and they had a cow on stage and a vulture. The lights would black out and the spotlight would be on the vulture. Then one of the crew would pull the chain, so the vulture flew up in the air. But the vulture was always biting the crew, so they started feeding it marijuana to calm it down. One night, the lights went out, the spotlight hit the vulture and it was hanging upside down, completely stoned. What a laugh!"

"Aerosmith, on the other hand, I don't remember fondly," Don admits. "They were supporting us at one time and I remember our roadie J.J. was doing monitors on the side of the stage. The wife of one of the Aerosmith guys stood beside J.J. and he kept asking her to move out of the way while he was doing the monitor mixing. He asked her three times but she wouldn't move, so he just grabbed her and threw her off the stage. On a later date we supported them and they remembered what J.J. had done, so they gave us a hard time.

"We were doing some shows together and we'd had some good ones, but the next one was the big one in the LA Forum. And they fucked us completely. They wouldn't let us have a soundcheck as they said they were trying new material, but they were just stalling. When we did eventually go on stage, the monitors were going off, things like that and, of course, it had to be that one in Los Angeles. We never had a good concert there. Aerosmith really fucked it up for us and, after that night, we realised that we would never make it in LA."

"We also did some shows with Status Quo," Don says. "We always had a really good relationship with them, but America treated them the same way as us. It was like taking coals to Newcastle."

"Quo and Slade would do a few gigs together, as both bands became what can only be described as fucking huge," Bob Young says. "Our paths crossed occasionally, including a few gigs (and parties) in America and, as always, we shared a strong bond of being two British bands that had fought against the odds to go on to sell millions of records and enjoy the rewards of the years of hard work."

"When we did those shows together in America, Slade had become hard-nosed," says Francis Rossi. "It's not a criticism; it's just how it was getting. Things were changing. In the late sixties/early seventies, people were very friendly with each other, but then we all began to realise: they are fucking competition. We went to a gig for the soundcheck, and as soon as we got there there were Slade doing *their* soundcheck for as long as they could, to hold us from ours. That's a thing that goes on. I'm not saying that as a criticism or a problem; it was just what happened – the realities of life, as we were actually in competition. Still, I don't think we ever got on with anybody as well as we got on with Slade."

"Status Quo couldn't do anything over there though," Don states. "They said, 'We are banging our heads against a brick wall in America, while losing the rest of the world. We are never coming back here again.' They had the right approach to that. If it doesn't work, why keep on trying? I honestly wish we had done the same, because they were so right in doing that. While we were trying to crack America, we did neglect our big markets in Australia, England and the rest of Europe."

J.J., Charlie Newnham, Robbie Wilson and Haden Donovan were the basis of the road crew at that point, with Swinn as the tour manager.

"They were a great crew," Don says, "but Robbie Wilson was sent to jail in New Orleans for two days."

"When we played New Orleans, the crew went out drinking and they got blind drunk," Swinn recalls. "It was a really posh hotel and it had a big fountain in the foyer, so Robbie Wilson and one of the American guys decided to get in the fountain. Nobody there tried to stop them. Then when they went up to their room, the staff double-locked the door so they couldn't get out and they brought in the police. Robbie was kept in jail for two nights. The band went on, but I stayed behind to get him out of jail."

"That was one of the things that was kept from the band at the time," Don adds. "We were just told that he went AWOL. Not all of our crew got in trouble. Some of them were not as hard as they looked. Haden Donovan, for instance. He is built like a man-mountain and he looks menacing, but basically he's a big, soft teddy bear. I remember on Haden's first American tour with us he was introduced to Peter Kauff, our American agent. Peter said, 'How are you finding America?' Haden answered, 'I love it. The only thing I'm worried about is about being mugged.' And Peter Kauff said, 'Jesus Christ! This is a rugby player, a man-mountain! Who'd mug him?' It was hilarious!"

"I went with Slade to America in 1973, 1974 and 1975," Haden Donovan recalls. "During the 1975 tour we went to Canada as well and, one night in Winnipeg, we were playing snooker in a youth centre. Suddenly, there was a fire alarm and there was smoke and we though we've gotta get out. We walked through a main corridor to the front door and there was a girl on the phone. Noddy tapped her on the shoulder and said, 'There is a fire. You want to get out. I've saved your life.' Swinn immediately called the pressmen in England and, the next day, it was front page that Noddy had saved the girl's life. Rubbish!"

"A thing I remember of Canada is that we had been in Vancouver for some days and I had to get everybody's work permits for America," Swinn says. "I got the band's and the crew's, but I forgot about mine. We went to the airport and they refused to let me on the plane, so the band went on and I almost shit myself. I thought, what am I gonna do? The last plane left about eight o'clock at night to LA; I ran to the counter about five minutes before they were closing the gates. You could do that at that time and, because it was so late, they only wanted to see my passport. So I got into America legally."

After months of separation, the wives of the band came to America in September 1975, when Slade were touring the Midwest.

"Nod's girlfriend, Leandra, flew to New York with Louise and Jan," Don says. "Jan had Jade, her and Dave's baby daughter, with her as well. The girls were very concerned about New York, but we had never seen any trouble there so we had said that they weren't to worry. They were booked into a hotel the first night and we had said that they didn't have to leave the hotel if they didn't want to, and we would be back the next day. But they went out to change some money in the bank and then there was a bank robbery. A guy came in with a gun and everybody panicked. They got down on the floor and the girls were in hysterics. Jan even had the baby with her. Then the cops came and started shooting. A bullet flew through Louise's hair and a woman lying next to Leandra on the floor was hit.

"The cops actually killed the guy, and then everybody just got up again and carried on as if nothing had happened. A few people in the bank were hit by bullets, but it was the cops who had shot them, because the guy who robbed the bank had a toy gun. That was the girls' introduction to America!

"Mari actually came to America as well, but she stayed with friends in Los Angeles while we were touring so we hardly saw each other. We only spent a few days together and, when I came off touring, she went back to England."

Slade now started rehearing in the Bronx, also recording an album and some singles at the Record Plant.

"We used to stay at the Essex House a lot, Central Park South," says Swinn. "We blew some money in those days. When the wives came over, the band then stayed in studio apartments."

"We stayed at a place called Shelbourne," Don recalls. "We had suites there as it was almost like a hotel, except you couldn't get room service. They were so cheap, so we stayed there for about eight weeks while we did the album.

"The rehearsals were done in a garage in the Bronx and it was so hot there. Mitch, one of our American crew, was from the Bronx and that was how we came to rehearse there. It wasn't a very nice area but Mitch was a good guy. He used to call Dave 'Henry' because we called him 'H'. But whenever we were rehearsing, Mitch would always be there lying on the floor and he had all his friends there as well. This way it wasn't like a private rehearsal, as we always had these people lying on the floor listening to what we were doing."

Slade released one album and three singles while they were in America. The first single, 'In For A Penny', with 'Can You Just Imagine' on the B-side, came out in November 1975, while the second, 'Let's Call It Quits', in January 1976, had 'When The Chips Are Down' as a flip side. 'Let's Call It Quits' was inspired by Allen Toussaint's 'Play Something Sweet (Brickyard Blues)', but the inspiration got a little out of hand and Slade were sued for having 'borrowed' the melody. The case was settled out of court and, eventually, 'Let's Call It Quits' charted at number 11 in England, just like 'In For A Penny'. The two singles were to become Slade's last Top 20 entries for five years. The third single, 'Nobody's Fool', with 'LA Jinx' on the B-side, was released in April 1976.

"Noddy came up with the lyrics for 'LA Jinx' because we never could get anywhere in LA with our music," Don explains. "That single fared as badly as our concerts in LA. It didn't chart at all."

The fruitful American album sessions produced all three singles, and both tracks on the third single were included on the *Nobody's Fools* album. To promote the album, the fan club put the origin of its title down to April Fool's Day 1966, and publicised it as the date of Slade's first concert, although their real inauguration had been March 19 1966. The record itself was released in March 1976 and went to number 14 in the album chart.

"I liked working at the Record Plant where we recorded *Nobody's Fools*," says Don. "That particular album is actually my favourite Slade album. I like the sound on that, and it was a bit different for us. It was more a studio album than anything, and that was a new experience for us, as it was a whole different recording technique in New York. It was very well produced, and it was also the first time we used girl backing singers. Tasha Thomas was the main session singer to be commissioned and she found the other two girls. They were so good. They came and listened to the songs, and Tasha came up with a lot of the backing herself.

"That album didn't do particularly well for us in England at the time. It made it to the charts, but not like the others did. Still, that's my favourite recording."

In late1975, Slade went back to England to record promo videos for the new singles.

"I spent months and months in New York without working while they were back in England," Swinn recalls. "I had fallen in love, with both America and a Jewish princess, so I stayed in New York. There, Jackie and I had an apartment on 96th Street and Third Avenue."

Finally, in April 1976, Slade were off to America again. For three months they toured the States and Canada, this time with groups like Blue Öyster Cult, Dr Feelgood, Nazareth, UFO and Thin Lizzy. Phil Lynott from Thin Lizzy caught hepatitis on the tour and the rest of the tour party had to go to hospital for precautionary jabs.

"At least I met Ringo Starr one time, at a show we did at the Shrine in LA in April 1976," recalls Don. "I was on stage playing away and I looked to the side and saw Ringo. I went all cold. My hero was on the side of the stage! When we came off, we had a drink with him and he was really nice."

But in general, the West Coast didn't take that well to Slade. The East Coast and the Midwestern states liked the band, but the West Coast was a whole different thing; when touring there, they would lose more than £40,000 in five months.

"The size of the audience varied a lot," says Swinn. "In St Louis we could play to 12,000-13,000 people. Other places, we were lucky to get 200-300. I remember a gig in St Louis where I had $18,000 in my attaché case. I hid it behind the couch and locked the door. When I came back after the show, the door was still locked but the attaché case had gone. We found it on the roof of the building and my camera and tape recorder were missing, but the money I'd put in an envelope and slipped in the back was still in the case. Again, I never told the band, as mishaps like that sometimes happened. Like Charlie being arrested once in Memphis. The local promoter would hire police for security, but the local fire brigade wasn't getting a hand-out so they would come in and put a 'no smoking' sign in the auditorium. Of course, Charlie was smoking and they arrested him. The promoter said, 'Let him do the show,' and they did. After the show, Charlie came to the dressing room and he hid in the wardrobe. The fire chief came in with his gun out and said, 'Where is he?' And as the good friends that we were, we said, 'He's in the wardrobe!' They arrested him and put him in jail overnight."

The happiest time of the stay was the month spent in Canada, when touring with the wives in a minibus around the mining towns of British Columbia. "It was fantastic," says Don. "A really great month. I was more or less single then, as things had been shaky between Mari and myself for a long time. During that tour we split. She'd started seeing somebody else anyway, and when she left me, she took my early diaries with her. That's why today I only have my old diaries from 1976 and on."

Don's diaries make interesting reading, explaining how things were on the road and at home in the life of a rock musician. To quote Hunter S. Thompson, "The music business is a cruel and shallow money trench, a long plastic hallway where thieves and pimps run free, and good men die like dogs. There's also a negative side." That's exactly why not all that's written in Don's diaries can be repeated here.

The music business is full of people struggling for years to make it and, when they finally do, they get too drunk and stoned to enjoy it. Half of what they have done they can't remember and the other half is too sordid to tell. It's populated by people who sometimes live in a state of 'convenient' amnesia: they either can't or won't remember what they have been up to. It is probably safe to say that Don's *real* amnesia was almost a blessing in his line of work in not having to remember everything he had seen and done in his life as a musician.

That said, most of the diaries are notes to Don from himself about what he had done during the day and what he had to do the next day.

And then notes on TV programmes: nearly one third of each page is about different films and TV shows that Don had watched during the day. He writes down not only the names of the shows and films, but also the cast, the guest stars and other details; watching TV thus became the most mentioned topic in the diaries.

When Slade came off the Canadian tour, they did a couple of shows in New York. At that point, they had decided to take apartments in Manhattan for the summer. During the tour, Noddy's girlfriend, Leandra, found out that she was pregnant, so she went back to England. "Send some flowers to Nod about the baby," Don wrote in his diaries, before continuing, "I hope it doesn't come out a bottle of brandy!"

With Leandra in England, Noddy preferred to stay at the Mayflower Hotel on the south-west corner of Central Park, so he took an apartment there. The crew also stayed at the hotel, as Haden Donovan recalls: "We stayed in an apartment hotel and every day the band used to come to our room, because we went out shopping. We had bacon and eggs, and the band came for us to feed them. It had got worse and worse every time we went to America. On the 1976 tour, we did a lot of clubs. The crew got a lot less money than the band, but we were feeding them! Don was there early in the morning, because he was up first, but he wasn't eating anyway. He was just there to hang with the crew. We had a few good laughs."

Of the crew, only Swinn didn't stay at the hotel, living instead with his girlfriend Jackie, close to Jim and Dave. They had both found apartments on East 75th Street on the Upper East Side. Don lived downtown on East 24th Street, just on the edge of Greenwich Village.

"I was so lucky to get that apartment," Don recalls. "When we finally decided to stay in New York, I hadn't got a clue. What do I do? Where do I live? It's not like in England, where you go to an estate agent.

"A lot of people over there, when they go to work somewhere else for a few months they sublet their apartments so they won't lose them, and that was how I got my apartment. Swinn's girlfriend, Jackie, was from New York and I might have mentioned it at one time. I said to them, 'Do you have any friends who'll sublet their apartments?' and Jackie said, 'I'll ask around.'

"There was this lady named Helen, who was an actress, and she was going to the West Coast to work. I went around to meet her and have a look at the apartment and she said, 'You can have it for that duration,' and that was wonderful. Everything was there that you needed, with a laundrette downstairs in the basement. It was perfect for me. She said, 'Just pay the money to my bank account and I'll leave the key with your office.' Then she took me around the area to show me different places and that was it. Done!

"We were in Canada when I was supposed to take over the apartment. When we got back, she'd left the key at the office in New York and then I just took it over.

"I loved living in New York," Don continues. "When we'd been over before I had never liked it, but that was because I didn't know it. Now I did. We used to go to a club called Catch A Rising Star, and Monday nights were talent nights and people would get up, either comedians or singers or whatever. Every Monday this girl dressed as a cowgirl came on, singing and dancing. She was a total joke, she was *so* bad – most of them were – but the interesting thing was that Bill Cosby was always in the audience, writing the jokes down. The comedians in there probably didn't have a hope in hell, but he was nicking their jokes.

"Chas was a big fan of Bill Cosby. He had turned us on to him. Chas had a lot of records of his and I think he lent quite a few of them to Dave. He never got them back, of course. Al Pacino was also always in that club. Monday nights were great nights; that was when it was really full in there.

"But in New York, when I first went there, you saw all the hookers on the streets. I'd never experienced that before. It was so open! It was amazing. They were talking, joking and laughing with the cops. I couldn't believe it! While in New York, I was dating a black stripper called Janice Hill, the same name as Dave's wife. When she was stripping her stage name was Lumumba, and because of that she used to call me Bwana, so I made her walk behind me! She had a great sense of humour. She was from Chicago and she came to New York to spend some time with me, but it was difficult being an inter-racial couple in the States. When we went out to restaurants, they didn't want to serve her because

171

she was black. The first time I took her out, she said, 'Do you think it is a good idea?' and I didn't understand what she was talking about. 'I'm black,' she said, and I still didn't get it as I didn't think it a problem, but she was right. I was amazed that it was still like that over there."

After a month in New York, Slade finally decided to go back to England for good. "We couldn't get any airplay in the States," says Don. "The singles were considered too raunchy for the AM stations that played Top 40 material, and they weren't progressive enough for FM stations that concentrated on album tracks. We didn't want to be there because they didn't want us. We were rammed down the throats of promoters who really didn't want us and it wasn't going to happen. If Nod, Jim and Dave were honest with themselves they'd agree with me, but Chas wanted us to crack America. Dave used to call him in New York to say that we didn't want any more. 'Do you want to throw the towel in?' Chas would ask. To Chas, it was a personal defeat if he didn't crack the US with Slade because he had done that with the other bands, both The Animals and Jimi Hendrix. In all reality, Slade not really cracking America *was* our biggest bugbear; in my opinion and in hindsight, we should have stopped touring there and knocked it on the head after about the third tour maybe, in 1973. We were constantly banging our heads against a brick wall and it was getting embarrassing. We had some good concerts in certain areas, but not enough to warrant the time we spent there. We lost the rest of the world and a lot of money while trying to conquer America."

Slade left the United States without having reached their goal. The vast country was still unconquered. Shortly after they left, the band's Warner Brothers contract expired. It wasn't renewed.

16

The Lean Years

When Slade got back to England in August 1976, they started recording their next album at Advision Studios in London. In the same month, Noddy married Leandra.

"A friend of Nod's had this beautiful old mansion-type place, and that was where the wedding reception was," says Don. "Swinn was Noddy's best man. At that time, I still had the old flat in Wolverhampton and I was moving some stuff from there to the flat in Hampstead. I had my big stereo speakers in my car and one of the wedding guests thought it was my car stereo!"

In December 1976, Leandra gave birth to a baby girl, Charisse.

Don himself was no longer single. On a flight from America, he had struck up a friendship with an air hostess, who declared soon after they met that she was pregnant. She lived with him for the rest of 1976, but the couple split up when Don found out that the baby she was carrying had been conceived before he met her.

"I had started drinking again and it got worse and worse," Don admits. "I kept writing in my diaries, 'Please, stop drinking!' but I didn't take my own advice. Sometimes I woke up in the morning on the floor, not knowing what I'd been up to the night before. There were so many lost days."

Still, Don took pride in keeping up with his work. In January 1977, the single 'Gypsy Roadhog' was released with 'Forest Full Of Needles' on the B-side. It charted at number 48, but the BBC declined to give it a fair airing as the lyrics referred to a coke dealer. 'Gypsy Roadhog' was the first release on the new Barn label, formed by Chas Chandler as part of his management company, which also included Barn Music and Barn Publishing, as well as a recording studio.

"It was the old IBC studio that he bought," Don explains. "That was where The Bee Gees and Status Quo used to record in the early days. The name Barn came from the barn belonging to Chas' house near Gatwick Airport, where we sometimes used to rehearse. The new label was distributed through our old record company, Polydor, but without promotion."

Coinciding with the single, the compilation double album *The Story Of Slade* was released in Europe as well, but failed to chart. A new studio album, *Whatever Happened To Slade*, recorded at Advision, was released two months later. The title quoted some graffiti that could be seen for years on one of the Thames bridges in London. Jim Lea disliked the title and, because it veered towards heavy metal, complained about the sound as well.

"He said that the album didn't sound too good," Don wrote in his diaries. "Too much sibilance, he said."

Punk had emerged while Slade were in the USA and they tried to match that with a heavy album, although not with any success. Even though Slade had influenced some of the punk bands, as The Sex Pistols later admitted, they were no longer popular.

"When we released that album, we had flyers and posters around on walls and boards," Don says. "On one of them, next to the title *Whatever Happened To Slade*, someone had painted 'pass'. Wonderful! *Pass!*"

The album was the first Slade album since *Play It Loud* not to chart. A month later, the single 'Burning In The Heat Of Love'/'Ready Steady Kids' was released and it didn't chart either. 'Burning In The Heat Of Love' was originally entitled 'Witch Queen'.

With the new album out, Slade lined up an English tour, but first they were sent to Norway and Denmark with music writers flown there by Polydor to generate some advance publicity. The Danish gigs went especially well, but the British press was dismissing the band anyway, probably because Slade played their American set which was very different from what the press was used to. The Scandinavian tour came to a premature end due to a newspaper strike in Denmark.

In May, Slade embarked on their first UK tour for two years, playing clubs and universities. By then, Dave had shaved his head as a show of solidarity with punk and he stayed bald for 18 months. When touring, he often called for Don to shave the back of his head. In his diaries he wrote, "Remember the light in the bathroom looks like H's head."

After England, they continued to a string of gigs in both West and East Germany. In Hamburg they bumped into Kim Fowley, who was there with his new project, the band The Runaways.

"It was great meeting Kim Fowley again," Don recalls. "He looked just the same. The first thing he said when we met him was, 'I told you that you were going to be big stars!' It was so typical Kim. He was great and so eccentric. He would never change."

Not everything in Germany was as great as seeing Fowley again, especially not in East Germany, as Don was soon to learn. "In East Berlin, we were to do a TV show and I was kicked out of the TV studio for chewing gum," he remembers. "They were shouting at me in German and pushing me out of the studio. I couldn't think what I had done wrong. Then I saw the guy who was looking after us from Polydor. I said, 'Please, talk to them, I obviously did something wrong.' He then said, 'Take the chewing gum out of your mouth. It's Western decadence.' I didn't know!"

Eventually, a 45-minute Slade special was aired on East Germany's youth TV channel, featuring a studio concert and overdubbed band interviews. The special was later released as *Live At East Germany Television 1977*, which is quite misleading, as the concert showed Slade miming to 10 tracks in front of a young studio audience, strictly controlled by DDR security guards.

On their return to England, Slade recorded a show in Ipswich for a live album before going back to Advision to record on and off during the summer. They managed to put down tracks like 'Not Tonight Josephine', 'Wheels Ain't Coming Down', 'My Baby Left Me'/'That's All Right Mama' and others that would be released over the next few years.

Outside the studio, the band didn't see much of each other. Apart from calling each other regularly to ask what was on television – which seemed to be a pet occupation of theirs – they didn't mingle. "In those days with Slade, we very rarely saw each other socially," Don admits. "We did go out sometimes, but it wasn't normal practice. We only saw each other when we were recording or touring. When we'd finished touring, we'd go, 'OK, see you next week, or see you in a month's time.' But it was good. It always kept up a freshness when we were together."

Instead of socialising with the band, Don hung out with Jim's younger brother, Frank. Frank moved in with Don for most of 1977, but Don's diaries from that period make depressing reading, as he hit rock bottom both personally and financially. At that time, Frank was the drummer with the group Slack Alice and the pair led a fast-paced life, mostly at Don's expense. Don was constantly drunk, sometimes stoned, and the amount of women going in and out of his two flats in London and Wolverhampton was beyond reckoning. Don let each girl think she was the only one; to be fair though, most of the girls only hung out with Don because of his fame, so both partners were exploiting each other.

Due to his amnesia, Don was the living personification of rock'n'roll during this period, constantly forgetting or covering up his own doings, and he felt awful. He suffered from insomnia. He was on a permanent diet, consisting of absolutely no solid foods, but he gained weight because of the booze. He had started smoking cigarettes and was constantly going to the dentist, as he kept breaking his teeth. Money was scarce as the band owed £350,000 in income tax. Don had replaced his Jaguar with a Mini and contemplated selling his flat in Wolverhampton. His diaries were quite disorganised; a lot of the time, Don's handwriting was so bad due to drunkenness that he couldn't even decipher it himself. Often, the many women in his life took over the diaries and wrote them for him when he wasn't able to do so himself.

Marc Bolan died that September, but his was the only one of the 'big' rock star deaths that didn't get a mention in Don's diary. Usually, he was very particular about writing down the dates of fellow musicians passing away, but September 16 slipped through. That was how far out Don was at the time.

In the autumn of 1977, Don went with Nod and Jim to have his ears tested at a clinic in London. "It was some company that wanted to prove that people playing rock music damage their ears," Don recalls. "We had to sit behind a screen with headsets on. We had a buzzer and, when we heard a noise, we were to hit the button. I remember sitting there hearing absolutely nothing. The doctor came out from behind the screen. 'Haven't you heard anything?' And I hadn't. 'You've got problems!' he said. 'I've been feeding things through to you all the time.' So my test wasn't that good, but as I'd had hearing problems since my childhood, the doctor said, 'I'm not saying that it is the music that has affected you that way, but it probably hasn't helped.'"

Despite Don's bad hearing, Slade continued working. The Elvis medley 'My Baby Left Me'/'That's Alright Mama' was released in October with 'O.H.M.S.' on the B-side. It charted at number 32, but all was not well. Chas Chandler was unconvinced by what they were doing in the studio.

"He wasn't too impressed," Don admits. "When we'd switched to Barn, Chas was basically slagging Nod and Jim's writing. He said, 'All you are doing is rewriting other people's songs, instead of writing like you used to write. You don't listen to me any more.' But the thing was that we had started to grow and to learn things, and wanted to do it our way."

"Of course, Slade was Chas' doing, but I think he did a lot of things wrong," adds Swinn. "One criticism was that he wouldn't let them mature as artists. He saw them as a pop band and kept them like a pop band. But they had a lot more in them musically. I told him once, but he said, 'They are a pop band. They make their money from what they are.' He couldn't see them being anything else and that was a shame. The business had changed but Chas hadn't noticed."

"I don't think it was all Chas' fault," Don ponders. "We had tried to develop since our return from America, but Chas always said, 'That is not what you are all about.' I understand what he meant, but we couldn't have carried on with the music from the early seventies. He wouldn't let us grow and, had we carried on like he wanted, we would have lost respect. We always had respect within the music business."

"I don't think Chas was very good for Slade," Francis Rossi adds. "He did lots of things to various bands, Jimi Hendrix being one of them. He was not very nice. He screwed Slade and I didn't like it. He owned a studio, where we recorded, called the IBC, and I think that years later Chas sold it all very, very cheaply, which again I thought was wrong. Some people in our business do that sometimes; they fucking don't care. That wasn't very nice to Slade; Slade really should have owned that studio."

"Chandler was useless," Haden Donovan states. "I'm not speaking ill of the dead, but I never liked him. I'm not gonna start saying he was a wonderful human being when I didn't think he was. He was bombastic. He knew better than anybody else. I didn't argue with him, but I used to think, 'He doesn't know what he's talking about.'"

The relationship with Chas worsened as the group felt that he was using them to keep his own company afloat. It was only because Slade were on Barn that he could persuade Polydor to give Barn money for other acts he signed.

A miserable 1977 came to an end; although Don had had a lot of fun with Frank Lea, he wasn't sad when Frank moved out of his flat in early 1978.

Don's drum roadie, Willie Wright, moved in, not least because Don thrives on the company of others and is not fond of living alone. In February, he met a stripper called Annie – "She preferred to be called an exotic dancer," says Don – and she became his steady girlfriend, although Don was still seeing other women as well. By then he had gravitated from wine to vodka.

In January 1978, Slade did the odd gig in Germany and one at Reading University, but most of early 1978 was spent rehearsing for an upcoming tour and recording the next single, 'Give Us A Goal', with 'Daddio' on the B-side. The band went to Brighton and spent two days filming a promo video at Brighton Football Club's ground in February, but when the single was released in March their efforts weren't rewarded. It failed to chart.

Don's diary entries from those months of rehearsals are filled with notes like "End of Monkeys tom-tom-roll onto cymbal before Jim's violin break. Remember to stop at the end of Jim's violin solo – small gap, then around the tom-toms before the bass break." Don's amnesia was getting in the way; in the end, Jim recommended he try Vasopressin, a memory-enhancing drug. It didn't seem to help, as from mid-March Don stopped writing diaries for three weeks. One of these weeks was spent at Tittenhurst Park in Berkshire.

"That was where John Lennon used to live," Don says, "before he sold the place to Ringo. We went there because Chas wanted us to. It was this enormously big mansion and I remember that on the front door there was a plaque saying, 'This is not here'. That was great.

"Tittenhurst Park had a big recording studio and you could live there, so when we had ideas we'd say, 'Quick! Let's go record it!' That was *so* good. We could walk from the TV room or whatever and just go record something. It happens so many times that if you don't put it down on tape, you forget it. Even if we just recorded 30 seconds, at least we had it on tape so we could finish it off on a later date. We had the drums in the hallway; we put mikes up in the corner, out of the way, to get the big-room sound like the sound on stage. But nothing was ever used from that session. We were just getting pissed every night and stoned. I remember Jim and I used to walk around in the grounds there and suddenly we saw a dinosaur. We could see it through the trees and I thought, 'Nah, that's not a real one.' It turned out that Lennon had placed sculptures of dinosaurs all over the grounds."

While Don was neglecting his diaries, Noddy had his second daughter, Jessica, and the band spent some time in Olympic Studios, going over live recordings from Ipswich and New Jersey. They embarked on a UK tour doing universities and clubs for almost two months, running at a loss, just to keep the band on the road. It became customary to pay off the last tour's debts by doing another and "the magic 500" became a mantra. With 500 in the audience at clubs they would break even, and then they lived off the university gigs where they could sell more tickets. Sometimes they were billed with Geordie, sometimes with Nick Van Eede (who later formed the highly successful Cutting Crew) or a punky group named The Depressions, all managed by Chas Chandler.

"They still gave the audience their all," Swinn says. "It's very strange with artists. With almost every band I've worked with, when everything is perfect they're going to have a lousy show. But give them an empty club and they will give you the best show ever. Out of pride, I guess."

The troubled financial situation led to Don selling his Wolverhampton flat as well as most of the furniture in it, except for a pinball machine which ended up in Chas Chandler's office. As money was still scarce, he eventually had to sell his share in an Indian restaurant in Birmingham. Dave also suffered from tight finances and had to sell his Solihull house and move to Albrighton. Nod and Jim were better off, as they had additional income from their songwriting royalties. The band kept working on the live album at Olympic Studios and started recording a new studio album at Advision as well. 'Ruby Red' and 'It's Alright Buy Me' were recorded during that period, as was 'I'm Mad', for which Jim asked Don to listen to the drums on The Beatles' 'Strawberry Fields Forever' and to be more loose at sessions.

"Don was always a listener and would always do whatever was required of him," Jim comments.

Nevertheless, it was not a happy time in the studio, with tensions building between the band and Chas Chandler. Chandler thought that they were obsessing about sound instead of turning out commercial records, and the two sides argued a lot. Finally, it was agreed that Slade would produce themselves while Chas would stay on as their manager only.

Don's freefall to rock bottom wasn't over, though. In mid-June, he failed a breathalyser test and was banned from driving. "It was the days of the 'Don't drink and drive' campaign and I'd been drinking," Don explains. "I'd had a bottle of wine in my flat in London when Frank called and wanted me to go out. So we went to a place called Emmanuel's, which was open until six in the morning, and on the way back we got pulled over by the police. I tried to sit up and look sober, but the policeman said, 'Don't bother. I can see you've been drinking. So I just have to sort this out... What's the number of the car over there?' And I looked: 'What car?' 'Right!' and then I was pulled out of my car. The officer had been pointing at a police car on the other side of the road and I couldn't even see it! Of course, I failed the breathalyser test and had to go with the police to the station.

"In the cell, they asked if I'd do a blood test or a urine test. If it was a blood test, I'd have to pay for the doctor myself, so I said, 'I'll wee then,' but could I? I couldn't. So they had to send for the doctor and he came and did the blood test at five o'clock in the morning. They kept a sample of the blood and gave me one to take to my own doctor.

"When I left the station with Frank, I asked the officers if they'd call us a taxi, as I couldn't drive. They said, 'No!' and threw us out. As we walked down the street, the same police officers who'd pulled me over were driving by, smiling and waving.

"Later, I called Dr Dymond, my GP, to hear the result of the blood test. He just said, 'Sell your car!' My blood test was 185 against the limit of 80. I was banned from driving for a year and given a £120 fine, but at that time I didn't even regard it as a bad thing. I just thought, 'Great! Now I can drink even more! Eventually, my Mini was sold."

17

"I Want To Leave"

It is safe to say that, by summer 1978, Don was a problem drinker with very little control over his life. Only when it came to Slade did he show self-discipline. His life revolved around the band and, even though drink and memory loss made him unsure of himself, he kept working steadily.

On June 3, Slade began recording on their own for the very first time, working in the IBC/Barn studios. Very fittingly, the song was called 'I've Been Rejected'. Later, its title was changed to 'Rock'N'Roll Bolero'. The band then flew to Denmark to do a couple of gigs before going on to tour Poland for three weeks.

"Nick Van Eede supported us in Poland," Don recalls. "It was only him and his guitar on stage and he was fantastic. One night, Nod and myself put overalls and hats on like cleaners and, while he was playing, we went on stage behind him, sweeping the floor. He didn't realise until he saw the reaction of the audience. Quite hilarious! Van Eede always wanted a band but Chas said, 'No, you've got to stay solo.' Later, when he and Chas split, he formed Cutting Crew and went to number one in America!"

Slade were the first Western band to tour in Poland, although other acts had done one-off shows. They played outdoor concerts to audiences ranging between 10,000 and 15,000. "Eastern Europe was the only market that was open to them after punk had taken over," says Swinn, "but in those countries, it was terrible the way they treated the kids. Security would draw a chalk line in front of the stage and if anybody crossed it, they were beaten severely. Once, security got one kid and held him upside down by his ankles and kept hitting him in the crotch. It was scary."

Before leaving for the tour Annie had moved in with Don, but that didn't stop him from getting laid, getting drunk and being miserable in Poland. "I'm not very happy playing with the group," Don wrote in his diary. "Remember to say, 'I want to leave as I don't enjoy playing.'" An income tax bill of £20,000 may have had something to do with Don's low state of mind, but in general his feelings came from the sense of being a burden to the band because of his amnesia.

"I wasn't very happy with myself," he admits, "because I kept forgetting things and messing up on stage. It was so frustrating. I don't think people really realised how it was. You had the band there and you're the one who's fucking up all the time, with three people relying on you on stage. And because of what happened, I couldn't do anything about it. It was very hard mentally. I don't think people realised what I went through. I was going mental."

During the stay in Poland, Don was not the only one to screw things up though. The road crew did their bit as well, especially when Pope Paul VI died.

"We went past this big religious procession with lots of nuns, and some of the crew members insisted on mooning them and put their arses against the window," Swinn recalls. "We almost got deported for that. And then we had this little lighting guy, whom we used to call 'Creeping Jesus'. He was five foot nothing and a beatnik. He decided to check in to the hotel naked. I had to apologise every day to the manager.

"In the hotel, we had to use the prostitutes that the concierge was providing, but one of our truck drivers insisted on bringing his own prostitute to the hotel, so they called the police to come and arrest him. Chas then decided to create a diversion and started a fight in the bar, which gave the driver time to get out of his room and cross the roof of the hotel. I talked to the promoter the next day and said, 'Why didn't you just talk to Chas to solve the problem?' And the promoter said, 'Because Chas *is* the problem!' But the driver got his revenge. There was a huge fountain running all the way around the venue and he emptied a bottle of washing-up liquid into it."

"There were clouds of foam everywhere," Don recalls. "We were on stage, but the audience turned around and watched all this foam coming down. They hardly noticed us."

"The food was awful as well," Swinn adds. "We had to drink vodka for breakfast to keep the bacteria away."

"It was horrible, both the water and the food," says Don. "We all had dysentery; even the promoter came out in boils. It was like living during the war. You couldn't get the most basic things. When we threw bog rolls into the audience, like we always did during concerts because it looked great, like big streamers, the audience kept them. They couldn't even get toilet paper there. It was really a bit of an experience, although not always a pleasant one."

Don can vividly recall a group outing to Auschwitz, accompanied by their Polish interpreter. "We used to call him George," Don remembers. "He was always dead straight, but that day when we got on the coach, he was knocking whisky back. When we reached Auschwitz, he had passed out and we left him in the coach. We went to see the concentration camp and it was strange. What they had been doing was experimenting – take an arm off someone and try to put it on someone else, giving him three arms. Horrible! I still find it hard to believe that nobody knew the camp was there and that the Russians found it by accident. Somebody must have seen the smoke from the gas chambers, as so many people were killed there. We were shown around the museum and saw those big piles of human hair, teeth, false limbs and children's toys. I think the people who lived there must have been in denial, because they must have known of the camp.

"When we left the place, we realised that there was no grass on the ground, no leaves on the trees, no birds. Nothing but dead quiet for a few kilometres surrounding the camp. It was as if nature knew of the evil that was there and stayed away. It was very eerie. In the bus, George was still passed out, but we found out later that he lost part of his family in Auschwitz and that was why he didn't want to go."

On their return from Poland, Slade did a few gigs in Wales, but it seemed that the band were running out of luck. On August 28 they played the Stoneleigh Club in Porthcawl, where a club bouncer got mad at Nod and broke his nose. Two days later, the band went to the police station to make statements and the bouncer was charged with assault. A year later, they were summoned to give evidence at the magistrates' court in Porthcawl.

"We were all called to the box in turn," Don recalls, "and two days later he got three months in jail for hitting Nod."

On September 7, The Who's Keith Moon was found dead, but only Chas Chandler went to his funeral, as Slade were gigging at odd clubs and universities. They also played a string of nightclub dates at Bailey's clubs in Watford, Leicester and Blackburn, where Don tried to keep up with a slightly altered live show. "Use my Chinese cymbal in Bizet to replace the clacker," he wrote in his diary, "'God Save The Queen' is at the end of the bass solo. Remember the violin solo has been changed to 'Beautiful Day'." Despite his notes, he was picked up by the other members of the band for making errors.

Slade's first self-produced single, 'Rock'N'Roll Bolero', was released in October, with the Chas Chandler-produced track 'It's Alright Buy Me' on the B-side. The single didn't chart and neither did the new live album, *Slade Alive Volume II*, which was released three weeks later. The album was recorded at shows in New Jersey in 1976 and Ipswich in 1977, and the band had worked on it for more than a year. It was to be their final release through Polydor, as Barn's contract expired in 1978 and wasn't renewed. From now on they had to find distribution independently. Chas Chandler used his own money to press up singles, then went to Pinnacle for distribution.

Keith Altham came back as press agent and Slade fan Dave Kemp started a new fan club to replace the original one, which had petered out in 1977.

The new fan club was called the Slade Supporters Club. It ran until 1982, had 2,500 members at its peak and published a bi-monthly magazine, *Slade News*, for which the band finally did interviews themselves.

During the last couple of months of the year, there was not much positive news to write about. Slade played only three gigs in November and one in December, and Don's diary was filled with depressed entries. "Had the most awful day at IBC recording 'Don't Waste Your Time'," he wrote on November 7. "Made a pillock of myself having to play what I had to. I may be aimed out of the group."

Indeed, Don seemed to feel that he was wasting not only his own time, but also that of the rest of the group. Slade were making no progress whatsoever and, in December, they even had a meeting about splitting up... but Don forgot to go.

By now, Chas Chandler had started throwing bits of session work Don's way, calling on him to put percussion on Nick Van Eede's track 'Rock'N'Roll Fool' at Advision studios. During this miserable time, the only positive thing to be found in Don's diary is a phone call from Jim, who called to tell Don that he and his wife, Louise, had had a baby girl, Bonnie.

The year ended turbulently for Don when he and Annie went to a party where one of Don's other lady friends, a local girl from Wolverhampton, showed up. She stayed with the couple for two days – she didn't have a problem with Annie, but Annie had problems with her. As soon as the Wolverhampton girlfriend had gone back to the Black Country, Don swore never to see her again. Don was not the only one with domestic issues, and he soon teamed up with a fellow sufferer.

"I, too, had some problems at home," Andy Scott recalls, "and I'd got my own place in St John's Wood. Don was living in Hampstead and we used to meet up in a pub called The Swiss Cottage, between Hampstead and St John's Wood, to drink. Then we went on having a couple of pints here and a couple of pints there. Once we ended up in West Hampstead, in a place that was predominantly a gay club. I remember us arriving at the door and saying, 'We're as queer as they come!' basically to get in to get a drink. I remember thinking, 'I know this area. Why do I know this area?' Then I realised it was near the Decca studios!"

"I don't even recall that," Don laughs, "but that just showed how badly we needed a drink. We would even pass ourselves off as gay to get one!"

The new year meant gigs scattered all over England, and whenever the band were on the road, they travelled in two cars: "the happy car" with Don and Nod from London, and "the hospital car" with Jim and Dave from Wolverhampton. The cars were named by the crew.

"Everybody wanted to drive the happy car," Don recalls, "because Nod and myself would always stop and have a drink somewhere. Nobody wanted to drive the hospital car, because all Jim and Dave wanted was to go straight home after the gigs."

When not gigging, the band were at Portland Studios recording 'Lemme Love Into Ya', 'Hold On To Your Hats' and other tracks for a new album. They were not the only ones using the studio, as Jim had started a new group with his brother Frank. They called themselves The Dummies and did their own version of Slade's 1974 song 'When The Lights Are Out'. Don went in the studio with them to put tambourine on the track. "He played on tracks by The Dummies on more than one occasion," Jim reveals.

Slade went on a tour of Germany, Yugoslavia and Austria in March and April and, on their return, went back to the studio to do overdubs for their next single. 'Ginny Ginny'/'Dizzy Mama' was released in May 1979 and, despite the collectors' lure of yellow vinyl, it did not chart.

It was a strange and trying time for both Slade and Don. All during the summer, Don was afraid of being kicked out of the band because of Roy Wood. "I think the others know about Roy Wood by the things they've been dropping out these past weeks," Don wrote in his diary. "I may look for a new job. Nothing seems to be going our way."

Don had known Roy Wood since the sixties, when Wood played the same clubs and pubs as The 'N Betweens with his band The Move. In 1973, Slade had also been pitted against his glam band Wizzard, whose Christmas hit, 'I Wish It Could Be Christmas Everyday', lost out in the Christmas charts to 'Merry Xmas Everybody'.

"What was happening was that Haden Donovan's brother Dave played drums for Roy Wood," Don explains. "I used to go down to the sessions and Roy and myself would talk a lot. There was a mismatch somewhere, so the guys from Slade thought that Roy was trying to get me for his band."

The fear of being kicked out of Slade recurred several times during that period and, in the end, Don did indeed start looking for other employment. When not in the studio with Slade, he began rehearsing with Steve McNerney. "We used to call him Steve Pleaser," Don says, "because he used to be with a group called The Pleasers, a very early Beatles-type band."

Don now joined McNerney and other musicians for the purpose of forming a new band. For a year, Don rehearsed each Tuesday with the group, who called themselves M.P.H. and soon had EMI, Hansa and Phonogram interested as well as Muff Winwood, Steve Winwood's brother, who was an executive at Sony Records. The band started recording an album and, for the first time in a long time, Don felt happy. "Had a great day recording," he wrote in his diary. "Everything went really amazing." Their tapes caught the eye – or rather the ear – of John Fruin, former president of Polydor, who was now on the distribution side of the business, and M.P.H. decided on *80 M.P.H.* for an album title and had promo photos taken.

But as soon as Don had to work with Slade, he was miserable. He kept feeling inadequate, and thought that he was dragging the rest of the band down. He sent for a memory concentration course but that didn't help, so the only way he knew how to boost his self-confidence was by drinking to get rid of his inhibitions. But of course that only made things worse.

During spring, the Barn group of companies went bust and Chandler found himself owing Nod and Jim a lot of money. "Because of that, they purchased Slade's back catalogue of the time," Don says. "They got Chas' share of the business, so to speak, whereas Dave and I only kept our original percentages. Nod and Jim then formed Whild John Music; they still own the Polydor catalogue and can do with it as they please. Dave and myself didn't know at the time, but what it basically came to mean was that Nod and Jim didn't have to work, whereas Dave and I have to."

"Financially it's a roller-coaster, and I wasn't even asked my opinion. Nod went to Dave's house to talk about him and Jim now owning the Polydor catalogue and needing to recoup what Chas owed them. He said to Dave, 'We haven't worked out how much we're going to give you and Don yet,' knowing very well that they would give us nothing. I wasn't asked, I wasn't told, but that was quite common within the band. I remember one instance: the four of us were having a meeting, discussing our 'direction', when Jim said, 'I think we should do this and that and take this direction, what do you think, H?' I was left sitting there, not even being included! I almost got up and walked out. I now wish I had done. Later Dave said to me, 'You didn't say much.' I said, 'I might as well have not been there, as I wasn't even included.' It was always like that, but anyway; Nod and Jim took over the Polydor catalogue, whereas Dave and myself are still on the same deal as when Chas took us over as manager and producer in the sixties!"

Chas Chandler became a partner in Cheapskate, a label formed by Jim and his brother Frank. It released The Dummies' first single, featuring Don. Slade were also releasing new material, as both a single and an album came out in October, but again neither charted. The single was 'Sign Of The Times'/'Not Tonight Josephine', and the album, which at one point had been called *The Good, The Bad & The Ugly*, ended up with the title *Return To Base*. It was the first self-produced album that Slade had ever released.

They embarked on a tour of England and Scotland, and among the gigs was one at The Civic in Wolverhampton. Afterwards, Don's girlfriend, Annie, would report that Chas had been saying that the gig was not too good. By the end of the year, Slade once again had serious discussions about breaking up. The band's Rolls-Royce had been sold to cover debts and their new single, 'Okey Cokey'/'My Baby's Got It', which was released in November 1979, did not chart.

During December, Slade did a few gigs in London as well as in Guernsey. Haden Donovan rejoined the crew. "I'd left Slade in 1976 and I didn't do another tour for a while," he explains. "Then, in October 1979, I got a phone call asking me to go to London to put Don's drums right, because they were in such a state. I did what I could and then I went to watch the show from up in the balcony. It was at the London Music Machine. After a couple of numbers, one of Don's cymbals fell onto the stage and the kid who was supposed to be the drum roadie did nothing about it. So I went down the stairs, walked my way through the crowd — it was pretty full — went on the stage, got the cymbal, put it on and tied it down. When Slade came off, Don said, 'Thanks for doing that. It wouldn't have been done otherwise.' That was how bad things had gone. Then it was Christmas and, after that, they automatically assumed that I was going to tour with them at the end of January. And I was back. I stayed with them for all the gigs."

To Don, those late-1979 gigs weren't pleasant as, once again his bandmates moaned about tempos. "I think I'm out of the band," Don wrote in his diary, and he was not totally wrong. By late 1979, Chas Chandler had called Noddy and Jim to his office to say that he thought they should break away from Don and Dave and form a new group. Noddy and Jim wouldn't have it.

"I don't know what it was all about," Don says, "but it affected Nod a lot. Jim as well, actually, because I remember Jim saying that he couldn't sleep after Chas had suggested that. I can't ask Chas now, God bless him, about why it was his idea to split us up. Maybe it was because of Nod and Jim writing, whereas me and Dave didn't. I don't know."

Seen with the benefit of hindsight, it was probably more a matter of money. Noddy and Jim now owned Slade's back catalogue and without Slade having any blockbuster hits, they didn't earn much for Chandler. The Slade name had become stale and chances of increasing his income may have seemed more likely with a new band.

With the new decade came a new woman in Don's life. In late January 1980 he met Carol, who worked for British Telecom, and eventually he split up with Annie. With Carol, Don experienced a more steady domestic life; in fact it was his happiest and most settled time since childhood, although it wasn't all roses. Don's finances were still in a shambles and he had to sell his Platts Lane flat and buy a cheaper one in Mill Lane; still he was unable to pay his bills, even those from Rose Morris, which distributed Ludwig in England.

Slade went to Hednesford for a few days to record 'When I'm Dancin' I Ain't Fightin'. While there, Chandler had Don, Jim and Dave line up for photo sessions to launch his new label, Six Of The Best, which specialised in releasing six-track mini-albums on 12″ discs.

Don did a few gigs with Slade around England in the spring of 1980, but in spirit he had left the band and was now concentrating on starting over with Steve McNerney. It still didn't pay the rent, so Don had to tell Slade's accountant, Colin Newman, that he had to get a job to survive. It was suggested that instead of royalties and other profits, Don could get a wage from Chandler. Don resented that. "I'm not going to have a wage from Slade," he wrote in his diary. "I'd rather leave."

"It caused a bit of a rift," Don recalls. "I talked to Chas quite a few times about it and he said that he just wanted to help me out, but I think it was more than that. I wouldn't have it, as it seemed unfair to cut me off from any of the profits made by our records."

When the 12″ disc *Six Of The Best* was released in May on Chandler's new label, it featured the tracks 'Night Starvation', 'When I'm Dancin' I Ain't Fightin', 'I'm A Rocker', 'Don't Waste Your Time', 'Wheels Ain't Coming Down' and '9 To 5'. It failed to chart, and Slade met to discuss their management. The general view was that their records failed to sell due to lack of promotion, and their feelings towards Chandler chilled further.

During June, Slade toured in England and Wales. Jim's brother Frank had now become their driver, as their regular crew had been let go due to lack of money. Don wanted out as well. "I want to come clean and tell them I'm leaving," he wrote in his diary, but he didn't have the guts to go through with it. Instead, he opted out of recording with Slade, calling Jim to say he would be rehearsing with M.P.H. instead. "He didn't seem very pleased," Don wrote in his diary. A week later, on July 28 1980, Don headlined his diary page with the underlined text: "The day I told everyone I'm leaving the band."

Again, Slade were supposed to be in the studio, but this time Dave didn't show up. He now wanted out of the band altogether. He didn't want to tour or record any more, and Don followed his lead. He called his bandmates, as well as Swinn and Chas Chandler, to tell them that he wanted out of the group. Nobody seemed surprised, as they were all busy doing their own things. "Nod has sung on a Roy Wood session," Don wrote in his diary, "and Jim was working on a Dummies session, recording an album with Frank and Louise, so everything is on an open basis with Slade." Dave was opening his own business, hiring his Rolls-Royce out for weddings, and Don carried on working with M.P.H. and helping out Chandler as well, as the latter had promised M.P.H. studio time at Advision.

"At that time, Sue Wilkinson had recorded 'You Gotta Be A Hustler If You Wanna Get On'," says Don. "The record went to number 28 in the charts and Chas wanted me to go on *Top Of The Pops* with her to help promote the song."

So he did, but only a few days later he received a phone call from Swinn that would alter his life once more.

18

Fame Revisited

When Swinn called Don on August 18 he no longer worked with Slade. Swinn had married his girlfriend, Debbie, the year before and taken the job as tour manager for Saxon, as they paid him £250 a week, whereas Slade could offer only £80. Still, it was Swinn who told Don that Slade had been offered a slot at the 1980 Reading festival.

"Ozzy Osbourne's band had dropped out and we were asked to fill in," Don wrote in his diary. "H refused to do it, and Chas spent hours talking him around."

"We had broken up by then," Don recalls, "but Chas said, 'If you are going to go out, go out on a high,' and it just went. We hadn't played together for a long time and we only had a few days' rehearsal, then we were off."

"Out of the blue, I got a call from Noddy," Haden Donovan remembers. "He said, 'Listen, what are you doing next weekend?' I said, 'Nothing. Why?' He said, 'We're gonna do Reading. Will you do it?' I said, 'Of course I will.' Noddy said, 'I want you to look after it. Swinn is in Germany with Saxon and he's gonna get back in the afternoon, but I want you to make sure that the crew is there.' I got there lunchtime and pulled a few favours, as everyone knew me and they made it very easy for us to get on."

"Haden was driving with the crew, as he wanted to be there and make sure everything was all right, so we needed someone to drive the band," Don remembers. "Haden then suggested his brother David, so he became our driver. We had no backstage passes though, and we had to park in the public car park. Whitesnake headlined the festival but nobody knew that we were on, as we weren't even billed. When we had fought our way to the backstage area, we were asked, 'What are you doing here?'"

When Slade finally got on stage on the evening of Sunday, August 24, they showed the world what they were doing there, although from Don's diary entry one would think that the concert had been a bit of a flop. He wrote, "Had a so-so show. Everyone disagreed. Chas was there. Everybody got pissed."

Of course, Don was drunk when he wrote the entry and, as he noted, everyone else disagreed with his opinion of the show. Actually, Reading ranks as one of Slade's greatest triumphs, and the following week the band were front-page news again.

"I came back to do the Reading show, although I no longer worked for Slade," says Swinn. "I remember talking to the manager of Def Leppard and he said the worst mistake he'd ever made was to let them go on *after* Slade. They had refused to go on *before* them, but now they regretted it, as there was no way they could follow their act. It was Lincoln all over again. Reading was a musicians' festival and they won them over. They had split up because they were broke basically, but Reading was the regeneration of the band. They came back as a heavy band and so much more like they were before their pop success. They returned to what they were."

"It was probably the most memorable gig I ever witnessed," Haden Donovan agrees. "It was out of this world. The next Tuesday, I got a phone call from Nod saying, 'A week from Saturday, we're gonna do a festival in France. Swinn is gonna be away, will you be in charge?' So I became the tour manager."

The Reading concert was recorded for the BBC. After the audiotapes had been mixed they were sent to DJ Tommy Vance, who played them on his radio show in September.

The Reading appearance changed everything for the band, but Don still carried on with what he had been doing, rehearsing with M.P.H. and doing a new *Top Of The Pops* with Sue Wilkinson, who was still in the charts. Don's pessimism regarding a second coming of Slade seemed to be justified when the band played a festival in Belgium in early September. "Didn't have a very good show," he wrote. "Everyone was down." So Don put his heart into M.P.H., as they seemed so much more successful. They were even approached by Tommy Boyce, one half of Boyce & Hart, who had been responsible for many of the early Monkees hits, as he wanted to produce them.

When Belgian TV came to Barn to film Slade that September, Steve McNerney was a bit worried about M.P.H.'s future, but Don put his mind at ease. Still Don rehearsed with Slade, but nothing seemed to rock his decision of sticking with M.P.H., especially as Jim missed some of the rehearsals to do the *Swap Shop* TV show with The Dummies.

On September 26, Don headlined his diary page: "The day we heard John Bonham was found dead. I can't believe it." On the same day, Slade released their first record on the Cheapskate label, the *Live At Reading* EP, a release that Chas Chandler had been against. It became their first chart entry for three years, climbing to number 44 in the UK singles listings. After that, Don was no longer that cocksure about leaving Slade. "Remember Chas and Nod talking to me about Slade," he wrote in his dairy. "I may have said I was out." Soon afterwards, M.P.H. were advertising for a new drummer in *Melody Maker*.

When the live EP was released, Slade were touring England and Scotland for a month with Haden Donovan and engineer Charlie Newnham as the backbone of the crew. "We did a tour of small venues," Haden recalls. "We did a lot of venues that we'd done in July with nobody in, and now there were queues around the block. And that was wonderful. It just couldn't be bettered. U2 supported us at one of the gigs in London. Just wonderful."

His brother Dave recalls those times as being not quite as wonderful, but highly amusing all the same. "I did Reading with Slade, as from 1980 I used to drive them. That's how I got to know them all really well. Jim always seemed a likeable guy, mean as a church mouse and insolent. Dave is a very nice bloke, but he's a strutting peacock. He doesn't know when he's on show or when he's private. Nod is a very funny man, but very true to his sign, which is Gemini. When he opened the door to get into the car, I never knew *which* Noddy Holder would get in. If it was the nice one, we would be chatting and joking; if it was the other one, I'd just chuck a pack of cigarettes on the dashboard and totally ignore him. That was the best way.

"One night, we went back into London after a gig and we dropped Noddy off at his place by the Thames and went north, up to where Don lived, in Hampstead, to drop him off at his flat. He was very, very drunk, and he realised that he hadn't got his house key hanging off his belt. So, in the middle of the street, he got his case open and he got everything out. He was well oiled and was getting very, very frantic about it. Dave Hill and Jimmy Lea were in the car and Jim said, 'Just come and stay with me.' So we got him back in the car and we drove to Highgate, where Jim lived.

"Jim's flat was on the top floor, three storeys, and Jim had his bedroom. Dave decided that he was quite happy on a settee in the living room and me and Don had the double bed in the spare bedroom. Which I wasn't looking forward to! I'd rather be on the other settee, but they were insistent that I stayed with Don. John Bonham had just died a very short period before of asphyxiation following alcohol consumption. So, I ended up in the bed with Don, which was all right as he went straight to sleep. I slept with my back to him. At that time I had very long hair; in the middle of the night, Don woke up, saw long hair and, in his alcoholic haze, he tried to mount me! It wasn't nice and he was very, very sorry when he realised! Then he went to the bathroom to let it die down a bit, I hope. The bathroom was on the opposite side of the corridor. I heard the flush go and the door shut, but it was the front door and I thought, 'Oh God!' So I put on my clothes and raced down to see him wandering down the street with absolutely nothing on. Luckily, I managed to turn him round and get him back into the flat. He was OK, but I slept in the chair all night!"

The UK tour was followed by a few gigs in Luxembourg and Belgium. Don's drinking was as bad as ever, as an entry dated October 26 bears witness.

In Haden Donovan's neat handwriting, it says, "Haden put me to bed and wrote diary at 3.15 a.m." The entry was written after a gig in Brussels. That was the kind of service Haden Donovan gave as tour manager!

"Don was changed after the accident," Haden explains. "He kept asking the same questions all the time, as he'd lost his short-term memory. When I became the tour manager and he asked the same thing two or three times, I said to him: 'Put it in the diary and look at it.' But sometimes, Don's writing was so bad, because of him drinking, that I wrote it down myself. If Don wrote it, you couldn't read it."

By the end of October, Slade demanded a new contract with Chas Chandler, who was not happy. Slade offered him 10% as manager, but he wouldn't accept that as he was used to a much higher percentage. He was very disappointed. He had just negotiated a deal with Polydor for the release of a compilation album, *Slade Smashes*, and when it came out in November, it became their first album to chart in four years. It went to number 21 and stayed on the charts for a year, selling more than 200,000 copies.

With renewed success, a new team spirit seemed to have emerged within Slade. They started seeing more of each other. They had to, because increased touring and recording also meant an increase in rehearsals.

It had always been routine for Slade to rehearse for a few days in the Midlands before touring or recording, and now Don's trips from London to the Black Country became more frequent. Usually they would rehearse in the village halls of either Cannock or Coseley, sometimes in the Lafayette Club in Wolverhampton as well. Whenever back home, as Don put it, he stayed at his parents' house and visited his brother, sisters and their families, especially his nephew Ian, Derek's son, who was close to Don's heart and almost like a substitute son for him. "I always used to play football or pool with him," Don recalls, "or take him with me for reheasals. We were very close."

When, on the other hand, the band were recording in London, Dave always stayed at Don's place for the duration, the two of them usually going for a curry before bedtime.

"I stayed at Don's occasionally," says Dave, "not sure whether we were recording or just down for some shopping for stage gear. Sharing a bed with Don was an experience, to say the least! His teeth used to chatter in the night when he was asleep; one night, I thought he was going to bite me! It was like sleeping next to a beaver! A bit like a sketch from *The Morecambe & Wise Show*."

Jim used to come to Don's flat as well, bringing the rehearsal tapes or borrowing Don's black suit for official dos and trying on his stage pants.

"Jim would never buy any clothes," Don laughs. "He always borrowed mine. 'Do you have a black suit?' 'Yes, Jim.' Me and Dave still joke about it, because he was such a cheapskate."

Only Nod didn't seem to visit Don's place, absorbed as he was in his family life in London with his wife and two daughters.

In early November, the band went to Barn to mix the crowd singing 'Merry Xmas Everybody' from Reading with 'Okey Cokey' for a new EP. The B-side was a live version of 'Get Down Get With It'. The *Xmas Ear Bender* EP was released on the Cheapskate label and went to number 70 in the charts. Chas Chandler got RCA to help promote the EP in exchange for The Depressions, a previous Barn label signing, being on the bill on Slade's next UK tour in November and December.

Before the Reading festival, Slade had sometimes played to audiences amounting to only a few hundred people, but now they could sell out venues with capacities of 3,000. A concert in Sunderland on December 6 had to be cancelled, though, as Haden Donovan had to take Jim to hospital with gastroenteritis after the show the night before. Two nights later, on December 8, Don headlined his diary page with the words, "John Lennon was shot dead in New York."

"When it happened, I had the radio on in the morning and every other record was a Beatles record," Don remembers. "It must be someone's birthday, I thought, but it seemed *too* many records. Then it came on the news and I felt really strange. I think everybody remembers where they were when they heard that John Lennon had been killed, almost like when John F. Kennedy was assassinated in 1963. I remember that it was Johnny Howells' father who told me about that. He said, 'Some bastard shot President Kennedy.' Things like that you never forget."

★　★　★

January 2, 1981, saw Slade starting the year in the studio, working for three days on a new single, 'We'll Bring The House Down'. Jim had been inspired by the ovation Slade had received at a show in Belgium where their encores had been delayed. Afterwards, the whole band went to Don's flat to talk about putting an album together in case the single took off. They also filmed promo videos at Granada Studios in Manchester, for both the new single and 'Mama Weer All Crazee Now'.

'We'll Bring The House Down' was released in mid-January with 'Hold On To Your Hats' on the B-side, and within a month it went to number 10 in the charts. It was their first Top 10 single in six years, since 'Far Far Away'. Slade appeared on *Top Of The Pops* and, shortly afterwards, started mixing their next album.

It was indeed a fertile time, and not only work-wise. In early February, Jim called Don to say that he and Louise now had a baby boy, Kristian. A couple of weeks later Dave was on the phone, saying that he and Jan now had a son, Sam, as well. By then Slade had finished the new album, although five of the 10 tracks were repeated from the 1979 album *Return To Base*. The new album was named *We'll Bring The House Down* and released in March. It charted at number 25.

A new single, 'Wheels Ain't Coming Down'/'Not Tonight Josephine' came out that same month, reaching only a disappointing number 60 in the charts. Both tracks had been recorded three years earlier for the *Return To Base* album. Noddy's lyrics to 'Wheels Ain't Coming Down' were about an experience he and Jim had in America, when they had come close to crashing in an aeroplane.

With the two new releases out, Don went with Noddy to Chas Chandler's office to talk about signing a deal with RCA. Chandler wanted to include a distribution deal for Barn and Cheapskate and, during the next few months, he and the band had several meetings about this. In April they reached an agreement and the band signed, although Slade dissented on the point that Chandler had made the distribution deal with RCA for the whole label and not for Slade only. A few days later, they went on a short tour of Switzerland and Germany as support for Whitesnake. Chandler was with them for some of the tour, but feelings were cold between the two parties. "Don't go to the office, as

Frank isn't in. I don't want to see Chas," Don wrote in his diary upon their return from the Whitesnake tour.

At that point it was mostly Frank Lea who looked after Slade. At Cheapskate Jim took care of the music, Chandler the money and Frank did everything else. When Frank realised that Chandler had done nothing to promote the new releases they had a big bust-up. The band were also extremely discontented about Chandler's seeming lack of interest in them. The final straw came when Slade wanted their next single to be 'Knuckle Sandwich Nancy'. Noddy had written the lyrics about the incident with the nightclub bouncer who broke his nose in Porthcawl, but Chandler was against the release. The single came out in May anyway, with 'I'm Mad' on the B-side, but it didn't chart. The band stood by their decision though, and felt it was now time for them to start managing themselves, since they were already producing themselves anyway.

A showdown with Chandler was put on hold for a few weeks while Slade did some UK gigs in May and June, as well as festivals in Holland and Belgium. They played 'Knuckle Sandwich Nancy' during the shows and Don wrote down in his diary how to remember cues for the song on stage: "H starts freaky guitars, I join in with the drum riff + bring the rest in as per record. The end, the others go to the front finagling, I bring them in with open roll + 3 end snare bits to the end." Laconically, he added, "Nod was trying to get me to elaborate on my drums intro to Jim's violin solo, I wasn't too keen as usual." Because of his amnesia, Don lacked the confidence to expand his intro.

In May, Slade went to Holland where their performance at the Lochem Festival was taped for Dutch television. Only three of the songs made it through to the TV screen but, as usual, what appeared on TV showed the band giving their audience the full whack.

On their return to England, Noddy was elected to tell Chas Chandler that Slade were finished with him. At the time nobody else was meant to know, because of the RCA deal, but during rehearsals in Coseley, the band talked extensively about their situation. Don noted in his diary, "We chatted about not paying Chas' commission on future royalties on the present RCA deal, which he said was through him. Nod said it would save a lot of problems if we did. H, Jim and myself didn't want to."

In the end, Chandler signed Slade directly to RCA and sold his interests in the Barn and Cheapskate companies. Slade would manage themselves thereafter, with the aid of their London-based accountant, Colin Newman.

"Actually, it was a great deal that Chas got us with RCA," Don admits. "The percentage deal was fantastic, so we were very content. We then formed Perseverance, our own holding company."

In August, Slade appeared at the Monsters of Rock Festival at Castle Donington, where AC/DC headlined. "We had a great show," Don wrote in his diary, "the reaction was great." Again, they were the darlings of the music press and they started recording a new single and an album at Portland Studios.

"It was almost like Reading," Don says. "We had a great gig and a great response. It worked well and, from then on, we were seen as a heavy band."

With the renewed success, Don's amnesia spawned new media coverage. In January, *TV Times* had printed a new interview with him regarding his amnesia and he did a few TV shows, among them *Where There's Life* with Adam Hart-Davis for Yorkshire Television. After the broadcast, Don got a letter from a lady named Valerie Austin.

"She had the same problem as me and had been cured through hypnosis by this American doctor named Gil Boyne," says Don. "He was in London doing seminars and Valerie Austin had already talked to him about me. I got his number and he said for me to come and see him.

"He hypnotised me for two and a half hours, but I thought it was only five minutes! I went straight away apparently. The doctor went right back to when I was seven, through the time in the Scouts, the accident and hospital. I was still sort of conscious when the things came out of me, but I didn't realise that afterwards. I didn't really remember what I'd said.

"Afterwards I felt great. Gil Boyne told me I had been talking about the accident and that he managed to clear a few things out of me. When I left the place, I went to the studio and overdubbed the snares to 'She Brings Out The Devil In Me' in the toilet – I could do it straight away."

As soon as Don got home from the studio, he started the lyrics to a record for his children's book. When Don was 22, he had started writing a children's book called *Bibble Brick,* as since his teenage years, he had had the idea to write something that appealed to both children and adults. The outcome was a quirky, funny tale about a beach pebble named Bibble Brick and his big adventures in the world of boxing. Steve Megson, the son of the owner of The Trumpet in Bilston, did illustrations for it, but now Don wanted the book to be accompanied by an EP. He even contemplated band names and ended up with Boulder Brothers.

"I think more than anything with the amnesia, it is a confidence thing," Don ponders. "When you are confident, it is knocked out of you. That is the hardest thing to get back, and I got that briefly from hypnosis. It didn't help in the long run though. I got some memory-improvement cassettes from Gil Boyne to work with, but maybe I needed to have been hypnotised regularly, I don't know."

Slade's next single, 'Lock Up Your Daughters', was released in September 1981 and charted at number 29. It had 'Sign Of The Times' as a B-side and was the first single to be released through RCA under the new contract. At Portland Studios, the band made a promo film for the record, using Don's big lounge mirror as a prop, before going to Germany to promote the track on a TV show as well. It helped Slade reach a whole new audience. This was heavier rock and, especially in the European territories, it became a big hit, often reaching the top three.

Back in England, the band went to Coseley to rehearse prior to the final recordings for the new album. By then, all improvement from Don's hypnosis had faded and he spent ages doing a drum fill. "I couldn't do it right until 9.00," he wrote in his diary. Don and Jim also recorded a track on their own. "Don and I often put down basic tracks between us, with me on guitar and him on drums," Jim recalls.

The record also included 'M'Hat M'Coat', an instrumental penned by Dave, who had by then realised that financial security depended on songwriting royalties.

While recording in London, the band met up with Henry Weck from Brownsville Station. "During the autumn of 1981, I travelled to London to begin pre-production work with the English band More for an Atlantic Records album," Weck remembers. "Before heading back to the States, I rang Don to see if we might hook up for a while. He said they were going into a studio the next day to finish work on a new single and invited me to stop by. I met them there, as they were doing the final mix, and the five of us went off to a nearby pub for a pint, or two, or three, or more. Don, I noticed, was drinking what I thought might be water, but soon learnt it was straight-up vodka. His accident had damaged his sense of taste, so the vodka went down like water. For a good hour or more we all matched one another drink for drink, sharing joke after joke and story after story.

"Eventually, we all had to part ways and head down our respective paths for the night. I had a room at a hotel near Grosvenor Court and planned to take the Tube there from the pub. Don and I had another 'one for the road', then off we went together to the nearest Underground station. On the walk there, it became obvious that Don's vodka had gotten the better of his motor skills, as he didn't walk in the straightest of lines. I feared he might slip on the curb and fall in front of a passing car, so I began walking my own not-so-straight path between him and the curb. It must have been a ridiculous sight to see me, who is a vertically challenged 5ft 7in, running interference between the towering Don and brisk evening traffic!

"Despite ourselves we made it to the station, where I needed to look at the map to find my proper connections. After a minute or so, I turned to say goodnight to Don. He was gone! I walked up and down the street, calling his name, and finally gave up and headed to the hotel. All the way there, I had horrible visions of Don falling into traffic or onto the tracks in front of an oncoming train.

"Early the next morning, my phone rang and I was relieved to hear a cheery voice on the other end of the line saying, 'Hey mate, how about a bit of breakfast on your way to Heathrow?' It was my friend Don – alive and well!"

Slade appeared on *Top Of The Pops* in England and on *Top Pop* in Holland, and finally they had a master copy of the new album through Pye Records. The master was a good one, but Jim suggested that they stick with George Peckham.

"George Peckham used to cut our albums," Don explains. "He had played with the second incarnation of The Fourmost, but then he started to work in the cutting room at Apple for The Beatles. When Apple folded, he came to work at Chas' studio."

It was Jim's brother Frank who had arranged for the cut through Pye. He had left Cheapskate to start his own label, Speed Records, taking Jim's solo efforts with him after four single releases with The Dummies through Cheapskate.

Slade's new album, *Till Deaf Do Us Part*, was released in November 1981 as their first album on RCA. It went to number 68 in the charts and its cover became the focus of some press attention, as it showed an ear with a large nail in it. "There was an article in the *Express & Star* about how bad the album cover is," Don wrote in his diary. The criticism seemed to strike even harder because the *Express & Star* was the local paper in Wolverhampton and used to support its famous fellow townsmen.

"It was a bit of a blow to the stomach," says Don, "but then again, we were on our way down."

19

Waiting To Explode

The renewed success following Slade's hit appearance at Reading was slowly petering out. Although this was probably obvious to the band at the time, it took them a while to accept it. Slade went back to rehearsing at the Lafayette for their upcoming tour and a tour programme was put together featuring rather tongue-in-cheek questionnaires. Don revealed his love for Joanna Lumley and his favourite red-light area in Ginza, Tokyo. He then went on answering: "Worst record: finishing in 30 seconds. First sexual encounter: finishing in 30 seconds. Biggest thrill: finishing in 25 seconds." Attaboy, Don!

Don bought his usual 10 packets of chewing gum and did his laundry before the tour, but his trip to the laundrette didn't go unnoticed. "There was an article in *The Sun* saying I was seen with my suitcases at West Hampstead launderette," Don wrote in his diary. "It said I was either on hard times or a man of the people!" People still didn't seem to realise that even rock musicians have to wash their clothes now and then.

The UK tour in December saw a concert in Coventry cancelled due to heavy snow, and at the show at Keele University Don broke two foot pedals and a snare drum on stage and had to have new pedals express-couriered from Rose Morris, the Ludwig distributors in London.

Their gig in Newcastle was recorded for an upcoming album and, straightaway in the New Year, Slade were back in the studio going over the tapes. They only spent two days there, as Jim had to go to hospital to have his appendix out. There were complications and Don sent him a get-well card: "I'll lend you my stomach, if you'll lend me your brain. Love to what's left of you." Jim was released three days later.

On January 25, 1982, Don was invited to the Scouts' 75th anniversary lunch at the Houses of Parliament, an event that even Don would find hard to forget. "Keith Altham called one day to ask if it was true that I used to be a Scout. He had this invitation from the Scouts movement to go to their anniversary and he thought it would be great if I went in a Scout uniform. I went to a dress–hire place and managed to get one with the short trousers, just as my uniform used to look in the old days. I then decided to go to the anniversary on the bus. I wanted to see if I could get half-fare when wearing that uniform! When I was standing at the bus stop, Frank drove by, screamed to a halt and shouted, 'Get in the car! What are you doing, looking like that?' He then took me to the Houses of Parliament. When I walked into where the reception was held, who was the only one there in a Scout uniform? All the others were nicely dressed and I felt the blood rush from my head. I just wanted to get out and come in again, dressed like the rest. I think it was the wife of the former Prime Minister James Callaghan who came up to me and said, 'Is it your own uniform?' I wished the floor had opened beneath me!"

Straight after the anniversary lunch Don went to the studio, where Jim had been cutting 'Rock And Roll Preacher' for the German market. The two of them now edited it, along with Noddy. Whether Don was still in his Scout uniform is, however, uncertain.

In February, Don attended the wedding of Slade's British promoter, Mel Bush, in Bournemouth. "Apparently we got up and played," Don wrote in his diary. "I played tambourine, David Essex played drums, Jim played bass + Nod sang."

"David Essex was Mel Bush's best man at the wedding," Don says. "He used to play the drums originally, before his solo career."

"There was a little band hired to play at the wedding and two members of the band Sky – John Williams' band – were present," recalls Jim. "One was the Australian guitarist Kevin Peek and the other was the legendary bassist Herbie Flowers, who played on 'Walk On The Wild Side' and endless Bowie tracks, not to mention being a top session player on loads of hit records. David Essex used to be a drummer and wanted to play, so he got on stage with Herbie and Co. Things were going along nicely until David shouted at me to come up on stage and play bass. I went up, but Herbie did not want to give me the bass and David said, 'It's only fair to give someone else a turn.' I picked up the bass but had not got a plectrum, so I asked Kevin Peek if I could have his. He didn't want to give it to me, but I insisted. So we began to play, the guitarist had blood coming from his fingers. Then I called Nod up to do 'Get Down And Get With It'. Don got up like a shot and told David to get off the drums immediately or he would hit him, or words to that effect. It is worth mentioning that Don drank a lot in those days."

"When we got on stage, David Essex said to me, 'Fuck off, I'm playing drums!'" says Don, "and I ended up only playing tambourine."

The following months were spent rehearsing and recording the next album, *The Amazing Kamikaze Syndrome,* as well as a string of singles. In March 'Ruby Red'/'Funk Punk + Junk' was released as a double-pack single in a gatefold picture sleeve on RCA, with the bonus single 'Rock And Preacher'/'Take Me Bak 'Ome'. It charted at number 51 and Don's dad mistakenly thought that the new single was called 'Red Duster'.

Slade prepared for their upcoming UK tour and Don ordered a snare drum, stand, stool, two hi-hats, foot pedals, skins and cymbals from Vincent Bach International. Earlier that year, Rose Morris had lost the Ludwig deal to Vincent Bach International and, when Don showed up to pay for his equipment, the new dealers gave it to him for free. "When I picked my things up, I talked to a guy named Kenneth Fitzhugh," Don explains. "I got my chequebook out to pay the 40% of the factory price and he said, 'What are you doing?' I told him that I used to pay the balance. He said, 'Do you have to *pay* for them? That doesn't seem fair.' So he sent a fax to Chicago to the secretary, Kay Holsten, and when I called him the next day he said, 'You're now a full endorsee. Just come and pick up your things.' It was like Christmas Day."

Christmas didn't last long, as the endorsement was cancelled altogether three months later. Still, Don was in a good mood. When rehearsing at Keele University, he wrote in his diary: "I wasn't the only one to make mistakes. Yeah!"

"Don's titanic struggle with his short-term memory was always a problem but, once again, it was always dealt with through his enormous sense of humour," Jim adds. The tour took off in March and Slade brought along Elton John's old mixing desk, which they had bought for £1,200.

On their return they went back in the studio Dave was again staying with Don and one night had a visionary dream. "H got up and said he had a dream last night about us in America," Don wrote in his diary, and that was actually not a million miles from reality. The band had already started having meetings with Sharon Osbourne, who – although she had married Ozzy Osbourne the year before – still figured as Sharon Arden in Don's diaries. Sharon was the daughter of the 'Al Capone of pop', Don Arden, and she had worked for her father before managing Black Sabbath. Sharon told Slade that the American Geffen and Epic labels were interested in their music.

In the studio, things had started to get complicated again. With Chas Chandler gone, Jim saw himself as the natural leader when recording and that didn't sit well with the others. The band spent hour after hour in the studio, and eventually something had to be done. "We all had a chat about the atmosphere between us all in the studio," Don wrote in his diary. "Especially Jim not having patience." In the end, Jim decided he could just as well record all the guitars himself, but that decision was not fully welcomed either.

"Dave didn't like that obviously," Don says, "but Jim had written the songs and he knew how he wanted them to sound. This way we didn't have to rehearse before we did a track, so it worked out quicker."

Still, months were spent recording and mixing the song 'Ready To Explode', putting car-noise sound effects on the 24-track, having DJ Pete Drummond overdubbing racing commentary and Don playing bog-rock drums. The track was to become Slade's longest ever – eight minutes and 37 seconds – the idea being to match the music on Meat Loaf's theatrical album *Bat Out Of Hell*.

"The problem was that when we started recording that and the other tracks for the album, there was no entity any more," Don says. "It wasn't the band recording and we lost our style. It could have been anybody really. The tracks lost personality and it was just another heavy metal album."

The trouble in the studio echoed troubles around the world. In May, Argentina attacked the British fleet heading for the Falklands and Don followed the war very closely. It was one of the only non-music related issues to end up in his diaries. Another was the doings of the Royal Family, especially the births of the new princes. "That's quite odd, actually," Don admits. "I never realised that I took that many notes on them, but I guess that what was massive in the media also went into the diaries, in order to jog my memory. All things poignant went into the diaries and that was usually births or deaths!"

Slade played a festival in Finland during June, but a planned tour of Israel had to be cancelled, partly because of unrest in the region and partly because their equipment would have been impounded for months, so Slade would have missed other work.

As touring was the major source of income for Don and Dave, they decided to form a band of their own to help their finances now that Slade spent more time recording than touring. They named the band Life and started working in Alan O'Duffy's Point studio. "Alan O'Duffy was the one who used to be the engineer of many of Slade's early recordings," Don says. "With Life, he offered us his studio for free and he engineered our sessions as well."

Life did a reggae track, went over some songs for Don's *Bibble Brick* and generally alternated between the Point and Portland studios, sometimes taking O'Duffy with them to the Slade sessions. When they were overdubbing ambient drums on the track 'C'est La Vie', John Bassetts put sax on 'Slam The Hammer Down' during the same session and O'Duffy joined the others on backing vocals.

During August, Chas Chandler sold Portland Studios to Don Arden, and his company Jet moved in. A month later, Carol moved in with Don and the two of them went to the *Guinness Book Of Records* 500 Number Ones party. Jim and Dave were not present as they went the year before, but Noddy was there as well as the McCartneys.

"The party was held at Abbey Road," Don recalls, "and there were no cameras allowed. Carol had one in her bag anyway, so I went up to Linda McCartney, saying, 'Would Paul let me have my photo taken with him?' and she said, 'Of course!' and had Paul come over. She then took the camera off Carol and took the photo."

All through the year Don worked steadily with both Slade and Life. Besides Don and Dave, Bill Hunt from Wizzard was among the musicians in Life, as was bassist Craig Fenney.

"I first met Don when I saw Slade at Birmingham Odeon in the late seventies, I think," says Fenney, "but the first time I played with him was in 1982 with Life. Don is a great guy, very down to earth. He has a wicked sense of humour and he is very generous, in all senses of the word. He always has time for everyone he meets. He is a rock-solid drummer; when he locks into a groove, he is a delight to play with. Life's guitarist was Adrian Ingram, who is a well-respected jazz guitarist, and the singer was Curtis Little, whom I had worked with in a couple of Birmingham bands – again, a very well-respected singer, mainly in the soul genre. Then we had a black singer, Millie, who was brought in when we recorded at the Point. I think we only used her on one track. She was a reasonable pool player though!"

"Curtis was a really good singer," Don adds. "He did a lot of reggae. He was a white guy, but he had a black voice."

"We were in London for some of this time," Craig Fenney continues. "I stayed with Don in his flat and Curtis Little ended up sharing a hotel room with Dave Hill, for some reason. I don't think Curtis has altogether forgiven me for that yet!"

Don wrote lots of lyrics for Life and work progressed satisfactorily, although the same could not be said for Slade. With the live album done, they now concentrated on their next studio album and some singles, but things were not easy. Dave noticed some volume dips on Noddy's voice on 'C'est La Vie' and again Jim put it down to sibilance. Jim wanted producer credits on the track, which annoyed the others.

While the months were ticking by, tracks were slowly finished for the album. In the meantime, Don did a public appearance in Battersea Park, throwing wellies and keeping goal. He was mistaken for Alice Cooper on the train from Wolverhampton to London and he got up on stage and played with Dream Cycle 7. Dave's wife, Jan, gave birth to a daughter, Bibi, and Jim released a single on the Speed label under the pseudonym The China Dolls.

Then finally in November the new single, 'And Now The Waltz (C'est La Vie)' was released. It charted at number 50 and *Sounds* criticised it for its overproduced grandeur. "They were just playing to themselves," Swinn comments. "They weren't selling the image like they were before." The single had the live track 'Merry Xmas Everybody (Alive & Kickin')' on the B-side and was released on RCA.

The following month saw the release of a new single coupling 'Okey Cokey' and 'Get Down And Get With It', this time through Speed, RCA having given Slade a lease so that it could be released on Frank's label. Despite an initial release as a limited-edition picture disc, the single didn't chart. 'Okey Cokey' had never been liked, not even by fans, who in general voted it Slade's worst recording ever, despite it being a good party song.

The live album *Slade On Stage* was also released that December, and serves as a fitting document of the band's 1982 stage show. Gered Mankowitz shot the cover photos on a deserted motorway near Dartford Tunnel and the album charted at number 58. It would be a year before Slade's next release, but they didn't know that at the time. Neither did they know that their next single would be one of their biggest hits ever.

The *Slade On Stage* album coincided with their traditional Christmas UK tour. The band used a new PA system and Don noted in his diary that it was very clean. The Australian band Cold Chisel supported them during the second half of the tour, but things were going wrong. Noddy had a head cold and Jim was very ill with a stomach bug, so they had to skip soundchecks at some of the gigs. After a concert in Bournemouth, the band was banned because of the noise and the mess left by fans, and on the last night of the tour Don had to go to hospital.

"After the show, we went for a drink and I fell down some stairs," Don explains. "I split the back of my head open. Luckily I was drunk, so I didn't feel a thing."

In hospital, Don had stitches and was kept in for a couple of days because of concussion. He didn't mind. "I opened some of my champagne to have with the doctors and nurses," he wrote in his diary. Admittedly, there was cause for celebration despite the head injury. Even though the tour had been problematic, Slade made the front page of *Sounds*. The music paper that had panned 'C'es La Vie' now ran an amazing feature-length article and review of Slade's Hammersmith concert.

Don's drinking was getting worse and worse, as Haden Donovan remembers. "Don was the ultimate professional, considering he was heading towards becoming an alcoholic. He never drank before he went on stage. But afterwards, he'd walk off stage and go into the dressing room, take hold of the vodka bottle and the largest glass he could find and he'd almost fill it with vodka. But my brother David used to do the tonic-water trick in the dressing room. When the band were on stage during the show, David would take the vodka and hide it; when Don came off stage, he'd find a glass of tonic water instead but he'd think he was drinking vodka. Some of the crew thought it wrong, but I think it probably helped keep Don alive. And I said to them, 'If it keeps Don alive, it keeps you in a job and it keeps me in a job.'"

The Donovan brothers were not the only ones to be concerned about Don's drinking. His girlfriend, Carol, was too, but that didn't stop him.

"I used to drink at Spiral's, the wine bar around the corner from where we lived," Don says. "Arthur Atkins, who used to be one of the team on *Candid Camera* in the sixties, owned the bar with his wife, Anesta. The pubs and bars in England used to close at three o'clock in the afternoon, to reopen around six o'clock, but usually Arthur just let me drink at the bar during closing hours. Sometimes he wanted me to go though, so he could get home and have a nap before the evening rush. If I had a full glass, Arthur said I could take it with me and then you could see me walking down the street, trying not to spill it. I almost looked like John Cleese, doing his silly walks! I got strange looks from people passing by. In the end, I had more than 30 glasses at home from Arthur's wine bar.

"One night, I was in the bar with Nod and Alan Heywood, an accountant working for Colin Newman, and we'd had a lot to drink. I was going to call Carol to see if she wanted to come for a quick drink before closing time. Spiral's was on two floors and the payphone was up the stairs on the balcony. I was so drunk climbing up the stairs, but I reached the telephone and put the money in. Then I could suddenly feel myself going down the stairs backwards and I couldn't stop myself. I just went bop-bop-bop until I got to the ground floor. The entire bar went dead silent as everybody was watching me. I was lying on my back, feet in the air, but I still had the phone in my hand! I'd ripped it clear off the wall. I jumped up, walked over to the bar and put the phone down. Nod was laughing. He said, 'Well, is Carol coming?' and I went, 'It's engaged.'"

"Don has an amazing wit," Dave Donovan says. "It's one-liner wit. When they were on the climb again, around 1982, we were on the south coast of England and they visited a radio station called The Three Counties. They were sitting in a room around a table, the DJ and the four of Slade. Before they went on air, the DJ was talking about Slade and saying, 'I've been through all the archives and I can't find any of the Slade stuff anywhere.' And Don – as quick as a flash, before anybody could open their mouths – said, 'Have you looked in the bin?' And he's like that all the time. He really is."

Don continued recording with Life at The Point. When Virgin heard their track 'My Love', the label freaked. Keith Altham volunteered to do their publicity for free. They had promo photos sent to WEA, and EMI promised to try for a European deal for the band.

Don did sessions with Steve McNerney, with the intent of recording Sandy Nelson's 'Let There Be Drums', and his children's book *Bibble*

Brick became the centre of attention once more. Tony Blackburn promised to narrate it for radio but, in the end, it never happened.

During most of 1983 there were problems with RCA, and Slade contemplated whether to re-sign with them. A supposed European tour with Bob Seger didn't come together, and RCA wanted Slade to work with a producer in the studio to finish their new album.

"RCA wasn't happy with the things that we came up with," Don sighs, "so they wanted us to have a producer, but they were only prepared to pay for studio time."

The band were forced to pay the producer fees themselves and relations with the label became very strained. Don wrote in his diary: "The way things went, I don't think we'll be together much longer. I think the band is going to split up."

Once again, the common feeling was that Slade was only working to keep everyone else afloat. In the end, it was decided to take the RCA advances to help the group members in their individual projects. Noddy and Jim went on to produce the all-girl band Girlschool and Don went into RAK studios to put down tracks with Noddy and Jim, enabling Girlschool to hear the songs. "It sounds like 'Brown Sugar'!" he noted in his diary.

"Don always liked to come to the studio whenever I was recording with other people," recalls Jim, "to sprinkle his gregarious wit and talent onto the session."

Don then contemplated joining AC/DC when there was an opening for a drummer in their band. "Dave Donovan had tried out for them," Don says, "and he asked me if I was up for it as well. It didn't materialise, because I spoke to their tour manager who said that AC/DC didn't particularly want an established drummer. It could have been interesting, though."

The fan club, which was now kept afloat by Haden Donovan, called on Don to write a letter dispelling the rumours of Slade breaking up. It coincided with the re-release of the *Slade In Flame* album through the Action Replay label which came with a new sleeve design and marked the 3M video release of the film, but it failed to chart.

Donald George Powell ITV/REX FEATURES

"The morning after the night before of one of our infamous after-show parties," says Don. "'Sleepy In Seattle' I call this."
ANDREW BIRKIN

Don, assistant manager Johnny Steel, Dave, Chas Chandler and tour manager Graham 'Swin' Swinnerton hang around on the set of *Flame*. "It was 10 minutes filming and seven hours hanging around!" says Don. GERED MANKOWITZ

Boarding a plane on tour in America, 1974. The guy behind Dave is Russ Shaw, the promotion man from Warner Brothers.
ANDREW BIRKIN

Slade's infamous but dedicated road crew. Don: "Many a time was spent getting them out of jail!" GERED MANKOWITZ

Jim and Don at a party, late 1970s. Don: "I was always first there and last to leave!" DON POWELL

"The support from the fans was incredible after the accident in 1973 that left me with amnesia and permanent loss of smell and taste. Here I'm reading get well cards at my parents' home in Bilston." MIRRORPIX

Don: "It was hard for my stepson Andreas to stay awake at Slade concerts when he was younger!" DON POWELL

From skinheads to being honoured with a degree from Wolverhampton University, September 2002. PA/EMPICS

Don backstage with Gene Simmons in Denmark, 2013. "One of the nicest and most together guys in rock." DON POWELL

Hanne and Don on their wedding day, December 6, 2010, on the tiny beautiful Danish island Aeroe. DON POWELL

A new Slade line-up in Don's new Danish hometown Silkeborg, in 2007: John Berry (bass), 'H' (being 'H'), Mal McNulty (singer) and Don. MICHAEL VON WOWERN

Don with Francis Rossi of Status Quo in Sweden, August 2011. DON POWELL

"Our kids" in 2013. Left to right: Emilie's boyfriend Jakob, Emilie (24), their son August (our first grandchild), Anne Kirstine (26), Andreas' girlfriend Marie and finally Andreas (20). DON POWELL

Don in full throttle in Bournemouth, August 2011. HARRY HERD/REDFERNS

Don reading one of his many diaries in Lise's home in 2011. "We are probably about to do an interview for this biography!"
LISE LYNG FALKENBERG

"I did the fan club, because everybody had stopped doing it," Haden Donovan recalls. "One of the things you can't get off Slade in any way, shape or form is decisions – I mean, there was nothing to do. There was nothing to put in it any more."

In September, Slade were introduced to their new producer, John Punter, who had worked successfully with Roxy Music in the past. Punter was to produce two tracks and Slade went to Coseley to rehearse. One track was 'My Oh My', a song that Jim had written because he wanted to do something similar to Rod Stewart's 'Sailing', with a melody going in a loop. The other one was called 'Black And White', almost a Celtic jig, for which Jim had found inspiration listening to Noddy and Dave tuning up in the dressing room. The song was later renamed 'Run Runaway'. They then went in the studio for a couple of weeks.

The first thing John Punter did was to bring in a Linn drum, a drum computer, which Don had to learn how to operate. "We spent ages getting a drum sound before we put the basic tracks of 'Black And White' down," Don wrote in his diary. "I'm not a big fan of drum computers, but I can see how you can get sucked into these kinds of things," he admits. "We were in the studio once and there were some modern bands coming in and they had a drum computer there. I was just playing with it, trying it for about 15 minutes and it was fantastic! Then I thought, '*What am I doing!? What am I doing!?*' So I understand why they use a computer nowadays. It's easy to use in the studio, it's so cheap and you can take it in a taxi, instead of taking the drums in. But one thing it does lack is the human feel. That's the only thing. It's a machine, and that's it. There's no human element there. But it's just the way things go.

"It's like computers, how advanced they go all the time. One time we were in the studio and we'd done a really good take, but there was a little squeak on the foot pedal. I thought, gosh, just oil it and do that bit again! But the engineer said, 'No, it's OK, I'll just take that tape and erase that.' Three hours later, he was still there with his tape, listening and trying to find it. I said, 'I could have recorded an album by now!' When you think The Beatles' first album was cut in one day, and now it takes days to find a squeak on a tape!

"In any case, the sound was a bit clinical when we worked with John Punter, because he was very much a recording man. What we used to do was use the drum machine just for the click track, and I put the live drums on afterwards. It takes away the live thing when you use a computer, basically, and we didn't like that. It was after we had decided to try to record properly. Just do the drums, or just do the guitars and the vocal on top of that – but it didn't swing so much, as it wasn't *the band* in there playing. Punter took a lot of time getting a sound and, although the album has a good sound, the way we used to work was so much quicker. We could have done this half an hour ago, instead of messing around with machines.

"But John Punter was OK. We didn't have to hang around all the time. He'd say to me, 'You don't have to be in before four o'clock in the afternoon to do the drums.' Nod always did the vocals in the evenings, they did guitars or whatever earlier in the day, and I didn't have to be there until they needed the drums. That was good. So much better than sitting around all day, waiting. When you're there, you want to do something. I'll put on the kettle! I'll do the sandwiches! Anything, instead of just sitting there! And then, when you're finally on, you have lost all enthusiasm. So that way John Punter was good, but he wasn't the band."

Of the recordings, Don especially remembers doing 'My Oh My', which also became one of his favourite Slade ballads. "I remember 'My Oh My', because it was only Jim playing and Nod singing. There was this song by Billy Preston called 'That's The Way God Planned It'. I think George Harrison produced it and he got Ginger Baker to play drums on it. It was like a ballad, but he really lets go on the drums and I said to Jim, 'I'd love to play that on "My Oh My",' and Jim said, 'Fantastic!' I used it for the intro and at the very end, and I played it on rototoms – narrow drums, highly tuned, and you have more control over the different sounds on them."

The tracks were mixed at AIR Studios and shortly after Don wrote in his diary, "Nod said we may re-record a short version of 'Cum On Feel The Noize' next week, for an ad for America."

Don didn't have a clue as to what was happening on the other side of the pond and how that would affect Slade in the years to come.

20

Cracking America

In mid-1983, Quiet Riot released a version of 'Cum On Feel The Noize' that became a number one hit in America. What Slade hadn't been able to accomplish 10 years before, Quiet Riot now did with the effect that Slade were asked to come back to America. "Jim called to say CBS were interested in Slade for the States," wrote a baffled Don in his diary.

'My Oh My' was rushed out as a single and it went to number two in Britain and number one in most other European countries. The B-side was 'Keep Your Hands Off My Power Supply' and a 12″ version was also released, including the bonus track 'Don't Tame A Hurricane'.

RCA wanted the album out too, but Jim still demanded a producer's credit, which dismayed the rest of the band. In the end he got his way and was credited as producer, except for the two John Punter-produced tracks. *The Amazing Kamikaze Syndrome* was released in early December and went to number 49 in the album charts, whereas the annual re-release of 'Merry Xmas Everybody' went to number 20 in the singles charts. The releases coincided with Slade's Christmas 1983 UK tour.

With two singles in the Top 20, Slade were busy doing *Top Of The Pops* and other TV shows in England, Holland, Belgium, Germany, France and Sweden. One of the shows became a classic TV clip, with the band appearing on stage less than sober.

217

"We did a performance of 'MXE' at a Dutch TV show," Don explains. "We got there early and they had a bar in the studio. We had to wait and wait to get on, so we had a drink, then one more. We were there for maybe two hours and when we were finally on, we were just so drunk! We went totally mad, especially me on the drums. It was great! Those were the days!"

Don's resemblance to Animal from *The Muppet Show* was striking, but for a hard drinker, like he was in those days, it was impossible to keep sober with the new goodwill of RCA, who were suddenly treating the band to champagne breakfasts.

A new stab at America was drawing close and the band met up with their accountant, Colin Newman, to go over a contract with CBS for America. "Sharon Osbourne got that contract for us," Don recalls. "Ozzy was on CBS and he was so successful that Sharon made them interested in us as well. It was a great deal percentage-wise and, with the videos and promotion, we were on the radio and MTV all the time. Sharon also got us a tour as special guests with Ozzy for eight weeks."

But before the band could leave for America, they had to shoot a promo video for the next single, 'Run Runaway'. "The video was filmed at Eastnor Castle, the same place as the wrap party where we got blamed for nicking the silverware," Don says. 'Run Runaway' was released in January 1984 with 'Two Track Stereo, One Track Mind' on the B-side and went to number seven in the UK charts. 'Run Runaway' was to become Slade's first release in America on CBS, along with a revised version of *The Amazing Kamikaze Syndrome* album. For the American market, the album was renamed *Keep Your Hands Off My Power Supply*, and had different sleeve art and a slightly amended track listing.

In early February, the band flew to America to see the ATI agency in New York and to meet with CBS. They did interviews and press photo sessions before flying back to England three days later to shoot another 'My Oh My' video, this time specifically for the American market. Then, finally, they were able to concentrate on rehearsing for the American tour.

Ozzy Osbourne's tour manager, Robert Alan, had got Don Ludwig drums for free for the tour, through Brent Webb at Vincent Bach International. "They weren't very happy about me not using Ludwig on *TOTP*," Don wrote in his diary. Now that Slade were back in the game, everybody wanted in on the action.

Slade did some gigs on their own in the States between March 21 and 27, before joining Ozzy Osbourne on the 28th. To illustrate the situation, snippets of Don's diary from that week read as follows:

21/3: in Lubbock: "Had a so-so first show – the power went off twice."

22/3: "We ended up on the plane for four hours, before we took off for Denver. The pilot couldn't take off because of snow in Denver."

23/3: in Denver: "A doctor came to see Jim and gave him a jab up the bum and some prescriptions."

24/3: in Colorado Springs: "The power blew twice while we were on stage tonight."

25/3: "Jim went to bed. Haden, Nod, H and myself watched *Cabaret*."

26/3: "The rest of the crew had arrived from Denver. I had coffee with them before I did some laundry."

27/3: "The concert in Reno was cancelled because of low ticket sales."

28/3: in San Francisco: "We had a dire show. We're going to come off the tour."

"That show was to be the first and last of us supporting Ozzy," Don says. "Jim became ill and, although we stayed on a little longer to do some interviews and promo work, he was really, really ill with hepatitis and we had to stop. Once again, America and Slade didn't hit it off and the whole thing was knocked on the head."

"They would have cracked America," Haden Donovan ponders, "supporting Ozzy, the biggest act on the road at the time. You just have to look at the supporting acts that Ozzy has had – every one has made it. They have all done well. And the fact that Sharon Osbourne was managing them; Sharon was amazing. Slade could have been up there. They would have been one of the big bands."

Jim Lea falling ill in America is often seen as 'the end of Slade' because it marked the end of the band's touring career. At the time, however, Jim's illness was regarded as a minor setback. Slade were set on conquering America and thereby the world. Don's diary goes on:

29/3   "We left for LA in Ozzy's bus. We drove for about seven hours."
30/3: "We spoke to Sharon about joining either the Billy Squier or REO Speedwagon tour in the near future. Sharon had been to speak to Jim earlier. He agreed to stay here to do the TV shows that were planned for us next week."
31/3: Don went to see Big Country in concert and at the after party in Los Angeles he met Carol Zimmerman, daughter of Bob Dylan.

"I remember somebody making a joke at the party," says Don. "Wouldn't it be funny if Dylan recorded 'Cum On Feel The Noize'? And they started singing it like Bob Dylan. I couldn't stop laughing!"

While Don enjoyed himself, Noddy hung out with Haden and Dave spent time at the Jehovah's Witnesses' Kingdom Hall. Dave's wife was a Jehovah's Witness and Dave had followed her into the religion.

"When Dave first became religious, I tore the last page out of his Bible without him knowing," Don laughs, "just to see if he noticed. He never did."

Don did interviews for *Kerrang!* and went to CBS and *Billboard* lunches. Finally, after five days, Jim emerged from his room. Slade then went on the *Solid Gold* TV show before flying to New York.

"When we reached the hotel, all the kids were outside waiting," Don recalls, "not for *us*, but for Duran Duran. John Taylor came to say hello and we had a drink in the bar with them. They were saying about being old fans of ours. In New York, we appeared on *Dance Party USA*. It was one of those Saturday morning kids' shows. They had a lot of those in America."

Slade performed both 'Run Runaway' and 'My Oh My' on the show, before flying back to England on April 7.

Back home, all was not well. An article about Don's fling with Bob Dylan's daughter was featured in the UK press.

"It wasn't in the papers until I had been back in England for a week," Don remembers. "Then there was a big story in one of the daily papers.

Carol threw it at me and just walked out. I thought, what's all this about? Then I saw the headline about 'Don Powell and Bob Dylan's daughter'. Oh God!"

Don and Carol had celebrated their fourth anniversary only three months earlier, but from now on they more or less led separate lives. Again Don dived into work, recording with Life and giving interviews to former *Melody Maker* writer Chris Charlesworth, a longtime friend and supporter of Slade, who was writing a book about them. Titled *Slade: Feel The Noize!*, it later became the bible for many Slade fans.

Although Jim was ill, Slade seemed on a roll. They decided to keep John Punter as their producer and were offered the Reading Festival as well as two shows with Elton John at Wembley. In May, the compilation album *Slade's Greats* was released by Polydor, reaching number 89. The band flew to Switzerland to appear at the Montreaux Golden Rose Pop Festival with Status Quo and Queen, and on their return went over the details of the festivals they were to play in Europe during the summer. They had meetings with Sharon Osbourne and planned an American tour with Billy Squier.

In mid–May 1984, Slade were back in the States and surprised to see that the video for 'Run Runaway' had gone to number four on MTV's video chart. "In America they released 'Run Runaway' first," says Don. "So they had the singles in reverse order. They really liked the video for that one, but over there they thought that the castle was where we lived. They thought it was our house!"

'Run Runaway' went to number 20 in the American charts, 'My Oh My' to number 37 and the album *Keep Your Hands Off My Power Supply* to number 33. In the seventies, Slade had only had two albums and four singles in the US Top 100, scattered over the decade; now, suddenly, they had an album and three singles in the charts at the same time – 'Slam The Hammer Down' being the third at number 92.

Slade maintained a busy schedule in America. In Los Angeles, they made an appearance promoting 'My Oh My' and 'Run Runaway' for *Solid Gold* and heard Quiet Riot's version of 'Mama Weer All Crazee Now'. They spent days doing interviews and appeared on *American Bandstand*, hosted by Dick Clark, before flying to Canada to do radio interviews and press for two days. Then it was back to America to do an in-store promo appearance at a mall in Buffalo; afterwards, they went to have a look at Niagara Falls.

"It was such an impressive thing," Don says. "When approaching the falls, we could actually hear the roar from a long way off and the view was just phenomenal. Unfortunately, we didn't have the time to go behind the falls. You could actually do that in a helicopter."

The band went to Cleveland to do interviews and a TV spot before playing at a carnival in a park. "It was absolutely awful," Don sighs, "because we had to mime to six album tracks. I remember at 'My Oh My', there is a gap before the drums come in and the guy who was working the tapes hadn't even listened to the record. So he stopped the tape. I counted the bars and came back in with the drums, and there was nothing there! Then he realised his mistake and made it even worse by starting the tape again, so the drum sound came in halfway through when I had started."

"A lot of bands were miming, but to see Slade mime! I thought, 'How terrible is *that*?'" Haden Donovan recalls. Don continues, "On the drive back to the hotel, Nod said, 'This is never, ever going to happen to this band again. If *this* is Slade, I'd rather finish.' At the time I didn't take any notice of it, because we'd all said things like that before.

"We went to New York that night to fly back to England the day after. When we reached the hotel, in each of our rooms there was a big bottle of champagne and a big bowl of fruit from CBS. They realised that what happened in Cleveland was wrong."

Don and his bandmates enjoyed the apology. "CBS had left us bottles of champagne which we took to the hotel restaurant to drink with our meal," he wrote in his diary. "We were contemplating selling them back to the hotel and splitting the money!"

"We flew back to England the next day, never to set foot in America as Slade again," Don adds.

Back in England, Don went with Jim and Noddy into Portland Studios to put down four tracks for the next album: 'Myzsterious Mizster Jones', 'I'll Be There', 'Hey Ho Wish You Well' and 'Love Is', the last of which never made it to the album and is now regarded by many as the unheard, 'lost' Slade track. "It was a rarity for songs that were written not to be recorded," Jim explains. "'Love Is' was one of those, as John Punter, the producer, was never happy with it."

The band recorded and mixed the album in different studios, such as Angel, RAK, Utopia, AIR and The Workhouse, throughout the year, but things were not going well. "My impression was that John Punter wasn't too happy with Jim while he was doing the guitar overdubs," Don wrote in his diary, before going on, "We heard the mixes from the last sessions, not very good. We all had it out with Punter, to say he was getting away from *our* sound."

"It wasn't Slade any more," Don recalls. "I wasn't happy at all and I remember Shaun Greenfield, our man at RCA at the time, said to Punter that they were great recordings, but the live feel had been taken away. And being a live band was what Slade was all about. John Punter was just a technical man; it works great for certain bands, but not Slade."

Noddy wasn't around much during that period, because he was going through a divorce from Leandra. Whenever he was in the studio, sessions usually ended up with him and Don going on a bender.

In July, Slade were lined up to appear on a TV show from the Grand Theatre in Wolverhampton with The Beverly Sisters, Frank Ifield, Roy Hudd and Julie Rogers. Don, Dave and Jim went to Portland to do the backing tracks prior to the show. "It was a complete joke," Don wrote in his diary. "H and Jim and myself put the medley of 'Take Me Bak 'Ome', 'Mama', 'My Oh My' and 'Run Runaway' down, but we decided we could say Jim was ill and pull the show." In the end, they didn't.

"It was like a variety show that we didn't want to be part of," Don explains. "They wanted us to play live, but we weren't sure what the equipment would be like. We said that we didn't want to do it, because we could end up looking like idiots. In the end, they did let us mime instead and Nod didn't have any objections like in America!"

At that time, Don was back with Ludwig drums. Brent Webb from the Vincent Bach International arranged a new deal, wherein Don got his sticks and skins free and 15 per cent off retail on everything else.

"One day Brent Webb called me," Don remembers. "He said, 'What are you doing?' 'Why?' 'Bill Ludwig III is over to do promotion for Ludwig in the European territory and he's in England for a week. Let's get together for lunch.' So we met and I reminded Bill Ludwig III that I had met him when he was a young boy in 1973, but he didn't remember. Then he talked about Ludwig's 75th anniversary and that they wanted to invite 75 drummers from throughout the world to come to Chicago. I got invited and I thought it was fantastic. Bill Ludwig III got Kay Holsten – she was still there – to send me all the details; I just had to book my flight and they sent me the money for it. Then I was told to send all my sizes through Vincent Bach International and I found that a bit odd, but the thing was that they were making dinner suits for all the drummers.

"On August 25 I flew to Chicago, but that weekend is totally lost to me, as it was in my drinking days. I got pissed on the plane on the way over and when I checked in to the hotel there was a big party with all the drummers, and they were all pissed and stoned. Don Brewer was there, Steve Palmer, Aynsley Dunbar, Roger Pope, Steve Negus and loads of others.

"We did a photograph shoot for a poster the next day in a big warehouse. Bill Ludwig II and III were there and Joe Morello, the famous jazz drummer from way back. All our suits were there, so we tried them on and had them altered to fit perfectly. Then they lined us up on big steps around a table with champagne on. Bill II and III sat at the table with Joe Morello, with the drummers in the background.

"They had security at the warehouse, because all the drummers tried to walk out with the dinner suits. We were told that these suits were not meant to be kept. I didn't understand that, because they were tailor-made for us – what would they do with them afterwards? But that was a lost weekend. Imagine 75 drummers at the same hotel. It was mad!"

On his return, Don sent Kay Holsten flowers to thank her for the invitation.

Although things had seemed fine when Slade got back from America, their new-found fame was dwindling. Summer came and went without them doing the planned festivals, and the Elton John shows were called off as well. When Slade's equipment finally came back from the States, Don's rototoms and their case with the guitar leads were missing. The rest of their gear was an absolute mess, as many of the flight cases had been damaged.

The band were having problems in the studio as well, mainly because Jim wanted more production credit on the material. "Ego me thinks," Don wrote in his diary, but eventually Jim got the producer's credit on 'Harmony', 'I Win You Lose' and 'Time To Rock', as well as credit for having arranged all of the tracks on the forthcoming album.

Slade recorded the video for their next single, 'All Join Hands', in Wandsworth. "The day Mrs. Ghandi was assassinated," Don noted in his diary. "I always thought she was a major player not only in politics but also in world society," says Don. "She was a key figure and that is probably why her death is mentioned in the diaries – the only one not of a rock musician. Usually, I never wrote down the deaths of heads of states or religion. When the Pope died, nothing. That's about how religious I am!"

The band appeared on *The Russell Harty Show* in Birmingham, but in general they did what they had always done when things looked dodgy: they buried themselves in solo projects. Don and Dave recorded with Life and Jim borrowed Don's Linn drums for some Gary Holton tracks that he was producing.

"I use the Linn drum to write on, basically," Don says. "And I also use it on stage, because of the things you can do with it. I can plug the drum mike into it and what I play on stage gets the Linn drum sound. It is a great thing to use if you're in a certain hall where you can't get a good acoustic sound. Then it sounds much better playing through the Linn."

As for Noddy, Don only saw him when they went out drinking with Ozzy Osbourne. "Went to Colin's and Nod was there," Don wrote in his diary in October. "Ozzy and Sharon turned up, we went to a fancy dress shop with Ozzy, so he could get a dress to go to the Iron Maiden show."

"Ozzy was going to sing with the band," Don remembers, "and he wanted a fancy dress to wear on stage. So we went to this shop and what was the first thing he tried on? A ballerina costume with pink tights and a tutu! Then he put a German helmet on and, although we said he looked silly, he kept it. We went to Hammersmith Odeon on the bus and Ozzy didn't care. That's why I love Ozzy; he would just sit there and talk in his tutu on the bus. At the bar at the Hammersmith Odeon, he was there with a Nazi helmet and the pink ballerina's outfit, drinking big glasses of beer and talking. Most of the people there went, 'Who *is* this?' It was great. And when he got on stage to sing 'Paranoid' with Iron Maiden, the place just went mental. It was incredible."

Don did a lot of drinking with Ozzy Osbourne in those days and he enjoyed it – being with Ozzy, you never knew what would happen next. "Ozzy and I always used to meet in Spirals, our watering hole on Finchley Road," Don recalls. "Ozzy lived about 100 yards one way and I lived 100 yards the other. Arthur, who owned the bar, always let us in about 10.30 a.m. so we could start our lunchtime sessions early! One day I was there getting 'happy' and saying to Arthur, 'Ozzy's late today,' and he agreed. Anyway, about an hour later Arthur came up to me and beckoned me to look in the direction of the entrance. Ozzy was standing there in all his glory, wearing a dress! Arthur and I were biting our lips, trying not to laugh, as Ozzy came towards us saying, 'My wife's got two cunts and I'm one of them.' It turned out Sharon had hidden all his clothes, so he wouldn't make our daily rendezvous. So he took one of her dresses and there he was. The power of the bottle, eh?"

It wasn't the only time that Sharon Osbourne objected to her husband drinking with Don. "Once Ozzy and myself were in the wine bar drinking," Don says, "and Arthur wanted to kick us out, as he wanted to sleep. Ozzy then suggested that we go back to his house to carry on drinking and that we could buy some wine off Arthur. Ozzy's driver, Pete, was with us. He was not drinking, obviously, and I turned to him and said, 'Is Sharon at home?' He went, 'Yes.' Then I asked, 'Do you think this is a good idea then?' 'No.' But Ozzy went, 'Fuck her!' Fuck this and fuck that. In the end I said, 'OK.' So we went to Ozzy's place and we walked up the driveway. I carried a lot of bottles of wine and I'd got my head down, walking. Then I heard Ozzy shout, 'Run!' I looked up and saw Sharon in the bedroom window with a shotgun. I just dropped the wine and ran down the driveway. We managed to get around the gate in time when she let a shot go. But the thing was that in the bottom of the driveway there was a brand-new BMW that the Osbournes had just taken possession of, and she blasted the whole side off it! I was shaking, but Ozzy was cursing and shouting. He went into the house and I could hear him and Sharon screaming and fighting, so I went home!"

Domestic problems weren't new to Don though, and in November, he decided to leave Carol for good. "I had started dating a girl who lived near Spirals," Don says. "One night I took her there and Carol was in there too. She was upstairs and I was downstairs with the other girl. And all the staff was killing themselves laughing, because they knew that Carol was there as well. The girl I was with went to the toilet. Carol followed her. Oh shit! Then Carol came over to me and she hit me, and then the other one came and she hit me too! So I had to leave the wine bar and I left the two of them drinking together."

In the end, Don moved in with his new love, leaving Carol in the flat. His diary entries were sparse around that time, as he left his diary in the flat as well.

Slade's next single, 'All Join Hands'/'Here's To...', came out in November on RCA. It went to number 15 in the charts and the band did *Top Of The Pops* and *Razzmatazz* in England, as well as a TV show in Germany, but the band was to suffer a new blow. On December 10, Don was more than baffled when he wrote in his diary, "H said Nod didn't want to tour any more."

21

Misery Seeks Company

Noddy not wanting to tour didn't really sink in with Don at first. He thought it was only a whim on Nod's behalf, as it had taken nine months since the last gig in America for Nod to say so. "Don's perception of Nod's touring attitude is bang on," Jim says. "It was a sort of 'cancer' growing within us."

"In August I started putting together a tour," Haden Donovan recalls. "The dates were all ready. Everything was done four months in advance and then, out of the blue, I suddenly got a phone call from Jim telling me that the tour was cancelled. I couldn't believe it."

Although the yearly UK Christmas tour didn't take place in 1984, Don was still busy working with Slade, recording and doing TV shows in England and Holland. The new year saw the band doing more TV in England, Germany, Finland and Norway, as well as filming promo videos for the tracks on the upcoming album. In mid-January, their next single, 'Seven Year Bitch', was out on RCA. It only went to number 60 in the charts and had 'Leave Them Girls Alone' on the B-side. By then, Don had left his new girlfriend and gone back to Carol.

In March, Don was called upon to appear on *This Is Your Life* for Alvin Stardust, together with Noddy. "I had never even met Alvin Stardust!"

Don laughs. "But I think they just wanted some known people to go on the show, to make it look good. I talked to Nod and we were both laughing over the phone. They wanted us to pretend we were long-lost friends of Stardust's, which was totally rubbish. I looked at *This Is Your Life* with totally different eyes after that!"

Shortly after, Slade went to The Trumpet in Bilston for the release party of the new album, *Rogues Gallery*. Although they did extensive promotion all over England, as well as radio and video interviews for Australia and New Zealand, the album didn't go any higher than number 60 in the charts. It was safe to say that the heart of Slade had been ripped out when they stopped touring. Gradually, it dawned on Don that this situation was going to be permanent. In April, the band went to a meeting with their accountant, Colin Newman, to sort out arrangements for an American tour, but Noddy still didn't want to get back on the road.

"I did a charity thing for Noddy in Birmingham for a children's hospital," Haden Donovan recalls. "We got Noddy to introduce one of the bands. In the end we got him to sing an encore with all the bands. There was Robert Plant, The Moody Blues, UB40 and George Harrison. After the gig, Noddy said, 'That was absolutely wonderful! I have to get back on the road!' A week later, he was in our house and Ozzy was on some programme in a dress and he looked awful. Nod said to me, 'I'm never gonna look like that. I'm never gonna go on stage again.' And that was it."

"It was so strange, because Dave and Jim never liked touring," Don says, "but when Nod decided not to tour, they wanted to carry on. Nod said, 'But you're the ones who never want to go anyway. You never want to go anywhere and now you have a go at me, because *I* don't want to do it!'"

"Nod just got fed up," Swinn comments. "Plus the fact that Sharon Osbourne was taking them back to the seventies again, playing in malls, and Nod never wanted to end like Ozzy – a pensioner on stage trying to rock'n'roll. He'll never go on stage again."

Although Noddy was far from being a pensioner – he was only 38 when he decided to stop touring – his decision was final. Slade's new-found fame in America ended prematurely because of that, and Don found himself in a vacuum. Touring was essential to him in order to survive financially, but with Nod's decision it had become impossible. Don tried to cope with the situation. He went to Wolverhampton with Noddy to open the new ring road, and he went in the studio with Chas Chandler to help programme his Linn drum for 21 Strangers, who recorded at Portland. Jim also needed his help in the studio, doing drum parts for his solo projects, but most of the time Don just tried to drown his sorrows.

He went drinking, either officially with Jim and Noddy at wine-tasting parties in London, or privately in wine bars with Noddy and Ozzy Osbourne. Don's recollection of that period is rather vague and, more often than not, his diary entries just say: "A day lost." His relationship with Carol suffered, and in the end they decided that it wasn't going to work with the two of them living together. Although they split officially, Carol stayed in the flat as she had nowhere else to go.

In July 1985, Don's life changed once again. The year before, Bob Geldof and Midge Ure had successfully founded the charity supergroup Band Aid to raise money for famine relief in Ethiopia. Their single, 'Do They Know It's Christmas?', had become the Christmas number one in 1984 and, although Slade had not been involved in the recording, they had performed with the band when doing TV shows.

"In July, we were invited to a Band Aid party," Don recalls, "and I went on my own. Everybody there asked, 'Why were you lot not on the track?' but the thing was that we hadn't been told about it. We would have done it, had we been asked, but we didn't know anything about it."

At the party, Don met a lady named Joan Komlosy, an antiques dealer who worked freelance as a reporter as well. Not only did she look a bit like Mari, she had features in common with Joanna Lumley as well; for Don, it was love at first sight. The relationship was turbulent though, as their work schedules often kept them apart. Slade had decided to accept an offer to record a Christmas album and, over the next three months, the band went in the studio.

"It wasn't easy to combine the band with Joan," Don admits. "She would never let me out of her sight and anything that had to do with the band was totally taboo. We were always arguing because of that.

Nod actually stopped calling me all together, because he knew how things were."

"Actually, she didn't tell him when Noddy phoned," Dave Donovan says, "or anybody else, for that matter. I phoned dozens of times, but she always told me that he wasn't there and I was never allowed to speak to him. She never told Don that I'd been calling and so we didn't stay in touch."

In late August, Don was asked to do a parachute jump for charity at Salisbury airbase, along with entertainer Kenny Everett and Spandau Ballet's Steve Norman and Martin Kemp.

"Keith Altham was calling me up," Don remembers. "He was laughing, 'Nobody will do such a jump, so I'll call Don!' When I agreed to do it, he said that I was mad. I don't like heights, but I thought it would be a good laugh and it was for charity.

"At the airbase the day before the event, we went through a brief instruction and training. We practised by jumping down from a platform a few metres up in the air. We were then told that the next day on the airplane, we had to climb onto the wing and grab hold of some handles. Then we had to throw ourselves backwards off the wing. Oh my God! That freaked me. I'd thought we would just be pushed out of the plane! The guy who trained us then told us all kinds of horror stories about what could go wrong with the parachutes. He was going on about someone once accidentally pulling the parachute while in the plane. It filled the plane up and the plane went down! It was in my drinking days, but that day I never touched anything! I stayed up all night trying to drum the instructions into my head. I really felt nervous about it."

The anxiety was reflected in his diary, where Don went to a great deal of trouble reminding himself what to do: "When we jump backwards, count 1,000-1 up to 1,000-6, then check canopy + we can steer ourselves. Land two feet together, knees bent, arms straight, roll left, legs following over straight. Run round to top of parachute to pull it down after landing."

"The next day, the jump was postponed due to wind," Don recalls, "and in the end, it got cancelled altogether, because of poor light. We

231

just sat there all day, waiting, and in the end we were told to go home, because it had started getting dark. We all went, 'That's a shame!' but we were so relieved!"

Since the car accident Don had suffered from insomnia, but after the day at the airbase he wrote in his diary, "I stayed fast asleep without even disturbing the bedclothes." A full night's sleep was so rare to Don that, whenever he got one, he actually wrote it down.

"I can't really think of why I never sleep," Don admits. "Maybe it is some nerve thing from the accident. In the beginning, I was a nervous wreck with the amnesia and I never slept, and the sleeplessness sort of carried on. I stayed up all night and watched the sun go up. Thank God that they had TV all night in England then! I also got a Game Boy, and that used to drive me mad! I had a big white one and I'd sit up all night playing that. I played like crazy. It didn't affect me though, going without sleep. And whenever we had two days off, I tried to wind down, not doing anything, just relaxing. It's a lot better these days and I do sleep a bit more now."

On November 2 came the laconic diary entry: "We got married today." Four years with Carol hadn't seen a wedding proposal, but after four months with Joan, 39-year-old Don stepped blindly into his first marriage.

"Don't ask me why!" Don laughs. "Maybe it was the proverbial love at first sight, I have no idea. But I do remember that when we agreed to get married, the first thing my father said to me was, 'Are you sure?'"

The couple were wed at Marylebone Register Office, with only the closest family members attending. By then Carol was out of Don's flat, which he had sold as he had moved in with Joan. The newlyweds worked together closely, Don helping his wife with her antiques sales and she going in the studio with Don to revive the recording of 'Let There Be Drums'.

"She knew Jona Lewie and he had a full-blown 48-track recording studio," Don says. "I didn't expect that, as he wasn't recording anything at the time. He lived in this big house in south London. When we rang the doorbell, we could hear five locks come off the door before he showed us into this enormous front room. I remember saying to him, 'How many rooms do you have here, Jona?' and he went, 'I don't know. Shall we have a walk around and see how many rooms there are?' He had lived there for years, but he had never been around the whole house. He'd done that song 'You'll Always Find Me In The Kitchen At Parties', but I didn't really get it until then. He had this amazing house, but he more or less lived in the kitchen. Jona is such a lovely person, but he is really eccentric."

"When Don said he was keen to do a version of 'Let There Be Drums', I was delighted for him to do it in my studio," Lewie recalls. "I had been good friends with Capital Radio broadcaster and presenter Joan Komlosy from around 1981, and when Joan started going out with Don, she and Don came over to my place for the evening, where my partner, Julie, and I had a lovely evening with them. Don was a very convivial and warm person, kind in conversation and very well mannered and polite.

"It was great working with Don in my recording studio. Here was the great drummer from Slade doing a classic drum track and renaming it 'Amnesia' to reflect his accident, which caused him to lose his memory. I remember our sessions in the studio were peppered with some great tales from Don about his global experiences with Slade, not without a bevy or two. The stories were not only entertaining, but in fact helped to make the atmosphere such a nice one to be working in. I just got drawn in and loved it.

"Don did some drum overdubs on a track I was working on at the time and it was remarkable how well he stayed on the beat, staying with a track that had already been put down. The precision was mind-boggling. With regard to the skill of timekeeping in drumming, I would put Ringo Starr and Don Powell at the top. I ended up adding the top line on keyboards for his great rhythms and the track ended up very differently from 'Let There Be Drums'! Very different drumming and instrumentation. In addition, it also had a vocal on it, whereas I seem to remember that 'Let There Be Drums' was only an instrumental piece."

"When I decided to rename 'Let There Be Drums' as 'Amnesia', Jona would say the word 'amnesia' in a deep voice on the track and end it with an incredible laugh," Don smiles. "It sounded like Christopher Lee from one of the Hammer horror films!"

"I initially sang the line," Lewie says, "but then persuaded Don to sing it himself, which he did really well, even though he never sang with Slade. The one bit of my voice that did remain at that time, in a guide mix, was when I said 'amnesia' at the end of the track. Once again Don, being the person he is, was very easy and convivial to work with.'"

"I've never finished the track," Don admits. "I would like to do that some day, maybe take some of the guitars off and alter it altogether."

"I think it could have had a strong chance of being a runaway single," Lewie ponders. "For starters, the marketing on it couldn't fail. Here was Don Powell reworking Sandy Nelson's 'Let There Be Drums' – both key drummers of their respective generations. It was by Don Powell, a name that was part of the British heavy-rock drummer fraternity, as it were, what with Cozy Powell of Sabbath and so on. Furthermore, this track anticipated the likes of such future dance classics as 'Born Slippy' by Underworld, a decade later."

Slade had finished their next single, 'Do You Believe In Miracles?', which was released in November. It went to number 54 in the charts and had the delightful 'My Oh My (Swing Version)' on the B-side. It came with a free single in a plastic double-pack containing 'Santa Claus'/'Auld Lang Syne'. The release was produced by John Punter, and when the new Christmas album came out a few days later he shared the producer's credit with Jim. The *Crackers* album went to a respectable number 34 and was released on the compilation-marketing label Telstar. The band did a TV ad for it at the Baron's Ale House in London, and for the rest of the year they did promo videos, as well as TV shows in Germany and England. Although Slade still worked together, Don seemed preoccupied with other matters, mostly his domestic situation.

Because the actual wedding had been a quiet affair, Don and his wife decided to throw a belated wedding party on November 13. "Our accountant, Colin Newman, also looked after Jet Records," Don recalls, "so I asked Colin if he would ask Don Arden's son Dave if they would let us use Portland Studios for the party. Dave Arden then gave us the studio for the day as a wedding present, which was really nice. My former drum roadie Willie worked at a rehearsal studio called John Henry's, and we arranged to rent three or four sets of drums and amplifiers and things like that from there. That was loaned to us as a wedding present as well. When we sent the invites out, we asked people to bring their guitars to do a big jam. Noddy and Swinn came to the party and John Coghlan from Status Quo, Steve McNerney, Mike Berry, Ozzy Osbourne and a lot of other people."

"George Harrison was there as well with his producer," Swinn adds. "They hid in the back and smoked joints."

"I didn't know," Don admits. "It was in my drinking days, so I didn't notice. Imagine George Harrison being at my wedding party without me realising! But it was a great night and I always remember Ozzy at that party. He was leaning against the wall and he kept sliding down, because he was drunk. Whenever he did that, he bumped into my new mother-in-law and she kept pushing him away. The youngest of Joan's three grown daughters then said to her, 'Grandma, he bites heads off bats!' and my mother-in-law replied, 'I'll bite his bloody head off if he carries on like that!'

"The next day when we woke up, Ozzy called and said, 'Great fucking party last night, Don! Brilliant!' 'But do you remember any of it?' 'No, but it was fucking great!' Only Ozzy could say that! Around that time, Ozzy and I had started going to Alcoholics Anonymous meetings together."

In his diary, Don wrote, "Stop drinking, as my darling is threatening to leave me," but the meetings didn't help him.

"I could never really understand the idea of AA," Don admits. "They didn't do anything for me. They didn't offer me any solution. It was just people talking about *their* problems. What's the point in that? Maybe it works psychologically for some, but not for me. Ozzy and I used to be like two little schoolboys, giggling in the back of the class. Then Ozzy would go, 'Do you fancy a drink?' 'Yeah,' and then we always ended up in a pub."

Don's drinking did stop eventually, on January 10, 1986. Six days before he had noted in his diary: "Phil Lynott died today"; now it said, "I stopped drinking today."

"I had wanted to for a long time, without being able to do it," Don says. "I'd had a couple of full stops and starts, but I'd been enjoying drinking too much. I'd had so much fun with it, and it doesn't matter if you go to the AA or not, unless you really want to stop it will never happen.

"Now I wanted to, one hundred percent. Joan and I fought so much about me drinking 24 hours a day that I decided to stop, not just for her sake, but for mine as well. I said to her, 'Give me a chance then. The only way I can do it is if I'm staying in. I'm not going to leave the flat. Any shopping that has to be done, you have to do it.' I was giving myself a week to stop and I got better every day, even after the first day. I didn't get any shakes or withdrawal symptoms, nothing. I just felt good. I knew I had cracked it after three days, but I thought I'd stay in for the week, just to be sure. And I have never drunk or even been tempted since. It just doesn't interest me any more. I think that if you really, really want to stop drinking, you can do it. And it is the best thing I have ever done."

Once again, Don's great will power, combined with his physical fitness, helped him like it had helped him cope with the effects of the car accident in 1973. "I had a medical exam a few years later and I told the doctor how I had abused my body," Don says. "The doctor did every test possible and he said that I was incredibly fit, and today my body is not affected by the many years of abuse. So many colleagues in the music industry have died over the years, mostly of abuse, and I wonder if I would still have been around had I continued drinking. I doubt it. I used to say that I drink for England. If it had been an Olympic event, I would have won gold every year."

Don and Joan spent the rest of January writing a B-side for 'Amnesia' for Polydor, and recording tracks with titles like 'Hold On' and 'How Long' at Jona Lewie's place with engineer John Madden. It all came to a stop though in April, when it turned out that Polydor didn't want 'Amnesia' after all.

For Slade's 20th anniversary in 1986, *Perseverance – The Story Of Slade*, a Music Box special hosted by Gareth 'Gaz Top' Jones, was aired.

It included videos from the band's career, as well as segments where Don teamed up with Dave and Nod, and with Jim, for two separate interviews. Don spent most of his time in April and May overdubbing with Slade at Portland, but when the studio went bankrupt, in May, Slade had to move elsewhere. They started using Redan Studios in May, Roundhouse Studios in June, Music Works Studios in July, Wessex Sound Studios and AIR Studios in August and Utopia Studios in September. All the time, the arguing between Don and Joan got worse because she didn't want Don to work with Slade.

When Don turned 40 in September, Joan had arranged a surprise party for him. Friends and colleagues had noticed his domestic situation, so they did their best to make things worse. After all, what are friends for?

"For my 40th birthday, Colin Newman and Alan Heywood sent me a strippergram," Don laughs. "We were recording with Slade at the time and, without me knowing, Joan had called both Nod and Jim to come to a surprise party for me. We had the party at our flat in Harley House and a few hours after the party had gone into full swing the doorbell rang. I thought it was more people arriving for the party, but it was a policewoman. I didn't understand a thing. She said, 'Mr. Don Powell, you have a car. Would you please come here?' I thought I'd done something wrong, but then her clothes came off. I had absolutely no idea. Colin and Alan knew very well what kind of relationship I was in, and it was a real wind-up to send such a stripper."

When Don and his wife weren't quarrelling they led a hectic social life, going to premieres and parties and giving dinner parties themselves. The couple went to concerts too, seeing bands like Black Sabbath, Queen, Status Quo, UB40 and Big Country, and they made many overnight trips around the country, looking for antiques for Joan to buy for her stall in Portobello Road, where she sold them every Saturday. Both Don and Joan dreamt of a house outside London and, on September 24, they took over Thorne Cottage in Bexhill-On-Sea, where they spent every free moment for the rest of the year getting the house in order.

In November, Don dispensed with the services of Colin Newman, placing his financial affairs in the hands of Alan Heywood, who used to work for Newman and had now branched out on his own. Earlier in the year, Heywood had got Don a great car deal on a Jaguar Coronet, but as Don kept getting speeding and parking tickets he had to spend time sorting out the fines.

For most of November, Don was at Music Works overdubbing tracks for a new Slade album. In December that year, the 'Okey Cokey'/'Get Down And Get With It' single was re-released on Speed, but it didn't chart.

The new year saw Slade compiling the new album at Music Works, and Joan was furious about the amount of time Don spent at the studio. "My darling doesn't love or care for me any more," Don wrote in his diary, "'cause she thinks Slade come first and they don't at all." When Nod called a few days later with a list of promotional duties for the record, it made things even worse.

In February, the John Punter-produced 'Still The Same' was released on RCA and it charted at number 73; the B-side, 'Gotta Go Home', was produced by Jim. It came with a free single in a 21st birthday commemorative gatefold double pack, containing facsimile autographs. The bonus tracks were 'The Roaring Silence' and also 'Don't Talk To Me About Love', with Jim on lead vocal. To promote it, Slade went on *The Tom O'Connor Show* in Blackpool, recorded a '21 years together' interview for Radio Luxembourg and did a *Superstore* show as well. Don went to Wessex Studios to overdub tambourine and tom toms on a Redbeards from Texas track that Jim was producing, and in March he was back putting a new track down at Music Works for the upcoming album.

In April, the single 'That's What Friends Are For' was released on RCA, with 'Wild Wild Party' on the B-side. It reached number 95. Roy Thomas Baker had produced the A-side and the B-side was credited to Jim. The single's A-side came from Slade's next album, *You Boyz Make Big Noize*, released in April 1987. It was to be their last.

"There was a sort of feeling in the studio that this album would probably be our last," Don recalls. "We hadn't toured for so long, so why were we making an album? The thought was that maybe it would kick-start us again."

Baker, who had co-produced albums for such varied artists as Queen and Dusty Springfield, was supposed to produce five tracks for the album, but in the end he only worked on two. "I liked it when we worked with Roy Thomas Baker in the Angel Studios in Islington in London," Don says. "It was great for the band, as it was a really live sound. We had a phenomenal drum sound, with just me in the studio and about 30 mikes on the drums. Baker put a close mike on the kit, then one a metre away, another two metres away and so on, going all around the studio. The drum sound was fantastic in the studio, but if you listen to the record, you wouldn't think that. The thing was that we didn't hear the songs until we got in the studio, whereas usually we would go away and rehearse first. Afterwards, when we heard the album, we thought of things we could have done differently to make it better.

"Baker worked pretty quickly, but he and Jim didn't get along very well. Not much of what we did with Baker was used, and I think John Punter actually mixed the tracks."

In fact, Don wrote in his diary, "Nod said CBS in America weren't all that impressed with Roy Thomas Baker's tracks."

"It didn't really come off like we had expected," Don admits. "Roy Thomas Baker was a big name, so he was very expensive and he wanted to use big studios. In the end we called it off, as it got too expensive.

"The title for the album we got from Betty, the cleaning lady at Angel Studios. One day when we were rehearsing, she came in and said, 'You boys make big noise.' We went, 'Yes! Take it down!' But it took almost 20 years before I realised that the track of the same name wasn't on the album. I never really played our albums when I got them. I'd had enough of recording them. Then I'll sometimes play them later on."

The album went to number 98. In July, the 'missing' title track, 'Big Boyz Make Big Noize', was released as a single on Cheapskate. It went to number 94 in the charts and featured Vicky Brown in a short duet with Noddy. It would be added to later editions of the album.

"Vicky was the wife of Joe Brown from The Bruvvers," Don explains. "Later, he shared some hits with his daughter Sam. The B-side was an instrumental version of the song."

Don and Dave did radio promotion in Leicester, Coventry, Birmingham, Worcester, Gloucester and Cardiff in late July and early August, and on August 11 Don was at De Lane Lea Studios to do backing tracks for the *Get Fresh* show. In his diary he wrote, "Spent a few hours going through the motions of recording the tracks."

Joan accompanied Don to Carlisle two days later when he had to do a TV show, but it turned out to be a bad idea, as she still had a hard time coming to terms with Don working with Slade. In fact she kicked him out of the hotel room, so he had to sleep in the room of backline roadie Mick Legg. Joan checked out of the hotel the next day and Don was then able to rehearse with the band and appear on the show, which was taped on August 15 in Border Television's car park for Children's ITV. The band mimed to 'You Boyz Make Big Noize' and 'Ooh La La In LA', using a stand-in for Vicky Brown.

"'Ooh La La In LA, was partly about me and Bob Dylan's daughter," Don recalls. "Nod wrote the lyrics and some of the song goes, 'There's George on his knees again, on the town with Miss Zimmerman, alert the media…' and so on. It didn't go down too well with my wife."

In September, Slade stopped using Keith Altham's services, and Don and Joan went to Paris for a week to visit antique fairs. When they returned, Nod called Don to say that he and Jim were financing another Slade single. 'We Won't Give In'/'Ooh La La In LA' was released on Cheapskate, with both tracks taken off the *You Boyz* album. Don wrote in his diary: "Nod called to see if I'd received the single, he thought it was bass light – I said, I thought it was ponderous." The single did not chart in England, but went to number 91 in the US charts.

In December, Slade were in Birmingham to perform on *Pebble Mill* and, of course, Don's wife resented that. In fact, the keyword to their marriage was jealousy: Joan being jealous of Don, Don being jealous of Joan and Joan kicking Don out of the Harley House flat almost every week, only to take him back a few days later. When they weren't fighting, they went to antique fairs and boot fairs all over the country, and continued giving and attending a lot of fashionable dinner parties as Joan knew everyone there was to know, among them Peter Stringfellow.

"He lived in the same building as us in Harley House," Don says. "He owned all the Stringfellows strip clubs, and he always gave a lot of parties. At one party, we bumped into Brian May and his wife, Chrissie, and she looked like she was down. I said, 'What's the matter, Chrissie?' and she went, 'Anita Dobson is over there. Brian really likes her.' Anita Dobson was a great friend of my wife's, so I took it totally the wrong way, totally innocent. I shouted to Joan, 'Can't you introduce Anita to Brian?' and that was the night when they got together. Oh my God! It was so naive of me! Brian divorced Chrissie in 1988 and married Anita a couple of years later. I have never seen Chrissie since, and I don't think I want to!"

Introducing Anita Dobson to Brian May might have been a bit naive of Don, but he was working on growing up. On January 16 he wrote in his diary: "I'm a big boy now, so must learn to spell sort (not sought) and if I write anything about my darling's paranoia, she will rip the page out!!!!" It didn't quite work though, as Don quickly went back to spelling sort as 'sought' and, as for his wife, she kept kicking him out and taking him back. When they weren't arguing about Slade, the topic was money. Mainly because they didn't have any. In fact, Alan Heywood called Don in February to say that his company, Don Powell Music, was almost out of funds and Don had to cut his credit cards up. He couldn't afford to have his drums in John Henry's warehouse any more and decided to sell them through Sotheby's.

It wasn't an easy time for Don, who felt the pressure from both his economic and domestic situations. Both were getting worse day by day, and there seemed to be only one solution to his marital problem. When Nod called in November to say that a new Slade single was being released on Cheapskate – it was 'Let's Dance (1988 Remix)'/'Standing On The Corner', which didn't chart – Don made up his mind. He called Alan Heywood to say that he wanted to leave Slade, and then he took the guitar that he had bought from Nod to be sold at Sotheby's.

22

Dying Twitches

From 1989, there was a change in Don's diaries. He still noted every death of any musician, wrote down big political events and whatever he had seen on TV, but the format of the diaries had now changed. When Don first started keeping a diary in 1973, he wrote his thoughts down in big ledgers, then changed to ordinary book size in 1978. From 1989, however, the diaries were only pocket-calender size. They were easier to carry and Don needed that, as he had to commute between London and Bexhill whenever Joan kicked him out. On January 13 he wrote: "Friday the 13th I got kicked out!!!"

Staying in Thorne Cottage, Don didn't answer the phone, which was a first. Usually he always answered as soon as his wife rang, but not this time. In the end the couple made up, but soon things were back to normal, with them arguing about Slade and money. On March 4 he wrote in the diary: "We didn't speak again 'cause I said we couldn't afford a swimming pool." In the end the pool was bought, and Don and his wife took out a second mortgage. In his diary Don noted: "I called Sotheby's for the result of the Rock'n'Roll sale. Nod's guitar went for £700, memorabilia nothing, stage jacket £120, One Armed Bandit £320, eight-track player nothing, the guitar Chas put in of Jimi Hendrix £2,000." The day after he wrote: "I found out the prices from Phillips

Rock'n'Roll auction: Merry Christmas platinum £420, collective of drums £180, stage jacket didn't go." Don needed every penny.

Malcolm Skellington had taken over the fan club by then and his first newsletter was for April. Whenever he talked to Don, it caused new arguments between the latter and Joan, but still the couple went on a work holiday to Paris in September, spending Don's birthday at an antique fair buying stock for Joan's business. But even buying stock was not without danger. Back in England, Don wrote on October 6: "Went to Amersham to buy stock; darling got into a bad mood 'cause someone recognised me!!!" The arguments continued for the rest of the year and the next one as well.

In 1990, the two compilation CDs *Slade Story 1* and *Slade Story 2* were released in Europe on the German Bear Tracks label. Produced by Chas Chandler and mastered by Tom Müller at Hansa Studios in Berlin, neither charted. In April came a new low, where the only entry in Don's diary for April 9 was, "Not a nice day." That was repeated the day after. It had to do with Joan's jealousy of Don working with Slade, of course. On April 11, Don did the *Pop Quiz* show with Nod.

Later in the month, Don checked up on the Phillips auctions: "I checked the Rock'n'Roll sale from Phillips: a white satin jacket + my Ludwig 75th anniversary jacket £150 + the bronze statue from Mel Bush + costume jewellery £160. I called Sotheby's re Rock'n'Roll sale: the eight-tracks was passed, the banjo + percussion case went for £300."

In May, Don received a £15,000 cheque from Perseverance in respect of a Polydor advance, which lightened things up a bit. On June 23, Don and Joan went to Wolverhampton to celebrate his parents' 50th wedding anniversary, but soon they were back to fighting again. As Don wrote in his diary on July 30: "We had another blazing row 'cause H called to say he was in London on Wednesday." Of course, Don didn't go and see him.

As they had the year before, Don and his wife went to Paris in September to celebrate his birthday and buy antiques. On September 25, Slade was given a plaque at the Walsall Town Hall, but although Don was back in England, he didn't attend the presentation. On October 4, he wrote in his diary, "Drove to have coffee with Frank who said Nod + Jim were in the studio producing The Mission. I went along – Nod had gone home. Put some percussion on the track." When he came back to the flat in Harley House, it continued, "My things were thrown at me. I packed the car + drove to the house." Don stayed in Bexhill for a week, then he went to see Colin Newman to go over a singles deal with Polydor. It caused another fight with Joan, and Don went back to Thorne Cottage, where he stayed for almost three weeks, following the events on TV when Margaret Thatcher had to step down as Prime Minister, with John Major taking over. Don opened a new bank account in Bexhill and he didn't answer the phone when Joan called.

On December 10, Don and Joan were suddenly back together again, but from then on humour disappeared from his diaries. Instead he took up interests in Genghis Khan, sharks and the conspiracy theories regarding the murder of John F. Kennedy.

"I didn't know that my humour was missing in my diaries as well," Don admits, "but I knew it was gone, because everyone noticed – mostly my family, of course. They all said that after I married, I lost my sense of humour. I changed a lot during my marriage. At that point, Slade hardly existed any more and I didn't even know what the others were doing. I was working with Joan in antiques, going to fairs, buying and selling and doing stock books. She had the stall in Portobello Road and we also went to antique fairs all over the country. We did the big outdoor ones, with up to 3,000 stalls in huge showgrounds in England. I was amazed how big it all was. It was phenomenal and so well organised.

"The big fairs always took place in the week, but if you were a stallholder you could get in on the day before, and that was when most of the buying and selling was done, as most of the business was done between the dealers anyway. We used to get there at four o'clock in the morning and there would be queues of cars and vans even then. People would go down the queues, buying and selling, as it would take five to six hours just to get in. Some didn't even bother to go to the fairs, they did their buying and selling in the queues; they could make £10,000 just from that. It was something completely different from what I had ever done before, but it was very interesting and I enjoyed the work very much."

In March, the album *The Slade Collection 81-87* was released through RCA, but it didn't chart and there was little indication that the band was destined to enjoy one more whiff of success.

For Slade's 25th anniversary in 1991, Polydor asked them to do two new songs. Don and Jim went to see Colin Newman about the new record deal. "We went over the contract and recording," Don wrote in his diary. "There is also an album deal imminent." The album was a greatest hits compilation on which the singles were to be included. Don felt very uplifted, but when visiting Nod a few days later he was a bit disappointed. "We had a long chat," Don wrote. "He said I should stay with Joan as what we had was great, as the group was nothing."

Noddy was now living in Manchester with his new love, Suzan, and maybe that affected his view on relationships. In any case, Don didn't take his advice and left his wife on April 4. The day after the break-up, Don went to Wolverhampton with Dave. For Slade's 25th anniversary, the fan club had lined up both an exhibition and a reception at Walsall Town Hall. Don and Dave visited the exhibition and did interviews with local television and press. After that, they went to a charity gig in Kidderminster.

"It was Dave who was going to that charity show," Don recalls, "and I went with him. Eventually we got on stage and played."

The reception at Walsall Town Hall the day after became a milestone in Slade history, as it was the last time they would ever be seen live on stage with the full original line-up. As usual, it didn't seem to impress Don much. His full diary entry for that date goes, "I got up 7.15. Dad was up. I popped to see Derek. I spent a couple of hours in W'ton. Came back to clean up. We left for the hotel in Walsall. We checked in our rooms. We all drove to the Town Hall for the reception. Cass and Mick Marson and Johnny Howells were there. We all stayed at the hotel. Went to bed 1.30."

Backstage witnesses could tell a quite different, more dramatic story. "In Walsall, all hell broke lose," Mick Marson says. Swinn agrees: "I do remember it. It was bad blood rising."

"There was sand in the air," John Howells adds. "I think they had a fight with each other."

The problem was that although the band thought they were merely going to attend a reception, it was a special party night and fans wanted them to perform on stage.

"They had a few Slade tribute bands on," Don recalls, "and then Malcolm Skellington, who headed the fan club, said that the kids would love for us to play something as well, but Nod flatly refused. Before the reception, Swinn had called to say that Nod wouldn't do anything and now Nod came in shouting that he was not going to sing. He was not going to do interviews, he was not going to do this and he was not going to do that, and I remember that one TV presenter from Birmingham thought there was a problem between us in the band because of that. Nod was shouting, 'I told you, I told you! I knew it would happen! I'm not doing it!' He was not going to go on stage. Jim, Dave and myself were up for it, and eventually Nod did agree, but it was totally under duress, believe me. We went on stage and all we did was the old 'Johnny B. Goode'. After that, Nod took off his guitar and walked out.

"We had a party at the pub of the hotel afterwards and there Nod was fine. He was the Nod that we all know, but he was just totally blank about going on stage and I have no idea why. I do understand if he would rather have people remember Slade for what it was, but still it was very strange."

Slade survived the Walsall Town Hall incident as a unit. They went to Jim's place to go over the new recordings, but the magic Holder/ Lea songwriting team had nothing to offer. Jim had some songs for his solo projects, so the band agreed on the singles' A-sides being Jim's and the B-sides being Dave's. Then they went to the Rich Bitch Studios in Birmingham to record for two weeks, and every day Don wrote in his diary, "Had a great day!"

Don really enjoyed being in the studio with Slade again. His personal life took a turn for the better as well, although his marriage had to go through the last spasmodic death cramps. Don sold his wedding ring, then went back to his wife, only to leave her again when discovering that he was broke. He took her back once more, but in August the couple broke up for good. By then Don had met Diana, who worked as a hotel manager in Bexhill.

"I used to go there every morning to have coffee and read the newspaper," Don recalls, "and that was how we met. One day I was sitting on the beach with her when a friend of mine came looking for me. He said, 'Thank God that I found you! You have to get out of town, because Joan is on her way.' She was coming to Thorne Cottage and she was to look up Di as well at the hotel, so Di called her boss and he gave her a few days off and sent us to their hotel in Brighton.

"While we were there, my wife came to Bexhill with two of her daughters and they caused a bit of a racket at the hotel, trying to find Di. My wife went to Thorne Cottage as well, where she got the neighbours to let her in with a spare key and she took some of my gold and silver discs, but I couldn't be bothered to try to get them back. I really couldn't go through any more with her, so I just had to have the discs replaced. The record company didn't have any of the old Slade albums left, so I spent a long time going to boot fairs and junk shops, trying to find them in order to have them coated. I got some strange looks, buying my own records! But eventually I got them. They were selling them for 90p for each album, but I knocked them down to 50p. Then they got coated, so I have them now."

Don also lost the alarm system, radio and CD player in his car around that time, but that was because his car was broken into in London.

"They didn't just rip out the CD player," Don smiles. "It was taken out professionally, and all the leads that they didn't want were folded up neatly and left in the car. There was a CD rack in the car as well, containing 10 CDs, of which two were Slade albums. And the thieves had taken all the CDs, except the Slade albums! I couldn't stop laughing. I called Nod and said, 'You never guess what has happened to me.' He was laughing as well, 'They must have known who you were!' That was the ultimate kick in the teeth, but so funny!"

Don moved to Tenterden with Diana. The manager of the hotel in Tenterden was going on holiday and Diana was sent there to look after it while he was away. She was then told by the hotel company that they wanted her to stay there.

"Tenterden is actually where we filmed the train scene in *Flame* back in 1974," Don says. "We spent a whole day there, going back and forth on a closed railway line. When I went back, some of the people living there remembered us shooting the film."

With Diana, Don experienced a much more harmonious and peaceful relationship than he had done with Joan, and working with Slade was no longer a problem. Diana fully accepted Don's line of work and the workload that he suddenly had with the band. Slade did photo sessions and shot the video for their upcoming single, 'Radio Wall Of Sound', spending all day and all night in London to get the clip done. In October the single was released on Polydor. Unusually for Slade, it featured Jim on lead vocals, and charted at number 21. The B-side was Dave and Bill Hunt's 'Lay Your Love On The Line'. The compilation album *Wall Of Hits* came out a month later on Polydor and made it to number 65 in the charts.

Slade were now busy doing *Top Of The Pops,* as well as other TV shows in England and interviews and television in France, Holland and Belgium. The day the band went to Brussels to shoot a Belgian show, Don headlined his diary: "Freddie Mercury had died very early this morning." Another one bites the dust.

December saw the release of Slade's final single, 'Universe', which was accompanied by the songs 'Red Hot' and 'Merry Xmas Everybody'. 'Universe' was penned by Jim and 'Red Hot' by Dave with Bill Hunt. The record came out on Polydor but did not chart. In his diary Don noted, "We go *Amadeus* on the video," which they did. Bill Clark wrote the script and the video has often been rated one of Slade's most evocative.

With the new recordings, Don felt far more optimistic about Slade. Finally, he saw a chance at getting back into songwriting, with him and Dave teaming up and doing some songs for future Slade releases. The year before, Polydor had started reissung Slade's back catalogue and that, combined with a spot at number 21 for 'Radio Wall Of Sound', was not bad.

Don immediately started writing lyrics for new Slade songs but, a week into the new year, the bubble burst as Polydor wouldn't take up the option on new Slade singles. Don seemed content with the band deciding to repackage some of the old RCA material though, and Slade went to Germany to promote 'Universe' and did promotion interviews in Norway as well. In March they went to Rich Bitch to re-record 'We'll Bring The House Down'.

"'House Down' was literally a house–dance-style version of the song, like Aerosmith's 'Walk This Way' with Run DMC," Jim recalls. "Once again, it never saw the light of day, but Nod did sing and Dave played guitar."

But these were all dying twitches. One day, Dave didn't show up in the studio. "H had a long conversation with Jim, about him doing everything and also Nod, who said he still won't work live," Don wrote in the diary and that was exactly the problem. The band was no longer a band when recording and, with Noddy refusing to tour, they were not a live band either. Slade was offered a prestigious slot at Castle Donnington, as third on the bill, and they were offered festivals all over Europe as well, but although his three bandmates were up for it, Noddy stood his ground. Slade hadn't toured for eight years and in his diary Don remarked, "Nod had told H he was scared of going on stage and blowing it." A fully understandable objection, as the band were completely unrehearsed for playing live. But touring was a necessity for both Don and Dave to make a living; Dave even suggested to Don that they tour without Noddy, but that wouldn't happen either.

"Nod didn't want to go on any more," Don says. "He had offers to do other things, and he would rather do that. Jim wouldn't go on without him, and that was basically it."

On March 23, four days after Slade's 26th anniversary, Dave and Noddy had a meeting at Colin Newman's office after which Don wrote in his diary, "H said the meeting with Nod resulted in no more Slade."

"Our record contract with Polydor expired and the aforementioned 'cancer' killed us off, so it was a slow process until 1992," Jim says. "In fact, it's myself and Nod who left the band per se, but really it was a metamorphic process."

23

Slade Too

When Slade finally called it quits, they had done much better than any other similar band of their era. They had enjoyed 21 Top 20 hits, six of which went to number one, in England alone. In other countries, their hits were even more numerous.

On the album charts, they'd had five in the Top 20, of which three went to number one and one to number two. They had influenced artists as diverse as Kiss, Quiet Riot, The Bay City Rollers, The Ramones, Oasis and Kurt Cobain, and for 26 years they had played to audiences all over the world with the same line-up. A truly remarkable achievement.

Although Slade had been the major part of Don's life since his teens, the split didn't seem to affect him much. Because of his restless nature, he had always been excellent at adapting to new situations, so when Diana took over the hotel in Tenterden as manager, he moved into the manager's cottage with her and started a new life as a bartender. Irony reared its strange face at Don, a former alcoholic, who now regularly lent a helping hand in the hotel bar at The White Lion.

"It was like somebody was trying to test me," Don laughs. "Let him work in a bar and see if it will tempt him. When you work in a bar, people often say, 'Take one for yourself,' and then I always replied, 'I don't drink.' 'You work in a bar and you don't drink?' But drinking was gone from me then."

Don loved his job and enjoyed learning about the hotel business, so when Dave called him in April to say that he wanted to form a new band, Don gave him his blessing without thinking any more of it. "I wasn't interested at the time," Don admits. "I had a good life in Tenterden, working in the bar, and what Dave originally wanted was to form an instrumental band like Sky with John Williams. He's one of Dave's idols. I did help him record a few things, but I was not interested in being in the band."

It took another month before Don came to the realisation that his days as a rock drummer were not over yet. In late May he wrote in his diary, "H called earlier about Suzi Quatro's husband Lenny calling him about a tour. I said I would be interested."

"In 1992, my friend Neville Martin, who was the editor of *Guitarist* magazine, said to me, 'I don't know if you'd be interested, but Dave Hill wants to go out on the road again and he's looking for management,'" Len Tuckey recalls. "It coincided with my divorce from Suzi, so I thought it would be interesting, as I had been managing her anyway and I knew all the people we would be working with. I called Dave Hill and we met at a hotel halfway between Essex, where I am, and Wolverhampton, where Dave was. I told him what I thought I could do and he said, 'OK, let's do it!'"

Two weeks later, Don found himself at a meeting with Len Tuckey, where he and Dave talked about forming a splinter group to do gigs. When summer came, the new band started rehearsing. "Spent all day having an awful time with the guys who we were supposed to do the show with," Don wrote in his diary in July 1992. "We decided not to carry on." An ad was quickly placed in *Melody Maker* for a new singer.

"I remember that I was the first of the 'new' members in Slade II," says Craig Fenney. "We were then joined by Steve Makin on guitar and spent two or three days at the Rich Bitch rehearsal complex in Birmingham, auditioning literally dozens of singers. By the end of the first day, we felt like a karaoke backing for some really unlikely singers. We then found out that these singers had responded to the advertisement in *Melody Maker* that mentioned Slade, so loads of them were just fans that had never sung in their lives before! But we did get the original Slade II singer, Steve Whalley, who was a great singer and played guitar and some keyboards, too."

Steve McNerney had also replied to the ad, but was thus beaten to the job by Whalley. When the new band finally emerged, it was now a five-piece band, consisting of Don, Dave, Steve Makin, Steve Whalley and Craig Fenney on bass. It was yet another irony that Don and Dave had left the old 'N Betweens in order to become a four-piece band like The Beatles, and now they were going back to a band with five members. By then Don had given up on Ludwig and was going with Pearl drums.

"They had stopped Ludwig as we knew it," Don recalls, "and besides, their drums cost a fortune. I remember talking to Bill Ludwig III about it. I said, 'How come Ludwig is so expensive? Kids who start these days can't afford them.' His answer was, 'It is just the way that the materials work. We cannot compete with the Japanese. They are doing things better than we are, and at a fraction of the price.' And now Ludwig is no longer. There are still Ludwig drums, but not as they were, and it is a shame because they were fantastic. Now there's Pearl and DW and such, and they are *so* good. There's so much choice these days. In the sixties and seventies, drums were never really cared about; not as much as guitars. Then all of a sudden there's Yamaha, Tama and the rest and it's so different for a drummer now. You *can* get good-quality equipment and it makes such a difference.

"When we started with the new line-up, I went with Pearl drums and I got a great deal. But none of the companies did endorsements any more. Maybe if you're a big name like Paul McCartney, but nobody else gets anything for free any more."

Don had to adjust to working with people other than Noddy and Jim. "With the new line-up, it was learning how other people worked. It was like an education for me. We were learning different styles of playing and singing, but to begin with it was a bit strange, because we somehow had to start over. With the old band we'd been together for *so* long. We knew exactly EVERYTHING about each other, so when we started to play, everything fell into place automatically. We'd go on stage and just do it. It used to be the normal thing, but that was not the case with the new line-up."

Indeed, nothing seemed normal any more. The guys who had been the core of Don's life for 26 years now became his opponents. "There are problems with Jim and Nod about using the Slade name," Don wrote in his diary in November. Don and Dave wanted to go on as Slade, but as Jim hated the idea of Slade becoming an 'oldies band', he wouldn't let them.

"I remember when the original Slade were as good as finished," Don says. "We were all on a flight back from somewhere and Dave, who sat next to Jim, said that he needed to tour and use the Slade name to make a living. Then Jim said, 'Use the name? I won't let you. And another thing; you'll be playing my songs and I'll stop you.' Nod was not so bad, but he'd had a meeting with Dave in his house regarding all the disgruntlement about Dave and myself having to carry on and still using the name. He'd said to Dave, 'What happens if you leave the band? What will happen about the name then?' No mention of me! But then again, whose fault was it? I never said anything. Later, we had meetings about the use of the Slade name. Jim never showed up, so only Nod and Colin Newman were there. I remember saying to Nod, 'Why won't you let us use the name? You are not going to use it for anything, so why can't Dave and I get the chance to set ourselves up for life, like you have done?' In the end he could see it our way, but he was in a tough spot, trying to be loyal to both parties."

"When Slade came back on the road, I was actually very interested in who was in the band," Andy Scott recalls. "I rang Noddy and he said it was Dave and Don. He said, 'I don't mind, but Jim's not happy.' 'But you can't stop them from doing what they do,' I objected and he agreed, 'I know. I just don't want to do it, but you have to make a distinction between the old and the new Slade.' I said, 'That will naturally happen. People aren't stupid.'"

In general, it was not a happy time for Don. When leaving the hotel one morning in November to go to Thorne Cottage, he hit a combine harvester. Diana got away with a hurt shoulder, but her Volvo was a total write-off and Don broke his nose.

"It was totally my fault," Don admits. "There was a tractor in front of us, I went around and there was the combine harvester. I tried to swerve into a ditch, but I hit the tyre of the combine harvester. I went down and hit the steering wheel with my nose and I heard a crack. I was in a daze; I was mopping up the blood from my nose off the floor with a tissue, trying to clean the car! The two guys in the combine harvester called the farmer who owned it and he moved the Volvo. When the police came they couldn't really tell whose fault it was, but the farmer had a talk to the officers and that was it. I went to hospital in Hastings to have my nose reset, but they didn't do a very good job as my nose now looks a little twisted."

The bad tidings seemed to roll in for Don. Although he had been separated from Joan for over a year, she refused to divorce him. By then, Don had filed for personal bankruptcy and was on the dole, as he didn't get paid for his work in the bar.

"When I first signed on the dole, I didn't really have any money," Don explains. "Whatever there was, it was tied up in my company, Don Powell Music. Although Joan had her antiques business and her flat in London, she wanted the house in Bexhill as well, so I stopped paying the mortgages. Her name was on the lease too, and if she wanted the house she should pay for it as well, but she wouldn't. I wouldn't either, as long as her name was on the lease, so we just had to see what happened — if the house was going to be repossessed or not."

To top it all off, Dave received a letter from Noddy and Jim regarding the use of the Slade name. "H sent a copy of the new letter of agreement from Nod and Jim," Don noted in his diary. "It was worse than the first one. Our advance money being withheld by Nod and Jim and Colin until we sign that letter."

"I remember Nod saying to me that after all we had been through, he never expected things to end like this between us," Don says, "but like my lawyer told me, it happens all the time in bands. If nothing is written down from the start regarding money, name etc, it is bound to happen. But when you start out, you just want to make a record. You never think about things like this, and you wouldn't think of something like that being able to destroy old friendships. Luckily, today we are past all that. We are friends again, but it was quite problematic at the time."

The name problem was solved by the end of the year, the new band calling themselves Slade II at Noddy's suggestion. Don now started recording and touring with them. Their first gig was in Umeaa, Sweden, on December 11, 1992.

"The best thing about the old band was that we were a unit, and for so many years we were the same unit, or the 'Slade animal' as I call it," Don says. "It was all we ever knew, the four of us playing together, so nothing could go wrong. After the success of the Slade-animal, it was difficult to start up with new people and, when we went on stage, I felt like I had never been on stage before. But we had two great days in Sweden. It was a rush and a great weight off my shoulders. It was just incredible. We just looked at each other and said, 'It's working!' It was a great feeling."

Two weeks later, Slade II went to Dortmund, Germany, to do a show with The Mamas & The Papas, Scott McKenzie, Middle Of The Road, Suzi Quatro, The Bay City Rollers, Showaddywaddy, The Hermits and Dave Dee on the same bill. In January 1993, the show was repeated with The Tremeloes and The Rubettes added to the bill.

"From the very outset, the band was always well received," Craig Fenney remembers. "Some of the first shows were in Germany, which then became like a second home for us. We got really bored with sausage though... It seemed to be on the menu at every gig!"

Before long, feelers were put out to ask Noddy to do some shows with the new band. He said he would think about it, but of course it never came about. In any case, Don was able to sign off the dole in February 1993 and head off to a concert tour of Australia.

Six weeks were spent down under. While flying to Perth, Don noted in his diary, "Most of Paul McCartney's road crew were on the plane, as he's on tour in Australia."

"Paul McCartney was already in Australia," Don says, "and the crew that was on the plane was the same that we sometimes used on our British tours. We played in Perth at the same time as Paul McCartney and he had the top three floors of the biggest hotel in town. In front of the hotel were three white limousines on 24-hour call. I used to walk by them every day and I'd say, 'Have you been used today?' 'No.' That went on for two or three weeks. Then, one day the drivers went, 'Yes!' A couple of the crew had come down and the drivers had taken them to McDonald's in the middle of the night so that Linda McCartney wouldn't find out!"

Slade II didn't enjoy the same kind of luxury as the McCartneys, as they had to travel by tour bus. The band played the West Coast for five weeks and then the North Territories for the remainder of the time. "Had a so-so first show at the Bindeon Festival," Don wrote in his diaries. Adjusting to life on the road was not that easy. Don found the muscles in his shoulder acting up, it being so many years since he had been touring. The vastness of the country was also difficult to overcome, with the bus breaking down due to fuel vapourising. As Don wrote in his diary about a concert in Port Hedland, "It was an outside show, the hottest we've ever known."

"Don was his usual self on the Australian tour," Craig Fenney insists, "played a storm, entertained us all, threw drumsticks at Dave Hill and drank his own body weight in coffee every day. We had some good days on the beach in western Australia too, as some shows were cancelled in other parts of the country, ironically due to bad weather."

The band played everywhere and anywhere, travelling out to all sorts of places, some not even on the map. "I remember a place in Australia, it was a like a café where truck drivers used to stop," Don recalls. "It was situated in the middle of nowhere, with hundreds of kilometres to the nearest neighbour. It was run by two elderly sisters and we were the first people they had seen for three weeks. I remember thinking, 'What if anything happened? What would they do with no one around within reach?' Because they hadn't seen anybody for so long, they were so happy to see us. They would do anything for us. We just had to ask and we'd get it. It was a wonderful experience.

"The strangest thing was, however, that there hadn't been a change over time. The Australians were still talking about *Slade Alive!* That was *the* album. But now people who had seen us in the seventies brought their children with them to our shows."

Just how popular Slade were down under showed itself on one occasion when the bus had to stop in the middle of nowhere for the musicians to relieve themselves. "We stopped to have a wee against a bush," Don says. "There was nothing around, we could just as well have been on the moon. All of a sudden, this fist came out from the bush with S-L-A-D-E written on the knuckles! I went, 'Whoa!' and weed on myself. Then an Aborigine guy came out from behind the bush. He said, 'All right, Slade!' and wandered off. I couldn't believe it. What are the chances of that happening?"

Back in Europe, Slade did a concert in Belgium in April with Golden Earring supporting them. That month also saw them record a TV show in Germany. May was spent touring Switzerland, Germany, Scandinavia and England. The gigs resulted in mixed feelings.

"I find it very difficult to go see Slade II," Haden Donovan admits. "It would take the magic away from what I remember."

"I saw the first incarnation of Slade II once," says Swinn. "It was a local show and the promoter wouldn't let me backstage. Dave was still so pompous, he hadn't moved away from the seventies, and musically there was nothing new. They were the same band from the seventies almost. I watched two or three numbers. Then I had enough."

"It *is* strange being in kind of like a time warp," Don admits, "but the thing is that the promoters want us to play the old hits. It's not very often that we have the chance to play new stuff. It is a bit of a problem. In a lot of the contracts, it even says that we have to finish with 'Merry Xmas Everybody' no matter what time of the year, because that is obviously what people want to hear. Although I'm not tired of playing the same songs over and over again, it would be nice to put new things on as well. In any case, I was having more fun on the road with Slade II than with the original Slade, because I had stopped drinking. I was really proud of myself, because I had stopped and I wasn't even tempted when we started touring. I got a real kick out of that."

With alcohol out of his life, Don gravitated towards other stimuli, although ever so briefly. "Once we stayed in the same hotel as Manchester United and we were asking their trainer about stamina in the footballers,"

Don explains. "He just said, 'Honey.' Before the Manchester United players played a match, they had half a dozen spoonfuls of honey. The trainer said, 'Then it's in your system and when your adrenaline starts to go down, the honey builds you up again.' I decided to do that, but I think I OD'd on honey because I needed to throw up on stage, so it only lasted for a while."

The rest of the year was spent touring all over Europe. Germany was especially good to the band, with Slade II playing there almost every month, which was a bit of an irony as the original Slade had never had a number one hit in that country.

Slade II went into Rich Bitch Studios in June to record, but although Don had been collaborating with Steve Makin on new songs, the ones chosen for recording were the Hill/Hunt-penned 'Hold On To Love' and the Chuck Berry tune 'Run Run Rudolph', written by Marvin Lee Brodie and John D. Marks.

"The equipment was so much advanced by then," Don recalls. "When in the early days with Slade we used to go on stage and play really loud, because the PA systems weren't like they are now, but we didn't need to do that any more. I still played loud though, and these engineers kept saying, 'You don't have to play so loud,' but I said, 'That's the way I play! You have to capture it, as I can't alter my style.' That's the way it was with the new band."

"Don is the same in the studio as live," Craig Fenney says, "loud and consistent. I remember we always seemed to finish the drum and bass parts really quickly and then sit in the control room, drinking coffee. This gave Don plenty of time to make wisecracks about the rest of the band when they made mistakes in their playing!"

The recordings were presented to the Belgian record company Play That Beat! Don wrote in his diary, "Len said, Belgium were over the moon about 'Hold On To Love'." It was now decided that the band were to do their first single for the record company.

By 1993, the original Slade was truly dead but not forgotten. In September, the comedians Reeves and Mortimer started doing spoof sketches about them on their TV show, cranking out their visions of 'Slade In Residence' and 'Slade On Holiday'. Don was played by Mark Williams, Jim by Paul Whitehouse, Noddy by Vic Reeves and Dave by Bob Mortimer.

"That was fantastic," Don laughs. "A call came to the office about them doing it – and would we mind? Nod called to tell me about it, but I couldn't envision it. I didn't mind though, as it would be a good profile for the band, Reeves and Mortimer being quite popular at the time. And when I saw it, I couldn't stop laughing. They must have done a lot of research, because it was us, in kind of a twisted way. It was brilliant. Especially Dave and Nod."

Don still kept in touch with Noddy and enjoyed listening to his radio show. Noddy had become a DJ at Piccadilly Radio in Manchester, doing programmes of seventies music. The relationship improved further when Noddy called to say that Don and Dave had money coming from Perseverance.

Slade II's first single, 'Hold On To Love'/'Red Hot', came out on the Belgian Emergency! Records for the Christmas 1993 sales, but it didn't chart. In fact, none of the Slade II releases ever did. Don enjoyed Christmas anyway, and for the first time in years he experienced a celebration that came close to the family gatherings of his childhood. At the hotel in Tenterden, he dressed up as Father Christmas for the kids in the hotel before going to the Christmas staff lunch.

"The hotel had a Christmas package," Don explains. "People would stay there from Christmas Eve to Boxing Day. They had a magician there, or somebody playing guitar, and they always needed someone to play Father Christmas. No one wanted to do it, so I had to. One time when I went to the bar, all dressed up and going 'Yo Ho Ho!', all the kids dragged me to the floor and started kicking me! I heard one boy say, 'That ain't Father Christmas! He ain't fat enough!' They tried to get my beard off, while kicking me. I hadn't seen that coming, as I wasn't like that when I was a kid!"

The last week of 1993 saw the band doing gigs in the Baltic countries. When Slade II arrived in Riga in Latvia on Boxing Day they were met with TV cameras, and for New Year in Estonia they were treated like kings. When the year came to a close, Slade II had done 80 shows all over Europe in one year.

The following year they played around 50 shows. For Don it started out with recording in Rich Bitch Studios, shows in Germany and a move. In January, Diana left the hotel in Tenterden to run another in Brighton and, a month later, she and Don moved into a company bungalow in Sompting, where they spent the next couple of years.

Slade II went on tour in Austria and Germany in March and did TV shows in Belgium as well. In April, Don and Diane went on a well-deserved three-week holiday in Spain. Back in England, they visited Don's parents on May 4 and spent the night in Lutterworth, as they were going to Pearl drums the day after. Don wrote: "I had a great day + met one of the main guys from Japan who gave me a £4,000 double kit for £1,700." The day after, Don's diary entry said, "Dad died today."

"Mum used to have a sleep in the afternoon, so Dad decided to mow the lawn, using an old push mower," Don says. "When Mum woke up, Dad was sitting inside the house, asleep she thought, but he was gone. The doctor seemed to think that when Dad mowed the lawn, he didn't feel too well and went into the house, where he died of a heart attack."

Don and Diane went to Wolverhampton to be with the family, and Don didn't sleep a wink that night. When he and Diane returned to Sompting, Jim had left a message. Don called him for a chat. He also called Nod and Swinn to let them know about the funeral details, but then Don had to fly to Germany to do a show with Slade II in Hanover on May 12. The funeral took place on May 16.

"Jim attended Dad's funeral with his wife, Louise," Don says. "I didn't expect him there, but I was pleasantly surprised when he came. That was actually the first time since 1992 that I had seen him. There was no bad blood between us because of Slade II; at least nothing was mentioned about it. We just talked the way we used to. Dave came too, with his wife – not to the service, but to my mum's house afterwards with some flowers. When Dad passed away, I remember we wanted Mum to move into a smaller place, but she wouldn't leave. She said, 'I can't leave, there's too many memories here,' and she stayed in the house in Green Park Drive until she followed Dad, five years later."

★   ★   ★

Slade II started recording a Christmas single at Rich Bitch Studios during May. While in the area, Don purchased a new car from his nephew Ian, who worked for a Ford distributor in West Bromwich. "I don't know much about cars, so I contacted Ian when I wanted to buy a new one," Don says. "He suggested a Ford Scorpio and he got a great deal for me. Ian then arranged for me to have the number plate MI3 EAT, my treat. At first I used to have the 'I' and the '3' together, but in England that is illegal and I was stopped so many times by the police. I remember one policewoman who said, 'I know it is very trendy these days, but it is not allowed.' Two weeks later, the same policewoman stopped me again and she was being really petty and patronising. She threatened to impound and de-register the car. I said, 'Please, explain to me what the problem is. I've seen many cars with the same kind of thing.' I thought I was being victimised, but it turned out that if the police photograph the cars to make checks on them, the satellite that reads the number plate can't read it if the numbers are too close. That made sense, but when I told a friend who was in the Special Branch of the police force, he just asked, 'Did the police have their hats on when they stopped you?' And actually they hadn't. He said, 'Then they have no right to pull you over and threaten you, because they are not in uniform.' Later, I got a call from the department that was handling the investigations and the guy on the phone wanted me to make a case against the officers for not wearing their hats. I wouldn't do it as I would have been victimised by every police officer in town, but he was really egging me on. Eventually, I had to put the phone down on him."

In the end, Don got a number plate with a gap between the 'I' and the '3', and the police left him alone. Years later, when Don replaced the Ford with a Volvo, he kept the number plate.

Slade II did concerts in Belgium and Denmark during May and the summer months saw them touring Europe, but all was not well within the band. Craig Fenney was fired in mid-July due to disagreements and in his place came Trevor Holliday.

"We knew Trevor in advance," Don says. "He'd been working with The Rubettes and he was a big friend of our manager, Len Tuckey. We'd actually been rehearsing with him before Craig got fired."

Slade went to Kiev to do a gig in August, and toured Germany and Holland before going to Belgium to record an album. It was recorded at Studio Impulse in the village of Herent, and the band stayed in a rented house in the historic town of Leuven. In his diary Don wrote, "Get sleeping bag and blow heater for house in Belgium."

"It was probably an OK place," Don ponders, "but I'm not the sort of person to sleep with the windows open. I like my bedroom warm, and it wasn't in Belgium. After the first night there I complained about it, so the people there suggested that I bring a fan heater. I used to leave it on while we were in the studio, hoping that it wouldn't catch fire!"

When not recording, the band did a few gigs in England and Germany, but most of the time was spent concentrating on the album. Don was still writing lyrics to tunes by both Dave and Steve Makin.

"Steve Makin and I used to work together a lot," Don says, "both writing songs and arranging the music. He was a lovely guy, but he was more into Bon Jovi, Van Halen and things like that. The other Steve, Steve Whalley, was into Little Feat and the two of them wanted us to do songs like that, but that wouldn't have been Slade. As for Steve Makin, he could play everybody else's stuff spot on, but there was no originality there. Not like Nod or Jim."

In December, Slade II went to Minsk in Belarus. By then the Christmas single was out on Columbia Records. It was a maxi CD containing three different versions of a Hill/Hunt song named 'Merry Xmas Now', not to be mistaken for 'Merry Xmas Everybody'. How the CD fared isn't documented.

January 1995 saw Slade II touring Germany. At a show in Gemünden, The Sweet and The Glitter Band got on stage with Slade to do 'Can't Get Enough'. On another trip to Germany, the plane was hit by lightning. "It was frightening!" Don states. "It had been a stormy day and the air was very heavy. We took off and it was a bumpy ride. I was sitting at the back next to a guy who must have been a pilot. Suddenly came a blue flash down the front of the plane and a loud bang, and the plane started losing height really fast. The guy next to me said, 'Don't worry. A lightning flash has hit the plane and the pilot has pulled out of automatic and is going into manual steering. When hit by lightning the plane doesn't know what to do, when it's on automatic. In the cockpit, all the pointers and needles are spinning like crazy, so the pilot has to switch to manual to dive down and get us out of the lightning.' He said that a plane can only take two or three hits of lightning, then it takes everything out and the plane drops like a stone. In all those years that I've been travelling with the band I'd never had that trouble before, and it was quite scary. It was not a very nice experience."

Don had another – if not scary, then at least strange – experience that January, when he visited the William Shaw company for the first time to see where his sticks were made.

"I'd never been to their factory before," Don recalls. "I was in the area and I was driving around trying to find it. I thought, 'This is so strange.' There were just normal houses. But I asked someone and they said, 'Yeah, it's just a hundred metres down there.' And it was just a house, a normal house where a family lived. And in the kitchen were all the computers and all the office works. Then there were two sheds at the bottom of the garden. And everything was made there. The daughter looked after the office and the accounts and the father and son did all the sticks. It was amazing."

The month was rounded up by Noddy calling Don to tell him that he and his girlfriend, Suzan, had had a little boy, Django, named after Django Rheinhardt.

March saw the Columbia release of a Slade II maxi-CD featuring three tracks: the Hill/Hunt-penned 'Wild Nites' and two versions of 'Hot Luv', which was written by Don, Dave and Paul Mellow – the alias of Paul Despiegelaere, Slade II's Belgian producer. It was to be the only Slade II track with Don's name on it.

"Dave and Bill Hunt wrote the bulk of our songs, so mine were never recorded," Don says. "Even 'Hot Luv' isn't really mine. It was Paul's song; I helped him finish the lyrics. We recorded some of my songs with Life and, apparently, the people at the record companies liked them, but we never did any of my things with Slade II."

The band did a single gig in Scotland in March as well as concerts in different European countries during the remainder of the year, but information on exact dates and venues is not available from Don, as he stopped writing diaries on April 9, 1995. Through the 22 years of keeping them, the diaries themselves had become smaller and smaller. Now they had disappeared altogether.

"It was a test," Don says. "I wanted to see if I could lead a coherent life without the diaries. I could, but today I wish I had kept on writing them, because you forget so many things over the years."

The album that emerged from the recordings in Belgium was *Keep On Rockin!*, produced by Paul Despiegielaere and released by Columbia. Of the 11 tracks, many bore titles resembling those of original Slade hits, such as 'I Hear Ya Calling' ('Hear Me Calling'), 'Miracle' ('Do You Believe In Miracles?') and 'Cum On Let's Party' ('Cum On Feel The Noize'). Although the songs didn't compare, everybody was pleased with the album.

"We basically did it in three days," Don recalls. "We'd been in the studio, playing together like we used to do in the old days. I remember that when Nod heard the album, he really liked it. He said, 'It sounds like you had so much fun recording it, because you were all in the studio together as a band. That was what we should have been doing at the end.'"

The only one who wasn't pleased was Makin. "Steve Makin is pissed off because of the album cover," Don wrote in his diary. As his services as guitarist had not been used on the album, he wasn't featured on the cover.

In July, Columbia released both a single and a maxi-CD with Hill/Hunt's 'Black And White World'. There were three mixes of the song on the maxi-CD and two on the single, on which one was renamed 'Who's To Blame' and featured the Belgian rap artist Daddy K. The latter's real name was Alain Deproost and he was a friend of Slade's Belgian producer, Marc De Bouvier. It was his idea to have Slade and Daddy K record a track together, in the same way as Aerosmith and Run DMC had done on 'Walk This Way', the influence of which is notable on 'Who's To Blame'.

The same year, Channel 4 aired a *Glam Top 10* programme, hosted by Alan Freeman and Tony Blackburn, which featured the most successful glam acts based on record sales. Slade were a clear number one. The programme included a 10-minute bio on the band, as well as individual interviews with the original line-up.

"Mine was filmed at the hotel in Brighton," Don remembers. "I was sitting there with my Pearl drums. That was probably around the time that we got a dog, a Sussex Spaniel. Some of the staff at the hotel had pups, and we got one off them and named it Ringo. I remember someone said to me, 'I wonder then if Ringo's got a dog called Don?'"

Slade kept on touring all over Europe, but nobody knows for sure just how much time Don spent with the band on the road. For the next five years, nobody really bothered to keep track of gigs, although the band were busy. Don's life seemed like an airport, with people coming and going all the time.

24

Comings And Goings

Don's life has always been turbulent, with people entering it, leaving and sometimes coming back again. It has been characterised by many hellos and goodbyes. Now a new goodbye was said, this time to Joan. After nearly five years, Don's divorce finally came through.

"God! That divorce took forever!" he sighs. "She just wouldn't let go. She wanted everything: the flat in London, the house in Bexhill, money from Slade, everything. She was on Legal Aid, so she could go on forever. Ultimately we *did* go to court, and it was fantastic. It was a lady judge and the first thing she said was, 'I can't believe this has taken so long to get this far. You are on Legal Aid. That is OK if it is genuine and it takes a few weeks or months, but this is nearly five *years*!' Then Joan's barrister got up and he talked about Slade's success and the biggest Christmas hit ever and so on. When he had finished, the judge said, 'With all due respect, what has that got to do with this?' Then my barrister said his piece and the judge said, 'OK, we're going to break for lunch, but this is going to be decided today. It is not going any further.' When we came back in, the judge decreed absolute divorce from that day. Joan was to keep the flat in London and I the house in Bexhill. She wasn't to have any future earnings from Slade and I was to have no claims on her antiques business. And that was it. I was stunned. Five years and then suddenly it was all over. What a relief!"

On July 17, 1996, another closure was reached, this time tragically. Chas Chandler died of a heart condition in his hometown of Newcastle, and it came as a shock to Don.

"I knew he had a heart condition," Don recalls, "but he got almost cleared at one point. Nod and I had seen him a few days before his death and he was fantastic. He was like the old Chas. When Nod called me up to tell me that he had passed away, I said, 'I can't believe it!' We'd had such a great night out, but he just had a relapse and went.

"All of us from the original Slade line-up attended his funeral. It was in Cullercoats, near Newcastle, and I drove up from Bexhill. Jim was already there and Nod as well. Dave came later.

"It was a very big funeral with loads of mourners; even Jimi Hendrix's father attended. He was the only black guy, obviously an elderly man, and I didn't know who he was. I asked, 'Who is that guy?' And when I was told it was Al Hendrix, I found it such a lovely gesture. He'd come all the way from Detroit to be there.

"Chas' wife, Madeleine, was fantastic. She was very composed. Stefan, his son from his first marriage, even did a speech from the pulpit. It was very touching. Nod also talked; he mentioned that when The Animals were in Japan in the sixties, everybody used to walk *through* the doors when they got drunk, because the doors were made of rice paper. They always knew when it was Chas, because he was such a big, tall man, much bigger than the rest, and in the basement of the hotel they had all those doors with holes shaped like Chas, like in a Tom and Jerry cartoon. I sat next to John Steele in the chapel and we just couldn't stop laughing."

Later that year, the original Slade line-up came together again but on a happier occasion. The Christmas edition of *This Is Your Life* was devoted to Noddy and, of course, the rest of the band were invited as guests. Characters from every era of Nod's life appeared on the show, and at the close the entire Slade road crew appeared. "We had such a great time," Don says. "We stayed there for the night and we all attended the party after the show."

The year also saw the release of *The Genesis Of Slade*, a compilation of the recordings of The Vendors, The 'N Betweens and Steve Brett & The Mavericks. The CD was released through The Music Corporation and had been compiled by long-time Slade fan John Haxby.

"For Slade's 25th anniversary in Walsall in 1991, I'd been surprised that people were interested in me and Mick and Cass," John Howells explains. "Until then, I didn't realise that people were interested in the past, but they are. They wanted to know all sorts of things: who played on the Vendors EP, what instruments we played, things like that. I think it strange that somebody would be interested in something that basically never happened. Some years later, I had a chat with a fan from Sheffield who told me that John Haxby wanted to make *The Genesis Of Slade*. I wasn't really interested, but the thing was that Don had come down for his 50th birthday and I found it a good time to run it by him. And Don said, 'Get on with it.' And we all know the outcome of that. *The Genesis Of Slade* fills in a little gap; I thought that if some fans are that interested in the stuff, then give it to them."

"I remember talking to Johnny about it," Don adds, "but that album caused a bit of trouble, because it included material not only made by our old bands prior to the Slade line-up, but also the recordings that we had made with Kim Fowley in 1966. We didn't know that in advance and, although it was done in our 'N Betweens days, we weren't very pleased with having the material out without permission from the band. But we didn't own the copyrights to those tracks, so we could do nothing about it."

In 1996, a new sound engineer, Robin Lavender, was introduced to Slade, firstly on a casual basis.

"I was working for The Rubettes in 1996 when I was asked to work for Slade, on and off," remembers Lavender. "The first gig I did with them was actually in Denmark, at The Locomotion in Aarhus. I got along with Don straight away because he is so friendly with everyone. You are instant mates with him, which is a really nice thing. Don is not pretentious. I remember once we were at the back of the stage and this young girl asked him if she could have a photograph. And Don went, 'No problem at all.' The girl then gave him the camera and posed with me! Don took the picture and afterwards she was so happy – she obviously had no idea who he is. When she had left, Don and I couldn't stop laughing. It was so funny!"

"We were on the floor in hysterics," Don agrees. "I'd got myself ready to pose, and then she wanted me to take a photo of those two!"

Don married Diana in 1997 and the couple lived in Bexhill, where she was back managing the hotel.

"We had the wedding party at the hotel in Bexhill," Don recalls. "Dave came down for the wedding, but Nod and Jim couldn't make it. Swinn was there though, and some of my family."

"I was glad when Don got married the second time," says his sister Carol, "because sometimes we all got a bit tired of Don's many women. There were only two whom we had really liked – Pat and Di, so we were glad that he married Di."

1997 was also the year when Slade II dropped the suffix and got back to calling themselves plain Slade. "We found out that we didn't need to call ourselves Slade II," Don says. "Our lawyer said that anybody can use the name, and if Nod and Jim wanted to stop us from doing it, they would look so small, trying to stop us from earning money. We were told that they couldn't do a thing against us calling ourselves Slade. At that time Nod wasn't bothered, anyway. With Jim, it was like he had put Slade behind him, dropping out of the public eye to study psychology instead."

The band toured Europe and, in 1998, the line-up changed once more. Steve Makin was voted out. "I agreed with it at the time," Don says. "Dave had spent so many years with Noddy as a second guitarist that he wanted another guitarist now. As Dave had had classical lessons off Steve Makin, that was why he was brought in. But Steve Whalley was playing guitar as well, and there were too many guitarists in the band. It got really crowded, so Steve Makin had to leave."

By then, Don had started using a gum shield when playing. "I'd never realised at the time, but when I play the drums I play with my mouth as well. Like singing the drums. I keep biting my teeth together and that kept breaking them. In the seventies, when I was chewing gum it was helping, but when I stopped with that, my fillings kept falling out. My dentist said, 'I can't keep on rebuilding your teeth,' so he suggested it. 'Why don't you have a gum shield like boxers?' And I thought it was a great idea, so I said, 'Let's try one.' He then made one for me and it is perfect. But I get strange looks from people down the front at concerts with these gleaming, white teeth. They're shining! A lot of people think that I'm still chewing gum on stage, although that's just me 'singing' the drums. You can see the bite marks in my gum shield. It is very strange, with the shield and the gloves on. When I go on stage to play the drums, it's like I'm going into the ring to box!"

So, while Don never became a boxer as he had hoped in his youth, he ended up wearing the gear on stage. Life has always had its little ironies with Don.

On October 6, 1999, Don's mother died, which shocked him more than anything.

"We had always been so close," Don says, "and I guess I'd been her favourite child. She had always been my anchor. I could totally rely on her and she had always been very supportive of me, so losing her was devastating. It shook my world."

"I remember, in the later years, a memory of Don's mum," Dave recalls. "I went over to her house in Bilston, because she wanted me to take her to visit Johnny Jones' mother, who was a friend of hers. Johnny Jones, or J.J. as we used to call him, used to work for us and had recently died. I had been best man at his wedding, so we both went over there and visited her. I remember Don's mum saying to me later, when I dropped her off home, 'Look after Don.' I think that was the last time I saw her."

"Since Dad's death, Mum had been lonely as the two of them used to do everything together," Don says. "Of course, my three siblings, who lived nearby, as well as my nieces and nephews, used to visit her and make sure she was OK, and I called her every day as well, but it wasn't quite the same. I remember my sister Carol saying it was a good thing that Dad was buried in a cemetery away from where they lived, instead of in the one nearby, otherwise Mum would have spent all her time there. She'd really missed him. Plus her body closed down, so she just died. It was awful. It was strange when I didn't have to call her every night any more. With her gone, it was like the end of the family somehow. To this day, her death is like an open wound to me and it is still difficult for me to talk about. I guess things like that take time to heal. I'm not sure I'll ever get over losing her."

On a happier note, a renewed interest in the original Slade started to bloom by the end of the old millennium. The Stuart Maconie documentary, *The Boyz From The Black Country – The Slade Story*, had been broadcast on BBC Radio 2 in 1998, with Toyah Willcox as the host. It became available as a podcast, hosted by Maconie, almost 10 years later. Another documentary, this time for television, was aired in 1999. It was called *It's Slade*, and Don rates this 50-minute BBC1 film as the best feature on Slade so far.

"The research is very thorough in that one," he says, "and they did some good individual interviews with us as well."

Although the documentary made it clear that it was the combined efforts of Don, Dave, Jim and Noddy that had made the band, Noddy as the frontman was the one that people remembered. He had become a beloved DJ, actor and entertainer in the UK, and was rewarded with an MBE for services to music in the New Year Honours list in 2000. Although fans wondered why only one member of the band was honoured, Don had no objections.

"I sent Nod a card," he smirks, "congratulating him on the MEB, MEB being short for the Midlands Electricity Board, a local electricity company. I wrote to him: 'Do I have to bow to you the next time we meet?'"

As the end of the 20th century approached, Don started doing cocaine. He had put his alcohol addiction behind him but now a new one emerged, quite ironically, as Don had been afraid of drugs in his younger years. "It was a bad habit and an expensive one," Don admits, "but it only lasted a few years."

It didn't prevent him from working with Slade either, and he kept the band's flag flying in the new century. In 2000, Trevor Holliday left the band; he had opened his own studio and would rather spend time on that. He was replaced on bass by Dave Glover, with whom they toured all over Europe. In November, they did a gig at the National Exhibition Centre in Birmingham as part of the Music Live show, which brought some familiar faces back into Don's life.

Since Slade's 25th anniversary at Walsall Town Hall, Don had kept in touch with Mick Marson, but now Carole Williams and Vicky Pearson came back as well. "One day I was strolling through the local store and I saw Dave coming towards me," Vicky recalls. "I thought, oh well, would he remember me? He walked up to me and said, 'I don't remember your name, but I know that I know you.' I said who I was and that I had recently been widowed, and wasn't in a great place at the time. Because Dave knew how close Don and I used to be, he wrote down Don's number and said, 'Ring him. He'd want to talk to you.'"

"Vicky came over the next night," Carole says, "and I rang Don. I hadn't seen him for over 20 years. I had lived in the next village to Jim and Louise during my first marriage, so we went over to each other's homes from time to time, but the rest of the guys were long gone. When I called Don, I tried to be all official sounding and formal, 'Hello, could I speak to Mr Powell?' but he recognised my voice and said, 'Hello, is that Caz?' We had a good chat and arranged to meet at the NEC in Birmingham, where they were playing. I was a bit apprehensive, as it had been so many years, but this tall, handsome guy with wonderful eyes just came and hugged me, and all the years vanished. Mick Marson was there as well; it had been 30 years since we'd last met, but we knew each other straight away. Since then we have kept in touch, going to see the new band whenever we can."

The year 2000 saw Don venturing into other areas than music. He was an extra in the BBC version of *Lorna Doone*, playing one of the bad guys.

"Some Slade fans were doing extra work on TV, and I asked if they could get me some as well," Don says, "just for passing time. The BBC was doing a big production of *Lorna Doone*, and I was asked to come down and take part. The filming took place on the outskirts of Cardiff and, as the hotel company that Di worked for had a hotel in the area, they put me in there.

"On the set, we were told what to do. We were lined up and the producer was walking by, as gay as they come, and he only took one look at me. He went, 'Oh, I like *him*! He has to be a Doone. Get him changed!' So I was dressed in black leather and I remember my job description was 'a bit of rough!'

"I was only an extra, but I had a great time. I knew a bit about filming from making *Flame*, of course, but I learnt something new as well. As it had to look like the 17th century, they had a lot of people riding horses, and when they did that they wanted chickens to run out of the way. But in order not to have the chickens run all over the place all the time, they had to control them. I didn't understand how they could do that, but the guy who worked with the chickens showed me. He took their necks and twisted them underneath their wings, without hurting them. When he did that they were basically stuck there. Then, when they get a soft push, the heads come out and the chickens start running around. It was almost like they were clockwork, but it looked very realistic."

In April 2001, Slade were playing in Denmark at a concert in the town of Silkeborg. Don met a local primary-school teacher. "Her name was Hanne," Don says, "and when our eyes met, we couldn't take them off each other. It was like that all night. I met her after the show and she said that she still had a drumstick of mine from 1974, when we played in Aarhus. I thought she was joking! She told me that in 1974 all her friends had got together to go to the show, but they had to buy Hanne's mother a ticket for the concert, as she was to drive them. Hanne's mum was a speech therapist at the time and she forced the girls to put gum in their ears to protect them from the noise of the concert. The gum sort of melted, so later they got into trouble with the school nurse, because they still had bits of chewing gum in their ears. Of course, I asked Hanne if she wanted a new stick off me!"

With two very busy and different careers, Don and Diane had slowly but surely grown apart. Despite all good intentions, their marriage wasn't built to last, so soon Don found himself dating Hanne instead, going back and forth between England and Denmark. "When I talked to my friends and said, 'I'm just going to Denmark for the weekend,' they would go, '*What!*' as if I were going to the moon," Don recalls. "They didn't realise that it probably took me longer to drive from Bexhill to London than it takes to fly to Denmark. That's how small the world is."

When Don met Hanne, his fling with cocaine ended. Hanne was a single mum with three kids who weren't to be exposed to things like that, so just as he had once stopped drinking, Don now stopped doing coke in order to be with his new love. The three children, daughters Anne Kirstine, born in 1987, and Emilie, born in 1989, and son Andreas, born in 1993, remember vividly when Don came into their lives.

"Mum used to talk about being a Slade fan when she was a teenager," says Anne Kirstine. "This way I knew 'Merry Xmas Everybody', 'Far Far Away' and 'Everyday' before I met Don."

Her sister, Emilie, agrees. "I too knew the Christmas song, but I didn't know anything about Don. At first, he and Mum only saw each other occasionally, but they talked on the phone quite a lot and then Mum would go meet him at concerts."

"I knew Mum had a boyfriend," chips in Andreas, "and I was looking forward to meeting him. I didn't know who he was though, except that he was a drummer and that was pretty cool."

"It was indeed very exciting," Emilie recalls. "Both Don's job and the fact that he was British. That was new and different. But he looked really weird with that huge, wild hair and his tight jeans. I had to get used to that. I was about 12 years old when Don came into our lives and I'd never seen a man his age wear tight jeans. He looked like an old rock star – which of course he was!"

"At first, I didn't understand what he was saying," Andreas admits. "He was British and he looked weird, but I knew he only wanted the best for my mum, and for me as well. I could *feel* his kindness. He wasn't just interested in my mum – he was interested in me, too. The first time he came to visit us, he was wearing these long leather boots and he went outside to play football with me, because I was into football at that time. And while we were playing, I happened to wreck those expensive boots. Oh my God! And that was our first meeting. But he was gracious about it. He was OK."

Despite his new relationship, Don went to the other end of the world in 2001, when Slade played in the Falkland Islands.

"That was interesting," Don says. "Before that, I was quite ignorant. I knew of the war, of course, but when we were to play there, I thought, where the fuck *are* the Falkland Islands? When you get there, you realise that the next stop is the South Pole!

"We all met at Brize Norton, the RAF camp in Oxfordshire, and we flew with a big jumbo jet in the company of a black comedian/compère, three young girl dancers and the next contingent of soldiers who were to go on duty on the Falklands. They only stay there for six months before they are sent somewhere else, and the jet was full of food for them. We landed in Port Stanley and there is nothing there, except for penguins and sheep.

"We stayed with the troops. Our quarters were very basic. There was one room with camp beds and a sink in the corner, and at the bottom of the corridor they had the showers and the toilets. When Dave saw it, he freaked! The first night, when he wanted to have his sleep, some of the troops were walking down the corridor singing 'Merry Xmas Everybody'. I heard Dave say, 'Will you keep quiet!' and the guys replied, 'Fuck off, you little cunt!' In the end Dave actually moved to the main quarters, so he could get some sleep!

"We did a concert in Port Stanley Town Hall and then two or three in Mount Pleasant, where they had a big restaurant with a ballroom. We got everything we wanted, and every day they took us out in helicopters all around the islands, pointing out where different events in the war had happened. When the Argentinians had taken over the islands, the Special Air Service was there before our troops arrived. They got dropped there secretly. There was a big lake on the island where six SAS officers had hidden, half-submerged in the water. At night they would go out and find information, so when the troops actually got there they knew everything.

"One guy lived on a farm close to the lake. One night, when he was watching TV with his wife, he heard little taps on the window. When he opened the door there were these frogmen standing outside, three guys from the SAS. They came in, sat on the settee in their scuba-diving gear and had tea and biscuits. They explained that they had been there for a week, hiding, as up the hill near the farm the Argentinians had got a post and they were trying to find out what was going on. The farmer said, 'Hang on a minute.' He got his jacket, put his hat on and got on his bike. He rode up the hill to the Argentinians and asked them what they were doing. They told him and he rode back down again and told it to the SAS. They had tried to find it out for weeks, and the Argentinians just told the farmer. It was mad!

"We learnt that when the troops had landed from England, the Argentinians had occupied one hilltop which our troops tried to take over. The Argentinians were just rolling hand grenades down the hill, but the English troops had a megaphone and they shouted to the Argentinians, 'If you don't give up, we'll send in the Gurkhas!' The Argentinians gave up immediately! The Gurkhas are really ruthless. They are only tiny guys but they are killers. It's instilled in them. They don't mind being hurt or killed. They just kill. Every army in the world fears them, because they have no thought of themselves.

"We stayed there for about a week, and the atmosphere between the immediate officers and the normal squaddies was like they were all the same," Don continues. "I found that great. They would just sit in one room, drinking beer together. But we used to eat in the officers' mess and that was very different. It said in our contract that we had to wear trousers and shirts for that, as they wouldn't allow jeans. They still had that typical British stiff upper lip.

"The officers' mess was like going to the Hilton. When you looked out of the window, it was this horrible weather and there was nothing but sheep, but inside they wore the red dress uniforms and had waiters bringing them all kinds of food. We were at the end of the world, but still they were so formal. One time I was sitting next to a high-ranking officer and I said, 'With all due respect, what was the war all about? There's nothing here. Is it some strategic point or what?' He just went, 'Offshore oil. The war was 20 years ago, but that's why we're still here. Every other week the Argentinian air force comes over. Then we just send our guys up and they go away.' I'd never even thought about that.

"We had a great time on the Falkland Islands, but we were told never to go off the paths because there were minefields. Before the Argentinians left, they mined the whole island. Almost every other army maps the fields, but the Argentinians didn't do that. The paths were safe, but the only reason why the troops knew where to look for mines on the rest of the island was when they heard an explosion and saw pieces of sheep going up in the air!"

Safely back from the end of the world, Robin Lavender became the full-time front-of-house sound engineer for Slade and the band got their own website, run by Belgian fan Philippe D'Hoeraene, which went live in August 2001. For the remainder of the year, Slade did over 30 shows all over Europe, including the yearly Christmas tour of England and Scotland. Often, Don's new lady would travel with the band, along with her kids.

"During the summer, I went to my very first Slade concert," Andreas recalls. "That was at the HSV Stadium in Hamburg, Germany, at an oldies festival. It was amazing! I was just a little boy and I watched all those people in the audience being *sooo* crazy! I remember seeing a huge man lying on the ground next to the stage, talking gibberish and peeing his pants! That was just such a lovely way of showing me the milieu in which I had landed! I was about seven or eight years old and I'd never known anything about fame or famous people, but Don took me with him on stage. Mum helped Don get his drums ready, so they asked if I'd like to go up front on stage. That was the first time I got that 'Oh fuck!' feeling! There were thousands of people in the audience and they all went, 'Aaawww!' from watching that little boy on stage. It was fantastic!"

"After that, we often went on Slade tours," Anne Kirstine says. "That way, we came to spend our summer holidays in quite a different way from how we used to, as we went with the band to Germany, France and many other places."

277

"A lot of parents from the school I was attending thought I was too young to go to Slade concerts," Andreas recalls, "but the way Don cared for us was amazing. He always saw to it that I felt safe. There was always some area backstage where I could stay and feel safe."

"It is, however, a bit weird with the age group that listens to Slade," Emilie thinks, "Most of them are middle-aged. I remember the first time I went to a Slade concert. My sister and I were watching all these *parents* acting as if they were teenagers! That was pretty strange."

"It is true that most people you meet at Slade concerts are old enough to be my parents or even grandparents," Andreas ponders, "but they are all so nice, and I have a great time with them. Slade fans are 'ordinary' people, who go to the concerts to have a good time with fellow Slade fans, drink some beer and listen to the music. Slade's music is all about having a good time. They are not out to make people angry or sad, they just want to make people feel good, and their fans are just the same."

"I haven't been on tour with Slade for a while," Emilie admits. "I only went when mum and Don first met. At that point, it was very exciting to get to spend the night in a posh hotel room, especially as you could bring your friends along; but when you've been on the road with the band for a while it gets boring. After all, you spend most of the time in a tour bus!"

"In the tour bus, Emilie and I would always sing," Anne Kirstine recalls, "and then Dave would sing with us, or one of the other band members, and it was so nice. If the hotel had a piano, we would bring song books and then we would be singing, some would be shooting pool and we would just have a great time, all of us."

"It has been very exciting getting to see how everything works behind the scenes," Emilie admits, "and besides, the entire band have always been good to us. They are nice guys, so we have had a lot of fun, just hanging out together. A couple of times I've been on stage, dancing with Dave Hill, as well. It was fun being up there, looking out at the crowds. Like getting a glimpse of what they experience as a rock band."

"I think the life of rock musicians is so cool, hanging out backstage and at hotels," Andreas says. "I didn't know anything about that kind of life before I met Don, and I never thought I'd get to know it. For some years I helped out selling T-shirts at the concerts, and that was a great way for me to earn a little money and get some amazing experiences. I wish I had the time to go with Don and Mum on tour a lot more than I do now, but as you get older you get your own life, and you put your friends over travelling with the band."

In 2002, Slade's website listed more than 80 shows all over Europe, but new territories were added as well, as the band played both Russia and Bahrain.

"The first time we went to Russia, we were asked, why didn't you come here in the seventies?" Don laughs. "But it's obvious why we couldn't be there back then. Now those markets have opened up and it's great. It's like they have been reborn. People go there to see us now. What's nice over there is, obviously because of the money situation, the government half-finances the concerts. This way they can keep the ticket prices very low, so people can afford them. It is fantastic that they do that. It's not a propaganda thing and it works.

"As for Bahrain, we only played for English people for one gig in a hotel complex. I thought it would be fantastic, because you just never go to such places. We stayed at a beautiful hotel, but the strange thing was that on one side of the street there were these amazing big houses, and on the other side there was extreme poverty. I wanted to go out and have a walk around but I was advised against it, because there had just been local elections and the people who lost weren't happy chappies. They had snipers on the building tops, shooting people. I thought, 'What am I doing here???' So we just did the gig and flew back the next day."

25

Home Is Where The Heart Is

Although it was a new line-up of Slade that now toured the world, no one ever forgot that the foundation on which this band stood had been built by the original line-up. To many a fan, the honouring of that group was long overdue. Overlooked and often scorned by the rock cognoscenti, Slade have somehow fallen by the wayside when it comes to handing out honours in the awards ceremonies that proliferate in the 'heritage rock' environment of the 21st century. In 2002, however, the original band finally got some of the recognition that should have been bestowed on them long before. On September 9, Wolverhampton University honoured them with fellowships for their contribution to music.

"A few days before, I called the rest of the guys from the original line-up and we were laughing, because how else could we have ever had such a university degree?" Don says. "We couldn't take it seriously. We all turned up for the day and had the hats and the gowns on and were given the awards as well. We were to walk through the crowds towards the stage and sit there until we were called up. Nod then gave a little speech and said something like, 'Who'd have thought that four guys from a rock'n'roll band would get such a fellowship?' It was something special, and I'm now don Don!

"A lot of people went for that event: my sister Carol and her husband, Swinn, Nod's lady, Suzan. Afterwards, we went to my hotel for a few drinks, but Jim didn't come with us. Soon after, he was to do a couple of solo shows, going on stage for the first time since Slade."

The year 2002 saw new releases from the band. In June came the maxi-CD 'Some Exercise' (three mixes), in September the single 'Take Me Home'/'Black And White World' and, in November, the album *Cum On Let's Party*. All the releases were on Virgin in Belgium. Where 'Some Exercise' had been penned by the Swedish songwriting team Lotta Ahlin and Tommy Lydell, the single tracks were written by, respectively, Hill/Whalley and Hill/Hunt. The album, produced by Slade, consisted mostly of tracks from the *Keep On Rockin!* album, with some added new tracks.

In 2003, the band emerged with a new bassist, John Berry. He replaced Dave Glover because of the press scandal concerning the serial killer Rosemary West. She was serving 10 life sentences in Durham jail for killing 10 young women and, apparently, had fallen in love with Glover after exchanging letters with him while in prison. Rumours of marriage between West and Glover were strong in the press, and eventually he had to resign from Slade in order not to hurt the band.

"Dave Glover was always on the computer when we were on the road," Don remembers. "It wasn't until it was in the newspapers that we realised that he had been writing to Rose West. I thought, *WHAT!!!* I called Len Tuckey to ask what all this was about, and Len just said, 'He's gone.' Apparently Glover had called Dave up a few days before, because he knew it was going to be in the papers. He was just warning Dave as to what to expect, but Dave never said anything to us, so we knew nothing. Glover both resigned and was fired at the same time. I think he thought Rose West was innocent or something like that. I have never spoken to him since. Instead, we got John Berry, who had played with lots of people like The Tremeloes, Mud and The Rubettes. He's a really nice guy."

"For Don, it doesn't matter so much that they've had a lot of different musicians over the years, because all the time Dave has been there," adds

Robin Lavender. "I think that makes it OK with Don. Although others may come and go, Dave is always there. And besides, the comings and goings of other musicians don't really change what Don does. He's just back there on the drums doing the same thing as ever. It's a good thing that he's a drummer, with his amnesia. As they say, in a band there are three musicians and a drummer! He just does his own thing. But admittedly, when John came in it was a lot easier, because we'd had a bit of trouble with the former bass player."

With John Berry in the band, Slade also got a new backline and stage manager, Tim Ramage, who was recommended by Berry, with whom he had worked previously with Mud. "Don and I work together closer than anybody," says Ramage. "Because of the amnesia, he'll ask me the same thing five or six times – he doesn't remember at all that he has already asked."

"That's right," says Robin, "especially if we are in foreign places. Don usually rings to hear what time we are leaving in the morning, and sometimes he rings you more than once to check things out. You might have a telephone conversation with him during the day and, when you put the phone down, he'll ring again and have the same conversation, forgetting that he has already talked to you. Don's amnesia doesn't affect his work, although I'm sure it affects the rest of his life immensely. But the drumming is one thing that remains."

"Don'll come down to the venue early with me, just to be sure to be there," Tim Ramage says. "If we have to alter things on stage, you can always see him look at me like, 'Are you sure this is what is right?' Yes, Don. The sequence of events is important to him. But when it comes to past history, his memory is incredible. If we hear some obscure song on the radio, he immediately goes, 'Oh yes! That's so and so and he did this and that.' He is very, very sharp that way. And then of course Don's onstage volume level – 130db+, akin to a Concorde landing in your lounge – is so loud, set to *stun*, that many is the time other technicians working on stage alongside me have expressed utter disbelief. During a performance, when either Don or I have to call attention to the level of his monitor, they assume this is to turn it down, but this is *never* the case. Don has a motto about monitor-volume levels on stage: *always up, never down* and *quantity not quality*!!! He says it every show! It is truly *cum on feel the noize.*"

"For me it is actually an advantage that Don hits the drums so hard," adds Lavender. "It makes it easy to get a very good sound. It is very easy to work with him."

"It seems that the name Powell is synonymous with very loud, powerful and hard–hitting classic English rock drummers," says Ramage. "Don is one, and Cozy, now sadly departed, is the other. I have had the pleasure of working as a tech for both of them. They both attack the kit in such a powerful and dynamic style; it has made working so closely with them on stage a great experience."

Slade's official website could boast more than 80 shows all over Europe in 2003, but rock'n'roll was still reclaiming its children. In January, Mickey Finn of T.Rex passed away. "We played a festival a few months before where he was on the same bill," Don recalls. "It was very sad actually. Mickey wasn't in a very good condition. He didn't know where he was on stage. Afterwards, we sat in the bar and he paid for our drinks, but then he gave me the change. I said, 'No, that's your change,' and he went, 'You just bought me one, keep it,' and that went on for a long time. I couldn't get him to understand that it was his change; I realised that I could be standing there all night, making quite a bit of money! But he was in a really sad state. He looked terrible, all yellow. It was awful, like the first time I saw Brian Connolly since the seventies. Again it was one of the big shows, with lots of bands on. I'd gone to the dressing room to get my stuff and was about to go back when this guy said, 'Hello Don! How are you? Great time in the seventies, wasn't it?' And I just said, 'Yeah,' because at first I didn't realise who it was. Then I suddenly stopped, realising that this was Brian Connolly of The Sweet. He looked like an old man in his seventies. It was awful. Now they are both gone. You know it is going to happen eventually, but with both Mickey Finn and Brian Connolly, it was no surprise at all."

2003 saw two new releases from Slade. The single 'Cum On Let's Party'/'Johnny Played The Guitar', both tracks penned by Hill/Hunt, as well as the album *Superyob*, released on YOB Records, an enterprise of Dave's. The album was a compilation, for which Dave had remastered and redesigned everything from Slade since 1992, including 'Merry Xmas Now', 'Hold On To Love', plus all of *Keep On Rockin!*

As 2003 came to an end, a Christmas edition of the TV show *Rock Legends* was aired on Central TV. The programme featured Slade, was hosted by Noddy and included new interviews with the four original members.

Noddy married his long-time girlfriend, Suzan, the following June, and Don went to the wedding accompanied by Hanne. By then Don had decided to move to Denmark, building up a new life with Hanne and her three children in the town of Silkeborg. The boy from the West Midlands had found a new home in the mid-west of Denmark.

Settling in Denmark on a permanent basis came naturally to Don. He quickly picked up a few phrases of the language, words like *lortevejr*, meaning crap weather, and *skat*, meaning both darling and taxes. But in general, he got by with his native language. "Everybody speaks English here anyway," he says, "so I don't get that many chances to practise my Danish. Even at home, Hanne and the kids speak English to me."

Home for Don was now a villa in the outskirts of Silkeborg, one of the most beautiful areas of Denmark, dominated by big lakes, forests and some of the highest points in the country.

"I think Denmark is a wonderful place to live," says Don. "I find it so peaceful here and there's so much going on. What I like is that the Danish authorities really care for young people and their interests. Once I was asked to go to a music school and talk about Slade's career and, when I got there, they had all this equipment, amplifiers and drums and guitars. The kids swap ideas and go on to play, taking turns and just jamming really. And I think it is wonderful.

"I did a question-and-answer thing from the stage, so they could ask about Slade's career and certain things relevant to having a record deal, which they were interested in obviously. Then I jammed with the young guys and one of them said to me, 'You're a fantastic drummer for an old man!' I almost wet myself laughing!

"Although people know who I am here in Denmark, they are quite surprised when they learn that I live here. Once a guy stopped me in the street, asking, 'Didn't you use to be Don Powell?' and I said, 'I still am!' But in general, there's a different respect in Denmark. When I'm going certain places, like the record shops or the cafés, people don't think they own me and have a right to butt in on me. In Denmark, even the Queen can go shopping like an ordinary housewife. You would never see that in England! Everybody is so down to earth, even the Danish Royal Family. I actually met the Danish Crown Prince once, as we'd been invited to the same event, the Danish Sports Awards. Some of his friends came over to say that he was a big Slade fan, so I talked to him and he was just a normal guy. I was totally amazed, as no way would it have been like this in England. Because people are so relaxed in Denmark and not boggled over by celebrities, I can now live an ordinary life, being a family man, where the family comes first and the music is just my job. I think that is great."

"Don has been living in London and in New York City, and then he ended up living in the woods in Silkeborg!" his stepdaughter Anne Kirstine laughs. "He isn't as restless any more after he has come to live here. The surroundings give him an inner peace. For years he used to bite his nails, but after he came out here in the woods, he doesn't any more. He is able to relax here, chopping wood and drowning the plants! He loves to water the plants. I'm sure Don loves it here. He has his peace and quiet. He likes the wood and the neighbours. They organise neighbourhood street parties each year and Don really enjoys that. He is happy and we are happy to have him. Except when Mum washes his stage clothes and puts them outside on the clothes line! Don's stage clothes are very tight, striped leggings; they look like something you'd wear in a circus! My sister and I find it *so* embarrassing! I actually think Andreas borrowed those leggings once for a fancy dress party where he was supposed to be Freddie Mercury!"

Andreas adds, "After Don moved to Silkeborg, whenever I went somewhere new with my friends, they would always introduce me, 'This is Andreas. His stepdad is Don Powell.' It was pretty annoying at times, because I didn't know if they wanted to be friends because of me, or because of Don. But I guess it will always be like that. I remember once I got a Slade CD and we used to play it on a CD player in class, and everyone would go, 'Wow, listen! That's Andreas' dad!' I thought, 'He's not my dad, he's my stepdad!' Sometimes I would say something, other times I wouldn't. We always played 'We'll Bring The House Down', but when you're in third grade and don't speak English it sounds like 'We'll bring the hamster.' We thought it was a song about a hamster! We thought we were so cool, running around singing, 'We'll bring the hamster! Woh-oh, woh-oh!' Mum told Don, who told the band and, of course, I became a laughing stock!"

Hanne's children were rather young when she and Don first met and Don came to love them as his own. "Obviously they are not my children, but they have taken me on board and I have taken them on board," he says. "I've got a good relationship with all of them; it is like a friendship more than anything else. It is a first time for me to settle down in a relationship with children that age. Joan also had children, but they were much older when I met her. Here in Denmark, I have more of a father function so to speak, although the kids see their father all the time. But I'm taking the kids to school, going to PT meetings and taking Andreas to football matches. I abhor football, but when I take Andreas, I quite enjoy it. It's one of the pleasures of being a parent. As long as we can sit in the box though! How anybody can enjoy a game when it's freezing cold, I don't understand, but it's OK from the box and you can see the whole field from there."

"Of course, I have my own dad here in Denmark," Andreas says, "and that has always been important to Don. Right from the beginning, he made it clear that he wasn't out to become my dad. He wanted to be my best friend instead and to make me feel safe, and that impressed me. He said to me, 'I respect that you have a dad and I won't try to make you like me more than you like him. I'll just be here if you need a friend.' It meant a lot to me that he handled it that way."

Emilie agrees. "I have a great dad, but then again, Don has no ambition of becoming my dad. At first he was worried that he would step on my father's feelings, as he spends a lot of time with us, especially with Andreas, to whom he has become a genuine father figure. It was different with my sister and me, as we were a lot older than Andreas. Don has never told me what to do and not to do and I have never had a row with him. He doesn't want us to feel that he can tell us what to do. Instead, our relationship has a very fine balance. To my sister and me, Don is a stepfather with whom you can talk and have a nice time, but as equals. And he and our father have a really good relationship as well. In that respect, everything has worked out nicely."

"Don is a great stepdad," Anne Kirstine says. "He is very tolerant. He just fits in and helps out where he can. He loves people and being around people. He wants to make everyone happy and he doesn't want anything in return. I think he'd find it embarrassing to make demands. He is very humble that way. I'm really impressed about the way he has managed his part as a stepdad, and I think he is enjoying it as well. He likes being a stepdad as he has no kids of his own."

"Don fits right into our family," says Emilie, "because we're all very musical, we have always had a lot to do with people from other countries and we are all interested in foreign languages, mainly English. Actually we've been playing English picture lottery since we were kids, because Mum lived in America for a while. This way we all spoke English, and we found it great to be able to speak it with Don."

"I think life would have been tougher in our family had it not been for Don," Andreas admits. "The only difficult thing is his amnesia. It is frustrating when he doesn't remember what he has allowed you to do! Don can be pretty confused and stressed, and it must be hard for him to live with that handicap. But I'm very happy that we have such a close relationship. I'm grateful for having a person to go to if I have issues that I don't like to involve my mum in. Don has always been great in supporting me and helping me out. I'm so glad that he and Mum got together, because he understands me; he has a way of telling me what is best for me without dictating anything. He trusts me to make the right decisions in the end."

Combining family life in Denmark with life on the road with Slade hasn't been as difficult as one would expect. "When Hanne brings the kids to our shows, they know that when I'm at work, I'm at work," Don says, "Then I'm Don Powell the drummer and I don't have time for other things. They understand that, which is good."

"He travels a lot, but it's like any other job," Emilie thinks. "He just has weird working hours!"

"I think that Don moving to Denmark is really nice," Dave adds. "He has moved to a nice country, living in a nice house with Hanne. Whatever makes him happy is the best for him. In the old days when we worked live, we were going around with our personal friends and we mostly only saw each other when we were playing, and it is the same with Don now. Whether he lives in England or in Denmark is not particularly different to me, as he's only a phone call away."

"It is actually a bit of an advantage that Don has moved to Denmark," Tim Ramage thinks, "because he always gets to the venues earlier than the rest of us. He always seems to be down there. The rest of us get flown in from England and sometimes we are late in the airport, or on the bus. So when Don's earlier than I am, he has a look at the drum kit or he'll call me and say, 'We need an extra amp for Dave,' or whatever. Often venues are an absolute nightmare, but it helps that Don calls me in advance."

During 2004, the band did about 80 gigs all over Europe, and life was never dull on the road.

"On one occasion, when we turned up to do an open-air show in Holland, we found that the dodgy promoter had neglected to supply a drum kit, assuming wrongly that we would bring our own," Tim Ramage remembers. "We were unable to borrow from the other bands as they had to leave before we played. So, with no one else interested in getting a kit – Dave and the rest of the band being safely tucked up in the hotel – it was left to Don and me to start asking around. Things were getting pretty desperate, as time was running out, so it ended up with Don and me knocking on the door of total unknowns at a house nearby! Can you imagine the expression of utter shock on the woman's face when she opened her door to find a famous rock drummer and me, his roadie, begging to borrow her son's drum kit so we could do a show up the road! Happily for us, she and her son agreed, so we immediately started to carry this young lad's drums over to the stage, with minutes to spare before the show started!"

Slade did about 80 gigs in 2005 as well, but in May Steve Whalley left them quite unexpectedly and a new singer had to be found. "Steve wanted to go on and do other things," Don explains. "He was into rock that was a bit softer and, even before he joined us, he did solo albums. That was what he got back into. To replace him, we got Mal McNulty. Apparently he sang with Sweet and I didn't know about it! It was Andy Scott who recommended him to us and he was a friend of our bass player John Berry as well. He approached him and we then rehearsed with him, which was fantastic. The first song we rehearsed was 'Cum On Feel The Noize' and when Mal started singing, I felt sparkles on my face. I looked up at Dave, and he was sparkling the same. It was like Nod singing! It was *so* strange! He could actually sing in the same keys as Nod."

"Mal started off as a bass player with Sweet, because he was a guitarist in a band called Weapon that I produced," Andy Scott explains. "I remembered his voice, because he has a real range. He was a natural for harmonies. Mal became the singer of Sweet sometime in the nineties and that lasted for a good five or six years. He was the obvious choice when Steve Whalley left. I said, 'You should try Mal.' I think he fits in brilliant with Slade."

By then, Slade had started doing shows with Sweet all over Europe, with the two bands billed as the Kings of Glam. "Slade and Sweet have done a lot of shows together," Andy Scott says. "It has been like a dream ticket the last 10-15 years. Slade and Sweet on the same bill. It provides a good audience in numbers as well, and the music from the seventies is historic. What else would you want?"

"With Mal in the band, it is almost a merger," Don laughs. "Sweet and Slade merging. And it was Andy Scott who recommended it! Maybe we should merge completely. That would be a new thing. When we were in the Bahamas and Andy was there with The Elastic Band, they were being looked after properly. They were in the nice clubs and were being paid. That's what it says of Andy, so maybe a complete merger would work for the better!"

While 'breaking in' the new frontman, Don decided to come clean about his private life. For years it was kept under wraps that Don was living with Hanne in Denmark, but the first time he and I met for an interview in my home in Denmark in the summer of 2005, he decided to tell all.

"It was bound to come out anyway, so I may just as well come clean," Don explains. "You kind of assess people when you meet somebody new, and as the chemistry was right between us, I decided to tell."

Meeting Don was indeed like meeting a long-lost friend, and it didn't take many months before he and Hanne asked me to write Don's biography. At the same time, Don asked me to edit *Bibble Brick*, after which the book was finally finished.

While working on the books, Don toured steadily with Slade and even found time to appear in *Bring Back The Christmas Number One*, a one-off TV show on Channel 4 in December 2005. Host Justin Lee Collins tried to bring together musicians of the seventies to do a Christmas hit. In the end, Mud's Rob Davis penned the song 'I'm Goin' Home', which was recorded with Don and Dave, half of Mud and all of Showaddywaddy, as well as David Essex on vocals and Jona Lewie on piano.

"Don and I met again on the TV production of *Bring Back The Christmas Number One*," Jona Lewie recalls. "Although the backing track had already been completed by Rob Davis and co, Don and I were nevertheless invited – for the sake of the TV programme – to record a few extra things for it. Don's incredible precision once again came to the fore, when he suggested to the producer that he do a hi-hat pattern throughout the track to an existing tempo, and it was a spotless take in one. Once again, the old warmth came through, even though we had not met for some years, and we exchanged numbers yet again. Were it not for the fact that he now lived abroad, we would no doubt have met up for a drink and a jam."

The song was available for download from the Channel 4 website, where it reached number one on the download chart.

In December 2005, Slade also went back to the Black Country. For the first time since the original line-up, the band were to play in Don and Dave's native area – in Bilston in fact, where Don had been born. As part of their yearly Christmas tour, Slade played a show on December

14 at the Robin 2 in Bilston, only two doors away from where Johnny Howells' father used to have his boarding house.

To Don, there was a feeling of finally coming back home. It had been a long and winding road: starting out as a young boy, rehearsing in a bed and breakfast in Bilston, and ending up playing there again more than 40 years later in a venue only two doors away from the old B&B.

"We'd been nervous playing with the new line-up in Bilston, for obvious reasons," Don recalls. "The old band had been so well-loved and respected there, so it was a bit scary going in with the new band. But it was a wonderful gig, and we played there every year on the Christmas tour for the next four years. Like the saying goes: you can take the boy out of the Black Country, but you cannot take the Black Country out of the boy."

26

Still Alive

For Slade's 40th anniversary in 2006, Union Square Music reissued all their albums with new photos and liner notes on the Salvo label. New and different compilation albums were issued as well, among them one that gathered nearly all of the single B-sides, including songs co-written by Don. To top it off, *Flame* was released on DVD in an improved version with an hour of bonus features, including interviews with the four original members, as well as Tom Conti and Richard Loncraine.

"We went to London to do the comments," Don recalls, "and it was great meeting Tom Conti again. He was so nice. Dave and Jim were there as well, and we all had a lovely day. I wondered why Nod wasn't there, but then I found out that he'd done comments for the film three years before and they were basing the interviews with us on what they'd done with him already, asking us the same questions as they'd asked him back then. It did make sense really, doing it that way. Unfortunately, they did Richard Loncraine's interview on another date, so we didn't get to meet. It would have been nice seeing him again and I would have liked them to interview Andrew Birkin as well, but all in all, Union Square really did a fantastic job with the DVD."

The band toured extensively that year and even did a long tour of Russia, playing from Moscow in the west to Khabarovsk, near China, in the far east.

"Once in Russia, Dave and Don were sitting on a couch, doing a TV interview," Tim Ramage recalls. "While Dave is chatting away to the interviewer, Don hands him a bottle of water, which Dave accepts. Don then hands him an orange, a few seconds later an apple and a banana, all of which Dave is now clutching in his arms, still talking on camera. Don then passes a huge bunch of grapes, which Dave also tries to hold, until we all burst into laughter. On the TV monitor, the close-up just looked like a pile of fruit with Dave's little eyes peering over the top… hilarious!"

Previously, the band had only done a gig or two in Russia and so, during the tour, Don got a deeper insight into that vast country. "We had to fly from Moscow to Vladivostok," he recalls. "It was overnight, a 12-hour flight, and it was surreal. It was just one country, but it took as long as it does to fly from London to Los Angeles. I was sitting there, wanting a cigarette, but smoking was not allowed. Then a steward came and asked, 'Do you want a cigarette?' I said, 'Where?' 'Follow me.'

"The plane was huge and we went down with this elevator to a lounge where all the crew was, smoking and drinking. I was standing there, having a cigarette, when one of the pilots came down from the cockpit. He took a couple of slugs of some vodka and went up again. Then the other pilot came and had a couple of slugs as well. Then he went back up. I thought, 'I don't want to see this!' It was quite frightening, actually.

"I remember another time in Russia, when we were waiting in an airport. There was this aircrew in the bar and I said, 'I hope they are not flying our bloody plane,' but they were. It's like they don't care. There are no rules. Their airlines are supposed to have the worst fatality record in the world and I wonder why!"

The day before Don's 60th birthday, the band were playing in the Czech Republic, so Don couldn't be with his family in Denmark until late at night.

"Hanne had organised a surprise party for me," Don recalls. "She picked me up at the airport that night and when we arrived at our house in Silkeborg, all my Danish friends and family were there, even though it was almost midnight. There was a band of young guys as well and they played a couple of Slade tunes. It was such a lovely surprise. Hanne and the kids gave me a dog for my birthday, a Golden Retriever named Rocky. I was a bit apprehensive about getting a dog. It's wonderful having one, but when Di and I had Ringo, it was difficult with her working long hours and me being away a lot with Slade. Ringo spent long days on his own, and that's unfair. So why have one? A dog is not a human being, but it is a living thing and you have to care for it. Hanne and the kids had to promise me that they would all take part in looking after it, then I agreed."

"Rocky is Don's baby boy," his stepdaughter Anne Kirstine smiles. "Don loves to play with him, but then again Don is probably the most childish person in our family, except for Andreas. He just loves to joke around. Once he and Mum were dining at an elegant restaurant after a Slade concert and there was this little boy there with his posh parents. The boy was bored, so he crept down under the table, and then Don crept down as well and sat there, waving at him. It's so typical Don!"

"Don really is the biggest child I've ever met," Andreas agrees. "The biggest baby you'll ever see! You know, I asked him, 'Are you sure you really want me to talk to Lise for the biography? Because I'll tell her how you really are!' and he said, 'I'd love that!' It is so great that Don has the energy to play and joke around. In the car we always sing – we do that in our family – but Don can't sing. Or he pretends he can't, so he always sings at the top of his voice, ruining everything! It is little things like that. When he walks past the door to my room, he always pops in his head and goes, 'Boo! He may be old on the outside, but he's young on the inside. A 16-year-old caught in the body of a guy in his sixties! He makes things fun, turns things into a game, so that everything is not just black and white. And I know it means a lot to Don to have us as his family. He enjoys having kids to play with as he doesn't have any of his own. He is definitely a family man, and it is so important to him that we all feel good about ourselves and our lives."

★　★　★

In 2006, Slade did their usual 80-odd gigs but, during 2007, Len Tuckey resigned as their manager. With new management, the number of shows dropped to around 50 a year.

"I'd been their manager for about 14 years then," says Tuckey, "and from the band, Don was always my best friend. I said to everybody, 'If I could have had a band full of Don Powells there would never be any problems.' Don never moans about anything. He is a fun guy and he's not just on time, he's always *early*. A lot of people are just moping and late, but never Don. He was never, ever late, not one time in 14 years. If you talk to people in the industry, they love him. I've never heard a bad word spoken about him, as there's nothing about him to dislike. When you're on the road with him, it's just joke after joke, fun after fun."

Tim Ramage agrees. "For several years, Dave would always carry his stage hat around himself in a Marshall amp carrier bag. He carried it everywhere. So one day, when I went to Marshall to get some equipment from their factory for Slade, I picked up about 20 or so identical carrier bags with Don in mind. We were on one of the Slade Christmas tours at the time, so I gave these bags to Don. Well, by the time Dave arrived at the venue, Don, myself, Robin, John, Mal, the support band and various other crew were carrying Marshall bags identical to Dave's, with Don mincing around with one over his shoulder, like a model at a handbag show! Don and I also hung five or six on hooks in the dressing room. Poor Dave kept looking in a bag, expecting to see his hat, only to find Don's pants or a bag of crisps! Naturally, we all fell about laughing. Dave saw the funny side, too... However, he does use a different type of bag these days!"

As the work rate slowed, Don also started doing side projects, one of them with Craig Fenney.

"I bought the Shaw sticks company in 2007," says Fenney, "and I had actually forgotten that Don used that make of stick when I last played with him. So that was a surprise, when a guitarist friend of ours who was working with Slade II as a guitar tech at the time reminded us both. We have since used Don in magazine advertisements for Shaw sticks."

2007 also saw Don involved in projects in his new home country, when he recorded a few tracks as guest drummer with the Danish rock band The Guv'nors, and guest starred in the musical *Oliver T* at the Team Theatre in Herning. The musical was the brainchild of Danish actor, director and theatre manager Mikael Helmuth, and it combined the storyline of *Oliver Twist* with the music of Slade with stunning results.

"When Mikael first mentioned it to me, I thought he was mad," Don laughs. "I couldn't picture a combination of Slade and *Oliver Twist*. But he did a fantastic job. It was incredible. For some of the showings he had invited school kids, and they didn't know Slade. They were too young for that. But they loved the music and they thought it was specially written for the show. That was a great compliment to Nod and Jim. I was really proud of being part of that musical."

Slade did about 50 gigs in 2008 in the UK, Germany, Belgium, Scandinavia and Russia, and appeared on the odd TV show now and then. In 2009, they still played around 50 shows in the Czech Republic, Norway, Denmark, Belgium, Germany and the UK. The year also saw two new releases from the original Slade. In October, the double album *Live At The BBC* was released on Salvo Music, a collection of BBC studio recordings covering the period 1969-1972. In November came *Merry Xmas Everybody – Party Hits* on Universal Music, a compilation album consisting of a mix of Slade's party tracks and greatest hits. It never made it past number 151 in the UK charts.

In the summer of 2009, Don went to Birmingham to participate in the charity event Stick It To MS, to help raise money for the Multiple Sclerosis Society. Together with 581 other drummers, he beat the old world record of 533 drummers playing the same beat at the same time.

"It was great fun," Don says. "Although the noise was devastating! I did, however, enjoy being in the company of so many drummers using *real* drums. Today, many bands use drum machines and it's frightening! But the thing is they're so good. It's not like it's rubbish. I remember one time, we got in the studio and I used to go the day before so I could get my drums all sorted out before the other guys came in. I went to the engineer's assistant when I arrived to take my drums in. He couldn't believe it. I said, 'What's the problem? What's wrong?' He said, 'You've got to use real drums?' 'Yes.' And then he said, 'I've never worked with real drums. I've only worked with computers.' But that's the way it is these days. A lot of records you listen to now have the same drum pattern. They have the same drum computer! I stick to *real* drums, though. Today I'm using a 22 × 18in bass drum and my rack tom is 16 × 16. My floor tom is 18 × 18 and I use the Pearl Piccolo snare drums. I use a 22in ride cymbal, an 18in crash cymbal and 14in hi-hat cymbals. That's all. I only play a very basic kit, but I'm always going to stick with real drums."

Don's personal contribution to music was honoured on March 11, 2010. On that day the Slade Rooms opened in Wolverhampton and, at the same time, Don and Dave got their names on the Black Country Wall of Honour at the Civic Hall in Wolverhampton.

"It's quite an honour and I'm very proud of it," Don says, "especially as it's in Wolverhampton. You never think anything like that is going to happen. It's like getting your first number one. When something like this happens, it's fantastic. Nod already had his name on the wall, and now it was Dave's turn and mine. Jim isn't there though. I don't know why."

Pretty ironic, as Jim was the one to write the bulk of Slade's music, one might add.

"Dave and I got on the wall in connection with the opening of the Slade Rooms," Don continues. "It's a 500-capacity music venue and it also has a classroom, used by music technology students from the City of Wolverhampton College. Dave and I helped launch the venue officially by cutting the ribbon, but it was Nik Kershaw who was the first to play there! Don't ask me why. It should have been us, of course, but I guess the venue is too small for Slade. It would have been nice though, to do half an hour or something, but it didn't happen."

Although Slade have yet to play the Slade Rooms, they did other gigs in 2010 in the UK, Germany, Norway, Sweden, the Czech Republic, Poland, Russia and a new destination, Monaco.

"We had never played there before," Don says, "but it was nice. It was a rock club, really, but when you got outside, you noticed this opulence. I guess we didn't quite fit in, but people were nice about it. I remember Hanne and me sitting outside a café at a casino, watching all the Rolls-Royces and cars like that go by. It was just incredible. They were so expensive! Then we wanted a drink and a salad, but when I got inside the café to order, everyone in there was in dinner dresses and tiaras and I was wearing denim shorts and a T-shirt! I hadn't even shaved! Luckily, it was no problem. They were fine with me ordering, but I really felt out of place. We went to see Princess Grace's memorial as well. I had never realised how small Monaco is; it isn't nearly as big as Silkeborg, and that surprised me. But of course, it costs a fortune to live there. The estate agents earn a lot!"

Touring came to a sudden halt in July. Slade were doing an afternoon show in Pyras, Germany, on the 10th in what was literally a heat wave.

"On stage, Dave acted strange," Don says. "When we got off, we weren't sure if he was dehydrated, as it was very hot. Hanne urged him to see a doctor, as she had a hint that he could have had a stroke. In the end, we called a doctor to come to the hotel. It turned out he'd had a mild stroke in the back of his neck. His wife came to be with him and he flew back to England as soon as possible to recover. We were really worried about him and work-wise it was a disaster. We wanted to go on working without Dave until he got well again, in order to make a living, like Sweet had done when Andy Scott was unwell or Smokie when Terry Uttley was ill, but Dave wouldn't hear of it. So that didn't happen and for three months Slade weren't able to work. It was a financial disaster. Then, finally, in October, Dave was fit enough to go on stage again, but all in all, we only managed 36 concerts in 2010.

The year ended on a happy note, however with a wedding. Back on Christmas Eve, 2007, Don had got down on his knees and proposed to Hanne.

"I think it was romantic to propose on Christmas Eve," Don blushes. "In Denmark, Christmas is celebrated on that evening. We'd had a traditional Danish family Christmas with Hanne's kids and family.

Obviously, Hanne and I had already talked about getting married, and I got the ring in England on the Christmas tour. I guess the thing is that I've had hundreds of partners and two wives, but in Hanne I've found a soul mate. When I proposed, Hanne's family were all weeping with joy. At least, I hope it was with joy! It was indeed something special."

After three years of engagement, Hanne and Don finally eloped on December 6, 2010, to the small Danish island of Aeroe, where they were married at the local mayor's office. Only Hanne's son and father knew because they were to mind Rocky, the dog.

"We got married then and there, because that was the time we had free," Don explains. "We had to do it on Aeroe, because it is difficult for Danish citizens to get married to foreigners, but on Aeroe the paperwork didn't take as long as it would in Silkeborg. Aeroe is a very nice island, by the way. It's so beautiful."

Don likes his life as a married man, too. He loves sitting at the end of the table as head of his own family, and he has finally found a way to handle both family and career.

"Don Powell the drummer and Don Powell at home are totally different persons nowadays," he explains. "I think it has to be that way. When I was engaged to Pat, many years ago, we talked about having a big family, but when we split up the attraction of having a family went from me. Then, when I met Hanne, I actually found it very easy to 'adopt' a whole family, so to speak. I'm not sure I could have handled it before, because it wouldn't have been fair, with me travelling all the time and drinking, too."

Hanne and her kids are happy that Don is now able to juggle both job and family, and the kids have come to see him as a very important person in their lives.

"My relationship to Don is very laidback, very peaceful and harmonious," his stepdaughter Emilie says. "Don has created his own role in our family and we all feel that we mean the world to him. He is always there to help us and support us, and that way he treats us as if we were his own kids."

"Don is totally down to earth and the most selfless person I have ever met," Anne Kirstine says. "If he can help us in any way, he does, even if it is demanding on him. He would do anything for us and it has been so since day one, which I find very impressive. I hold Don in great respect."

"Because I was so young when Don and Mum got together, he and I are very close," Andreas says. "I am very grateful for that, as I'm sure he has made me a better person. He is such a big part of my life, because he has always been the friend you needed if you couldn't talk to your mum and dad. Someone to talk to and have fun with. I've definitely grown as a person because of him and my life would have been totally different without him. He has helped me so much and I am so grateful for that."

"At first it was quite a surprise for us when Don moved to Denmark," his sister Carol admits. "We were fond of Di, but it didn't work out and Hanne is such a lovely girl – beautiful as well. Besides, Denmark is such a wonderful place. The country is beautiful and peaceful, and the people are so nice. It's like being in heaven. I've never seen Don as happy, healthy and relaxed as he is in Denmark with Hanne and her children. I'm so happy for him. I'm sure Mum would have loved it, too. She really loved Don, he was truly a mummy's boy!"

In 2011, Slade did about 40 concerts in the UK, Germany, Austria, Belgium, Norway, Sweden, Poland and Russia, and made their debuts in Portugal and Bulgaria.

"They were both nice places to play, "Don says. "It's so terrific these days. The early records of the original Slade were such big hits all over Europe, and everybody knows the songs. That's why we still have a big following, also with the present line-up. The fans from the seventies bring their kids to the concerts, and that is how we've got a following in the next generation as well."

"It pays the rent," Swinn quips, "and being on the road has become a natural way of living. That's how Don keeps up with the pace."

"We have a good time and the audience has a good time," adds Robin Lavender, "and we've been at it most of our lives. I always have my travel bag next to my bed. It's a way of living. We've spent so much time on the road together that I'd say the relationship I have with Don today is both a working one and a friendship. It's a big portion of both."

"I'd love to think that we are certainly mates," Tim Ramage agrees. "Don has a good heart. If I'm struggling with the equipment, he always gives me a hand. Other people would stand and watch, but not Don. I'm always going, 'No, Don. You shouldn't be doing that. You're playing and I'm doing this.' He is a very likeable guy."

"He is a lovely man. Of all the band, he was the guy whom the crew loved," Haden Donovan states. "It doesn't matter who you speak to; all the crew would say that. I mean, Jim could be very funny and he could be worse – we'd never know. Dave was full of himself but, to be honest, he mellowed. And Noddy… I always liked Nod and I always worked with him, but there was another side to him…"

"In my opinion, Don Powell is a hugely underestimated force within the context of Slade, as both a drummer and founder member," Keith Altham says. "Without him, there would probably never have been a group in the first place."

"Don Powell is an outstanding drummer," states Gene Simmons of KISS. "He is a very physically hard drummer. You'd hear the crack of the drums and the huge power of the kick drum. It hit you in the gut. Don's style is very similar to John Bonham as a player. He is a force of nature, who served as the driving power and engine behind Slade's music."

"Without his physical presence, Slade would never sound the same," Keith Altham agrees. "It was made abundantly clear to me in 2008, going to a gig for Slade II in London. Even without Noddy Holder's amazing vocals and Jim's inventive bass, the distinctive Slade musical stamp was still there, driven by Dave Hill's guitar and Don's powerhouse percussive style. What was really good to see, after all these years with Slade, was Don and Dave on stage, still getting a kick out of playing all those old hits live and hearing that powerhouse sound once more, which only Slade could deliver from the back to the front of house. I could almost hear their late manager intoning from above, 'Yoos see, Keith, even half a Slade is better than none, and much better than most!'"

Altham is not the only one to praise the new Slade concerts. As Vicky Pearson says, "The concerts with the new band are just great fun. I'm always telling people to come and watch them and have a good time. To me, they are just as good today as they were back then. If people really, really love the songs, they should come and see them. It is what it is and they *are* Slade. It is a great show."

"I love the new band members," Carole Wiliams agrees. "John Berry is such a great guy and Mal McNulty seems nice too, although we have only met a few times. I see the new band whenever I can. To think that we met in our teens and are now in our sixties. Many years passed when we lost touch – in fact a lifetime – but when we met again, all that melted away. It was like we just saw each other the week before. That is how it always seems."

"It is a lovely thing to be part of and it has been a major part of my life," Vicky Pearson states. "I'm always very proud when I say, 'I'm gonna see Dave and Don.'"

"I go see them whenever they play Bilston," Mick Marson adds. "Then I get a good chat with Don. He's not that quiet any more, at least not when he is with me! We always chat and joke. My memory is not that good and, of course, neither is Don's, but between us we still remember a lot of the old times and I always appreciate seeing him."

"Don really is a lovely bloke," Carole Williams says, "and I am very happy that he seems so settled nowadays. After everything he has been through in his life he is just the same as that great guy I met all those years ago. He is more outgoing now, still very funny, and definitely not the shy guy hiding at the back any more. There will always be a little corner of my heart reserved for Don."

"I met Dave a couple of years ago in the Guardian Centre," John Howells recalls. "I said, 'Hello, how are you doing?' He said, 'I feel I should know you.' I went, 'Oh, forget it!' and walked away, although I can forgive him for that. We all get older. But when I met Don again a couple of years ago, he remembered me. When I first saw him, I said to myself, 'Hasn't Don aged?' but then I thought, 'Bloody hell, so have I!' You remember people how they looked when you last saw them, and at least Don is young at heart. He used to be just like me and Mick and the rest, but there was a big jump from that to the success to the accident. I think today Don is almost like he was in the old days – a progression from how I knew him. He's just an older version. He has had a lot of ups and downs, but he keeps in touch."

"The wonders of e-mail help with keeping in touch, and we certainly do," Craig Fenney says. Henry Weck adds, "Don and I both look forward to getting together over tea, as we bore our wives to tears with our rock'n'roll war stories! We are survivors…"

"I haven't seen Jim for many years, but Don, Noddy, Dave and I manage to hook up every year at the annual lunch for many of the musicians, etc, who have survived in the music business from the sixties through to today," Bob Young comments. "It's organised by Keith Altham and it's been a great way to ensure that we all keep in touch. The stories that are, and could be, told by these legendary figures sat around the table are endless. If those four walls could only talk… we'd all be in deep shit!"

"Don was always the good-looking one of the band," Suzi Quatro adds. "Girls always seem to go for the drummer and the reason… perhaps they think all that power will translate to the bedroom! And *power* is the word. When Don hits the drums, they stay hit. But more important, he's a special human being. Wouldn't have minded him in my own band. Mmm, now *there's* a thought!"

"I remember talking with Suzi once about having a little side project," Andy Scott adds, "and on the drums it had to be Don. I think he is possibly the best drummer in rock; I have never heard a louder one in all my life, and I've stood alongside Keith Moon, John Bonham and all the others. He has the most minimal kit but gets the most out of it. So both Suzi and I went, 'It has to be Don.' That still could happen."

"Don's the perfect musician," Len Tuckey states, "and I'd say – OK, I managed him – that he's my best friend and hopefully he'll be my good friend to the day I die."

"All the time I've seen Don he has always been very calm, laid-back and easy to get on with," Jona Lewie says. "In addition, he has always appeared well mannered and, put simply, plain decent. I would describe him as a warm person, but I've also been of the impression that underneath would lay solid strength. He would not be afraid to speak his mind if it were ever necessary. That is to say that it would be a rare thing if anybody ever managed to get one over him or exploit his nature. If he were ever crossed, he would remember and be able to deal with such a situation. Today, we have the sort of relationship where either of us can ring up and say 'hi' anytime. We lead very busy lives, but on the other end of the phone would be the guarantee of that sympathetic voice. Long live Don Powell."

"Don is just the nicest person in the world," Dave Donovan adds. "Full stop."

As for the original members of Slade, Don still keeps in touch with them, although he doesn't see Noddy and Jim very often.

"Nod and I mail and phone each other," Don says, "and I usually see him at Keith Altham's yearly Christmas party. Nod still lives in Manchester and does lots of TV work. He has settled down with his wife and their son and, as his two grown daughters are from where he lives now, he sees all his family. He's happy now.

"Jim is still married to Louise and I follow his career. Since 2006 he has been doing solo albums again, and I think what he does is great. The tunes are typical Jim and are very well done. Nowadays we don't see much of each other, but we aren't strangers."

"Whenever I've met Don, after the demise of the band, he was always his joking, affable self," Jim comments. "He is dependably unchanging, which is surprising, as people from the past can sometimes metamorphose into complete strangers."

"When I talk to Jim on the phone it is like the old days, as if no time has passed," Don adds. "I like that. Dave I see all the time, of course. We've been together for so long, so obviously there's that chemistry there. We both know what we are gonna do, without even talking about it. It's like an unwritten thing. It's not only the playing, but also the camaraderie. It was the same thing with the original band and it does show on stage. It is a magical thing."

"Actually, one of Don's great pastimes on the road is his ongoing teasing and cheeky comments to Dave Hill," Tim Ramage reveals. "This is done in the way that only two guys who are great lifelong friends can. Dave had a bad cold a while ago, so Don went around telling everyone that Dave had pygmy flu! Another time, when we were waiting around at an airport, Dave went off to buy some new sunglasses. He came back to where we were sitting and asked Don what he thought of his new shades, to which Don replied, 'Well, they make you look much taller,' and we all fell about laughing! And then, of course, Don will put a chair on a table in a dressing room, borrow my marker pen, climb up and write, 'Dave Hill was here' as high as he possibly can, so we all fall about giggling at the idea of 'little Ronnie Corbett', as Don refers to Dave, doing it!"

"Dave's still the same," Don smirks. "One time we were in Vienna, doing a concert, and Dave was having a stroll around the city. Then this hooker came up to him and said, 'It's 5.50,' and Dave looked at his watch and said, 'No it isn't! It's half past three!' He had no idea what was going on. He'll never change."

"What is special with Don and me is that we've managed to stay together," says Dave. "Whether it has been playing together, reforming the band or whatever we have been doing, there has always been a connection between the two of us. With all the travelling we have done and all the special times we've had together, we have a strong bond – a union. Don was always there for me and has been close to me. We have been together a very long time and been through many changes. We have weathered many storms, had some wonderful experiences, and our relationship today is stronger than ever. We are, in a way, like brothers. We have kept true to the music and each other. Since Don and I have been on our own together, we have been able to visit some wonderful places and played some really superb venues. All of these experiences together have only served to enrich and strengthen the bond of friendship between us.

"All the hardships that Don has gone through have made him strong. He has improved in a lot of things and I think he is happier now than he has ever been. He's in a situation now where he's settled and, working together, we've kept Slade alive and strengthened. Because that's what Don does – he plays the drums, and his abilities as a drummer are great. He is truly a monumental drummer with an original style, which is an integral part of Slade's music, and his broken drumsticks still hit me on the back of the head as they fly off. I'm still considering taking out insurance! I'm very pleased that we are, to this day, still touring. It's Don moving forward and me, too."

"They are still nice blokes," Francis Rossi adds, "but I think they should have kept on playing together in the original line-up. I don't know whether it's naughty, because Noddy doesn't want to do it, but I think it's a big mistake that they have made. Some people don't like the idea of being our age and still being in the business, but the problem is you still reach that age! Then you go, fuck, I'm an old person doing it Noddy and Jimmy are great little writers, and I just wish they had stayed and done it longer, as they would have been able to do well for themselves. They should have considered it 10 years ago and I think it's a shame that they didn't."

"People always ask us to do a reunion tour, and I *would* love to do a concert with the original four members," Don ponders. "That would be something special, for me as well, but I doubt it will ever happen. But to think we were four schoolboys when we started out, and now the youngest member of the band is a grandfather of three! I can't believe it."

As Don gets older, he finds that living with amnesia is never going to be easy, but at least you learn how to cope with it.

"I used to be very insecure, because of my memory loss," he says. "I get the upper hand when I joke around. Then I'm on safe ground. But I'm not just the quiet guy who can crack jokes. I have opinions on things and I have feelings, too. Although Don Powell the drummer and Don Powell the private person are two very different guys, my insecurities somehow rubbed off. When I'm the drummer, people just wanted to talk about Slade and my stories about the band; somehow, I became like a machine in front of other people, even my family, only able to talk Slade. I still have problems with that. It is as if I'm programmed, and just repeat my Slade stories over and over again like a parrot, but I'm working on it.

"At least the amnesia isn't that bad anymore, although it is sort of unpredictable. It's never the same. It comes and goes. I remember one time in England when I had parked my car. I had some errands, but when I got back, I forgot where the car was. I went round looking for it, but I couldn't find it, so there was only one thing to do – get a cab. I explained the situation, and we drove around to find the car. And the strange thing was, the cab driver told me that I was only his second customer that day, but the one before me had been the same. He couldn't find *his* car, either!

"Nowadays, the amnesia mostly pops up when I am stressed, so I try to relax as much as possible. My drinking days are over and I've stopped smoking, too, so I relax with sweets and camomile tea. I always thought I was fine when smoking, but now that I've stopped, I've realised that I wasn't. I'm awful when it comes to sweets though, and as for the camomile tea, I can drink up to 60 cups a day! When we're on the road, promoters often line up wine and beer for the band, but I bring my thermos with my camomile tea. That's rock'n'roll for you!"

Although Don has turned his back on the rock'n'roll lifestyle, he has no plans of turning his back on the job itself.

"People always say, 'Haven't you had enough? When are you going to retire?'" Don smiles. "But I've never even thought about it! My policy is that as soon as I stop enjoying it, then I'll finish, but I enjoy everything about it. I've been around the world like four times, and I've been so lucky to see all these different countries that I only ever saw on TV, or read about. I always say that has been my education. And it is amazing how music is one common denominator wherever you go. No matter what nationality, the music is one common denominator all the time. But I've seen so many musicians who say that they don't want to play, really. How can they do it? How can they put their heart and soul into anything when they don't even wanna be there? I couldn't do that, just go on like a robot. I love playing drums and I have the best job in the world, but as soon as I stop enjoying it, I *will* finish."

★ ★ ★

Don finishes his cup of camomile tea and gobbles down a final piece of Danish. He is dressed in jeans and a T-shirt advertising a Danish music festival. Although in his sixties, his physique, his clothes and the long, curly hair give the image of a much younger man — an image supported by the humorous talk and outbursts of giggles. It is a grey October day, I am

307

sitting in Don's living room in Silkeborg and we have just finished the last of our talks for this book.

Two days later, Don is back at work; this time, it's a gig in Germany. The dressing room is full of people, not only the band, but also their local friends and hangers-on, and Don is laughing and joking while he strips off his clothes. He rids himself of jeans and T-shirt and slips into his stage clothes: a short top and a pair of tight spandex trousers. He puts on his ladies' gloves, tapes them to his wrists, then pops his gum shield in his mouth, transforming himself from family man to rock'n'roll drummer.

Don is concentrated now. He focuses on the upcoming job: to pass on the myth and the music of Slade to the waiting crowds. He leaves the dressing room and walks down to the stage. He is the first one to walk on. The middle-aged audience, accompanied by their children, break into thunderous applause, cheering and clapping when they spot him. Don smiles in disbelief at the eager crowd, then mounts his drum stool. The myth is still very much alive.

Author's Note

When Don and I first embarked on writing this book, the year was 2006. I had expected to finish the work within two years, which is the time I normally take for a biography, and had someone told me that I would still be at it five and a half years later, I wouldn't have believed it. But the logistics of getting together – not only with Don who was touring most of the time, but also with the many people who have graced this biography with their comments – turned out to be quite complicated and in the end it delayed the book by more than three years. Hopefully, you found it worth the wait!

I would like to thank Dave Donovan, Haden Donovan, Dave Hill, John Howells, Robin Lavender, Anne Kirstine, Emilie and Andreas Lundby, Mick Marson, Vicky Pearson, Tim Ramage, Francis Rossi, Andy Scott, Graham 'Swinn' Swinnerton, Len Tuckey, Carol and Gerald Watts and Carole Williams for granting me extensive interviews. I am truly grateful for the hospitality and frankness with which they met me. I would also like to thank Keith Altham, Andrew Birkin, Craig Fenney, Jim Lea, Ric Lee, Jona Lewie, Suzi Quatro, Gene Simmons, Henry Weck and Bob Young for having enriched this book with their comments. Their kind help has been very much appreciated.

A special thank you to Ian Edmundson and Chris Selby for taking their time to proofread, for helping out with research AND maintaining our friendship throughout the process! Thanks also to Wilfried Mende, Philippe D'Hoeraene, Per Christensen and Søren Mosegaard for their help and support.

My greatest gratitude goes, of course, to Don Powell, for his confidence, openness and friendship. Not only did he trust me with his diaries, he and his family also took me in and made me and my family part of their lives. I'll always cherish that and I hope this book reflects the chemistry between us that made us want to write it in the first place.

Research sources:
Don Powell's diaries; *Slade: Feel The Noize!* by Chris Charlesworth; *Who's Crazee Now?* by Noddy Holder; *'N Between Times* by Keith Farley; *The Slade Papers* (the collection of fan-club newsletters from 1970-1976); and *Flame* by John Pidgeon, as well as articles and interviews from newspapers, magazines and TV shows too numerous to mention.

October 2011, Odense, Denmark

Lise Lyng Falkenberg